THE SILVER REVOLVER

THE SILVER REVOLVER

JOHN SHIRLEY

ROUGH
EDGES
PRESS

The Silver Revolver
Paperback Edition
Copyright © 2025 John Shirley

Rough Edges Press
An Imprint of Wolfpack Publishing
1707 E. Diana Street
Tampa, FL 33610

roughedgespress.com

Cover design by Rough Edges Press
Editing by My Brother's Editor

Paperback ISBN 978-1-68549-663-0
eBook ISBN 978-1-68549-561-9
LCCN 2025947114

For Micky

Special Thanks to
Michelina Shirley, Jennie Goloboy, and Paula Guran

AUTHOR'S NOTE

The lyrics to "One Step Ahead of the Devil" have been used with permission.

AUTHOR'S NOTE

The lyrics to "One Step Ahead of the Devil" have been used with permission.

"I mixed myself up in everything that came along.
It was the only way I could forget myself."
Doc Holliday to Bat Masterson in
The Sunset Trail (1905)

THE SILVER REVOLVER

THAT HUMID SUMMER MORNING, I brushed my teeth, showered, consumed bran cereal, drank some coffee while reading the lead paragraphs on the front page of the *Chronicle*, and took the Muni to work in downtown San Francisco. A little later that day, I was going to the emergency room to see my son. A little later yet, I was getting drunk beside a pool of blood.

The editors meeting with Rowse, the vice president of Ledbetter Publishing, took place right before I was notified that my son was hospitalized. Thinking back, it was like all during the meeting that information about Frankie was right there in the air, just hanging there like a headline suspended in space; barely out of view, a blur I couldn't quite read in the distance, but there all the same.

That's probably because Frankie had been headed for a fall, and I could sense him spiraling down, despite all the reassurance from his counselor, his mom, the soccer coach, his English teacher—and from him.

Maybe that feeling was why, even though I hadn't gotten the news, the meeting was so nerve wracking But then, I was a book editor, sitting in an office with my superior, who was laying down the law, and that was always about me holding myself back. Tension on the leash.

There hadn't been a necessity of constantly holding myself back with old Lawrence Ledbetter, though. The president of Ledbetter publishing hadn't always agreed, but we spoke straight up, and we understood each other. He tolerated my acerbity.

Then Mr. Ledbetter retired and sold the company, just a couple of months before this morning's meeting.

"As you know, Slim," Rowse was telling me. "Book publishing is changing. Has already changed dramatically." He snapped his lower lip with his rabbity front teeth and slowly turned an empty Pepsi can under his right hand, as if trying to screw it into the desktop.

For this meeting, he sat behind his leather-topped desk, fingers tented—a cue that was not lost on me. Peter Eickhoff from marketing sat to Rowse's right, on the leather sofa of the compact office, nervously patting his threadbare blond comb-over. I sat at the apex of the triangle, in an office visitor's chair, like an outsider. Being seated there was another cue that found its way home. Cues and omens.

Don't worry about it, I told myself. *You got the editing job, been here for years, Texas State Prison is way behind you. Your job is safe.*

There was a window that might have shown summer in San Francisco from about six stories up, but the curtains were closed, and the office was gloomy. It could have been a room in winter.

Rowse's suit jacket was over the back of his chair so that, in his vest and shirtsleeves, he could affect his notion of an actual publisher. The slick, pernicious prick.

Me, I wore jeans and cowboy boots and one of my

cowboy shirts that day, the rusty-red pearl-buttoner with the black, ornately silver-threaded panel along the top. Not typical office wear at Ledbetter, but they put up with it. And I wear glasses. Wire rims. Which have now come through an amazing lot of hell intact, whereas if I'd just been hanging around the house, I probably would have sat on them.

Rowse was talking, and I was nodding at the right intervals, but my mind was on Frankie. If you have a teen, you find yourself anxious at the kid's standoffishness, their constant signals that they want to have their own space. All the while, you know that it's a dangerous world. And me...I've seen people die, right here in front of me. Not just that once, in prison. I saw it on the street a couple of times. Talking to your teenage son, you're doing a tightrope walk between trying to instill some sense of real-world danger without coming off like a harrying authority figure.

Thinking about it took me back to better times with Frankie. I remembered a few years ago, browsing the pet store—Frankie was pretty well up on aquariums—and admiring the freshwater crabs, the African Butterfly Fish, and the Dwarf Puffer. Just the feeling of two people enjoying the world together, one comfortably as a dad and one comfortably as the son. It was like singing in key together, an octave apart—an effortless, good feeling.

And that time we went white-water rafting, riding on wildness together—

Eickhoff cleared his throat and looked at me. Then I realized Rowse had asked me a question. Something about the fall titles.

"I'm confident in our fall titles," I said, hoping that covered it.

Rowse grunted. "But have we got a leader? Our top sellers..." He droned on, and I nodded.

Eickhoff looked back at the clipboard on his knee and waited. He wore a butter yellow shirt, a brown tie, brown slacks, and loafers. Prominent wedding band. He had one leg tightly crossed, almost knotted over the other, and he seemed like he was breathing a little too fast, like if I stood up too quickly, he might scream.

Tightly wound-up guy, I thought.

He was wound way tighter than I realized. I misread the guy. Lots of people did.

Rowse was polite but also unfailingly disdainful. Does all that show some hostility to these two guys? Maybe so. It wasn't because they were the suits, and I was the editor with the glamorous "understanding of the artists."

See, I was used to businessmen. Mr. Ledbetter, my old boss—my boss for eleven underpaid but honorable years—was a business guy. He liked to make money, but he was not a slick, pernicious office vulture. In fact, he knew I'd done some time—a little less than two years, but still real State Pen time—and he hired me anyway. He'd read some book reviews I'd written. I was the *Dallas Morning Star*'s pet inmate reviewer for a while, and he dug my style. That figured into it, but Ledbetter was just trying to give me a chance. Would Rowse have hired me eight months out of prison? Fuck, no.

I tried to get back on task, dutifully chiming in, "Change can be good for a business."

"Ledbetter Publishing is still Ledbetter Publishing, though it has been purchased by PolyMedia International," Rowse went on.

I couldn't resist saying something to that. I should have maintained airtight integrity in my pressure suit. But I said,

"It's still Ledbetter Publishing? Although...Mr. Ledbetter is no longer connected with Ledbetter Publishing."

I smiled to show it was a friendly observation, though it wasn't.

"Right," Rowse said, eyeing me speculatively. He glanced down at my cowboy boots. Every time I'd met him, he'd always acted like he wanted to tell me not to wear the boots and then remembered the company had agreed to keep Ledbetter's casual dress tradition. "But, uh...though we do want to maintain Mr. Ledbetter's deservedly respected standards, we have to face realities. We've got to seriously reduce overhead."

I glanced at Eickhoff. He was squirming a little, like he had to go to the bathroom. I felt like telling him, *Just get up and go, dammit.*

As I watched Eickhoff, his eyes snapped to the window, and back to us. There was a distant sound of a siren somewhere south of Market, and his hands tightened, knuckles white on the armrests.

"I..." Eickhoff began. "There are, yes, in fact, certain realities..." He seemed far away in that moment. As if trying to remember what those realities were.

You work with guys day in and out, but you have no real window into their real lives: their homes, their families, their past. I took pity on Eickhoff, turning my attention to Rowse. "Who're we going to be realistic about first?" Thinking, even as I said it, that I really ought to gentle up my tone.

They could be thinking about getting "real" with *me*, after all. Ledbetter Publishing had been taken over. A takeover usually led to layoffs.

Maybe part of me was hoping they'd fire me. It might give me time to visit Austin. I'd been thinking about Texas a lot. The delicious contradictions of Texas.

In Austin, a college town with a college rock scene, most people disdained cowboy boots and hats. So, of course, I was the guy who wore them. I understood the cool of anti-cool way early.

Austin. I thought about the warm nights. Cicadas droning. Brash, noisy grackles, like a gang of bratty children, stealing your sandwich buns right off your plate at the picnic table behind the barbecue place where Janis Joplin used to wipe grease off those powerful lips. Bats at sunset, multitudes of them strobing up into the sky from under the bridge to the *oohs* of tourists, the *ee-ews* of children holding their noses at the mustiness of a million guano-sticky leather wings hitting the air at once. Sudden changes of weather, like a sultry woman just going with her moods. Undergrads laughing amiably at me in the college bars, where I was a half-assed grad student—already an older guy—because I talked earnestly about how westerns, in movies and books, were America's only true native art form, except maybe for Texas barbecue. English major and binge crystal-sniffer Slim Purdoux, sitting in the bar holding his cowboy hat and holding forth about the honest romanticism of westerns, the "sacred austerity of instinct." Students in vintage R.E.M. T-shirts laughing at me, and buying me drinks, always glad to see me, though they insisted I was full of shit.

I've heard Austin has changed. Sprawl, philistine incursions, thugs. But still, I wanted to go back.

That was a fantasy. I couldn't go back, because Meredith and Frankie were in San Francisco, in the little house she'd bought when she filed for divorce. She was invested in the foggy rolling hills of the Sunset District. She wasn't moving, and I wasn't going to move away from the boy, separation or no separation.

I needed to see Frankie safely to at least nineteen years

old. There had been no one to see me through except Mom, the old man having died when I was eleven. Mom was there as much as she had to be, and not a jot more.

Rowse was nattering on about something—how we had to please Amazon more than Barnes and Noble or the independent stores. Darwinian publishing.

I nodded noncommittally. I was still thinking about Texas—and Frankie. Wishing I could show Frankie all of Texas's rich embarrassments, like the town of Crawford, and its embarrassing riches. But even if I could get Meredith to let me take him out of the state for a visit, all my friends would've moved on. I was clean and sober, hardworking Slim Purdoux now. I didn't take drugs anymore, and maybe Austin would no longer have that throb of intimate, relentlessly experimental energy.

"The kind of books we need for the new publishing era," Rowse was saying, "are going to be plotted with AI and..."

Books. I remembered reading to Frankie when he was little. He had an unquenchable thirst for stories, just *good* stories. Maybe he'd have become a storyteller, a writer someday. Something I'd wanted to do, and never seriously could.

I remembered going to father-son camp with him when he was eleven. After the separation, I hadn't been able to afford it again. But that one summer, we were happy. The two of us laughing at the chirpy summer camp staff; splashily paddling canoes; me and him, the two members of a two-member gang. I kept my authority by a thread, but he was there with me; right there with me.

That winter, his mother decided I was a bad influence on her and him both. Would barely let me see him.

Eickhoff cleared his throat, glancing at Rowse, who nodded almost imperceptibly.

A little red light went on inside me, and I said, "Wait! Did you say *plotted with AI?*"

"Oh yes," Rowse said, studying his fingernails. "Poly-Media's very big into that. Moving on, we'll get some work for hire writers to turn the AI plot into novels. They wanted to let the program do it all, but...uh...I talked them into trying this first."

What a brave man, I thought bitterly.

"We're thinking," Eickhoff said, looking hard at his clipboard. "with the cutbacks, isn't any room for Mark Dustin in the Ledbetter general fiction line, or Judith Mayfield."

"Say what?" Then I remembered *gently, gently.* I leaned back and made an ever-so-gentle hand gesture that meant, *I understand, but after all*, and said, "We should remember that Mark Dustin *sells.* He has a following. *The New York Times* reviewers love him."

"He's been slipping," Rowse said, shrugging. "A lot. Sales figures don't lie, Slim."

Eickhoff nodded stiffly. He squirmed in his seat.

I took off my wire-rimmed glasses to wipe the lenses as I spoke, so I didn't have to look at him. "I am not going to work with AI generated writing. Never. Nada."

Eickhoff abruptly stood up, making Rowse's head jerk back in reaction to the suddenness of it. "Just want to..."

"Go ahead, right down the hall to the right," I said.

"The men's room..."

Rowse looked irritated but waved him on. Eickhoff almost bolted through the door.

"Too much coffee or something," Rowse muttered, looking after Eickhoff. "He's been very edgy lately. We had a bit of a...he walked off the job yesterday."

Now I was genuinely surprised. "That guy? He comes off as such a milquetoast."

"Seems to be having some kind of issues with his wife."

"It's going around," I said.

"You need to take some time and think about the AI component, Slim," Rowse said. "It's the coming thing—"

The phone on Rowse's desk chimed. I knew he would answer it. He always took calls during meetings. During meetings with mere editors, anyway.

It was PolyMedia for Eickhoff. "He was just here. Just ran off to the little boy's room for a moment. He should be on his way back by now. Hold on." Rowse pressed his intercom button. "Kenny? Is Eickhoff coming back down the hall? He went to the men's—"

"Peter Eickhoff?" came the tinny voice from the box. "He didn't go to the men's. He went out on the balcony. He's out there pacing and talking to someone."

We shared the balcony with Renquist Investments. Just a few chairs and little tables out there, and one sickly potted palm tree. The six-story building contained two businesses, dividing the building vertically in half, like a big condo. Ledbetter and Renquist. We saw little of them, though I was friendly with their receptionist, Betsy, a patient, efficient white-haired lady in her sixties who came out on the balcony for a smoke sometimes when I was out there drinking coffee. We'd chatted about children—hers were grown—and about Texas. She was from Dallas.

Rowse frowned and stood, took a step to the window, moved the curtain, and tilted his head to look along the wall to the balcony. "He's out there all right, but there's no one out there with him. Must be talking on a Bluetooth." Eickhoff must have seen him looking, because Rowse made a *there's a phone call for you* gesture, holding his hand against his head. Then he sat back down at the desk, picking up the phone. "Yes, uh, he'll be...okay, I'll tell him." He hung up. "Whatever. He took a deep breath. "So—Slim. I've read some AI produced material that was not much worse than, you know, a great deal of what's out there in the market..."

"The whole concept is denigrating, Rowse. Christ, AI in the arts—man, it'll go through our culture like a flesh-eating bacteria."

Eickhoff came in, face mottled. He sat down, avoiding our eyes, looking just as squirmy as before. But then, he hadn't gone to the bathroom at all.

Rowse glanced at him. After a moment, he said, "You got a call—"

"From Alice?" Eickhoff interrupted, snapping the question.

"Alice? No, from Ferris at PolyMedia, but he said he couldn't hold. You can call him in about an hour."

Eickhoff squeezed his eyes shut. Then he nodded way too briskly. "Oh, great. Gee, thanks. I'll...yeah. Good."

The phone rang again. Rowse answered and frowned when he learned it was for me. That was two not for him. "Yes, Mr. Purdoux is here, but he's in a meeting...what kind of emergency?"

I sat up straight. Who the fuck cared what kind of emergency? *Give me the fucking phone.*

But I simply sat there, waiting. I hadn't crossed over yet.

Rowse said grudgingly. "All right, hold on. Slim, it's for you. You can take it on that phone on the little table next to you there. Just press...there ya go."

I knew the woman was a nurse the moment I heard her voice. "Mr. Purdoux? We've admitted Franklin Purdoux here. We're at San Francisco General."

"Is it...what is it? What happened?"

"He seems to've overdosed on something. It may be a mix of things, but we think fentanyl is involved. He's in the critical ward, third floor, B wing."

"Critical! Is he..."

"That's all I can tell you on the phone, sir. You'll have to speak to the doctor."

"Frankie!"

"Will you be able to—"

"Yes! Yes, I'm...coming. Now!"

I hung up, and the other two had adopted the expected expressions. "Go ahead on over there," Rowse began. "Don't give it a second—"

I was on my way out the door before he finished the sentence.

2

THE DOCTOR WAS a small South Asian man with a small mouth and a smaller smile. I'm sure he is an intelligent guy, a fine doctor, and a grand family man. But I wanted to strangle him because I knew what he was going to tell me. I could see it in his eyes.

He looked at a clipboard. "Mr. Pur-*dowks*?"

I wasn't going to correct his pronunciation right then. "Yeah, yes. Where is my son?"

"I—"

"Jimmy?" It was my ex, Meredith, interrupting. Looking squinty-eyed and pale in the other doorway, she stood there hugging herself. Tall and wiry, like me, but with lank dark hair that stood sharply out against her pale skin. But for both being sort of tall and skinny, and wearing glasses, we didn't have much else in common. Except we both came from Austin.

She had been intensely progressive, politically. I voted her way, but told her I was a member of the "cynical party." She took classical music appreciation classes and knew a scherzo from an adagio. I liked All Them Witches, Clutch, and the Velvet Underground. I used to play bass in some raggedy-ass punk bands, and I thought Frank Zappa was classical music. And of course, I could get into Hank Williams, Johnny Cash, and Steve Earle.

Meredith was a Wiccan. Not long after we moved to the Bay Area, she went all goddess-worshipping feminist. Fine by me. I was a kind of vague deist, like Thomas Jefferson.

Right now, she was wearing a dark-blue work shirt, jeans, and sandals, and an Isis moon goddess pendant around her neck. I don't even know how the hell we ended up married. But Frankie was our son, and we both loved him.

I knew when I saw her squinting that way at me that he was dead. And I knew that somehow, she was going to blame me.

"It was a fatal CDI, combined drug intoxication," the doctor said in a soft little voice. "He tested positive for two drugs. One was MDMA. We think they're both from the same pill. He had two in a little bag in his pocket. The one that killed him was fentanyl."

"Well, for fuck's sake," I snarled. I just heard myself say it. It was like I was out of my body, listening. "Did you try naloxone?"

He didn't even blink. He nodded to say he understood how angry I was and put a gentle hand on my arm. "Much too late. He was already gone."

"Did you try to revive him?"

"Oh, yes."

I heard myself say, raspily, "You're saying...you're saying he's dead."

"We tried for nearly half an hour to revive him. Every-thing, sir. Everything. There was a blood clot in the lung from a broken blood vessel there, and the blood clot went into the artery, stopping his heart. We tried to break the clot up, restart his heart, but he came to us already quite gone."

Frankie...

I turned to look at my ex. She was gazing mutely at the floor tiles. "Where did he get this fentanyl shit, Meredith? Exactly *where* did it happen?"

My own voice sounded to me like a poor recording. The room was a box with some white walls and white lights overhead. There were three people in the box. Me, this little doctor in the white suit, and my ex-wife. We were in this box and always had been. We'd always been here, talking about my dead son.

"He went off to..." Meredith was making long raspy asthmatic gasping sounds in between phrases. "A party without..." Pausing to breathe between what I now recognized as sobs, sobs of a depth that I'd never heard from her. "Without my permission."

A gasping sob. "He went from summer school...after class...to...some party of Victor's. Victor's mom was working a night shift somewhere. Nobody was home. I think Victor was the one who got them the...I don't know. I was frantic... didn't know...where he was. Police...called. He collapsed at the party...when he was dancing."

"Maybe some more," the doctor put in softly.

"Drugs. When did it go from pot to this opioid shit?"

I was in a state of raging detachment, though I stood statue-still. And now my voice was more than detached. It was flat as the surface of a subterranean lake. "I thought you had a counselor working with him...some flake from Marin. Meredith, right?"

She looked at me with a murderous emptiness. "I...*You.* You were his hero, the party animal."

"I have been clean and fucking sober for eleven years. You're going to say he did this to be like me?"

"I will leave you to talk," the doctor said. "Remember, grief makes people angry. I will be in—"

I grabbed the doctor's bony little shoulder. "Doctor, listen to me. I want to see him. Now."

The doctor looked like he wanted to refuse. Something to do with proper morgue procedures and authorized doctors' exams and death certificate signings or something. But he didn't say it. He was wiser than that.

He nodded and gestured to a metal door, a door painted very, very white.

———

Meredith didn't come along. I figured she was calling her sister or her life coach. Or her Wiccan girlfriend.

The hall contained Filipino nurses and a middle-aged white doctor who darted by as if I was going to ask him for pain meds for my dying mother. Then there was a room, a cool room, with three gurneys in it, with sheets pulled up over three faces, making me think of three-card monte: pick the right shell and under it...is your dead son.

The doctor pulled back the sheet on the nearest body.

I was surprised by how much expression there was on Frankie's face. He looked puzzled, a little angry, betrayed. Cheated. There was a certain dulling too, like a shape in wax when it's just a little warm. That was death, softening the edges of that final expression. Death undefines us.

But it was my Frankie lying there, so very still. A dynamo of a young man, now so *very* still.

Skateboarding, he'd practice the tricks over and over until he splintered his skateboard into a ruin. Dancing to reggaeton. Playing softball. He'd been awkward at every other team sport, but something would snap into place when he played softball, and he became Fred Astaire as a shortstop.

He dropped out of the team last year because Coach Glausinger was a judgmental old bastard, and Frankie took it personally.

Frankie took my divorce from his mom personally too.

I'm sorry about that, kid. Your mom and me breaking up. I didn't think it was like breaking up with you too. But I guess you felt like it was.

Had I ever told him I was sorry about it? I couldn't remember. My mind was jammed up by memories fighting for center stage.

I tried to make myself kiss his dead, cold face. I couldn't even touch his hand. My body wouldn't bend over. My hand wouldn't lift up.

I didn't need to confirm he was dead. He was long gone. There was no Frankie Wayne James Purdoux left in the world. There was just that tire-print of a parting expression.

I had one other thought right then. That he was born into drugs and died in drugs. Because I had gotten Meredith pregnant with him in college, when we'd both been doing some MDMA. X. Stoned, she'd been yielding and intellectually open and full of possibilities while her bitterness slept. She got pregnant in a waking drug dream. Frankie died in a torturous mix of MDMA and fentanyl.

The doctor's almost tender touch on my arm steered me away from the body, and I went out the door into the warmth of the hall. Away from the room where I'd seen Meredith.

I found an exit—emergency only. Its warning bell rang when I pushed through it. I was fine with it ringing. The hospital should be filled with that clangor, all day and all night. It should be required.

I decided I needed to be moving. I had to keep a step, two steps ahead of the feeling that was coming. The thing trying to catch me.

I decided to go back to the office so I could quit the job, face-to-face. After Ledbetter retired, I only kept the job for my boy's sake. And while I was there, I could just coincidentally get the Jack Daniels I had in my desk, a retirement gift all wrapped up to send to Mr. Ledbetter. I wasn't going to send it to Mr. Ledbetter now. Mr. Ledbetter was on his own. I was going to drink some Jack and blow off my sobriety, because nothing else was conceivable in that moment. When you're in enough pain, you look for a painkiller.

Yeah, the office. For starters, that was someplace to go.

I moved my body through the places it needed to go through to get back to work. I could go in and quit the job and get the Jack and split.

And then what? Oblivion in one form or another.

I walked a few blocks, waved down a taxi, and took that. The driver was a late-middle-aged White guy who looked like he was having to work at not drinking on shift. His hands were white knuckling on the steering wheel. He tried to talk to me, but then he looked at my face in the rearview and shut up.

I arrived at the building and wordlessly paid the cabbie. I went upstairs in the elevator, scribbled a note to Rowse, and handed it to Clueless Kenny, the vapid young guy who was Rowse's assistant.

Rowse:

My son has died. I am done here. I stayed so I could be sure of a job, so I could provide for my child. And maybe be a role model: a working dad.

I'm not a dad as of today. That's all gone. My parents are dead. I'm divorced, and only two things were meaningful to me: my son and my chance to cultivate good books. The world took my son from me, and you took the other. You're making books meaningless. Let us indulge in tautology and repeat that word. <u>Meaningless.</u>

Sincerely,

Slim Purdoux

Dated: Whatever the fuck this day is. And who the fuck cares?

Kenny read it, even though it was addressed to his boss and not to him, and blinked back at me in graceless confusion. "Uhhh...Are you, like, sure you don't want to, you know, talk to him? He'll be back in a second. He just went down the hall real quick to—"

"Just give it to him." I turned my back and walked away. I went to my office, got the wrapped package from the desk drawer, tore it open, poured a coffee cup full of whiskey, drank off three belts, and *wham.*

It was good timing. I had just finished shuddering, was just lowering the cup from my lips, when the gunshots started.

It sounded to me at first like an irritated carpenter was really whacking something resistant with a hammer. Rap! Rap-*Rap!* Rap-*RAP!*

"Huh," I said. Some maintenance guy with a nailgun?

Was that a scream? Maybe he nail-gunned his foot.

I poured some more Jack. When had I last talked to Frankie? On the phone last night. The last thing I ever said to Frankie was something like, "You gotta go to the damn summer classes if you want to graduate to the next grade, man. You screwed off most of the school year."

Something like that. *You screwed off most of the school year.* The last thing his dad said to him before he died.

I felt something catching up to me and had to keep moving out ahead of it, and curiosity was a way to keep moving, a couple of steps in front of the thing that was coming. So I let curiosity pull me to the banging sounds. Definitely not a nailgun. I knew guns. That was an automatic pistol. There was a smell in the air that drew me too. Gunsmoke.

Carrying the bottle and the mug, I went into the hall and saw Eickhoff, about forty feet away, with a big automatic pistol in his shaking hands, standing over the body of Hal Renquist, CEO of Renquist Investments. Blood swirled, pooling around Eickhoff's loafers, right in front of the Renquist HQ reception door. Renquist was lying face up, sprawled crookedly across the hall carpet.

I had met Renquist for a second or two at a Christmas party—both companies were invited—and had thought he was a vainglorious dickhead. But this...

Eickhoff was panting, staring down at Renquist's shot-up body. Three wet wounds in his chest. I felt sick, but not surprised. Maybe I couldn't feel surprise right then. But after the meeting in Rowse's office, Eickhoff's killing people seemed to make some kind of perverse sense to me.

"You going to shoot me too?" I asked, more interested than scared. I took another drink of the Jack D. "What the hell, it's your gun. I'm just asking. You want some of this here, Pete?"

Yew want some of this here, Pete? I was also interested to note that my Texas accent and diction returned a little when I got drunk. The first drinking I'd done in a high stack of years.

"I believe..." Eickhoff licked his lips, staring at the bottle. "I *would* like a drink. Yes."

I handed him the cup. I was aware that he hadn't yet answered my other question. He seemed in no hurry to kill me, but...

I could smell Renquist's blood.

I was a little afraid of how little I was afraid. Maybe I was hoping he'd shoot me. And I was very drunk.

Eickhoff took a drink, looking at me with wide eyes over the cup. His face was tear-stained.

I felt I had to say something. Talking kept me busy, kept me moving in some way, ahead of what I needed to stay ahead of. "My son's dead, Eickhoff. Yep. He died today. Poisoned by some shit he got into last night. He was, you know, all I stayed at Ledbetter's for. All I fucking stayed *straight* for. That and the idea that I might be contributing a little something to the arts. *That* idea is gone."

"I'm sorry about your son," Eickhoff said vaguely, kicking at the puddle of blood so that it spattered the blue carpet and the moldings.

"So what do you think of them apples, Eickhoff?" I swigged from the bottle. "My son's dead, and he was all that was keeping me alive. He's gone, Eickhoff. Wiped off the face of the earth. My Frankie."

He nodded sympathetically. "That really sucks, Slim."

"You just about nailed it there, Petey."

Eickhoff cocked his head at the sound of sirens. "You know, I just killed my wife," he said conversationally. "Alice was having an affair with Renquist here. But it wasn't just that. She was leaving me for him. And I heard him laughing in the background when she told me on the phone about, you know, leaving."

"Yes," I said, still not surprised. "Renquist was an

asshole, and your wife did you wrong, but I can't say I approve of your remedy." I took a swig and grimaced. "Well, hell, Pete. I take it something was bothering you even before all that."

I heard distant sirens. They were coming closer.

Eickhoff nodded gravely. "Bothering me for a long time. I haven't slept—I mean, really, *no sleep*—in so long. You see, my Alice left me and wouldn't talk to me. I've always had some problems, and they started to come back lately, but it's so goddamned hard to concentrate when I take the medication." His voice broke. Tears streaked his cheeks. "I can't *work* on the meds, so I cut back on them, and then certain kinds of, you know, *behaviors* start up, because I stopped the meds. And then she left me for Renquist. She was working in his office and...you know how that is." Eickhoff spoke faster and faster. "I called her today, and she told me she had a restraining order against me because I was yelling outside her window. So I said that was the last straw, and it really was, and I came here and I told her I had this gun, and if she didn't come out to talk to me, I was going to start killing hostages. And she didn't, so I did." He looked at the gun. "I did tell her. I warned her about that."

"Hostages?" I looked toward the Renquist inner office.

"Oh, I didn't take any *hostages*. I gave up that idea. I just shot whoever I ran into. They've been protecting Alice and Renquist, you see. There was that woman, Dorothy, who works in their IT department, and there was an intern, a pimply, rude young man, and there was that guy with the magenta hair who does their viral marketing. I shot those three, because they were in the way. And there was...I don't know who he was."

All at once I felt very cold. "What about the receptionist? Betsy?"

"Didn't shoot her. She ducked under her desk. I think she's still there. I was in a hurry to find Alice. And I shot a security guard outside, because he said he wasn't to let me in."

The blood continued to pool around his feet. As quickly as it pooled, it was soaked into the carpet, but then some more kept coming, refreshing the red pool.

Eickhoff held out his cup, and I poured some more Jack. Some part of me was playing him. I had it in the back of my mind not to die just yet. There was something I needed to do first, and I had an instinct to keep him from shooting anyone else by talking to him.

I was in a kind of existential groove with Eickhoff. He and I were both stricken, and he and I knew a certain truth we probably couldn't have articulated for one another. Having to do with being trapped in a big existential machine that was flying apart around us, its pieces cutting into us. And he and I both didn't give a fuck anymore.

Eickhoff took another drink.

"Whew...hard stuff," Eickhoff said. "You want my gun?"

"Your gun?"

"See, I finished the killing. It's all done and I don't want to do anymore. And--I don't want to talk to the police. And they're on this by now, pulling up outside. So..." Eickhoff held his gun out to me." I'd appreciate it if you'd shoot me. I don't seem to be able to do it."

I felt like a magic token was being passed over to me. A powerful talisman of some kind.

I took the gun, thinking that if I had it, he couldn't shoot me or anybody else with it. I didn't think I wanted to live, but I didn't want to be squirming in an office building, gut-shot and dying, either.

"I put a fresh clip in it," he said helpfully. "You can be, like, a hero. Say you took the gun from me."

It was a chunky semiautomatic .45, heavy in my hand. I was comfortable with guns.

I'd had a pistol and a Winchester rifle back in Austin. I got them as soon as I was legal to have them—everybody in Texas has guns—and spent a lot of time shooting at paper targets. I even went to an instructor for quick-draw and accurate shooting. After a year, I got second place in a Practical Shooting competition. USPSA quick draw. Next year, first place. This was before I got into the street drugs.

Later on, after we got married, Meredith made me get rid of the guns. Couldn't blame her for that. All the mass shootings—the lunatics weaponized by the NRA.

Police sirens yowled right outside the building.

I squinted at the gun. It seemed to swell and shrink and swell in my hand. Most certainly, I was drunk. "Where's the safety?" I was drunk and not so drunk. But drunk enough, I was having trouble seeing straight and figuring out the safety.

"It's there. See it? But why would you want the safety on? Can I have another drink?"

I gave him the bottle. The whiskey was giving me a headache anyway.

Then came the amplified police voices from downstairs, and shouts, all with an official tenor. You could hear their nervousness, their own fear, in it. I imagined Kenny and Rowse and the others at Ledbetter were hiding behind their desks, office doors locked. That was the sensible thing to do.

Eickhoff glanced toward the end of the corridor, where the cops' voices were bouncing around. He was swaying, beginning to shake. "Alice..."

I started to wonder how many other bodies there were. "Say, uh, Peter...you said you shot a security guard?"

"Just Renquist's security guard."

"Louis. Didn't really know him much. Too bad, though, you shooting him."

"Yes, I'm sorry to have shot him. I am. One favor, Mr.—Wait, I might have to throw up. No. No, it's passed. Mr. Prodocks—"

"It's pronounced Per-doo."

"Sorry. Trouble talking."

"No big thang there, Petey. So, uh...what favor?"

"It's just...could you please shoot me?"

"Oh."

He looked pitiful and like he needed to be put out of his misery. How would a guy like him do in prison? Like as not, he'd hang himself at the first opportunity.

I thought about Frankie. I raised the gun and pointed it at Eickhoff.

But I didn't have it in me to shoot him. To shoot somebody, it has to be *in* you, has to come out of you. It didn't seem to be in there for me to shoot Eickhoff, not in that moment. If he'd sold dope to Frankie, he'd already be dead. But he was just a guy who didn't take his meds and hadn't slept and lost his wife and flipped out.

I could shoot lots of *other* people, though, if they fucked with me. I could shoot just about anybody who fucked with me. I could shoot whoever had taken Frankie from me. Frankie had made everything meaningful. Having Frankie meant I didn't have to live with a lot of regrets. I didn't have to regret marrying Meredith, because that would mean regretting having Frankie. And I didn't regret having him, even now that he was dead. At least there'd been Frankie for a while.

It almost caught me then, the feeling, the rearing wave of pain. But it didn't, because that's when the cops started shouting through bullhorns down at the elevator. I couldn't see any of them yet.

"Get down on the floor!" came the amplified voice. "Throw your gun aside and get down!"

"Stay out there or I'll shoot this hostage!" Eickhoff shouted shrilly at them, though I was the one with the gun.

"Peter..." I began. But I wasn't sure how to advise him. "I can't do this for you." Then, in a boozy kind of way, I had an idea. "I know! The cops'll do it for you! Here, take the gun back."

He shook his head. "No, you keep it. Kill me before they get here, please!" Eickhoff licked his lips. "Please, oh please. I'm scared of them. I might fall down and beg them not to kill me. I'm not scared of *you*. I could let you do it."

I didn't understand that logic at all. But Eickhoff hadn't been taking his psychiatric meds. He had his own logic.

The booze made me dizzy when I shook my head. "No, man. It ain't in me to kill you in, like, cold blood. If you had another gun and threatened me with it, then I could."

"This is the San Francisco Police Department!" came the bullhorn from the crossing hallway. "Come to the door and talk to us in there! Do not hurt that hostage! If there are wounded people inside, let us help them! Don't make this any worse than it is!"

"How about..." Eickhoff stumbled to the receptionist's desk, splashing in the blood, and found a dagger-like letter opener. "I could stab at your eyes with this."

Eickhoff was just full of helpful suggestions.

The room spun a little when I shook my head. "No, Peter. Look, we gotta...we gotta surrender here." I stepped over Renquist into the waiting room. "Seriously. Enough people have been hurt."

Then Eickhoff came lurching toward me.

"This is SFPD. We are going to come in there. Drop your—"

Eickhoff slashed at me with the letter opener. I stepped instinctively back, and the gun went off in my hand. Eickhoff shouted in triumph and fell on his face at my feet.

Shot down. *I'd shot Eickhoff down.*

A pale, very young cop's face showed at the door of Renquist's reception. The SWAT guys hadn't gotten here yet, and this helmeted young guy was staring at me with his pretty blue eyes.

"Shit!" the cop swore. "Fucking hell!" Mad that he'd failed, so he thought, to save the hostage.

"No, I'm not the kil—" I began.

But a vase on the desk behind me exploded. The young cop was already shooting at me. He'd seen me shoot Eickhoff. He assumed I was the guy shooting people here.

I jumped back behind a doorframe. Another shot cracked past. "Throw your gun down!" he shouted.

Well, shit. Wouldn't you fucking know it?

If I surrendered, maybe I'd live, but they'd assume I'd done all the shooting. They'd assume I was the mass killer, my fingerprints now on the gun and all. They'd jail me in a little tiny cell, and oh my fucking god, I could not face that again.

It's not as if I thought this through, but it all went through my head in a second like a fiery meteor shower, and I was out of my right mind, if there is such a thing. I had been out of my goddamned mind since I saw Frankie on the slab.

A bullet smacked into the wall near me.

"You sons of bitches become cops so you can find some fucking excuse to shoot people!" As I shouted, I was moving into the back offices of Renquist, past a strip of cubicles, backing down the aisle, gun in hand, hearing the cops shout to one another just around the corner of the hall. I stepped over two bodies. A woman and a young man. I heard a scrabbling sound and was aware of people hiding in a conference room. A woman was whispering to someone.

Then I saw the door onto the balcony, and I was out the door and climbing over the rail of the balcony onto a motorized window-washing scaffold, where I found the switch and made the scaffold go down, way down to the alley.

I jumped down onto a closed dumpster from there, and —running almost joyously ahead of the black wave inside me—jumped on the hood of a parked cop car, denting it. Down from the car, I ran past the two startled cops sitting in the cruiser, hiding the gun in my pants under my untucked shirt, and around a corner to a crowd that was gathering.

I ran into the crowd, laughing, laughing uncontrollably.

Frankie. Frankie.

Stay ahead of it. Run! Run and get some ammo, reload that gun, and use it on the ones who killed Frankie.

Everyone in the crowd, not seeing the gun, just ignored me, dismissing me as some flaky street guy. They just got out of my way. I ran down into the BART train station, tossed my phone into a trash can, and ran to the turnstile.

3

STILL DRUNK, it took me two tries to get the ATM to work.

The ATM was one BART station down the line. I took out four hundred bucks, all it would give me at once. I knew the police could trace my whereabouts from that, but I wasn't lingering here. I was going to quickly move on and on and on some more. Keep moving. If you're moving, you can keep ahead of the pain front, like trying to outrun a tsunami.

Shoving the money in my pants pocket, I noticed a guy watching me, looking at that pocket. He was standing against the farthest wall. He wore a ball cap, something about hockey on it. Maybe thinking about jacking me up. Then people came sweeping between us, hurrying from a train.

I puffed up the grimy concrete stairs to the street, cutting between cars and prompting angry honking. I got to an alley, hurried past a drunk sleeping in a puddle of urine, got to a street, turned right, crossed to another alley, turned again...

I hustled my ass to the Tenderloin district. I was sweaty

in the humid afternoon, but so was most everyone else. I was sobering up from the exercise, sweating out the booze. My thoughts were racing in circles like a dog chasing its tail.

You're in it now because you flipped out when Frankie died, and if he were alive, you'd have dropped the gun and surrendered, but you wanted that gun. You wanted a reason to hit the streets with it, and now they think you killed people. You could've surrendered and explained, and they could've tested Eickhoff's gun hand, maybe found gun smoke residue, and maybe the gun was registered to him. But the cop saw you, and you ran, and so you're in it now because you flipped out when Frankie died and...if he were alive, you would've...

Like that.

I saw a thrift store on one side, used clothes and every manner of junk, a TV on behind the counter.

I ducked in, wondering how soon my face would be on the breaking news cycle. The sallow-faced, pot-bellied man behind the counter nodded to me and went back to talking to a skinny Black lady who was hugging an enormous purse by the cash register.

An ancient air conditioner wheezed in a side window, pushing around sluggish air that smelled of bug killer.

Do this quickly, I told myself.

"Why this weather on us like this?" the Black lady was saying. "It's sittin' on us like a fat old lady. Where the breeze from the bay?"

"Weather been crazy the last five years," allowed the man at the counter.

I picked out a used Levi jacket, a used white Resistol cowboy hat—a little worse for wear, somebody else's sweat marking the base of its crown—and some dark glasses, faux Oakleys.

I went into the one changing booth, a tiny little thing with a thin, tatty curtain, and had to step around a syringe with a bent needle someone had left on the floor. I pushed it into a corner with the tip of my boot and closed the curtain.

A long, narrow, cracked mirror hung on one wall, its cracks dividing me into two crooked men. I took off my shirt and undershirt and put on the jacket. Now I was bare-chested in an open Levi jacket. In the Tenderloin, it wouldn't seem strange. Just another crazy streety. Hands trembling, I put my regular glasses in the pocket of my jacket and put on the sunglasses. I got out two twenty-dollar bills from the wad in my wallet.

I tucked the twenties into the jacket chest pocket. I rolled the shirt up, put on the cowboy hat, and turned to look at my cracked reflection to make sure the gun in my waistband was hidden under the coat. It seemed to be, but I didn't like it being behind me in this jacket. I did up the three bottom buttons on the jacket, then stuck the gun in my waistband in front. I tugged down on the jacket. Yeah, it hid the gun fine. I put the rolled-up shirt in my jacket pocket.

Then the smell of the booth, and of me, my sweat and booze and the memory of the bodies I stepped over in the Renquist offices...

My gorge shot up, and I vomited a little, just a spurt I caught in my mouth. I spat it at the syringe. Trembling all over, I laughed a little and suppressed a sob.

Frankie.

The bodies in the office, a sprawling woman and a young man with his arms flung akimbo...

It was all a single phenomenon to me. Like if a train hits a bus, two things become one. The train crashes, and people die. The bus smashes and people die. That's how it's going now, I thought. For me, for this country.

For Frankie.

I closed my eyes and forced myself to take long, slow breaths. Something seemed to click inside me. I could almost feel gears mesh, click-clack.

Some sons of bitches needed to die. Not random sons of bitches. The ones who killed Frankie. There's no justice in a train wreck. But maybe I could make some justice happen anyway. Just my little corner of justice.

I came out to see the shopkeeper glaring at me because I was wearing his goods without having bought them. I walked over to him and said, "How much for the jacket, the sunglasses, and the hat?"

"You *gotta* buy 'em now, because you fucking got *sweat* all over that jacket and that other stuff," the guy said, leaning toward me. "Thirty dollars."

I took the two twenties out of the coat pocket, and then I noticed that there was a row of used knives and knuckle dusters in the glass case between us. One of the Buck knives was labeled with *8 doller* handwritten on a sticker. I pointed at it. "I'll take that Buck knife too."

I handed him the money, and he said, "There's some tax."

I said, "Keep the two bucks for that."

He passed over the knife. I slid it into the chest pocket of my jacket, turned on my heel, and strode out the door, conscious of the gun under my jacket.

I dodged between streeties talking to themselves and past Tenderloin folks talking to one another. I weaved between the little igloo-shaped tents of the homeless. Partway down the block, I came to a very narrow alley with a large, overfilled dumpster almost blocking it. Overfilled? It was a cornucopia of decay and dismissal. It flowed from the dumpster onto the cracked asphalt. Fast-food remains formed veins in its plastics and Styrofoam. I admired its boldness for a moment, then slipped into the alley, where flies buzzed up from the dumpster, outraged I'd disturbed their idyll. I sidled past the dumpster, retching a little at the smell from it, then stepped partly behind. I took off the jacket and went to work with the Buck knife.

It seemed to take a long damn time to cut the sleeves off the jacket. But I wanted to look like a streety dressed for the heat. I had an old stick-and-poke prison tattoo—a skull wearing a cowboy hat—on my right upper arm. On the left arm, more professionally done from my days competing in Fast Draw, was a coiled rattlesnake with the word Peace-maker curved under it. Blurred and bluing out with time, the exposed tats were all to the good to create the impression of a streety. I tossed the sleeves into the dumpster and, sighing with regret, put the rolled-up pearl-button cowboy shirt in there too. I put on the jacket, now more of a vest, checked to make sure my gun was covered, pocketed the knife, and went back to the sidewalk.

My mind was whirling again, telling me I could still turn myself in and explain. But if I did that, they'd still take me into custody, and even if *eventually* they decided I didn't do it, I'd be alone for hours and days, maybe months, curled up in a cell thinking about Frankie. Seeing Frankie and me in the canoe, Frankie and me reading a book together...

Frankie dying at a party. Victor's party.

I remembered Victor. I knew where the kid might just be. I was going to make use of that knowledge.

I dodged a waving, ranting, bearded guy and

approached the next corner, where a shop window said, "Hot Slices!"

And that was the first time I saw them. The woman and her man and their crony.

They were standing at the sidewalk pizza-by-the-slice window, and I knew something was up. The three of them were drinking sodas, and the stocky Black-Asian guy, standing close to the Black woman, was eating a slice dripping with cheese.

I knew they weren't just loitering, this tall, willowy Black girl with the corn-rowed hair and the short blue summer dress and her stocky boyfriend with the gold-lensed, gold-framed sunglasses, voluminous short pants that went past his knees, and a long LA Lakers jersey that could be hiding a pistol like my jacket was. He was maybe forty-five, a little too old for his clothes.

I noticed their probable associate—a squinty, red-faced White guy in a dingy red windbreaker and red flat-bill cap that said "Montreal Canadiens" on it—talking in under-tones to the gold shades guy. I recognized Hockey Guy. The guy who'd been watching me at the ATM back at the BART station. He must have followed me, and seen me go into the thrift store.

Now he gave Gold Shades a Look with a capital L, and then started walking toward me, as if just heading past. But he was trying too hard to look disinterested. He passed on my right, striding up on the sidewalk, and then I heard him stop. I guessed he'd turned around, was coming up behind me, making eye contact with these two finishing their sodas at the pizza place a few steps farther.

Maybe my face was already buzzing around cell phone internet, a wanted man with a reward. But I didn't think it could happen that quickly. I'd only slipped the cops half an hour or so ago. They'd still be sorting things out on the killing floor. I walked past the pizza slice window, past Gold Shades and Cornrows. I noticed she was a head taller than her companion. I took three more steps and turned the corner onto the avenue.

"Hey there, cowboy," said a voice behind me.

I turned around and saw that Gold Shades was coming up on me, the girl close behind him, the grinning Hockey Guy siding her.

"What's up, Tex?" Gold Shades said.

"You can call me Slim," I said, aware that it sounded like dialogue from a western, and liking it.

I noticed my senses were impossibly sharp now. The gut sickness was gone. I was so *there*. So present, so awake. The only thing blurring that *presence* and that rootedness in *being there* was the smoke that rose from inside me and sometimes fogged my head. It's funny how cold fury burns hot.

But right then, everything looked crystal clear: the scraps of fast-food wrappers on the sidewalk, old chewing gum pressed into blackened flat stamps, the posters for *MC SWEE-TOOF* on the wall of the alley. Every wrinkle in the sloppily glued paper etched in my mind—the rapper's carefully selected angry grimace, his gold and diamond grill.

Fuck it, I thought. *Let's not run from this thing. Let's do it.*

Maybe I could get a jump on my mission here, or go down with a gun in my hand. There could be some satisfaction in that. A little satisfaction was all I could hope for now.

To the right was a doorless doorway into a charred hallway. There was yellow caution tape lying on the sidewalk, ripped down by someone who'd decided to go into the burned building to hit up some dope.

"That doorway looks like a good spot for you to jack me up," I said mildly, as if we'd all known each other forever. "Let's do it there."

And I stepped into the doorway, turning so I was facing the street.

Now the three jack-buddies were in front of me, on the sidewalk, seeming both confused and amused. It stank so much of urine in the charred hallway, I almost gagged, but that would've looked bad. I didn't let myself gag.

I just opened my coat and put my hand on the gun.

"That's not a cowboy gun," the Black girl said. Just an observation. She wasn't scared of me or my gun.

"The motherfucker, he's *fou*," the White guy observed. He had some kind of accent. French Canadian, maybe. His upper lip squinched up like he was smelling something bad.

"*Mm-hmm*, going in there like that, he out of his damn mind," the Black girl agreed. "What you think, Wendell?"

Gold Shades, Wendell, shrugged and shook his head. He had a gun out already, a .38 revolver just dangling by his side, pointing at the ground. He didn't even have his finger on the trigger.

"What're you talking about, we going to jack you?" he said.

"Talking about y'all should find a stupider target," I said. "Canadian Red there was watching me at that ATM, saw me take out a bunch of Jacksons."

"How'd he know I'm from Canada?" the French Canadian asked.

"How people know Chinese from China, you dumb bunny," Cornrows said, chuckling.

Because I knew it would show my confidence to good

effect, I reached slowly up with my free hand, took off the counterfeit Oakleys, put them in the coat pocket, then replaced them with my wire rims, never taking my eyes off Wendell. "There isn't much more in the ATM account this time of the month, so you can forget the part where you try to get my card and my PIN number. Just try for what I got. Go for it. Then the bullets'll fly from me to you and you to me." I looked at Wendell. "Because I sure as fuck do not care at all."

Wendell looked into my face. After a moment, he nodded. "It would seem you don't give a fuck." He shrugged. "Why don't you just kick with us then?"

"You'll jack me first time I look away. But I tell you what. Why don't you go in with me, help me on my mission? It's going to take me where there's a pile of money. And you can have the money. I figure there's got to be some-where between ninety thousand and three hundred thou-sand. Dealer money."

"The man's on a mission," Cornrows said, shrugging.

Mostly, I was just fronting with them right then, dangling a carrot so I could get some kind of leverage. A play for time so I could decide if I was going to ditch them or if they could get me where I wanted to go. I only 49 percent wanted to die right then. Fifty-one percent of me wanted to go on my mission.

"How *much* money you say, player?" Wendell asked.

My turn to shrug. "How much money does a drug dealer have in his house? That's my mission. Take down this dealer. He got on the wrong side of me."

"Who's he with?" Wendell asked.

"What I hear, this guy's not connected anywhere special. No one to come after you later." I had no idea if that was really true.

"You got somebody in mind?" Cornrows asked. Her face was expressionless. The whites of her eyes were ivory yellow.

"Yeah, I just got to confirm a few things," I said, which was even more unmitigated bullshit. I had nothing to confirm since I had no idea who the actual dealer was. Or who the next level dealer was behind him. I wanted to get as many of them as I could.

"Latesha," Wendell said, "you let me ask the man the questions."

"Just askin'—"

"I said shut up." He kept his eyes on me. "Tex...Slim... you want to get a drink?" As he asked it, he put his little revolver away under his shirt with one hand, made a kind of roller-coaster motion with the other hand, to show the row of thick gold rings on it, to bling at me, maybe, and to say we can roll easy. I kept my hand on Eickhoff's .45.

"I need to put something in my stomach," I said. "Had three or four shots of Jack Daniels an hour ago. I'm out of practice with that shit. Giving me a sour belly."

I saw an SFPD cruiser ease by behind them. I took my hand from my gun, blocking the cop's view of it with my arm. I set to looking down at the ground, like a tweaker looking at the white spots, so that my hat brim would hide my face.

The cops went on by. They looked bored. It's safer for everyone when cops are bored.

Wendell, who wasn't stupid at all, glanced back at the cop car after it was almost passed, and then looked at me.

I put my hand back on my gun.

"Ah'ight," he said. Like, I get it.

We waited for the cop to be gone from the block. Then I said, "So I tell you what..." I smiled like a Bible salesman. I was going to get over on the people who were set to rob me. I was going to pick them up in my slipstream and draw them along with me. A smidge of satisfaction, right there.

"I'm buyin' dinner, if y'all want some," I said. I had to pretend I was equal to anything, so I dropped my hand from the gun and walked past Wendell, feeling him watching me.

Forty-nine percent of me wanted them to take a shot at me.

I started down the street to a little Chinese place on the next corner. I needed to get my face off the street. There could be an APB out on me any minute. Wendell and Latesha caught up and walked beside me as I said, "Y'all like Chinese beer?"

———

Standing behind the "Order Here" counter, the chunky Chinese lady who ran this Tenderloin greasy spoon had an expression on her face like she was very, very sorry to see us.

Latesha, Wendell, and Canadian Red were working their way through steamy piles of sweet and sour pork, Mandarin beef, and spicy shrimp. I managed to get down a bowl of wonton soup, the kind with the big gooey lumps floating in it, and half a potsticker.

It wasn't easy. The dead in the Renquist offices kept floating across my mind.

Focus on Frankie. You didn't kill anyone at Renquist. That was Eickhoff. And you shot the crazy prick.

I skipped the beer and drank the thin Chinese restaurant tea. I needed a clear head.

"Not much appetite there, Tex," Latesha observed, glancing up at me. I could see a prison tattoo on her forearm, a cross with a weeping Jesus over it. Which was maybe why she asked, "Where you learn to bluff that way? 'A good spot for you to jack me up?'"

"Texas State Pen, Huntsville," I said. "I was there just under two years. Possession with intent to sell, but in fact it was just intent to use it all myself."

She snorted. "I hear that."

They drank four Chinese beers each, none of them acting like it was strange at all that a guy they'd been planning to rob was buying them dinner. Because in the Mix, all kinds of things happened, and you never knew who was your friend and who was your enemy, not for long. I hadn't been on the street like this for more than thirteen years, but except for some new slang, it was the same old bullshit.

You could have all kinds of fun with people in a place like this, as long as you didn't turn your back on them or go to sleep with them in the same room.

I heard another siren whipping past. I started wondering what would happen late tonight or tomorrow when I ran out of strength to keep going.

I fronted like I didn't give a damn about anything, but there were a few things I was scared of.

I was scared to sleep. Scared of the dreams.

Asleep, I'd be vulnerable in other ways. I didn't know what'd happen if I fell asleep around Wendell and his friends. It could be they were the kind of people who'd decide that the best, most logical, most prudent course of action was to disarm me as I slept, beat me to death, and take what money I had instead of chasing my big score pipedream.

I was even more worried about the drugs. In this neighborhood. Around these people. On this mission.

How could I even contemplate taking drugs after what happened to Frankie? All I can say is: *That's dope.* You can hate it and still unquestioningly spend all your time and money trying to get it. It's a part of your brain that starts nudging you and thinks up rational-sounding reasons—not actually rational at all—why you should take your drug of choice again.

If I got into drugs out here, chances were I'd lose sight of my mission, lose sight of anything but more drugs, another hit, more drugs. Plus, I was a lame, highly unprofessional drug user. I couldn't really take drugs and be functional, because I always did too much. If I started taking meth or coke, my drugs of choice, I wouldn't stop until I was psychotic on them, thereupon attracting the attention of the police, who were looking for me right now, anyway.

I'd just lucked past those cops at Renquist's, just happened to hit on the wide-open moment. Another forty seconds and the cops would've had that place sewn up tight.

It was just possible, I thought, using my fork to squish the insides out of a potsticker, that the SFPD hadn't even identified me yet. The other office hacks hadn't been around. But pretty soon, they'd figure it was me.

"Skinny White guy in a cowboy shirt? That sounds like Slim Purdoux. I'm not too surprised. He was a bitter guy, and he was bitching about the PolyMedia takeover a lot. I heard he used to take drugs, though I guess he was in recovery. And no one's heard from him either. Oh, wait, look at this weird note that he wrote Rowse. Well, there you go...And I heard his kid just OD'd or something. Wouldn't surprise me if he gave that kid the drugs that killed him."

And what was Frankie thinking about when he died?

When he collapsed on the rug at that party and heard people around him laughing as he clawed at his chest before they realized how serious it was. Had he yelled out for his daddy?

His mom could be so brittle, so judgmental about me, even after my years clean. But she softened around Frankie. We'd watched him try out for a skateboard competition together a few months back, both of us pretending we weren't afraid he was going to hurt himself veering and leaping in that hard pool of skull-busting concrete. And her eyes, when she turned to me, had some of the old, lost tenderness in them.

Frankie must have thought of his mom as a completely different person from the woman I knew.

Had he called out for her when the blood started filling his lungs?

I was glad when Latesha broke into my thoughts.

"I'm fittin' to go outside for a cigarette," Latesha said, taking a pack of Newports from her purse.

"You don' smoke cigarette in here!" the Chinese woman barked. She was half Latesha's size, but she wasn't going to take any shit from her.

"I jus' *said* I was goin' outside, woman. *Damn!*"

Wendell and I both chuckled at that. "You watch out, she don't kick your ass," I said to Latesha.

Latesha took it good-naturedly and stood up. "I am watchin' out too."

Wendell said, "While you at it, you get Dulcet from the Fat Pussy."

"That fuckin' place a mile from here."

"It's no fucking mile, girl. Just get over there."

"Shit, I'll go get her," Red said, licking his lips.

"No, you won't," Wendell said. "You'd disappear into that place, start paying all your money for lap dances, grab somebody's titty, get into a fight with them bouncers."

"No, I fucking won't fight with no—"

"Just drop it now, Red." He looked at Latesha like, *You still here?*

She shrugged. "I'll go, but I don' know Dulcet wants to leave. She's makin' good money."

"You bring her. We'll be in the Boxcar."

Latesha fingered her unlit Newport. Her nails were long and curved and spangled. "Why don't you call her, see if she—"

"Why don't you shut the fuck up?" But even as he said it, he reached into a big side pocket of his short pants, or long shorts, or whatever those things are called—I never figured it out—and he brought out *three* small cell phones.

"That phone like to be no good now," Latesha said, pointing.

He tossed the one she'd indicated onto his greasy plate and tried one of the others.

"This one's inactive too," he muttered. He tossed that one with the first and tried the third one. That one seemed to work. But whoever he was calling didn't pick up. "She's not pickin' up."

"Probably out on the pole."

"You get your ass over there now, girl."

"Ah'ight," Latesha said.

"We'll go over to the Boxcar. Wait for you there," Wendell said.

I'd seen the graffiti-splashed entrance of Boxcar Cocktails and Dancing on the way from the BART station, just off Market. From the outside, it looked like a good place to go if you had an urge to get stabbed and lie bleeding in beer-soaked sawdust.

Latesha went outside, cigarette in her mouth, provoking the Chinese lady by firing the cigarette up with a Bic lighter before she'd quite gotten through the door.

Red looked mournfully through the window after Latesha as she walked down the street smoking. "Shit, I wouldn'ta—"

"Red, I'm tryin' to talk to the man here," said Wendell, though he hadn't said much to me since we'd sat down. But now he turned to me and said, "You talk like a player. You going to deliver what you promised there, Tex?"

"I don't have to deliver anything to you, Wendell," I said. "But if you're there with me, you can rake in something good."

"And you don't want the money?"

"I have another interest. I owe a man a bullet. The man killed my son."

He gave me another searching look. Then he shook his head in wonder. "I believe you, and I don't know why."

"I don't," Red said.

We ignored him. "Wendell, you can take it or leave it. But it's a lot of money."

Red looked at Wendell, apparently surprised that Wendell sat still for someone talking to him like this. But again, that look passed between me and Wendell. Two guys who really didn't give a fuck. Wendell knew he could probably kill me, but he couldn't intimidate me.

Wendell said softly, "I do need a score right now. Got some things to pay for."

I went on, my voice soft, "You got to go with me somewhere first. I need to confirm one thing."

"Go where?"

"Over in the Sunset District. You got a car?"

"Bensur, we gotta van," Red said.

Bensur? After a moment, I realized it was his version of the French *bien sur*.

What were the chances, really, somebody wouldn't spot

me from some web news shot and call the cops on me, running around town like this?

Again, I thought about turning myself in. But I was on a mission. I could turn myself in when it was all done.

Wendell drummed his fingers on the table. "I can't be running around the Sunset not knowing what I'm doing. The SFPD going to stop us in that neighborhood. You never heard of 'racial profiling?'"

"So let Red drive."

"Ah, sure," said Red. "But you know, there's some skip tracer motherfucker looking for us."

Wendell turned him a look of disgust. "Shut your froggie Canucky mouth! Between you and Latesha, always running your gums. You stressing me out."

A skip tracer? A bounty hunter working for a bail bonds outfit. That could make things interesting.

I pointed something out. "He going to look for you in the Sunset District? Probably not. He going to look for you around here? Probably is."

Wendell made a grimace that meant I just might have something there, but he had to think about it. Then he shot a narrow-eyed look at me. "So you was in Texas State Pen. I got a connection was there. You know Bran Tangles?"

Luckily, I did know him. "He was there. Big man on campus. Tangle Gang boss. I had a run-in with him, but I had Choo-Chee with me. He spoke up."

"Bran's my uncle. Married a woman in Dallas, got himself busted there. I heard about Choo-Chee. How you hooked up with him?"

"First couple of months in the unit, there were guys trying to bitch me. I had to fight, got beat up a lot. Then somebody came after Choo-Chee—four of them. I was there, and I stepped in. Got my ass kicked again, but it slowed them down. The guards got there and maybe saved Choo's life. So Choo sided me. Kinda found me entertaining. Called me the Lone Ranger. And he spoke up for me. I bet that up, for real."

"You got no tats I can see."

"I gotta tramp stamp of John Wayne."

Wendell stared at me. I laughed, and he realized I was joking and laughed too.

"No, see..." I went on, "I was always about getting a straight job when I got out. And I had one for a long while, editing books. But then...shit happened."

"It does that." He pushed the beer aside. "Let's get outta here, get a real fucking drink. The van's over by the Boxcar anyway."

————

Early evening, it was a balmy night, everybody in shirt sleeves, lots of bare chests.

I walked along with Wendell and Red. I could smell Red, sweat that had decayed and then covered over with a fresh layer. He didn't bathe much. Wendell smelled like a high-quality cologne.

We walked past the corner of Hyde toward Ellis. Five Cambodian teenage boys—that was my guess, anyway, Cambodian—were sitting around a boombox on plastic milk crates, listening to hip-hop. Swee-Toof.

I always hadda way
I sho always know
A mothafuckin chump
Fumma real high-roll...

The Cambodian kids might or might not have been a

gang. They were wearing white or gold ribbed tank tops, nose rings, and gold necklaces.

They looked at us with a loaded emptiness. I knew better than to make eye contact or even nod. Stay in neutral.

We kept on until we came to an asphalt basketball lot, cracked and infiltrated by weeds. Red and Wendell paused to watch a pickup game that was at some point of primal testosterone explosion, Asian kids and a few Chicanos whipping around each other, grunting and shouting, whipping in and out of the melee so fast I couldn't follow the moves.

"That boy with the dreadlocks, he got some game, ay?" Red said. He took a circular container of smokeless tobacco from a shirt pocket and thumbed some under his lower lip.

I was looking nervously up and down the street, checking the people out. I saw a Black drag hustler with afternoon stubble but eyebrows plucked pretty much to nothing, sashaying on big, muscular legs, out of uniform in cut-offs and a sweatshirt with the sleeves missing, prison tattoos on her biceps. When she passed people she knew on the street, she said, "Hey Boo-Boo! How you, Boo-Boo!" in a sort of Yogi Bear voice. They all grinned back at her and waved.

A couple of meth tweakers, a sagging White woman and a gaunt Black man were fighting over trash can bottles. I didn't see any cops. But it wouldn't be long before the prowl car rolled on by again.

"How's about, let's get off the street," I said.

Wendell looked at me, shrugged, and led the way again. I was walking a tightrope. If I fell off, I'd be lost in Frankie dying, Frankie dead. If I kept moving, kept my mind always focused on the next thing and the next thing, I stayed on that tightrope. It was not good to stay in one place for long, and not only because of the police.

I was afraid of five in the morning. I was going to have to go to ground somewhere...

Just keep moving. Eyes on that tightrope.

Then we went into the Boxcar. I put on my regular glasses and looked around. It was almost a shock how much better it was inside than it looked outside. It was a surprisingly comfortable place, with a fireplace. Okay, the fire in it was fake, just rotating lights under red plastic logs, but it looked nice glowing at the far end of the long, dimly lit boxcar-shaped barroom. There were only a few high windows, set with purple and green stained glass, giving the room a mellow art nouveau sort of glow. The bar was a nice one of mahogany. An expansive mirror behind the bar reflected some high-toned liquors. The well booze was down below. There were plush black leather booths at the back of the lounge.

I was relieved to see no bar television. I didn't want to look up and see myself on a news flash.

There were only half a dozen customers. The usual shaky old men, a bored middle-aged Black guy in janitor's coveralls, one trembling skeletal White woman in a skanky outfit who might have been a whore. She looked like she'd probably been up for a few days.

"Looks like they decorated for a different clientele," I muttered.

Then I thought, maybe that wasn't the smartest thing to say to Wendell.

But he laughed. "You got that, Texas boy. New owner got it like this cheap. The people who put it here, they thought the neighborhood was, you know, uh—gentrifying."

I nodded. "Figured it was gentrified before it was.

Looky there, with its own little spotlight on it, a print from..." I started to identify the industrial still-life as Ozment, from the Purist school, one of the post-Cubists—I had three years of art history at UT Austin—but I decided that might make Wendell think I was showing off. I didn't want him primed to have to prove anything, any more than he already was. "Some art-catalog crap."

"They got that decorator shit going," he said distantly, as we took bucket seat leather barstools.

The bartender was a slender young Asian guy in a Hawaiian shirt who kept chewing his lip. It was like he was waiting for someone in particular. Wendell ordered Rémy.

True to form, Red ordered Canadian Club. "That's real patriotic of you, Red," I said. "As for me, I don't drink Texas beers." I got an Irish coffee. The only coffee he had was the burnt-tasting stuff for drunks who wanted to try to sober up.

"Yeah, this place," Wendell said, making a point of paying for the drinks. "It had a cigar room, where they had a deal that it was legal to smoke in there. It's still there, but there's no cigars left. They gonna put a pool table in there."

"Whassup, Wendell?" the bartender said. "You gonna get us a new pool table?"

"I got a call in on that pool table. I told you that. Don't you get it nowhere else," Wendell said.

"Some bars, I heard, serve only oxygen," I said. "Flavored oxygen from a tank. You pay to suck air from oxygen masks. In New York and Japan."

"Now you fuckin' with us," Wendell scoffed.

"No, I heard that too," the bartender said. He glanced at me. Had he spotted me when I was standing at the door looking around? Remembered me from some news flash and called the cops? Is that who he was waiting for? SFPD? But he hardly seemed to notice me, except to look at my cowboy hat. "I like your hat there, Tex," he said.

"Tex likes to be called Slim," said Wendell, who was genuinely fucking with *me* now.

"It's true," I said, "about the oxygen bars."

"It get you high?" Red asked.

"No," I said. "Might give you a headache."

"And people, they pay for that shit, ay? I like to get into that business," Red said. "Selling air. Maybe they buy some farts from me, ay."

Wendell laughed. He was looking at the door too, like the bartender.

I wondered about Wendell and Red. How'd those two improbable associates meet up? In prison? Not impossible, but I'd done my time in Huntsville, and though that was a long time ago, I was sure it was the same scene anywhere, anytime. Black guys stayed with Black guys for protection. White guys stayed with White guys for the same reason. Hispanic with Hispanic and so on. Most likely, they'd hooked up in the Mix, in the tumbling dice of street life, probably around drugs, which brings all kinds of people together. Which drugs, in this case? That was an issue. Some drugs were safer to be around than others. But then, did I care what was safe to be around?

What about what Frankie was safe to be around?

Oh sure, I tried to protect him. But why hadn't I warned him more about dope? I *did* tell him, but I should have drilled it into his head until he was past sick of hearing it, and then told him some more. He'd known dope was a roach motel, theoretically. But a kid sees his friends getting high and nothing *apparently* going wrong with them, so he figures maybe the adults were lying. Or if he's mad at his parents, and most teenagers are going to get mad at them, he doesn't care anymore if it's dangerous. Maybe he wants to do it *because* it's dangerous.

I didn't go into it much because I didn't want to lose my son's friendship. So I lost my son.

"Well, fuck *me*," I said aloud, with an ugly chuckle.

Wendell glanced at me incuriously. I shook my head, not wanting to explain, and he looked back at the girl at the end of the bar, maybe wondering if she was worth the trouble to recruit.

He struck me as a kind of jack-of-all-trades, who never hesitated to pimp his women but who didn't like to work at any one thing too long in any one place. Always a step ahead of something, which was maybe something else we'd recognized in each other.

I drank some of the brackish Irish coffee. The bartender hadn't put any cream or sugar in it, and looked at the stained-glass windows straining streetlight through in purple beams, and thought of a funeral chapel.

Eickhoff saved me from having to go to Frankie's funeral. I didn't want to see Frankie Wayne James Purdoux in a coffin. I didn't want to talk about how he had loved life —which would only be about half true—and about how it was a loss to the world, but he'd always be with us and...

I started getting seriously restless in this funeral chapel of a bar. I was starting to *feel* too much. There was a drunk-tank full of unwashed, retching, babbling feelings in me, fighting one another for the little window in the door.

"How long we got to wait in here?" I asked.

"She be along," Wendell said. "Whyn't you tell me what you got going. The details, you know?"

I shook my head. "Maybe somewhere private."

The bartender licked his lips, looked at his watch, and then asked Wendell, "You watch the bar for a second,

Wendell. I got to go to the bathroom. I don't trust that hustler down at the end."

Wendell thumped fists softly with him.

The bartender slid off to the bathroom. He looked, frowning at Wendell once, as if wondering, just before disappearing inside.

I reckoned bartender-boy was going to shoot up some dope or maybe do a line of speed.

Wendell got up, stretched, went confidently behind the bar, tapped the cash register keys in some pattern that made the cash drawer open, reached into the back of the drawer for the larger bills, and shoved them in a pocket.

He looked at me. I shrugged.

He looked at the other people in the bar in a very flat kind of way, and they got the message. Like it was rehearsed for simultaneity, they all looked down at their drinks.

He closed the register and came around, and I thought sure we'd split then, but he just sat down.

"Now, I can watch the bar from those booths there. Let's sit there alone, and you can tell me what you got going, Tex."

The dark wave was close to catching up with me inside, and I thought, anything, anything.

"Yeah, sure."

Wendell and I got up and went to an oversized black booth under a window. The tabletop had only a few knife marks and cigarette burns on it. Almost like new.

I leaned back and improvised the pitch. "There's a drug dealer who takes his own shit. He's all fucked up. Bad security. Got a pile of cash around him, maybe as much as three hundred grand."

Wendell grunted. "Sounds good. What kinda dope?"

"All kinds. He's nobody you know, probably, and there's

no way to connect us to him. He don't know me either." I was making most of this up as I went along, except the parts about there being a dealer and this hypothetical dealer probably not knowing us. "I just don't want to go in alone. You never know for sure. He might, after all, have some-body to back him up. Might have an AK-47, something like that."

Wendell looked at the table. He sipped a little Rémy. He looked at the door.

"You could be a cop."

"You know I'm not," I said.

He thought about it and nodded. "But I don't think you're any kind of pro in the life either."

"Not for a long time. I did some time. But you're right, I was not a pro. But I'm a good pistol shot, and I keep moving till I get what I'm going after or I go down. I do what I say I'm going to do."

I considered telling him about what had happened with the cops and Eickhoff. It might dazzle him.

Or it might discourage him. He might figure I was too hot to chill with, so to speak.

"You don't fucking know me, and I don't fucking know you," Wendell said, not saying it out of concern, but more just finding it remarkable.

He drank some of his Rémy and went on, "But I'm so fucking bored, and so close to the bottom of the pocket. I told Red to watch the ATMs and score for us. He didn't even get that done. I got some debts to pay. So...Tex, where in Texas?"

I pushed my glasses back on my nose with one finger. Something self-deprecating in it. "I'm from Austin."

He snorted. "Bunch of college students and hippies. I was born in Dallas, but I left there when I was a kid. I been

back to Texas a few times. See my uncle. Got a lot of rela-
tives with something like your accent."

"So are we good to go?"

"*Maybe* good to go. *Maybe* could be. Got to wait for my
girls. Think on it. I don't like to be fucking rushed. I like to
do the rushing."

We didn't say anything for a while. Then Latesha came
in, blinking in the sudden dimness, herding ahead of her a
bottle-blonde White girl, black streak in her hair. Her name
was Dulcet.

She was maybe thirty-two and had her hair rubber-
banded up in those two little fanned-out tufts on the top of
her head, kind of a rave thing, that curious-puppy-ears look
that was an ironic mock of innocence. Her expression was
distantly annoyed, understatedly depressed, and there was
some kind of impudence in her eyes that she used to keep
the depression at bay. Her face was long, like a lamb's. Her
ears stuck out a little. But she was pretty. She had nice eyes
if you didn't get lost in the expression. She was at least five
feet nine inches, buxom, and a little overweight. Her clothes
were another burlesque: a little girl's blue and yellow frock,
way too small for her, with the top unbuttoned to show her
cleavage, and white tennis sneakers with little white socks
folded down at their lacey tops just above the shoe.
Stretching between the sneakers and the horizon of the
billowy little skirt were nicely turned legs in blue stockings.
Each long fingernail was painted a different color, like the
little girl had been playing with her mama's manicure kit.
She carried a small, shiny plastic Barbie purse with a
picture of Barbie and Skipper frolicking on the side of it, on
a long yellow strap.

"She wear that outfit on the street?" I asked. "Around
here?"

"She got a little backup pistol in that little toy purse," Wendell replied, in a soft aside to me. "Anyway, people know who she belongs to."

It was unlikely that Wendell ran the Tenderloin in any way. If anything, the Cambodian gangs ran it now. But I nodded.

"Who's the four-eyed cowboy?" Dulcet asked, looking at me with no social shyness whatsoever.

I thought her accent was maybe Florida. She didn't wear much makeup. Her lips were naturally dark pink. She had hazel eyes, and it looked to me like one of her cheekbones was slightly lower than the other. You had to look closely to see it. That might be from an operation that went wrong. Or a beating.

She had one tattoo on her upper arm of Betty Boop.

"Slim Purdoux," I said, and put out my hand.

She did a little girlish curtsy, ironic as her outfit, and briefly shook my hand. I could feel hand lotion still drying on her plump fingers.

"Pleased ta meet you, Cowboy Curtis." A mock of a little girl's voice. "I am Dulcet Groans."

"She got an act, when she strip," Latesha said, seeming to feel an explanation was necessary. "Does that little girl thing."

"Complete with lollipop?" I asked.

"I'm her motherfuckin' lollipop, and the only one. You keep that up there in your cowboy hat too," Wendell said, not bothering to put a threat in his voice. "Unless, of course, I say she give you some."

Dulcet said, "Can't afford a shirt, cowboy?" Dropping the little girl tone.

"A matter of personal style, and a hot day," I said.

She looked right at the place where the gun was under

the jacket, nodded faintly, and then opened up her purse—and got out some candy. "You like sour candy? This is super sour, this stuff."

"No, thanks."

I glanced at the bar. Red had that skinny whore on his lap, grinning at her with all his tobacco-discolored teeth. She was chattering away and didn't seem to mind him. Her hand was on his back, not so far from his wallet. Red had a certain obtuseness, but my guess was that meth girl would be sorry if she tried to lift his wallet.

The bartender hadn't come back from the bathroom yet, I noticed.

An old Black man got up from his stool and went to the restrooms, opened the men's room door, and there was the bartender on the floor, slumped against the wall, nodding. Not dead, just in dreamland.

I looked away, so I wouldn't see Frankie, and watched as the people in the bar got up and, taking turns looking at the bartender, went around behind the bar, one of them at the cash register, another grabbing high-priced liquor.

Red dumped the whore off his lap. He'd pretty much forgotten she'd existed, you could tell, before she even hit the floor.

"You fuck!" she shouted, rubbing her fanny.

Red went behind the counter, grabbing bags of peanuts and a bottle of Irish whiskey.

"Get me that Rémy, Red, yo," Wendell called over to him.

The old Black man had the Rémy bottle and tried to hold it back. Red cold-cocked the old guy in the forehead with the bottle he already had and caught the other bottle falling in the hand that held the peanut bags without losing the peanuts. Arms crowded with all this, he came back around the other side of the bar, waiting by the door.

"Let's go then, ay?"

Dulcet watched all this without reacting, except she clicked her front teeth together, click-click-click, sort of meditatively. She had a way of doing that.

"That jus' like the boy," Wendell said, "getting peanuts. Without me that all he do—steal peanuts."

Latesha barked a laugh again.

"How come you made me leave work, Wendell?" Dulcet asked, chewing sour taffy like gum. "I was making some money for you."

"I s'pose we gonna go out to the Sunset, see what we can see," Wendell went on. "Let's get the van."

He led the way to the door. I let him lead the way, right then.

I glanced behind the bar on the way out of the place and saw the old man sprawled back there, his head bloody, stirring a little, cursing softly. He'd live.

I looked into myself and saw no feeling for the old man, which was interesting. I was different today. I was, for sure.

Mostly all I felt right then was relief at moving, staying one step ahead of that certain something.

When we left, the whore was in the bathroom with the door open, going through the bartender's pockets.

4

WENDELL HAD stops to make before he was ready to go on my mission. A lot of them. We trundled around town, stopping here and there to pick up money and goods. He had a team of teenagers boosting for him, and he picked up the shoplifted health and beauty goods from them. Four shopping bags' worth. He took them to his man, who sold the stuff online, and collected money from him for yesterday's sales.

Wendell co-owned a massage parlor and spent about an hour there arguing with the manager about receipts. He told us the place was losing money and sat in the van a while talking to prospects who might want to buy the place from him. Then he went on another roundup. The day wore on like that.

Latesha, Dulcet, Red, and I were gummed up a long, dismal time sitting in the van, waiting for him, the engine running for the air conditioner. I tried not to think about Frankie and pushed away flashes of Eickhoff and Renquist's bodies. Dulcet and Latesha gossiped, Red trying to get in the conversation and mostly getting cold-shouldered.

Wendell would come back, and we'd drive on, stopping in a couple of bars for some kind of lottery scam I never did suss out. None of it added up to a lot of cash. A little less than six hundred dollars by the time it was sunset. Time to go find Victor.

It wasn't just luck finding Victor. I had dropped him and Frankie off at this little shopping center before, and I knew Victor was here almost every day after school until the cops ran the kids off.

"You can smell the ocean," Dulcet said, rolling down the van window. She was in the front of the old Ford van, beside Red, who was driving. Wendell, Latesha, and I were in the back seat. "Ohmigod, ya get so hot and bothered with doing stuff in the city you forget about the ocean being right there."

"That's true, girl," Latesha said.

We were about twenty blocks from the ocean, in the parking lot of a shopping center dominated by a Safeway. The big red letters, lying about safety, shone morosely down at the parking lot. The supermarket was flanked by a dry cleaner and a taqueria. The shopping center had a shoe store too, and a couple of shops that had gone out of business with For Lease signs in the windows. Fogtown Comics 'n' Cards had not made the grade.

On the right side of the parking lot from us was a Shell station, and behind it, the teenagers congregated, with skateboards and Bluetooth speakers. And there was Victor, as always, with half a dozen other guys and one defiantly-smoking, pimply White girl with cerise hair. She was sitting on an overturned plastic bucket, flipping a green-glowing light stick up over her head, catching it, flipping it up again.

There was an impromptu line of skateboarders doing

grinds and ollies against one of those little concrete bars they put at the end of parking spaces.

"Whoa, shit stain! You can't do a spinner on that?" That was Victor, heckling some kid. "I can do better than that, blood!" Victor was a medium-sized kid with a slack mouth and spiked hair, brown toward the roots, the tips bleached white. He wore a zip-up windbreaker hoodie with the hood up, over a Juji T-shirt, the same kind of loose shorts as Wendell had, and Vans brand skateboard shoes.

We pulled the van up near the boys, as if we were just watching the skateboarding.

"Mother*fucker!*" Victor was yelling as he piled up, trying to do a grind, scraping his palms. "Nigga, get out my way!" This to a portly White kid.

"How come," Dulcet said, "all the shoes the kids wear now are, like, too big for their feet?"

"Those shoes not too big on the inside," Latesha said. "Just the outside. Too fucking big for they little bodies."

Wendell lit a blunt and offered it to me. I shook my head. Still holding the smoke in, he passed it to Red.

Victor was looking toward us.

"That's him there wearing the windbreaker," I said. "Go ahead, Dulcet."

She opened a window and lazily leaned her cleavage out the window. "Hey sugarbone! You Victor?"

He looked at her with a visible mingling of lust and naked suspicion. "Uh...yeah?"

The portly kid laughed. "He's not sure who he is."

Dulcet idly fluffed one of her puppy-dog hair tufts with her hand. "I'm from Big-Ass Skateboards. We're looking to sponsor you," Dulcet said. "We heard you were good. You want to come with us and try out?"

"I never heard of no Big-Ass Skateboards," the girl said, scowling at Dulcet. "They're all hoaxing you, Vic."

"I think I heard of it," Victor said, though Dulcet had made the name up. He snapped the skateboard up with the tip of his foot, caught it in his hand without looking at it, and walked over to us. "Y'all get the ska'ers to try out at night?" he asked, seeing Wendell and Latesha through the window.

"That's Big-Ass Skateboards for you!" Dulcet said. "That's our lifestyle! Come on, cutie. We're going over to the skate park."

"Which one?"

"Nearest one, fool," Latesha said. She opened the back door of the van.

I leaned back, keeping my face in the shadows, my hat brim tilted down.

Victor nodded, mouth open, eyes half glazed. His nostrils twitched at the smell of the pot. "Oh, that new park out at Sutro Baths? Fuck it, les go. I'm your nigga."

Wendell laughed softly.

He climbed into the van and squeezed in between me and Latesha. Wendell was in the seat behind us. Latesha closed the van door with a slam that made Victor jump, and we drove off, toward the beach.

Wendell leaned forward toward Victor. "So...you my nigga, huh?"

"If y'all want to sponsor me for skateboard competitions and shit, yeah, nigga. Shit yeah, dog. Can I have a hit off that blunt?"

Latesha laughed and passed it to him. "That a blunt, huh?"

I said, "I thought a blunt was one of those little cigars, with some marijuana stuffed in it, and some other dope too."

"It used to be," Dulcet said, nodding, watching the boy smoke the dope. "Now the shit's legal for grown-ups. They got these big pre-rolled things. Got so it just means reefer, I guess."

Wendell was watching Victor with hooded eyes.

Victor looked at us, his mouth dropping open. He finally noticed me. "Mr. Purdoux?"

"That's part of me," I said.

"Yo, you the one recommended me to be sponsored?"

I chuckled. "I recommended you, all right."

"Is Frankie going to chill widdus at the skatepark?"

I looked at him for a long moment. Finally, I was able to answer him. "Frankie's dead, Victor. Fentanyl's what killed him. It was mixed in with the Molly you guys took."

Victor coughed up smoke. "What? He's *dead?* For serious? You're fucking with me!"

"Yes, he is, Victor. I saw his body. He's dead. There's a lot about him and me you don't seem to've heard about."

Victor gaped at me. Then something occurred to him. He looked out the window. "This ain't the way to the skatepark."

"Hey, bingo, ay!" Red hooted.

"What's up with this shit, motherfucker?" Victor asked, with his best imitation of street bravado.

Wendell leaned closer to Victor. "What up with that gangbanger shit you talking, you little cracker bitch boy?"

Victor blinked. The pot had slowed his reactions. "Uh... fuck. You dudes ain't sponsoring shit, are you?"

"That's right, Victor," I said. "That was an untruth."

"But I was good, wasn't I?" Dulcet said.

Latesha laughed. "Yeah! Damn! 'That's Big-Ass Skateboards! That's our *lifestyle!*'"

Wendell chuckled appreciatively. "That's my baby girl."

Dulcet stuck her hand out toward Victor. He recoiled. She said, "You want some sour candies?" She opened her hand to show him a couple of wrapped-up sour taffies.

He took them automatically. "Uh, cool. Thanks." He looked at me. "So if you're not, you know..."

I nodded sagely. "We are on a whole different mission, Victor. I have some information in my head, and I need you to confirm it. You can do that by telling me where Frankie got the drugs. From you, right?"

"What? Fuck no! We both got 'em together. But he took more, and he...I don't know...I threw mine up."

Latesha laughed.

Victor scowled and added defensively. "Yo, I was drinking hella forties, man! Too much of that shit, so I throw up."

"Oh shit, he drinkin' 'forties' too," Wendell said, shaking his head. "Boy, can't you find your own culture?"

"Who'd you get the fentanyl from, Victor?" I persisted.

"I...we...we got 'em from Abel at the Bike 'n' Board. And I don't know where he got 'em."

I looked at him, and I knew he was lying about not knowing where Abel got them. "Yeah, you do, Victor. Where'd Abel get 'em?"

Victor looked at the door. I'm pretty sure he was imagining slamming that door open and jumping from the van. We were driving slowly down side streets, zigzagging toward the beach road.

I shook my head. "Victor? Forget it. Don't think about going for that door. That's not going to work. Think about what I asked you."

He glanced at me, then away. When he looked back at me, there were tears in his eyes. "Frankie's really dead?"

"I saw his body"—my voice caught—"in the..." I cleared my throat. "Yeah. He's dead."

Victor looked into the middle distance, likely thinking about Frankie being dead, and I could see him peering, for a moment, into eternity.

He whispered, "Whoa. Fuck."

"Where'd he get 'em?"

Victor shook his head very slowly, twice. "I so totally really don't know. I really don't, Mr. Purdoux. Please."

I believed him. I patted his shoulder. "Okay. I'll ask Abel."

Wendell looked out the window at a passing car. "That one not a cop, but who knows when one ride on by and get curious." He sighed and drew his pistol. A Baretta niner.

Victor was trying to seem unworried, unwrapping a sour candy.

"Hey, boy," Wendell said. He smacked Victor on the side of the head with the gun, hard enough to get his attention. Latesha barked her laugh.

The boy recoiled, shouting at the impact. Blood stained his scalp almost immediately.

"What?" he yelped.

"What else you know, 'my nigga?' Huh?"

I looked inside myself again to see if I cared. I saw nothing there for Victor. Felt nothing for Victor.

But I said, "I believe him. He doesn't know where Abel gets it. So I'll ask Abel."

I leaned back in my seat to wait. We drove along the beachside highway. There were few lights here.

Victor's eyes were sliding to their corners to see Wendell's pistol. His slack jaw was trembling, dropping a little spittle into his lap.

"That kid looks comical, doesn't he, Latesha?" Dulcet said, as if fondly amused with a toddler.

"He's going to pee his pants."

"Hey, now. He don't fuckin pee in my van, ay!" Red called sharply over his shoulder. His voice was a little slurred by the smokeless tobacco he'd just thumbed under his lip.

We were just pulling into a strip parking lot at the beach. There was a faint scribble of silver on the waves from the young moon, and far down the beach, a fire burned in an old steel oil barrel. I could just make out bottles glinting as they were lifted to firelit faces.

Red turned off the van and switched off its lights. We sat in a little glow from a streetlight about a hundred feet away.

Latesha peered at the fire down the beach. "We way far off from those people," Latesha said. "They can't see no license number from here. Maybe give him a bust in the chops and push him out, Wendell."

Wendell shook his head. "I don't think we should let the kid go. Names been spoken. Faces hangin' right out to look at."

"I won't say anything, not to anyone, ever!" Victor said pretty believably.

Wendell turned a glare toward me. "You don't know shit about this dealer, do you, Tex?"

Red mimicked the glare at me with one of his own. "I don't trust this cocksucker, Wendell. 'Tex.' 'Slim.' He don't even know his own name. He's lying about shit, Wendell. He's making all this shit up, eh? I don't want to be around him if we don't need to."

I ignored Red. "I know what I need to know, Wendell,"

I said, figuring that was the right degree of ambiguity. I looked him in the eyes and waited.

Maybe Wendell had figured I had flat-out lied about the money supposedly just sitting there for the taking. Maybe it would end here, in this van on this dark beach, with a scream from Victor and an exchange of gunshots.

So big deal. Let's do it then.

Wendell looked at me, his face hard to read in the dimness. "You know what you know, huh. You just a White guy lost his kid, looking for revenge. That's some fucked-up shit for me to get into."

"Mos' def," Latesha said.

I shrugged. "The money's there. I stand a better chance of coming out of it alive with the money if I have some help. But you do what you want."

But Wendell smiled. "Well, shit. It's like I said, I got nothing else on. Let's see what we see."

"You guys, listen..." Victor began.

"Oh, now it's 'you guys' and not 'my nigga?'" Wendell observed.

Red turned in his seat and pointed his finger at Wendell. "You don't shoot his brains all over my van, Wendell, eh? I said you the boss, but this fucking van is all I got, ay?"

"Just shut the fuck up, Red. I'm gone take him over to that dumpster there. You get the motor runnin', but keep the lights off—"

"Hey, whoa!" Victor shrilled. "Don't!"

"Got to, brotha man," Wendell said, grinning. "Because we going to have to kill some motherfuckers around all that dope money. If they is any. And with you knowing about us...Uh-uh. Noooooo...."

I looked into myself. Was I going to let them do this?

The side door made a rumble-rumble-*chunk* guillotine sound as Wendell slid it open, and then he and Latesha were pushing Victor out. Victor yelled something I couldn't make out and tried to run, but Wendell had him by the shirttail.

Latesha was looking after Wendell and Victor with a sort of blank sadness.

"Ooh," Dulcet said, pointing at the floor. "He dropped one of my candies, still wrapped, on the floor there. Hand me that. I've only got a few more on me...Thanks, Latesha doll."

Wendell was dragging Victor over to a dumpster in the parking lot about fifty feet away. Cars passed, but Wendell and Victor were in the darkness on that side of the van. He was dragging Victor away from the streetlight into deeper and deeper shadow.

Victor yelled, "Mr. Purdouuuuuuux!"

I remembered Victor as a boy of twelve on a trip to the Marin County Fair with me and Frankie, waving with Frankie from a whirligig ride as the garish ride-car whipped by. *"Yo, hi, Mr. Purdoux!"*

I remembered him and Frankie showing me skateboard moves. Victor, who had no dad, was just as concerned as Frankie to have me watch him do a trick. *"Watch, Mr. Purdoux!"*

I sighed. And I drew my gun.

Latesha saw that and reached for a gun somewhere low, stashed somewhere I couldn't see. She did it so I'd notice.

I said, "Just simmer. I want to shoot the little prick myself. He got my son killed."

Latesha relaxed and nodded sadly.

I got up and climbed out of the van and, hiding my gun in my left armpit, strode over to catch up with Wendell.

Victor was on the ground, Wendell standing over him. Victor tried to get onto his feet to run—in the position of a sprinter—and Wendell kicked him hard, knocking him over against the dumpster. "Ow! Shit, please! Don't! I'm not going to tell anyone anything!"

"Wendell?"

He turned to look at me. I could just make out that he was frowning.

His gun hovered in the space midway between Victor and me. It might turn first to Victor. It might turn to me.

5

I MADE MY VOICE APOLOGETIC. Man-to-man friendly. "I used to make sandwiches for this pitiful little fuck here, Wendell. He's got a single mom. She's...she was pretty nice to my kid. So I'm asking you not to kill hers. Nobody's going to backtrack all the way to this dumb little asshole. And he'd never go to the PD on his own."

Wendell looked at me, thinking. Victor was breathing hard...and listening hard.

Wendell looked past me at the van. "I don't think I can do it, Tex, after I walk him over here to do this."

Victor wailed, hearing that, and tried to crawl away.

Distractedly, Wendell kicked Victor in the head so that he sagged, gasping, stunned.

"I understand," I said. "They're watching. I told 'em I was going to ask you if I could do it. Like a favor. Long as it's, like, under orders from you, right? I'll make it look good."

Wendell thought about that, frowning.

Finally, he shook his head in quiet amazement. "Look at that! I am just letting you fuck with me. I must really like you, Texas Slim. But you second-guess me one more time? That's the end of your ass. You understand me? I'll just step up behind you and shoot a tunnel through your head."

I played it like one businessman negotiating with another, all reasonableness. "Yeah, of course. I hear you. I'm just asking a personal favor. This once."

He looked at me, then at the van. Then he nodded. I glimpsed a flicker of relief on his face. He said loudly, so the others would hear it, "You going to do it, Tex? Then fucking get it done! I want that shit done, motherfucker!"

I nodded vigorously. He walked back toward the van.

Victor was blinking, coming back to himself. He turned to look up at me.

I hated the sight of him. Too simple to blame it all on him, but if it hadn't been for him, Frankie would probably still be alive. And it was easier than admitting who the real culprit was right then. I said slowly, thoughtfully, "Actually, thinking about it...I really *should* kill you, Victor. I know you're the little prick who got Frankie started on drugs."

I raised the gun and pointed it. Victor screamed.

There was a ragged rust hole in the dumpster, hand-width, right next to Victor's head. I shot into the rust hole twice, whispering between the shots, "Act dead, dumbshit."

Victor, whimpering, sagged as if dead. But you could still see him breathing.

"Hold your breath till we're gone, moron," I muttered.

Victor sucked it in and held it.

I strode with a grim, satisfied air back to the van.

The people at the fire down the beach were shouting something I couldn't make out. They'd heard the gunfire, had seen the muzzle flashes.

I half expected Canadian Red to drive off without me,

but he waited, though the van was moving when I jumped into it.

Red U-turned and drove out onto the highway, then down a side street, before switching on his headlights—and before I finally got the side door shut.

Dulcet looked at me and then winked. She leaned over and whispered in my ear, "You're so cute, pretending to kill that boy. Letting him go. I'm glad."

———

We were cruising slowly by Fort Mason, where yuppies and bohos went to see small, chic theater productions and orchid shows. We passed the complex, turned left, and another block or two took us to a strip mall.

Barry White was rumbling around a classic on the soul station. Wendell was singing softly along with it. "I admire that man," he said. "Barry's got style. He know how to talk to a woman."

I saw a mocking smile ghost over Dulcet's lips when he said that.

"There's the Bike 'n' Board, right there," I said, looking at the strip mall.

I'd taken Frankie to this shop for the best skateboard trucks, the hottest ball bearings, and a T-shirt that said "Arrest Me, I'm A Skateboarder" on it. And he'd reluctantly accepted an Element helmet and shin guards, which he'd only worn once. For some stupid reason, I'd been way more worried about him killing himself from cracking his head open skateboarding than getting into dope.

Red pulled up across the street from the shop. There was a light on in the back room. I could see it over the unfinished wall behind the counter.

Frankie might have grown up to be a comic book writer. He might have grown up to be a doctor who worked for Physicians Without Borders. Or he might have been a shop owner, selling bicycles and skateboards in a little strip mall storefront like this—and loving it, and perfectly fine, perfectly happy, safe as anyone is safe.

"I don't know what the point of this is, ay?" Red muttered, looking in the mirror at Wendell. "There's not going to be much cash in that place. It's just another place to get noticed by the cops, you know, eh?"

He might have grown up...he might have been...

"Red got a point," Wendell said. "We going to follow this up, let's go over to Richmond where the fucking money is."

"Red." I looked at Red. I thought it might be time to make a move with respect to Red. I could feel he was the loose brick in my building. "What's the appeal with Red, Wendell?"

I said it that way, talking about Red like he wasn't there, just because it would piss Red off.

And I needed to get started pissing Red off. Because Red didn't like me around, so I didn't like Red around. Which meant I had to push him so he made his move when I was expecting it, and not when I'd let my guard down. It's a pretty basic equation, really.

Red looked at me in some amazement. "Who the fuck you think you are, cocksucker?"

Wendell snorted. "Red's a good driver, and he's got nerve. He always been loyal."

"I ain't loyal to this Texas cocksucker," Red said.

"Red, find another epithet," I said, genuinely irritated. Cocksucker I could just barely tolerate, for a brief time. But *Texas* cocksucker?

"Whoa-ho, listen to that, ay? Epithet! Suck my dick, Texas cocksucker!"

I decided this wasn't the time to escalate it further. "Wendell," I said, letting all feeling slide from my voice. "I need to find out from this guy Abel exactly where the dope money is and when it's going to be there. They'll have pickup days."

"Now that's a point," Latesha said.

"Shut up, Latesha," Wendell said absently. "Maybe he doesn't know about that part of it, Tex."

"But he might. Let me ask him."

He considered briefly, and then he nodded just once. "Okay, but I ain't here for any mission of vengeance for angry daddies," Wendell said.

Meaning I was on my own in there with Abel. That suited me.

"I hear you, man," I said, getting out of the van.

"And don't fuck around," Wendell said. "We leave if we don't feel comfortable, you know?" he added, as Latesha slammed the door behind me.

I walked across the street, looking up and down the avenue for cops.

No cops, no cars of any kind. I put my hand on the gun in my waistband.

The front of the shop was dark, just a small neon clock over the back counter. Mountain bikes hung from racks. Skateboards lined the wall over the counter. There were cases of skateboard trucks, wheels, and special ball bearings.

I walked around behind the shop. I remembered what Abel looked like, and I saw him through the back window. He was using an electric screwdriver, tightening the truck screws on a skateboard vised to a workbench. There was a finished one next to it. He was making house skateboards with his logo on them.

There was a bong on the bench with smoke drifting from the top of it, like the last smoke from a chimney just after the factory shut down.

I could hear music playing from a radio on the shelf over the bench. It was a local metal-rock station, which called itself "The Bone" for reasons no one but its marketing department understood. They were playing Pantera's only radio hit.

The back door was open. "Hi, Abel," I said cheerfully as I came in behind him, like I was an old pal coming for a visit.

He jumped, spinning around with the electric screwdriver poised out in front of him like a knife.

"Fuck! Who the fuck are you, sneaking up on me like that? I am fucking closed, dude! Back the fuck out that door!"

I laughed. He made a funny sight, all worked up like that with that little whirring tool in his hand, especially considering how I felt about him now. "What you gonna do? Unscrew me?"

Abel was an ex-surfer. Now, at forty-something, a small-time entrepreneur in the skateboard resurgence. He was chunky, darkly tanned, his head shaved on the sides, blond hair long on top and back. He wore surfer shorts and an open bowling shirt. Under that was a T-shirt for Dogbreath Skateboards with a picture of a cartoon dog riding a skateboard and flipping the world off.

Wendell had said don't fuck around, so I pulled the gun and closed the door behind me.

"All right, that's it, asshole," Abel blustered, setting himself for a fight, but looking more scared than angry.

Especially after he noticed the gun. "What the fuck? You going to rob me? It's not worth the trouble."

"Abel," I said calmly, "You killed my son."

He took a step back and went pale. "Who the fuck...No, dude. What?"

"Or you and I killed him. You more proactively, selling him dope. Me passively. Working together without knowing it, you and I, to kill my son. Eventually, the police are going to take care of my part of the justice, what with the shit I'm getting into. But I think, really, it's up to me to take care of your part. Don't you?"

He was stoned, and it took a while for all this to sink in. "Man, you...got me totally mixed up with somebody."

"I know you, Abel. By sight. Victor says you're dealing fentanyl. Mixed with X or speed or something."

"Victor! That little fuck! Victor is full of shit!" He looked at the gun in my hand. "He's full up to his little pinhead with steamin' shit, bro! You think I'm dealing drugs, call the police on me!"

"I don't have time for that."

"Goddammit, what do you mean, killed your son?"

"You know my boy, Abel. Knew him. Frankie Purdoux? He's dead. He got the dope that killed him from you."

"Look, I smoke a little weed. I might even sell a little Thai stick now and then..." He was going onto the balls of his feet, probably thinking about jumping me, jabbing at me with that electric screwdriver. Maybe catch me by surprise before I shot him. "But I never—"

"Where'd you get the shit, Abel?"

"Um...I don't know. A guy I knew. He moved out of state."

I took a step toward him and pointed the gun at his crotch. "That is such an obvious lie, man. It's as big and obvious as a billboard for a casino guaranteeing good luck. So where you want to be shot first? I'll give you a choice. The crotch or your right kneecap."

His lips went white, and he started to pant. "I...Those guys...No—"

"I don't care." I cocked the gun. "I'd just as soon shoot you as not anyway. Tell me. I'll know if you're lying."

He stared at the gun and then closed his eyes. "A warehouse in Richmond. Banyan's place."

"Who's Banyan?"

"Just some raver asshole."

"What's the address?"

He told me. "Ricky Kwai's the fenty. Banyan's the X. That's all I know."

He was almost hyperventilating. And he was thinking too hard. You could see the strain of it on his face, trying to estimate: Could he jump me?

"You can't, Abel," I said. "The safety's off. I can't miss at this range, and if you twitch, I'll shoot a hole in you. Now put that Home Depot sale item down."

I raised the gun to point at his face. If I had to shoot, I'd probably drop the muzzle to the center of his mass, to be sure of hitting him, but the psychological effect of a gun pointed between your eyes is profound.

I looked into myself to see if I felt bad about any of this. Nope. Not at all.

"Okay, you're not going to drop the tool? Then I'll say goodbye right now, Abel."

He dropped the screwdriver from slack fingers, his eyes now riveted on the muzzle of my gun. It was like he was trying to literally see down the dark barrel, see the tip of the bullet.

I thought about Frankie, and sorrow was utterly indistinguishable from rage—and I felt like pistol-whipping Abel to a pulp. And he kept looking down into the barrel of that gun.

I kept my voice carefully flat. "You ever think about what happens when a person gets shot, Abel? You better think about it if you plan to keep anything back having to do with that certain little warehouse. A bullet, Abel, is like a battering ram. You know? Like for a castle?"

He nodded numbly, staring into the muzzle.

I went on, genuinely into my subject. "The bullet, like the battering ram, *smashes into* its target. It breaks through. I mean, in movies, they make it look like punching a neat little hole, almost surgical, but really it's a *smashing*. It *smashes* through the skin, it *smashes* through the soft tissue, it *smashes* through the organs, and it *smashes* through bone. Can you imagine how that'd feel? A flying battering ram bashing *into* you? And with a big ol' .45 caliber like this? It sets up shockwaves that explode through the body outward from that hole that's smashed into it. Sometimes it smashes right on out the other side." I paused and bent closer to him. "Think about what else I might need to know."

Abel made a squeaking sound in his throat. "I think..."

"Yes, Abel? Go on."

"I think they pick up the money Thursday night. Maybe four or five guys get together, count it and shit, at the warehouse. They got a whole route they go on, and that's the last...the last stop. To count it, turn it over to..."

A whole route? That would please Wendell. Lots of money. Me? I didn't give a fuck.

"And?"

"I swear that's all I know. But don't tell them. If you tell anybody that I told you this shit, they'll—"

"You are worrying for nothing about that."

He relaxed a little until I went on, "Because I'm going to kill you right now, man, for what you did to my son."

"Hey, people buy shit off me they *know* is not pharmaceutical!" He was waving his hands now, his voice getting loud and shrill. He was edging toward the door behind him that led into the front of the shop. "I don't make nobody take it! And he musta done that shit wrong!"

I nodded understandingly. "I would generally agree that an adult, they take their own chances with drugs. It's their lives, Abel, right? But a kid Frankie's age? He didn't know what he was doing. And you didn't really care to tell him. You don't really care about anything or anybody."

"There's money right there. In that metal box there. See it there, on the workbench?" He wanted me to look away from him. "See it? I can get more tomorrow. A whole buttload more!"

I shook my head, and my hand tightened on the gun—and he bolted for the door to the front room of the shop.

I have a thing about shooting people in the back. Not that I'd ever shot anybody dead before, unless you counted Eickhoff. I didn't count him, because that wasn't intentional. But I'd known that I would shoot somebody someday. Some people just know it.

"Hey, Abel..."

With my left hand, I scooped the finished skateboard from the worktable, slapped it toward him so it spun down under his feet.

Abel tripped over it, fell down in the doorway, and turned toward me. Scrambling up, he squeaked, "Don't! It was your own—"

They say that it's hard to shoot someone the first time, and after that, it gets easier. They're right, up to a point.

Maybe it's especially harder for certain people, their first time.

He looked pathetic, scared. His face drawn into a white, involuntary grimace of fear.

But there was a big momentum in me, a momentum that was like a wall of black volcanic glass, shoving me onward. And they didn't really matter, those feelings that made me hesitate. They were just some extra, peripheral feelings.

The main thing was feeling like I wanted to kill this motherfucker.

I shot him twice, carefully. The first time he yelped, like a kicked puppy. Before the second shot, he put his hands up instinctively to protect himself, palms outward.

I fired, and one of his fingers disappeared. The bullet that took off his finger finished its work, a battering ram smashing into his chest.

Abel fell back and convulsed like a fish just yanked from the hook. I was surprised at how much he shook there on the floor. After a minute, he lay still. I could smell the shit as his bowels let go.

I looked at him. What had he started to say? *Don't! It was your own...*

My own fault? Was that what he was going to say? If so, he had a point. But it was something I already knew.

That's when I saw it. That finger I'd shot off had been carried along in some kind of slipstream of velocity, and the bloody upper half of it, about from the middle knuckle up, was lodged in one of the holes in his chest, right over his heart, flipped around.

Abel's shot-off finger was pointing out of the wound on his chest, and right at me.

Life simply likes to *fuck with you* sometimes.

I was distantly aware that Abel's radio was playing an old Blue Öyster Cult song.

The chorus was saying, over and over:

One step
Ahead of the Devil
One step
Ahead of The Man
One step
ahead of Evil
You can only run as far as you can...

I wanted to shoot the radio then, but I just grabbed the metal box Abel had pointed to, put the safety on my gun, stuck the gun in my waistband under my shirt, and went out to the van.

I had to keep moving.

You can only run as far as you can...

I'd just killed a man. Once before, I'd shot a guy in the leg, years ago. I'd never killed one before.

If I'm honest, I felt a little high.

———

"Four hundred and six dollars and change," Latesha said, as she finished counting the money from the little metal box.

"Ey, big fucking deal, okay?" Red snorted.

"You can have my share, Red," I said. "Buy yourself a new personality."

It's not the line. It's the delivery. Dulcet laughed.

"Hey, fuck you, cocksucker. I'll *take* your fucking share."

I smiled like Buddha and said softly and sweetly, "It was an offer made in all sincerity, Red."

Wendell chuckled at that and shook his head. "Crazy editor boy."

I wished I hadn't told them over dinner that I'd been a book editor.

We were crossing the Richmond-San Rafael Bridge from the Marin side, soaring over the blue-black San Francisco Bay on an arc of steel.

"So that warehouse was on Google Maps, Dulcet?" I asked. It was time to ignore Red again.

"Sure, if they haven't moved." She shrugged, peering at an old iPhone with a pink glitter case she'd pulled out of the Barbie bag.

"That's where the serious money is."

Red snorted. "Yeah. Maybe."

Dulcet turned and lolled her head over the back of her seat and pouted at Wendell. "I want to get high, Wendell."

"You get high sometime, Editor Boy?" Latesha asked me.

"Not really. Lost control of that shit a few times."

"Shit, I always lose control. Wasn't for Wendell, I be shaking my heels at the ceiling for that glass pipe."

Dulcet laughed with a sisterly fondness.

"That skateboard shop guy going to talk to anyone, Editor Boy?" Wendell asked.

He gave me a particular look, which I understood to mean, *You kill this one for real?*

"No, he isn't going to talk to anyone," I said. Seriously wishing they'd stop calling me Editor Boy. "He's not even going to ask what's for breakfast."

I gave him a little nod that meant, *For real this time. He's dead.*

I looked inside myself again. Still didn't find any regret about Abel.

What I did feel, though, was tired. And I was still afraid to sleep.

Maybe some drinks would help. I had to keep out ahead of that thing that was trying to catch up inside me. And if I slept, it'd get me for sure. Maybe a gallon or so of Irish coffee...

"How come they callin' you Editor Boy?" Dulcet asked.

I sighed. "Because when we ate dinner, I was still a little drunk, and I made the mistake of telling Wendell I was a book editor. Till recently. After I got out of jail, I got a break from the chief of...of a publishing house."

"Ooh! A book editor. You edit anybody famous?"

"Depends on what you mean by famous. Joel Spaulding. I'm not his usual editor, but for one book—"

"Joel Spaulding! I love his shit!"

"She always reading something," Latesha said affectionately.

Dulcet said, "Did you edit *Devil May Care*? I loved that one. When that guy turns into a tiny little bug-man and crawls into people's bodies and eats them up while he's in there, and they can hear him saying, 'How you like that, how you like that?' That's some funny shit."

"Damn girl, you makin' me sick!" Wendell said.

Red was taking the first exit off the bridge, toward Point Richmond.

We circled around and down, followed the freeway for a while, and then drove along the underpass beneath it. The towers and tanks of a refinery rose on one side. They always made me think of tubes in the back of my grandfather's old TV set, writ large.

If I'd been driving around with Meredith, I could have remarked about how some artifacts, like industrial technology, only made you think of older kinds of technology. That was the referent that came first to mind. It was that far removed from human warmth. Though these people would have understood the remark, because they weren't stupid—with the possible exception of Red—they wouldn't have seen any point in saying it. But Meredith liked to talk about ideas for their own sake. Something I'd liked about her.

Too bad I hated her now. Thinking about that, I hoped she hated me too. That'd be justice for Frankie, if his parents each hated the other.

"There's the warehouse," Dulcet muttered. There was an almost sexual huskiness in her voice. Maybe it was for the money in warehouse.

It was a squat, rectangular, tin-roofed wooden place. A rust-pitted metal sign, from maybe thirty years ago, read "Kwai & Sons" over the loading dock at the parking strip. On one end wall, there was one of those old billboards they painted on the sides of buildings, kept for vintage charm. The faded, peeling face of a cherubic boy brandished an orange soda bottle, and under his grin was the slogan, "FANTA, now that's refreshment!" complete with the quotation marks.

"Shouldn't be too hard to get in there," I said.

The warehouse looked pretty run-down, though not abandoned. Run-down is good because it means the place is porous. Lots of holes, ways to break in. Less chance of an effective alarm system or cameras.

Not that I wanted to get in and out without coming across anybody. There was no point in it for me if the dealers weren't around, even if there was a big pile of unguarded money sitting in the middle of the floor. I just wanted to get the drop on the sons of bitches.

Sure, I thought about how I'd come from standing in the midst of a mass killing, to looking to kill people myself, all in one day. How that would seem to people. But I'd been simmering about killing the dealers involved in Frankie's death from the moment I saw him lying in the morgue. Not at the top of my mind, but it was there. Then, when the police started shooting at me, and I felt the gun in my hand...

I mean, if they were going to blame me for the Renquist killings, why not at least get some justice for Frankie?

We drove slowly around the warehouse, just once. I could see a light in a painted-over corner window, where the office might be. No sign of security cameras. Nothing much else to see, except an outside door into the corner office—a last resort.

There was a big blue SUV parked in its weedy strip of gravel parking, one of those bull-like six-wheeled Ford pickups with the extended cab. Its license plate read BLUE OX.

Across from the warehouse was a storage-rental business with a chain-link fence around it. It was late. No one was around, though they might have a security guard. And CCTV.

Behind the building was a vacant lot waist high with weeds. Flanking the warehouse were cinder block buildings. One was a modest plastic toy manufacturing plant, judging from the Tammy's Tots Toys sign. The other, a used car parts business.

"Your skateboard man say when the cops patrol through here?" Red asked.

Latesha looked at me. "You ask him that?"

"No," I admitted. "But he wouldn't have known. Cops aren't here now, so maybe we should just go with the momentum. It's quiet. We could just...go in."

"Now?" Dulcet asked, her eyes shining. She liked the idea.

Wendell shook his head. "Not yet. The money's not all piled up yet."

Dulcet said, "Can we go over to Leon's? He's so close."

"That what I'm fittin' to do," Wendell said, annoyed that she'd anticipated him. "We party a mite and rest up, and we go in tomorrow night."

But I didn't think I could make it that long. Not without blowing my brains out.

Or somebody else's brains. At least.

Still, we went to Leon's place, half a mile away, and thinking about it now, I'm pretty sure that the bounty hunter was already watching the place when we got there.

6

I WAS HAVING to watch myself because, after years of sobriety, I'd lost most of my ability to keep my mouth and my impulses in check under the influence. I had downed a couple of shots of Jameson, and I was already on my way to drunk.

Red was snoring on Leon's sofa. The rest of us were out back. We sat under a naked yellow lightbulb on the big wooden back porch, talking and drinking, the others smoking pot laced with cocaine. Wendell in a rocking chair, I was in a canvas deck chair, and Dulcet, wrapped in a long coat, lounged in a hammock. Latesha got up from her deck chair, to go into the kitchen.

Leon was a tall, very Black guy, muscular, but with a roll of beer fat, and close-cut hair salted with gray. He was sagged in the overworked deck chair with a tumbler in one hand, a cigarette in the other, but he kept looking at me like he wanted to say something about what the fuck was I here for and did they know anything about me and was I maybe a cop—and then kept thinking better of it because Wendell had vouched for me.

Leon's was up on the east side of the ridge that sheltered Richmond from the bay. There weren't any houses really close by. It was an old two-story wooden house, good-sized, with an up-sloping backyard, the front yard choked with flowering azalea bushes. The house was recently painted white, and the picket fence was half the same color, as if they'd run out of the extra house paint partway.

Leon, who was even older than Wendell, had some Marvin Gaye softly playing on the living room stereo. Between songs, there was the distant sound of cars, and there were crickets in the ivy. I could smell the white flowers on creeper vines that had overgrown the rose bushes in the up-sloping backyard. They say that parasites dominate the biosphere.

The air smelled sweet up here. The night, though, was wearing thin. My head hurt from the liquor, and I was getting hungry—and at the same time, the thought of food still made me sick.

I figured there was an APB out on me by now, thanks to Eickhoff. The people I was with weren't prone to checking the news. But eventually, they were going to hear about a Purdoux who was being sought by police. And the idea that I was a mass killer would change their whole attitude. They'd think of me then as a grenade with the pin pulled. If I could get my own mission done before they found out about me and the cops, that would be enough. Turn myself in to the police, or maybe Wendell would decide I was a liability and step up behind me and make that tunnel through my head.

Leon was Wendell's cousin, and he was part of the reason Wendell had picked the Bay Area after his crew's sudden exodus from Miami. From the general talk, I gathered Wendell had ranged across the south—Texas, to Atlanta, to Orlando, to Miami.

Came the day he had to get far and fast from Miami. Two of his people had been picked up and were doing time in Union Prison in Raiford. I didn't pick up on the details of the sudden exodus from Miami, except that it had as much to do with dodging Cuban gangsters as ditching cops and bounty hunters, which was why Wendell needed me. He was no kid anymore, and he'd lost most of his money in Florida. He needed a fat score.

"My man Leon here, he put me up for six, seven weeks, when I first got here," Wendell said.

Leon took a drink and grunted, then said, "More like four months, but who's counting?"

"You are, OG. You got some black tar?"

Leon hesitated. Frowned at me again.

Latesha made a dismissive flick of the fingers. "He's all *right*, Leon, *fuck*."

He grunted. "And you know this how, girl?"

"She's an intelligent young lady," I said.

Leon made a noise deep in his chest as he stood up. He had the look of a guy who was going to ask if I was implying something about him.

"Just simmer, Leon," Wendell said.

Leon glared at me, then looked at Wendell. Then he pointed his finger mutely at me and gave me a don't-fuck-with-me look, and went into the living room to turn the record over. It was an actual vinyl record on a turntable. Not one of the newly fashionable kinds. This one had been purchased in the eighties. But he had the latest 90-inch TV.

Had Leon seen me on the television news on that big TV? Was that what was behind the hostility? But he'd have said something about it. *Wendell, you know this mother-*

fucker went postal, shot a bunch of people at work? You can't trust a wacked-out motherfucker like that.

But Leon's mistrust was probably more a matter of policy, made more pungent by the fact that I was a strange white guy who didn't act like the White guys he usually dealt with.

I was getting terminally antsy again. Maybe I should tell Leon, "Fuck you, I'm a cop. Here's some cop action if that's what you want." And then I could shoot him in the head, because I gleaned that he sold black tar heroin. He was a part-time dope dealer. Just a sideline. His main job was AC Transit bus driver.

Leon came back and sat down with a double grunt.

I was about to just get it all over and done with—and I even started moving my hand toward my gun—when Latesha came out with a joint for Wendell and a fresh tumbler of Johnny Walker Red and Coca-Cola for me, smiling. I drank some of it, and I felt like chilling a bit then. Wendell took his hit, handed her the weed, and she said squeakily, through the exhale, "You want a hit of this, Editor Boy?"

I shook my head. "Y'all please stop calling me Editor Boy."

"What you going to do if *I* want to call you Editor Boy?" Leon said. "Do tell."

He was checking me out by pushing me this way.

I shrugged. "I'm gonna ask you to call me Slim or Jimmy."

"How about Slim Jim, like those chewy things?" Dulcet said, winking. Taking up the little girl voice again, "You a big, bad, stinky, chewy stick, Slim Jim!"

Latesha laughed. "Slim Jim."

"If you must," I said, "Slim Jim. But not Editor Boy."

Leon grunted. "I said, what you going to do? *Make* me call you different, Editor Boy?"

I glanced at Wendell. He looked up at the moon and studiously said nothing.

I shrugged. "You know, I don't think I'm going to get into a fistfight for anything. I'm not up for it. I'm fading too much. I don't think I should *shoot* anyone just for giving me a stupid nickname. Doesn't seem right. Especially as you're Wendell's cousin. So what does that leave me? I guess you call me Editor Boy."

"Oh, Leon, call him Slim," Dulcet said. "Or Tex. He's from Austin."

"Shut up," Leon said, just the way Wendell did. "Wendell, your ho is back talking me."

Wendell said, more dutifully than angrily, "Ho, shut the fuck up."

Dulcet chuckled, seemed to get a certain satisfaction from hearing that, and shut up when she heard it.

"'Kay," she said faintly.

"We going to have some harrow-ron?" That's the way Latesha said heroin. "Or not?"

"Editor Boy going to have some?" Leon asked.

I had some rationale or other for saying yes. Social necessity of the moment or something. But I probably just wanted the dope. Like I said, it makes no sense. It has its own logic. Like, for example: *I'm going to get high on something different this time, and since it's not what I used to take, I won't get addicted to that.*

Or even: *I am on a mission to kill the dope dealers who killed my son. I hate dope. So now I'm going to take some dope. And that's why I hate it, and why I want to kill people who give it out, because it makes me want some now, even though dope killed my son...and that's why I must now...must now...must now have a hit...a big, strong hit...*

Drug logic.

I leaned forward in my chair. "Yeah, I'll take one good hit, Leon." It wasn't my drug of choice. I wasn't going to trigger into a binge on that stuff. And I thought I needed to show Leon I wasn't some kind of undercover cop. But maybe all that was just a load of addict rationales.

Leon pointed his finger at Wendell. "I bring out my dope, I get some pussy."

"You get some pussy anyway," Wendell said, starting his rocker going. It creaked on the wooden back porch, as if in reply to the crickets.

Latesha looked up at the moon and said distantly, "Whatever my man say." Dulcet shrugged.

"I don't want no motherfucking stripper pussy," Leon said. "Last time she said all that weird shit to me, I couldn't keep my motherfuckin' wood. Made me feel like a goddamned child molester. I want some cash too, Wendell. I'm almost outta shit. I can't afford to give shit away."

Wendell shrugged. "Latesha, give him half that cash Tex here got today."

"Okay, baby." And Latesha got up immediately, went into the house, and out front to the van. Less than two minutes later, she came back and handed him the money I'd taken from Abel. She'd probably sensibly pocketed fifty or sixty dollars too.

Leon folded the money without looking at it and put it in a shirt pocket. He waited a while, so he could show he was in charge and hence would get the dope in his own sweet time.

Eventually, Leon grunted to himself, got up, stretched, and lumbered into his bedroom. A few minutes later—

Dulcet watching the doorway the whole time, waiting—he came back with a small metal tray. On the tray was a lump of black tar heroin, a small sheet of aluminum foil, and a torch lighter. Leon got to work using a pocketknife to lay some of the lump out on a piece of foil.

Latesha said, "Wendell don't allow needles."

"That black tar'll give you abscesses if you shoot it," Dulcet said, unconsciously rubbing an old scar on a bare thigh. She was watching Leon's every move.

"We jes' chip on it, like ol' pros," Latesha said to me. She was watching Leon too.

Leon made the smoke rise, and Wendell inhaled it from the foil. He leaned back, his eyes immediately dimming.

Her voice husky now, Latesha added, "Wendell don't let us do the hard narcotics too often."

I nodded approvingly. Going to use dope, it's good to have a dope nurse.

We each chased the dragon rising from the burning black tar. It tasted like opium to me, but harsher, and it wasn't all that different.

I was already fucked up from the whiskey.

I sagged back in my chair, feeling like I'd crossed some kind of moral Rubicon. But more like if Caesar had crossed the Rubicon, marched a while, then said nah, and went slinking back over.

That's right, it was doing *dope* that made me feel that way, not killing Abel. I had no qualms about killing Abel.

Stoned, slumped in a deck chair, nose itching, slightly sick to my stomach, I told Wendell about the finger sticking out of Abel's wound. Abel's shot-off finger, pointing at me out of the bullet hole.

"You full of shit," he said, laughing.

"You watch, it'll probably be in the papers." Then I thought, *Purdoux, don't mention the newspapers.*

"Because you *stuck* that finger in there, with your hand, motherfucker. That shit is ballistically impossible."

"Improbable, I grant you. But it *can* happen, because it did! It's like synchronicity. One of those weird coincidences that make you think life is playing games on you."

Wendell nodded solemnly. "I do know that kind of shit for sure."

I almost told him about Eickhoff then. That was life fucking with me too. But I bit that one off. Best he not know until he had to.

I was getting sleepy from the dope and whiskey, but I was nowhere near actually sleeping. There were whirligigs dancing around the edge of my vision. Scimitars flashed in the darkness. The moon breathed and exhaled, sucking in and out. I thought I saw Frankie slipping through the ivy. I thought I saw him riding that small luminous gray cloud across the sky. I thought I heard him crying like a small child...

Daddy...

It was the heroin. Just the breath of the dragon.

I took off my glasses and rubbed my eyes. I looked up at that moon, not quite full. Without my glasses, the moon was all distorted, doubled and tripled, so it looked like a fat yellow spider, the double exposure of its edges splitting to look like the spider's legs.

About this time, I'm guessing, the bounty hunter was slipping up the side of the house. Maybe he'd called the bail bondsman who'd hired him a little earlier, and said, "I got 'em, and I'm going in." Just to establish that this was all his. And he had that in his mind as he crept up the walk with his shotgun in his hands. *They're all mine, and that's a big hunk of payday...*

Stoned and drunk, I just started talking. It flowed out of me in the warm spring of dope and whiskey.

"When I was a kid, just, like, a teenager," I said, barely aware I was saying it aloud, "I wrote some poem about how when I took off my glasses, the blurriness, my nearsightedness, made things...sinister, weird. Like, when I looked at the moon without my glasses, the moon all double-imaged-up so it looked like a spider. Just like now...just like now too. Glasses on or off, man, I always felt like the world was... alien, weird to me anyway...then. Even now, a lot of times. But shit, back then I was 'specially...dissociative. I didn't feel a physical connection to things. I didn't identify with being a person in the world. Other people felt ordinary, and I envied feeling ordinary. I never *felt* ordinary. I mean, I wasn't *special* or wonderful. It was more like...out of it. Lost. Disconnected. Like some kind of bird blown from its migration path into a big empty desert. The bird ended up in a desert when it was supposed to be in some lush tropical place. Things that were normal to other people—like dances, school events, TV, shopping centers—they all seemed strange to me. Cars seemed strange conveyances, weird shell-like accretions. I couldn't understand why sports weren't important to me. I never felt comfortable anywhere. I wanted the same things other people wanted—love and admiration and acceptance—but always there was that feeling of everything being, like, out of focus, distorted a little, like I'd lost some other pair of glasses. But when I got into books, *then* I felt a connection. It was like I heard the music of life for the first time. It's that connected feeling I want. When I was younger, I found other things, things that made me feel connected—drugs and rock 'n' roll and guns. I used to do some second-story work when I was really young, mostly stealing office machinery, petty cash from some lawyer's desk...and that's when I felt awake and connected. But then I had this kid, I had a son, my boy Frankie...and I felt connected to *him*. I loved him, see, so I did what I had to for him. Went straight. But now he's gone. They took him. And when they told me he was dead, it was like I was falling into this hole in myself, like I had a black hole with its super gravity in my gut and my body, my mind—it was all sucking into it. Imploding. I was swallowing myself. And I knew that to survive, I could either go into...into not feeling like I belonged on the planet again, or I could...I could go on. Y'all know what I mean? A mission. A memorial mission for Frankie. And then the black sucking mouth was left behind, and I...if I pushed out the edges, if I looked for somebody to kill, something to go after...for 'Some Weird Sin' like Iggy said...If I was on the edge of completely going off, like today with that prick Abel, then, that's when, that's when...that's when I felt like I was in my own...my own...Like, I was real again. I was...like I had my glasses back on. I could see things right again. It wasn't all just a...just a threatening blur..."

Latesha was laughing silently. "He *so fucked up*! Cowboy all stoned up! The 'bird is blown out of its migration!'"

I laughed too. We both laughed at it. It was ludicrous. It was funny.

Then I stopped laughing abruptly, feeling something crumbling inside me. I thought I heard Frankie's voice again when an owl called, and the wind picked up, and a fence post squeaked...

Dulcet turned her body completely around in the hammock stretching between the back porch posts, so her head was near me, and asked softly, "Cowboy, you feel bad about your boy, huh?"

"I...said way enough already."

"True that," Leon muttered.

"Let's talk about something else, Dulcet," I said.

She moved her hand like a hula dancer and said lazily, "The boy's dead. I'm gonna be dead. Everybody going to be dead. Boogie man eats up everybody." Her eyelids sagged, and so did her lower lip. She'd sucked three dragons down to my one. I wanted to bite into that ripe lower lip.

About that time, I think, the bounty hunter must have been setting himself in the darkness nearby, deciding how he was going to handle this. And hesitating, not wanting to bring the cops in, but probably thinking maybe he should, and wishing he'd called his partners to help him after all.

"But maybe there's life after death," Dulcet said, not sounding as if she believed it.

Latesha said, "Why, sure there is..." She said it so softly I could barely hear it. "Across the Jordan."

"I don't know if I'd want there to be life after death," I said. "Life after death's just as likely to fuck with you."

I was looking at Dulcet because when I looked at her, I didn't see Frankie anywhere. She held my attention. "Dulcet, your last name isn't Groans. Is it?"

"Ohmigod, no. It's McNair. But Dulcet's my real first name."

Life after death, across the Jordan. Was Frankie anywhere now? Was he across the Jordan?

I shook my head. I managed not to think about Frankie most of the time, anyway, at least with the top part of my mind. It's a skill you get. Like, suppose you have a ripped-up, badly injured leg that hurts all the time, and can't be fixed beyond the stitches. You get good at putting your weight entirely on the other leg, at balancing on one foot like a crane. You don't even know you're doing it after a while. You lean away from the pain, and you do it expertly. That's something you can do inside yourself too.

But still, in some part of yourself, you knew you were maimed.

I plunged on. "Personally, I think this life is all there is. I'm an existentialist, I reckon, though not devotedly."

I noticed distantly that Wendell and Leon had gone inside and were talking softly near the turntable in the living room. Maybe they were just discussing a choice of music, or maybe they were up to some shit. Hanging with two guys like that, you should always know where they are and what they're talking about. But I didn't care right then.

I could feel the weight of my gun in the pocket of my jean jacket. There were, what, two bullets left? Just aim carefully, is all.

"What's that? 'Existentialist?'" Latesha asked, taking over the rocking chair. "I heard the word a lot."

Dulcet said sleepily, "People use it all kinds of ways. Doesn't seem to mean one thing."

I chuckled, and my chuckle sounded crazy in my own ears. "You got it nailed! It's come to mean whatever people want it to, like Zen has. But what it's *supposed* to mean... Something like...Well, in modern times it's, uh, it's a philosophy of, uh..." I couldn't seem to access that part of my brain just now.

Dulcet said, "Ohhhhh, it's about authenticity. Being real. Making decisions that make you more real. Seeing everything kind of absurd and making your own reality and shit. Recognizing that it's all up to us in this life, 'cause death is certain and final and all that."

I looked at her.

She tinkled a laugh. "The stripper went to college and actually remembers some of that stuff! Yeah, two years, almost three. But I'm *tooooooo* happy being little Dulcet to do anything I don't wanna do." She added dutifully, "Unless it's for Wendell."

Latesha said, "What you said that existentialism is, that's like Wendell is. He don't believe in anything but being Wendell as much as he can. Being real—that a big thing with him."

"That's right, but nothing's seeming real right now," Dulcet said, staring into the grass.

Latesha kept on talking about Wendell. "He don't believe in nothing but this life. I try to save his soul one time. He said, 'Girl, you can't save my soul, and if you keep trying, I'm gonna save *your* motherfucking soul by sending your ass away from me.'" Latesha's voice was breaking. She was close to crying. As she rocked, the mournful creaking sound of the rocking chair made a torn paisley shape in my mind.

I thought I saw the moon climbing down the sky, on its eight white legs, but when I looked again, it was just squatting up there in its pale, dimly seen web of stars and stringy clouds.

"So you believe in heaven?" I asked her.

The light bulb over my head seemed to hum a song I couldn't quite name. The light from the living room window rippled as a shadow crossed it. The shadow looked three-dimensional, palpable. I drank a little more whiskey and cola.

"I surely believe in heaven, Slim Jim," Latesha said. "I ain't *goin'* to heaven. I chose the life, and I chose Wendell, and this is my life, and that's all there is."

"If you believe in heaven," I said, on an obscure impulse,

"you could go and...find your way to—I don't know—some-place where you could feel you were going to go to heaven when you died. A church of some kind."

"Oh, I know where I'd go! The Easter Hill Church of Our Loving Savior, right down there in Oakland." She pointed over her shoulder, toward Oakland. "I ran off from Wendell one time, went to this gospel church down there, and I could feel the Lord moving. But I called Wendell, and he was just so sad. So I went back. I went back to him, and he was rough, but he's my man, and just for him I'll go to hell for all eternity."

She said it with complete conviction.

"So you think Wendell's an existentialist, huh?" I said. I could see Wendell through the open door, back in his chair, seemed like he was napping. "He's an interesting kind of player anyway. He dresses like a rap video, but he seems to me like...old-fashioned."

"He's fifty-two. He oughta be old-fashioned," Dulcet said.

Surprise almost penetrated my dreaminess. "Y'all are yanking my chain. No way, girl. I thought maybe forty, forty-three or..."

"People always think that," Latesha said. "He's going to live forever. He fifty-two."

I drank a little whiskey to make the taunting song in the lightbulb go away. "What happened in Miami?"

Latesha shrugged. "He was working a thing with us, me and Dulcet. We pick up on tourist guys, and then we slip 'em something, make 'em sleep, take all their shit." Her voice was bland, as if she were giving work experience in a job interview.

That's when the record ended. It was suddenly very quiet, except for the crickets and the birds. The rising and falling sound of a motorcycle passing somewhere way below us; then a truck whining on the freeway.

Latesha went on, "The thing we had going, it worked damn good too. Dulcet got them in easy. But one of 'em woke up in the middle of the thing, in his hotel, an' he go a little crazy—that GHB shit, you know, it can make you crazy—and he grabbed my purse and took my little piece, got a shot off at Wendell. So Wendell grab the gun away and beat his shiny white college boy ass dead with it. I don't think he plan to kill him, but...Well, this was a Cuban kid visiting his auntie, and his family, they got their paid-for peeps in the local police to grip on that shit like a dog with a rat—and Wendell got arrested. He put up the bail, and then he jump bail. And we come out here because he owns a condo here. He kicked the people renting out and moved in. Comes over here to this end of town to do some business, but he goes back most nights. He loves that place, but that shit's expensive. And he's about to lose it, he don't get some bigger cash flow. That why when you come around with—"

"You talk way too fucking much, you dumb little ho," Leon said, coming out on the porch. "Wendell, you hear that shit what she say? She tell every motherfuckin' secret you got."

Wendell muttered, "Shit!" as he came out.

He walked up to Latesha, shaking his head in disgust. His eyes were lost in deep shadow as he lifted his arm to backhand her for babbling his story out.

And I was poised on the edge of doing something about it—or just turning away.

But I couldn't just stand there while he beat the woman up.

Wendell snorted and dropped his hand. "Woman—"

"Look!" Dulcet said, pointing. "It's a little boy in the bushes! Looking at us!"

My heart stuttered, and I looked. We all looked, even Wendell, frozen with his arm still raised to strike, and I saw what did look, in the moonlight, sort of like a boy's face looking at us. But when the face shifted position a little, we saw it was a gray fox, poking its head up above the ivy, checking us out. Its face was delicate, its eyes gleaming gold. The fox opened its mouth as if to speak, but only panted.

"Look at that. It's a *fox*," Wendell said with a city dweller's awe.

I thought he seemed grateful for the interruption, as this way he didn't have to hit Latesha.

Leon grunted. "Sure, we got foxes and raccoons out here getting into our shit all the time. Motherfucking raccoons mess with the garbage can."

He picked up an empty flowerpot to throw, but the fox was way ahead of him and ducked into the bushes, vanishing.

"Wow, a fox," Dulcet said, with something like authentic childlike wonder this time.

"Y'all freeze right there, every last one of you!" quavered a voice from the darkness.

I was looking for the fox still, and the man's voice from the night didn't register on me at first as quite real. It seemed like another heroin illusion. "A gray fox, Dulcet. Beautiful animals. I wish...Frankie could see..."

A shout this time. "Everybody, stand up and put your hands on your heads!"

Shit. That's real.

"Fuck!" Wendell said. "It's that motherfucking skip tracer."

Then it sank in. I stood up and saw Wendell reach

behind for his gun and pat his bare waistband. He realized he didn't have it on him. The bounty hunter had stepped into the light now.

The first thing I noticed was that he was a tall, refrigerator-sized guy with a big belly. Fat, colorfully tattooed arms in a sleeveless shirt. A safari hat. A short, sharply trimmed black beard. The second thing I noticed was his shotgun. I looked down into its muzzle, the way Abel had looked into my gun.

The bounty hunter had another gun on his hip, and what looked like a taser, pepper gas, a cell phone, and a beeper all attached to his belt.

"This asshole has a fucking Batman utility belt on!" I said.

Dulcet laughed, her eyes bright. She got up from the hammock, but she didn't put her hands on her head. She hadn't been carrying her Barbie purse a few moments ago, but now she had it over her left shoulder, with her left hand on top of the purse. She had that little gun in there.

Latesha was already standing up, open-mouthed, her eyes wide. "That same motherfucker!"

"Y'all were dumb to come here, Wendell," Leon growled, shaking his head. "What you think? The motherfucker not going to find your cousin? Come to your cousin's house?"

"We thought you were in Dallas for a long time," the skip tracer said. His voice was kind of high-pitched. He seemed genuinely scared, his eyes darting around. "They're still—"

He broke off, realizing he'd given something away.

Wendell said, "I think this dumb cracker is the only one here."

I took just one sidestep toward the door and stopped. Waited.

"No, you're wrong, Wendell," the skip tracer said. "I've got all kinds of backup here. And I can get the Richmond police here in five minutes. Now we're gonna do this easy. You folks are going to get down on your knees, put your hands behind your backs."

Nobody moved, though, except me. Wendell and Leon were now blocking much of the bounty hunter's view of me.

I took another sideways step to the back door. And stopped. Moving made me realize how stoned and drunk I was. Every step seemed to spin the world like a globe on a stand. My stomach seemed to revolve inside me too.

But on a certain level, I was feeling good. Probably because I wasn't thinking about Frankie in that moment.

"Where's the other one?" the bounty hunter said. "The red-haired Frenchie Canuck."

"He went for beer," Wendell said, instinctively lying. "Maybe we can make a deal, my man."

The "red-haired Canuck" was snoring like a little lamb a few feet from me, just inside the door. As I side-stepped through, I squatted, putting my hand over Red's mouth, and he instantly came awake at the contact. He stared at me for a moment in furious shock.

I put a finger on my lips, then whispered, "Bounty hunter." I tilted my head toward the back of the house.

He turned his head, under my hand, to look toward the back porch.

I went in a low, slow crouch through the house.

It seemed to take a long time. The light was mostly in the back of the house, behind me. I was moving through a dark wooden corridor, past the shadowy shapes of unidenti-fiable furniture that seemed to change proportions as I passed. It felt like a long time getting to the front door, each step requiring some concentration. I was still stoned, and the smell of Leon and dope smoke and dust on old wood seemed thick as wool in the air.

But I got to the front door, and thought, *Don't fumble with this. Stop and think, Slim.*

I could just make out the doorknob in the yellow-white of the streetlight shining through an old glass transom. I found the knob with my fingers, the contact almost electric with sudden metallic chill, and turned it.

I heard a shout from the bounty hunter and an answering laugh of derision. "You all alone, ain't you, motherfucker?"

I got the door open, went out on the front porch, and looked around. If the skip tracer had backup, he had them well hidden. I forced myself to move against the current of my altered state, and slid into a primitive stalking mode, prickling energy rising up. A sense of the fullness of the present moment took hold of me, filling me with the night's breath. Life gains sharp definition with the imminence of death.

Still crouching, I went up the walkway along the side of the house toward the back, my gun in hand.

I saw the bulky shape of the bounty hunter, a silhouette from here, his left side to me. He was lifting the shotgun to his shoulder, forcing the issue.

Trying to make his voice deep and scary, he barked, "Get down *now*, or I swear I'm going to blow your fucking head off, Wendell!"

I was creeping up on him, and I felt good now that the spinning had stopped. I was centered, awake, alive.

Made for this. I was made for this.

Now he was looming over me like a building.

I put the muzzle of my gun against the back of his neck.

He shivered, and I heard him hiss, "Shit!"

I said, in a reasonable, soothing tone, "That's right, big guy, you're in it deep. This gun is primed. Toss the shotgun aside. Do what I say, and you get out of this in one piece."

He was breathing hard, chest rising and falling fast. "You give me your word on that? The part about me not getting hurt?"

"What's your name, man?"

"It's...Tuck. People call me Tuck."

"Like Friar Tuck? My word on it, Friar Tuck. If you cooperate, you're cool. We'll just leave you somewhere to chill for a while, and you'll be fine."

I could see the outline of his Adam's apple go up and down very distinctly. Then there was a rustling thump as he tossed the shotgun aside.

I stepped behind him, reached slowly across to pull his pistol from its holster with my left hand.

"Now drop that Batman belt. Slow."

Hands shaking, he dropped his belt, just as Red came out of the back door with a MAC-10 autopistol in his hand.

"I'm surprised you came here alone, Tuck, with all of us here," I said, genuinely curious. "Don't you guys usually come in packs?"

Tuck made a hissing sound through clamped teeth. "They wouldn't leave Dallas. I knew Wendell was here, but they wouldn't listen." He added wistfully to himself, "I almost had the collar."

I heard Dulcet laugh from the porch. "He wants to be the hero and get 'em all by himself! What a cute little safari-hat guy!"

Red was grinning, and he was cocking the MAC-10.

The machine pistol was pointed at Tuck's gut. "I don't like fat guys following me around. The smell bothers me, ay?"

Tuck must have seen something in Red's eyes.

"Don't!" Tuck said. "He gave me his word, man! Don't do that. I'll blow this case off. You can leave me tied up somewhere!"

Tuck's trunk-like legs were shaking. I could hear the cloth rustling as his thighs rubbed together.

"Red," I said, "I don't believe in much, but I do believe in keeping my word. We'll truss him good and be long gone."

Red shook his head. "It's not what you say." He kept the gun leveled and kept looking at me and Tuck, but tilted his head and spoke out of the side of his mouth to Wendell, who stood behind him on the porch. "Wendell? What you want me to do?"

Leon said, "Better just take his ass quietly off this property. And I mean fast."

"Look," Tuck said, "I'm fucking *outta here*! I've already forgotten you guys exist. I'm not really cut out for this job. I just, you know, I blew everything else I tried. I thought I'd try this, but—"

"Shut the fuck up," Red said. "We don't want your whiny story, ay? What I do with him, Wendell?"

I heard Wendell sigh.

I figured Wendell didn't particularly want to execute anybody, but he couldn't seem weak. He'd already compromised too much.

"You know what to do, Red," Wendell said. "Just don't ever put it on me."

Which meant, kill him, but if it goes to court, don't say I gave the order.

7

TUCK WAS BREATHING HARD.

I said, "Wait a minute, goddammit. Wendell, I gave my word—"

"But here's a thing, Wendell," Red said, ignoring me. "Maybe too much noise here, eh, Wendell? Then there's this big fat slob's body. When you were eating all those cheeseburgers, you didn't think about other people having to haul that fat ass around and dig a hole for it, bounty hunter, ay?"

The moon seemed to spotlight Red somehow. His grin was getting wider. His knuckles were getting whiter.

"I...Look, you could ransom me," Tuck said. Tuck was breathing through his mouth, faster and faster.

"Ransom? That's a sucker game, least in this country," Wendell said.

"*What if,*" Dulcet said gleefully. "You gave him his gun back and let him fight with you! I'd fight with him too! We could play army! With real guns!"

I'm pretty sure she wasn't kidding.

Leon snorted. "Motherfucker. You see what I mean

about that woman, Wendell? She out of her mind. Y'all get this motherfucking bounty hunter out of here. I don't want to *know* what you going to do with him."

Tuck was wheezing now as I put the automatic in my waistband and shifted his pistol to my right hand.

Red meditatively thumbed some smokeless into his mouth, and said, "There's a cliff over the ocean, on the other side of that hill there, you know. We could take him there, tie something to his feet, and shoot him right off the edge. Take care of his big cheeseburger-eating ass and get rid of him all at once."

"That what you do, then that what you do," Wendell said. "Whatever you gonna do, get to it."

Tuck made a bleating sound and tried to rush Red—

And the MAC-10 barked and rattled in Red's hands.

The skip tracer staggered back under the multiple impacts, screaming, his safari hat, cinched under his neck with a leather string, falling to hang awkwardly off the side of his neck.

I shouted, "Red, you fucking *weasel!*"

And I leveled Tuck's gun at Red, only barely registering what kind of gun it was. A .45 revolver with a silver finish.

"Back away from him, Red!" I yelled.

I had the drop on Red, and he shrugged and lowered his gun, grinning. "Bounty hunter's good as dead."

"Goddamn all this noisy shit!" Leon was hissing, looking toward the street.

Tuck was on his knees now, clutching his gut, writhing. He was squealing, "*Ee, ee, ee-ee...*" over and over.

I wasn't sure which way to jump. Tuck was on his side, clawing up the ivy, thrashing. It made me think of Abel. Only I felt kind of bad for Tuck, and I hadn't felt a thing for Abel.

"Goddamn it, mother*fucker*," Leon said, growling it and stamping the porch so you could hear a board crack. "My neighbors going to be calling the motherfucking police, all that noise. Wendell, that's all now. I'm gone tell you straight up. Take your shit-brains crew and this dumb bleeding motherfucker of a half-assed bounty hunter and get the *fuck* right on out of here!"

"Ah'*iiight*, Leon, shit. Just fucking simmer and let me think how we going to do this," Wendell said.

Tuck looked like a salted slug on the ground, and I could almost read his mind. *I fucked up everything in my life, and then it ends like this, people laughing at me while I bleed to death.*

I was starting to laugh, in fact, but at myself. *Thought you didn't fucking care about anything, Purdoux.*

Tuck was still squealing and didn't seem ready to die. Red was looking at me and at the gun in my hand, and I realized I still had it aimed at Red and wasn't even conscious of it.

I mean, if you're going to point a gun at somebody, you should at least be mindful about it.

Red looked like he was gauging when to swing his MAC-10 toward me.

Tuck was doubled over, fetus-like, around his wounds.

"Y'all ever see that movie *They Shoot Horses, Don't They?*" Dulcet asked. "I never saw it, but I remember the title. I mean, the idea comes to mind."

And Red was poised to make his move. He was going to take me out.

And Tuck was squealing, bleeding, thrashing...

"Motherfuckers, do *something*," Leon hissed.

Wendell said, "Okay. What we gone do is—Slim? Yo."

I nodded. I lowered the gun but kept it between me and

Red. And I looked at Red and then jerked my head toward Tuck.

Tuck wasn't going to live, even if he got to an emergency room.

Red stepped up to Tuck, put the gun against Tuck's head. Tuck looked up at him, and then squeezed his eyes shut and waited for it.

Red grinned and blew Tuck's head open, and after that, Tuck was quiet, except for two or three final spasms.

Red straightened up and squinted at me. "You were pointing a gun at my head there, Tex," he said softly, looking at me like a man looking at a dartboard in a bar, calculating the throw. Like it was no big thing, just a question of when and how.

I remember exactly what thought went through my head then. *I'm gonna have to kill Red for real. Because the second I turn my back...*

There was a silence as everyone listened for sirens and tried to think about what to do next.

"Hey!" Dulcet said. "Look! Slim Texy got a cowboy gun!"

I looked at Tuck's pistol more closely. It was a Colt .45 double-action revolver, a working reproduction of a gunfighter's Peacemaker. She was right. It was a damn cowboy gun.

———

Leon agreed to deal with the blood in the yard if we did the rest fast. There was an old scrap roll of vinyl flooring in the crawlspace under the back porch. A black widow spider walked daintily away from it as we rolled Tuck up.

"Roll him up just like a burrito," Red said. "Feels like he liked burritos, the fat fuck."

"Red," I said. Just that. *Red.*

At the other end of the roll, he glared coldly at me and then grinned. "Yeah, you'll get your turn...Editor Boy."

Red's idea about the cliff still applied. He knew the way. He'd been there once before, on an errand.

Wendell was at the wheel now. He backed the van up to the edge of the beetling granite cliff. Red and I silently pulled the linoleum out of the rear of the van, letting it thump to the ground. Swearing softly, we dragged it onto the rocky outcropping over the bay.

Wendell drove the van back over to the road to wait. I could see Dulcet watching out the van's backdoor window. I guess Latesha didn't want to watch. Red looked at me now and then, and looked away, but I knew what he was thinking. *Why do we need this asshole now that we know which warehouse it is?*

I shivered. My high was mostly gone. Sounds still had a certain reverb quality, and everything I saw—trees waving in the breeze, a shadowy house frame, the curve of the road, the rocky cliff edge, the setting moon, the bay, Red, the roll of vinyl—all was some kind of insignia, in a code I couldn't understand.

The dawn was turning the sky to cobalt and aluminum above the East Bay hills. But the sun hadn't yet shown itself in person when the vinyl roll containing ol' Tuck and about two hundred pounds of new brick—intended for a chimney that would never happen that we'd added to the Tuck burrito for extra weight—went bouncing end over end down the cliff side and into the bay.

I had given Latesha the automatic, and I had Tuck's Peacemaker in its holster. A holster in a gun belt that went with the gun. Tuck's gun belt had the leather loops filled with bullets, the whole shebang-bang.

I was looking down over the edge of the cliff to see if the roll sank. It did, vanishing like the Cheshire Cat's grin.

And I realized Red was very quiet, and he was behind me.

I straightened up, not too fast, saying, "Tuck's gone. It's cool," as easygoing as I could. And I gently put my hand on the butt of the Peacemaker, stepping back from the cliff.

Then I spun, jerking the pistol. Red had the advantage because he had his gun ready.

Wyatt Earp said that the man who took his time and aimed with sure deliberation was the man who won the gunfight.

Wyatt was right. Red fired a burst jerkily at me, but the bullets buzzed past me like confused wasps, into the sky over the bay.

I aimed at the center of Red's chest and squeezed the trigger. It was a fast draw shoot—but with the competitions, they use wax bullets. This was a steel jacketed slug.

At that range, the round hit him hard, and he was slapped right off his feet, backward, dropping the MAC.

I went and picked the autopistol up and stood over him, watching to be sure.

"Don't," he said. "Don't. *Je suis rien*...Don't..."

But he was staring at the sky, and I had the weird feeling he wasn't talking to me. Maybe he was talking to a memory.

It took him about thirty seconds total to die, I think. "Don't," he said, one more time. And then he was done with his dying.

I grabbed him by the collar, felt the ebbing warmth of his body on my knuckles, and turned him sideways to the cliff edge. I used one cowboy-booted foot to roll him over a couple of times, then right off the edge of the cliff. He splashed into the sea, bobbing up to float just above the spot where Tuck had sunk. He'd killed Tuck, and now he was sinking into the sea with him.

Then I looked at the van, maybe a hundred feet away. Were they going to take revenge for their old crew buddy?

But Dulcet waved a come-on motion from the back. "Hurry the hell up, Tex!"

I holstered the gun and walked back to the van. It was all cool, because Red had fired at me. Fair is fair.

I looked inside myself again to see if I was sorry I'd shot Red.

Nope. Not even a little.

8

EDITOR SOUGHT *IN MASS KILLING*

The newspaper was on the counter in the Travelodge's office. I glanced at the headline, and then I looked hastily back at the registration form I was signing for the Sikh clerk. The turbaned clerk was a reticent man with pockmarked skin and a pointed beard.

Dulcet, who was wearing a coat and playing my wife, saw the newspaper too. She only smiled mysteriously.

I told the Sikh gent we'd been driving all night from Missouri, so we were going to get some sleep, even though it was morning. I could smell the coffee from their continental breakfast nook. The clerk nodded. He didn't care. He never glanced at the newspaper or looked closely at me.

I took a chance booking that motel room. Using my credit card with the Eickhoff thing hovering in the background. But I didn't care anymore. I was terminally exhausted.

I was still scared of sleeping, but the exhaustion had come like a deep layer of volcanic ash, falling at first lightly, then more and more heavily, each black snowflake, weighing near nothing, but adding up, conspiring to become the weight of the world, bearing me relentlessly down.

We got a room with two queen-size beds. It was pretty much like all eighty-nine-dollar-a-night hotel rooms. I got it for two nights so we wouldn't be disturbed.

We pulled the thick curtains really snugly, so it was dark in there, except for a couple of milky shafts of light cutting down at the dun carpet from the edge of the window and the light from the TV. Dulcet had switched it on the instant we'd come in.

Latesha showered. I sat on the edge of a bed, trying not to think about incompetent bounty hunters begging for their lives, trying not to see my son's waxen face in the hospital morgue. I sagged where I sat, barely able to keep from sliding to the floor. Wendell lay on his back on the other bed, remote in one hand, gun lightly under the other, flipping around on the TV. I thought he'd see me on the news, but he started watching *Sesame Street*, laughing sleepily at the puppet vampire.

I could hear Dulcet peeing as she talked to Latesha in the bathroom. I heard the toilet flush, then the squeak of her feet on the tub as she got in beside Latesha, and their tired voices as they washed each other.

Latesha came out first, with only a towel around her. She tossed it onto a chair and lay naked on the bed near the bathroom beside Wendell. Then Dulcet came out, barefoot in her panties, braless, and went yawning hugely to the bed I was sitting on. Wendell turned the TV off, pulled off his shoes, and lay beside Latesha, spooning and muttering to her, his gun under his pillow.

I made myself stand up. I tottered into the bathroom, undressed and showered, handwashing my clothes in the shower at the same time. I wrung them out and hung them up over towel racks.

Wendell had turned off the TV, and I went naked through the semidarkness to the other bed. Naked anyway, but for Tuck's gun in my hand, which made me feel dressed enough. I put the gun under my own pillow and kept my hand on it as I lay down next to Dulcet, spooning just like Wendell with Latesha. She had one hand under her own pillow.

"Maybe we should roll a joint. Could we, Daddy, please?" Dulcet suggested, talking to Wendell, a little girl's voice in the darkness.

"Girl, shut the fuck up and go to sleep," Wendell said muzzily.

"'Kay, Wendell Daddy."

"'N' if that White boy wants to fuck you, you just let him fuck you. I don't want no arguments waking me up."

"'Kay, Wendell Daddy."

He was already snoring even as she said it. Latesha was soon snoring in a kind of duet with him, her alto to his bass.

We all lay on top of the covers. If we had to jump out of bed fast, the covers would just get in the way, and it wasn't cold.

Dulcet reached back, found my left arm, and pulled it around her. It was not unpleasant.

"Tex...Slim Jim..." Dulcet said sleepily.

"Hmmm..." The ashen weight was mummifying, petrifying me.

"Know what? I'm glad you got rid of that Red. I didn't like him. He was always asking Wendell to make me fuck him. I hate red pubic hair. And his mouth was all gross with that smokeless shit he chewed on."

I was almost asleep. "Glad to...be of service."

"Know what else?" Her whisper seemed to come from the blackness behind my closed eyelids, as if she were sharing my personal darkness.

"Whuh?"

"You know that Leon? You know what he said? When we were getting ready to leave, and I was in the van, and you were loading the back of it, and he was talking to Wendell up front?"

"Don' even fuckin' care whuh he said..."

"He said, 'That Slim Jim boy is all right, after all. Y'all better off with him than Red.'"

"Did he? I'm...all aglow from ...self-esteem."

She snickered softly at that. I was almost asleep, the fear of sleep perched somewhere like a raven in the night.

Then she said, "How many them people you kill in the city...at that publishing place? I saw it on TV in the dressing room at work."

That brought me more awake. I whispered, "Do...the others know?"

"I didn't tell anybody. I like secrets." Her voice was a play-whisper. "How many you kill? Tell me!"

"Not any. Well, one guy in self-defense. The guy who did the real killing. The cops misunderstood the...the situation."

"That your story and you stickin' to it?"

"'S true..."

"Don't have to pretend with widdoo Dulcet. It's all right. They're all happier now...those people. They're happier dead."

"If you say so."

She was quiet for a few moments, just softly humming to herself, thinking it over. "So you were there, and you saw those dead bodies after that crazy man did his thing?"

"That about sums it up."

"That stuff, I don't get how that works. I understand saying, 'Say hello to my little friend,' and shooting some motherfuckers. That's business. But people going to work or some school and just shooting everybody. Where's that shit come from?"

"I'm as puzzled about it as everybody else. But my son had just died, and somehow it all seemed like part of it. The world was falling apart, and the shootings didn't surprise me so much. Just seemed...my own apocalypse, I guess. I just wanted to get out and find the guys who gave Frankie the shit that killed him."

By the end of that question, all my fatigue had rolled insistently back onto me. I wanted to change the subject. "You like being a stripper and lap dancing and all that?"

"Like it? No. Better than working for a temp agency. I did that for a min-min once or twice." She yawned noisily, seeming to enjoy the sound. "You want to fuck me?"

"Honored...by the...offer...but...I'm too...I'm too..."

"That's okay. We got time tomorrow night or some other night."

I went to sleep, thinking that we probably didn't have much time at all.

I slept without dreaming. Then I came almost awake, just enough to surmise, a few hours later, that Wendell had awakened with a hard-on. He had anyway unzipped his pants, shoved himself with no preliminaries into Latesha from behind. I heard her grunt with the entry. It must have hurt some, without the preamble, but she dutifully pumped her hips for him until he came in her, moaning, "Ooh, bitch. Give it to Daddy..." And then he was asleep again, sawing logs almost instantly. He probably hadn't been fully awake for any of it. And Latesha, too, was asleep a minute or two later.

Dulcet seemed aware of this brief sexual interlude, and she squirmed against me, in case I wanted anything, but I only hugged her a little, and she commenced snoring softly again.

I heard kids laughing as they walked by outside our second-floor room. I heard their flip-flops slapping on the concrete.

They're coming back from the swimming pool, I thought. Frankie loved to swim...

Then I slipped back down into the pit of ashes again.

———

"I've joined a special group of people who have a very, very special relationship to God," Meredith told me matter-of-factly. "And just for the record, Slim, I don't like it when people call it a cult."

"You said *special* twice," I said. "That's so special."

We were in a sunny wooded park, sitting at a picnic table. It was a hot summer day that buzzed to itself—bees, maybe. Cicadas. And the day groaned too, an airplane passing overhead. I saw a water fountain in the background with flies thick around it, but the flies weren't buzzing. They were whispering. I couldn't quite work out what they were saying.

Meredith glanced over her shoulder at the place in a thatch of ivy where two men knelt in a flowerbed, sawing at something. I didn't recognize the men. I could just make out the glint of tools in their hands.

I knew they were sawing down deep into Frankie's

body, though I couldn't see the body. I wondered distantly why I wasn't angry about it.

"You know," I said, "when my mom died, I didn't feel anything. No grief. Or I didn't know I was feeling grief. But then I had trouble concentrating on anything for weeks, even watching a movie. I couldn't finish a book. I was weirdly clumsy. I kept dropping things, and then I realized...that was it. That's how it showed itself."

"We can cleanse you of all that," Meredith said. "All that's necessary is a special operation. Do you see this little scar on my abdomen? Of course, sometimes..." She glanced toward the two men, the body.

One of the men was throwing red bits of body parts in the air, showering himself with them, and gibbering something that might have been some kind of prayer.

Meredith went on, "Sometimes the operation goes wrong. But if you'll just trust us, without thinking or feeling or caring, but leaving all that behind, we can promise you endless bliss...endless bliss...endless bliss..."

Then the two men stood up, and now they were someone else—or had they been Red and Abel all along? The lumpen ex-surfer and the obtuse French Canadian gunsel...dragging soggy red bits of Frankie toward me.

"Dad?" said a bird on a bush. "Dad, please. I can't breathe. Help me, I'm so cold. I can't breathe, Daddy. I'm sorry...Please, just...help me..."

"Don't," Red said. "Don't." Grinning as he said it, coming closer with something in his hand. Something—

"Tuck is one of us now," Meredith was saying.

"Daddy..."

———

It was one of those dreams you have to wriggle free of, like Houdini from a straitjacket. I woke up with Dulcet straddling me.

"Hey, Tex," she said, smiling down at me. "Poor ol' Slim Jim! You having a bad dream?"

She was pinning my arms with her knees. Her hair was bed-frizzled. Her breasts were pointing at me like they might go off.

She had my gun in her hand. She aimed it at me.

"Boomy!" she said.

She laughed and spun the silver revolver on her finger, like in the movies, but awkwardly.

"Don't do that," I said. "It could go off."

"You need to brush your teeth," she said. "I've got some toothpaste and a brush you can use. We brung it in from the van. Your clothes are not completely dry, but I hung 'em over the heater. Wendell's in the bathroom." She looked at the shiny gun as if she was trying to see her face in it. "e always gets constipated after doing some of that kinda dope. Latesha's bringing us back some food and coffee."

I pulled my arms out from under her, gently taking the gun from her hand. "I hope it's a lot of coffee."

"Do you want to smoke some pot?"

"No...no, thanks."

"Want a hair of the dog? Got half a bottle of really hairy hooch."

I shuddered and shook my head. "*Fuck* no. For God's sake, don't even talk about it."

"'Kay, Cowboy-ee!"

My stomach lurched. "What time is it?"

"About seven p.m."

"You're kidding."

"No, I'm not *even* kidding, Mr. Big Saddlehorn

Cowboy. We got to get it together, Wendell says. They're going to be bringing all that dope money to that place tonight. He says, at least you better hope they do." She lowered her voice, so she sounded like a child actress from a sitcom, and said behind her hand, "He didn't wake up in a very good mood."

"Me neither." I wriggled out from under her, trying to think about the mission, so I could forget about the dream.

"Do you wanna fuck *now*?" she asked.

It was her way of being polite. Hospitable.

"Nah, I'm...hungover and...No thanks, hon. But I do thank you very kindly, and I mean that."

"'Kay some more!" She reached out and tugged my forelock playfully. "Hangover owie! Come on then, Mr. Little Bighorn Cowboy Guy. Wendell's finally getting out of there. I'll show you the toothpaste and where Wendell put the extra bullets."

9

WE SAT in the van for an hour, in a wedge of warehouse shadow cast by moonlight and streetlight, half a block from Kwai & Sons. Wendell was at the wheel, me riding shotgun, the two girls in back. Latesha smoked Newports. I wanted to ask her not to smoke in the car, but decided it was probably better that she had her nicotine fix. Her hand would be steadier.

We chilled without radio or lights, just watching. We could see the little gravel strip parking lot. The Blue Ox extended-cab pickup was there alone. That one light in the corner window.

I was feeling a little hungover still, spaced, and sick to my stomach. The almond-paste croissant I'd eaten seemed to haunt me now. I was still just slightly stoned. And all the coffee was churning in the mix too.

But I sat there. We waited. It sucked. Hard to stay out ahead of the pursuing thing when you're just *sitting* somewhere. An hour seemed like a year. It seemed like that fucking hour had seasons. I was only up to autumn when Wendell asked me the second time about the autopistol.

"You sure you don't want that MAC-10 of Red's?" Wendell asked, putting his plastic coffee cup down. "That fucking six-shooter only shoots...six."

Latesha laughed. "'Six-shooter only shoots...*six*!'"

I shrugged. My clothes hadn't dried completely, and the damp cloth was making me itch. I shifted around, scratching my back against the seat. And I said, "Nope, I'm gonna use the Tuck the Bounty Hunter Memorial Pistol. I got a pocketful of his shells. I might take along that shotgun of his."

"'Tuck memorial pistol!'"

I could hardly sit still. The razor-edged wave of black glass was looming up inside me again, and—

Daddy?

I needed to stay out ahead of it. I had to get moving.

Wendell glanced at me and muttered irritably, "You're squirming around, man. You making me nervous. You got to pee? Too much caffeine or what?"

"I'm just antsy to get going. It's got to be after ten."

He looked at his watch and shook his head. "Fifteen to ten."

Still had the winter of that hour to go through. Fifteen minutes that lasted three months.

"You want some chewy sour candy?" Dulcet asked. "I've got a few pieces left."

"No thanks. I don't think you want me to be sick in the van."

"You nervous about this, huh, Slim Jim?" Latesha asked. "You don't need to be. I looked up in my astrology book— using Wendell's birthday, my birthday, what day it is. We cool."

This annoyed me more than it should have. I almost snapped at her that astrology was bullshit, and didn't she claim to believe in the Christian God, and lots of Christians thought astrology was a tool of the devil to get innocent people into the occult—that kind of mean-spirited remark.

But Wendell saved me from myself. "What the zodiac say?" Wendell asked, interested.

Latesha held a little penlight over an open supermarket register paperback. "It say, 'A syz...' What this word, Dulcet?"

"Uh...Syzygy."

"What the fuck is that?" Wendell asked.

"I think it's about, like, conjunctions of planets."

"Tha's interesting," Latesha said. "Wasn't sure about that part. But it's good. It's all good. Horoscope says, 'A syzygy of luscious convergences pours forth the fruit of the glowing abundance of good fortune on your enterprise. Wealth is a *possibility* if you play your cards right and do the footwork.'"

"That sounding pretty sweet," Wendell commented. "But y'all better shut off that motherfucking light."

She shut the little penlight off and lay back. Dulcet sat beside her, stroking her cornrows with the tip of a finger.

"'Wealth is a possibility!' That shit sounds *good*," Latesha said cheerfully. "What gun I got, Dulcet?"

"I guess you can have the MAC. The cowboy don't want it."

———

A cold, bleak handful of minutes before ten, the black SUV pulled into the gravel strip at the warehouse. It parked beside the pickup, snug to the old loading dock. Its lights were on for almost a minute, then switched off.

A tall, crewcut blond man in a tailored powder blue

suit got out of the SUV from the driver's side. A short, chubby Asian dude in black jeans and a black button-up shirt got out from the passenger side. He was talking, the other nodding. And the blond guy was carrying a leather satchel.

Okay, Frankie, I thought. A meaningless gesture is better than no gesture, sometimes. It's all I can do. Here goes...

Wendell murmured, "You think they bringin' in some money?"

"Yeah, and counting it with what's already there," I said. "Let's go." I put my hand on the door handle.

He reached out and laid a hand on my arm, not too hard. There was respect in the touch. That was worth something.

"Hold your horses, cowboy. Give 'em time to get comfortable. Talking to the people inside, distracted."

"Makes sense." But I felt like I was going to explode if I didn't get out of that van.

To keep my mind busy, I tried to start a conversation about something, you know, meaningful. "Hey, uh, Wendell...Did you ever notice that even if you *know* you have a self-destructive tendency, a character flaw, you usually can't do anything about it, and you keep doing it, keep acting out and like exhibiting that same fucking flaw even if your therapist has made you see it?"

Wendell looked at me. "You picking *this* second to say some put-down shit about me?"

"You?" I was confused for a moment. "No, man. I was making conversation. About my favorite topic. Me. Not you, me. I just spoke, like, in the second person. I meant, it's true for anybody, anyone."

"Anybody? I thought you said it was you."

"Hypothetically, anyone but especially me, okay? I just figure most people...are the same."

Latesha said, "I sure as a bitch know what he means. I have a lot of behavior shit I wanted to get rid of and never fucking could."

Wendell turned in his seat and scowled at her. "Something to do with me? About how you behave for me?"

"No, I—"

"Everything you *do* supposed to be for me, ho."

"I didn't...That's not what I meant, baby."

I felt sorry for Latesha. And I found myself wondering if I was hanging out with a pimp now, a misogynistic choice of companions, because I was so infinitely angry at Meredith.

I said, "I meant, Wendell, all my life I've had a tendency to just lurch into things. Haste and...and impulse. I had it in check for a long time, for my family. But now...now that I lost them...it's like it was waiting. I just want to plunge into the shit. I mean, there's running in bravely where you have to, and then there's dumbfuck *mindless* bravery."

Wendell was laughing silently now. "Tex, you are one weird White man. Shut the fuck up, get out the car, and let's go."

"I'm wid dat, dog," I said, doing my best Victor.

I turned to see if Latesha thought that one was funny. She looked solemn. I'd had a feeling she'd regret our having to kill Victor. Maybe at some point, I'd tell her I hadn't killed him after all.

But Wendell laughed aloud at my Victor impression. As he laughed, he did a chamber check on the .45, making certain a round was ready and waiting.

———

Wendell jimmied a small pane out of the way so he could reach in and crank the window open. Dulcet caught the pane so it wouldn't break and make a noise. I admired their well-practiced, almost silent teamwork. Wendell waved a hand to send Dulcet in. Enjoying herself silently but to some kind of ludicrous excess, she climbed in, and a dozen deep breaths later, she opened the back door from inside. No alarm went off. Wendell, Latesha, and I slipped in past her.

The main room of the warehouse had a small fleet of vintage cars in it, and nothing else, illuminated in the big, dusty room by a couple of high ceiling lights. They were classic cars, most of them in perfect shape: a Lincoln Continental, maybe from '71, an old, cherry condition '67 Thunderbird, a '57 blue and white Chevy Bel Air, a really nice 1960-something flat-black Ford Falcon, a Bentley touring car, maybe 1955, not fully restored, and an old Rolls-Royce Silver Shadow. There was even an old Packard.

Dulcet patted her hands together and did a little football player victory dance, seeing the cars. Wendell made the fanning-himself *that's hot* wave and grinned appreciatively. They assumed that they'd come out of this with a nice car or two now, as well as cash.

Me, I assumed that some of us were going to die.

They followed me through the shadows along the closed corrugated metal gate of the loading dock. I wondered how they'd gotten the cars in here, then I remembered there was a ramp that went up onto one end of the loading dock, just wide enough for cars.

We padded slowly toward the upright rectangle of light that was the open inner door to the office.

I glanced back at the others. Wendell had the .45 automatic in his hand. Dulcet had the AMT .38. Latesha had the MAC-10.

I had the Peacemaker in my hand, worn cowboy boots on my feet, and my cowboy hat on my head. My wire-rimmed glasses firmly on too.

Latesha's expression was all business, focused. Dulcet, though, was big-eyed with delight, chewing her sour taffy, almost skipping. I was glad she didn't have the autopistol—not something to play with.

All my dope spaciness, all my hangover, was gone now. Burned away in adrenaline. I could hear my heart thudding.

We got close to the open door, out of the line of sight of whoever was in the office. I heard voices.

"We got the Sweet Flash," said a deep voice. "Lot of people going to be there with money."

"I haven't decided on that one," said a smaller voice. "That's so high-profile. There'll be celebs there. This dope at that event might get some attention we wouldn't want, 'specially if something goes wrong."

"Oh no, we *have* to serve Sweet Flash if they want it," said another man with a fruity, self-congratulatory voice. He sounded high himself. "The more celebs, the better! Let them celebrate freedom!"

"You know, I'm starting to wish we didn't have to have this clown here," said a man I thought might have been Dutch, judging from the accent. "Here or, I tell you, anywhere. He takes the wrong shit. Takes that X bullshit."

"We're going to a rave, after all. Or am I mistaken?" said a fruity voice. "Ecstasy is the communion wafer! Oh, my friends, open yourselves up to the moment!"

"Yeah," said the deep voice. "He's already high as Elon Musk."

I knew they were glaring at the Oh-My-Friends guy,

then. They had their eyes on him, so I stepped into the doorway, the Peacemaker leveled. And now, they all had their eyes on me. Four pairs of astonished eyes.

"Yeah, gents," I said with a soft voice, scaring myself with my own confidence. "'Open yourselves up to the moment.'" I added in my thickest Texan accent, "And will *y'all* all kindly put your hands up?"

Just as we'd rehearsed it, Wendell moved up close behind me, but on the other side of the door, down on one knee with his pistol out at the end of his arms. Latesha stood behind him, aiming the MAC over his head. She was rock solid. Dulcet knelt beside Wendell, between me and him, but a little back, grinning over her little pistol.

All four of us with a target selected, all of us visible, though I was the most vulnerable, a little bit out in front.

I'd been half expecting Wendell's crew might hang back and let me take some fire.

The four men in the room stared at us, and one by one, raised their hands. One of them was a Black guy, with the overstated bulkiness of a hardcore weightlifter. His close-cut hair was dyed in stripes of white and blue. He wore sweatpants, a muscle shirt under an open Las Vegas Raiders bomber jacket that partly concealed a .357, probably a Smith & Wesson, in a shoulder holster. I was peripherally aware that Latesha had her weapon aimed at the weightlifter. The guy had a calculator in his hand instead of a gun.

Wendell was aiming at a big square-headed blond guy with angry blue eyes and rubber-banded bundles of cash in each of his ham-sized fists.

I figured the Asian guy for the boss, with his aura of immaculate authority. The one ultimately responsible for what had happened to Frankie. I had my gun aimed at him.

He was twitching visibly as he looked at the gun, his empty hands opening and closing.

Dulcet was aiming at the fourth man who stood on our far left, the one with the droopy, frozen smile. A tall—I mean, six feet five, at least—middle-aged, stooped, clean-shaven, bald White guy, totally missing his eyebrows, in a very old tie-dyed Moby T-shirt and blue jeans. He had a fanny pack too.

Not one of them had a gun in his hand.

They stood around a big oak desk, gaping at us, and the desk was cleared off to make room for all those stacks of money.

They had been counting the dope money. It looked like at least a week's take. I could feel Wendell's happiness like a space heater in a cold room at the sight of the skyline stacks of money on the table.

Wendell said, "Must be at least three hundred thousand. You see how a little planning, and waiting for the right time'll, how that pay a man, Tex?"

"When you're right, you're right, pard," I said.

I saw there was, after all, something else on the desk, behind the stacks of cash.

I was pretty sure it was an Uzi. I could just make out the muzzle and breech.

Behind them was another door, which I thought went out to a little wooden porch. I wasn't sure if it opened anymore. On the floor, near the door, was an open cardboard box, and in it were four big plastic jars, with something white in them. The dope or something to cut the dope with.

The muscular Black guy was staring at me. "It's a motherfucking cowboy," the guy muttered in wonder.

Dulcet tittered behind us. "He is! He's a killer outlaw! He kills all kindsa people!"

"Shut up, ho," Wendell said mildly. He cleared his throat and went on, "Y'all lift your hands, move your asses back away from that desk, and anyone does anything not on that list is the first to get hisself cut down."

Then came the inevitable moment when they had to think about that.

They hesitated.

With easy deliberation, I cocked my gun. It made a loud noise in the waiting quiet.

The Asian guy heard it, looked at my gun, and raised his hands. The others followed suit, though I saw the Dutch guy glance at that Uzi as if to memorize exactly how it lay.

We didn't want any shooting during the robbery. One or two of us would go down if the shooting started. Then, some nearby patrolling security guard could hear the shots and call the Richmond police. Cue the car chase scene. No, thank you. A nonviolent robbery was less problematic.

Except, of course, that I planned to kill these strangers, all four of them, after the robbery, once Wendell and crew were safely on their way with the money.

Until then, if we could just ease quietly through the robbery part...

"We really should talk this over!" the bald middle-aged raver chimed in. His red mouth—one of those mouths that look like they have lipstick on them when they don't—barely moved when he talked. It was like he was talking out of his dilated eyes. He looked vaguely familiar to me. "Because what's up is, we all are working for the same thing, freedom and love and—"

"Banyan," the Asian guy said, licking his lips. "Please be quiet now. Be very quiet, and just do what we do."

Banyan? Was that some kind of exotic first name, or his family name?

Banyan blinked and seemed to consider the recommendation that he shut the hell up. Then he shook his head and looked pityingly at us all. "'Do what we do?' It's yes and no with that, isn't it? There's a time for harmony and a time for individuality…" He cocked his head, and his face got vacant as he spaced out on that.

I let out a long, slow breath. "Now y'all step real slow and carefully back, like Mr. Steroids here told you."

Letisha laughed. "Ha! Mr. Steroids!"

They glanced at each other. They were unnerved, I think, by what a good time we seemed to be having, which was the idea. We hadn't rehearsed that. But effective criminals should be natural psychologists. If I lived long enough, I thought I might write an essay on that from Death Row.

The Asian guy moved back. The others followed suit.

"Line up," I said.

"Why?" the Asian guy asked, starting to lose his veneer of control.

"Not so we can shoot you," I said. "So we can keep an eye on you." That was half true.

"Mr. Steroids," Wendell said to the weightlifter. "Reach your left hand, use two fingers—and I am going to count to see is it just two—and you take that piece out by the tippy end of the butt, and you toss it on that desk there."

The weightlifter's eyes clouded over. He was getting pissed off.

Wendell shifted his gun muzzle from Dutch over to the weightlifter. He caught Latesha's eye. "Girl, you help me kill Mr. Steroids there? We get him first and then that Euro trash motherfucker."

"Yes, baby," Latesha said. "I'm fittin' to shoot his crotch first."

The Black dude seemed to sag in his clothes. He eased his left hand to the shoulder holster and tossed the big gun on the desk.

"Can I ask 'em one question?" Dulcet said, chewing her sour taffy.

"Go ahead," Wendell sighed. "Just git it out."

She beamed at the four men in the office. "How come you pissy puppies drive those dumb ugly trucks and those big-ass Jeep things when you could be driving those pretty cars back there?"

"Those are *my* cars!" Banyan said. "Aren't they beautiful? They're a present from the Spirit of Ecstasy. I was planning to give one as a present to each of these guys, but you know what, there are plenty of cars in the world. Would you like one? All the keys are in that desk there. Let's talk it and walk it—individuality in harmony!"

"Banyan, shut up!" the Dutch guy said.

"Amen to that," I said.

Dulcet laughed.

"I got a question or two myself, and then we can get to business," I said. I looked at the Asian guy. "You Ricky Kwai?"

He just looked at me, chewing the inside of his cheek.

I said, "I could always check the ID off your body."

He blinked. Then he nodded. "I'm Ricky Kwai."

"And that stuff in the jars, in the box there, that more of the shitty X and fentanyl you mixed together? The stuff that killed him?"

"Tex," Wendell said warningly.

I knew what he was thinking. If these guys thought I

was on a vengeance mission, they'd figure they had nothing to lose by going for the guns.

And as each second ticked by, we were perpetually half a second away from a bloodbath while things stayed like this. The mutual exchange of death. I knew that too.

"What does he mean, 'shitty?'" Banyan asked, genuinely puzzled. "It's the best pharm X, friend."

"Oh fuck," the Black guy muttered.

I nodded. "I get it. They didn't tell you they were not only stepping on the shit, they were mixing it with poison?"

Banyan frowned. "I..." He looked at Ricky. "You poisoned someone?"

"If you guys want the fucking money, take it and get the fuck out," the Dutch guy snarled suddenly.

"I believe the man's right, Tex," Wendell said. But he didn't move.

Banyan looked at me like he was a Baptist painting of Jesus, and said, "I thought it was good to make money on it because the X brings people together. It's a gift from the Spirits, to save us all, a communion wafer—"

"It makes you blab on and on like an idjit," I interrupted. I took another step into the room. My arm was starting to get tired, holding the gun like that. "Boss, get your money."

Wendell nodded happily and stepped into the office, coming at the money with me and Latesha covering him.

But if there's a bunch of cold-sober guys in a hard situation and one stoned guy, the stoner is always the one who fucks things up.

So the baldheaded guy, with his droopy earrings and his droopy smile and his nebbish face, came half-stumbling toward us. "I am here to tell you, we're all going to glow as one when the solar system in each of us becomes the galaxy of all of us." At least I think that's what he was saying, improbable as it seems.

I'm not sure, because my attention had riveted on the Dutch guy, who was using the blundering distraction of Banyan—

Banyan lurched, sparkle-eyed, toward us with arms spreading for a group hug.

The Dutch guy scooped up the Uzi and, in the same motion, squeezed off a long burst at Wendell.

Most of the bursts missed Wendell, sizzling the air around us, chewing up the frame of the door. I felt a hot poker burn my right ear. I heard Latesha yell in surprise and pain.

Wendell caught three rounds, stitched across his left shoulder, his chest, his right side. He shouted, "Fuck, shit!" and fired at the Dutch guy, catching him in the forehead near the right temple, the .45 round chiseling a corner of the Dutch guy's skull away so that bits of yellow and blue-white calcium and droplets of red sprayed back on Ricky Kwai, who was covering his head with his arms and cringing.

Dutch staggered back, fired another burst at nothing in particular, making a stack of money burst into the air like a flock of startled butterflies. He didn't fall immediately, blinking as if simply surprised, his hands still swinging the Uzi around, maybe spasmodically or maybe in one last act of will for another burst at us, as I aimed at Dutch and squeezed the trigger.

The six-gun jumped in my hand, and the round punched right through his esophagus. His head jerked back, and he spun and fell with a heavy thump.

As shot-torn bits of one-hundred-dollar bills drifted down like parade confetti between us.

The weightlifter had just closed his hand on the pistol

he'd tossed on the table when a burst from Latesha's MAC made him do a sort of odd little dance, like his part of a mating dance with her, and he fell back against the wall, randomly firing the pistol...so that the window exploded outward.

Dulcet was half skipping into the room, her little gun making popping sounds, as she pumped rounds into Banyan, who was off in a corner, to my left, waving his hands at the gunshots as if to shoo flies away.

Ricky was crawling...crawling toward that back door, breathing hard. "Take the fucking money!" he rasped. "Just take it!"

I saw the weightlifter was still alive, sitting on the floor with his legs splayed, shakily raising that gun again. I cocked my gun and aimed at his head. He moved as I fired, the round smacking into his right eye.

The eye socket instantly became a crater gushing blood, but the round had gone downward, missing his brain, and he was firing the pistol, sloppily, though. The rounds whistled close, made pieces of ceiling rattle down—

I squeezed off another round into the weightlifter, and he bounced back against the wall, closing his remaining eye.

Gunsmoke snaked up into the air from the silver muzzle of my Colt and stung my eyes.

I heard Dulcet singing something and turned to tell her to get back into the big warehouse room. But I found I couldn't say anything to her right then.

"Happy trance!" Dulcet chanted as she fired her little automatic. She was dancing around to music only she could hear—and shooting.

"No, that's...it's..." Banyan said between each impact, sounding as if he was trying to explain how sadly wrong she had gone.

A number of small holes on his torso spouted blood. He was on his knees, his mouth open, looking so sad, so disappointed. It seemed to affect her.

I heard the Black guy coughing wetly. The son of a bitch was game, pard. He wasn't dead yet. I turned to see his remaining eye burning up at me as he tried to say something, not getting the words out. But I knew he was telling me he was going to kill me.

He raised his Uzi. The little submachine gun was wobbly, but it was pointed at me.

I aimed carefully, quickly but with deliberation, and, without time to cock the gun, I squeezed the trigger hard. It was harder to pull the trigger without cocking the gun.

But the Peacemaker bucked in my hand, and this time the round caught the weightlifter between the eyes. A nice round hole, a couple of red oozing cracks zigging from it.

He quivered, dropped his gun, and went still. His remaining eye stayed open this time, rapt. As if he were attentive. Maybe he was.

The room was choked with gun smoke now, smelling of gunpowder and blood. I felt hot wetness running down from my right ear.

Dulcet squatted close to Banyan, who was coughing blood. Dying. "Want some candy?" she asked, sounding completely sincere. She took the half-chewed sour taffy from her mouth and put it in Banyan's, as if to share.

He chewed once, twice, and he smiled thinly up at her. He reached up with bloody hands and patted her forearm. "That's so...It's sour, but...you're so...sweet. My dad likes..."

Then he stopped talking and went limp like a remote-control toy with the batteries pulled.

"Ohmigod, he got blood on my blouse," Dulcet said, pulling it off. She was naked from the waist up.

Latesha was on her knees beside Wendell, who was trying to sit up. Her face was wet with tears. It was screwed up like a weeping three-year-old's, and for a moment, I saw the little girl she had been, once, in that face. A little girl in Florida, waiting for her parents to come home.

Ricky was pulling at the lock on the door to the outside. I walked toward him. "Ricky, turn around."

He got the lock open now and was jerking at the handle. Fumbling.

He was clumsy with fear. I almost wanted him to get away, he was so scared.

But I hadn't come this far to let him go.

"Ricky...you killed my son. His name was Frankie. You killed him with fentanyl. They say the dead can pray for you. I hope he prays for both of us, Ricky Kwai."

"Shoot him, Tex!" Dulcet shouted gleefully.

That made me want to let him go too. "Shut up, Dulcet," I said.

I walked over to Ricky, cocked the gun...

At the sound of the gun cocking, he tried to make himself small, cringing down and away from me. "Reno!" he said shrilly. "In Reno!" I didn't think about why he was saying that. Not until much later. I wanted to get this over with.

I reached out, spun him around, shoved the gun into his open mouth, and pulled the trigger.

I admit it. I closed my eyes. As an existentialist, I should have taken responsibility, and watched his brains explode out the back of his head to run stickily down the door.

I didn't watch it, though. But that's what happened to him.

I looked to make sure it was done, and then I let him

drop and turned around to face, at least, the wreckage behind me.

10

LATESHA WAS STILL WEEPING over Wendell. He was cursing her, telling her, "Get me up, you damned fool woman..."

And Dulcet was raking all that money—what wasn't shot up or badly bloodstained—into the three satchels it'd come in. Then she turned to the jars of fentanyl and X.

"Dulcet!" I said sharply.

She pouted at me.

"Leave it for the police to confiscate," I said. "That's nonnegotiable. That shit will kill you dead. It's killing kids. Needs to be off the street."

Dulcet hesitated. She hated to leave all that potential money.

Grimacing with pain, Wendell snarled, "Dulcet, forget that shit dope and get your skinny little ass out to the motherfucking..." He broke off, gritting his teeth.

I knew we ought to be running—and right now. Even in an area with few people around at this hour, that much gunfire was going to attract the cops.

But as I walked over to Banyan, every step was a

struggle against a current that wanted to push me back, push me down on the floor...with the dead.

And I wasn't sure I wanted to leave here at all. I figured I really ought to stay and greet the cops.

My boots made sucking sounds in the blood on the floor as I walked unsteadily, slowly, over to Banyan. I stared at all those little holes Dulcet had shot into him.

What had Banyan been saying at the end? It was like he recognized me in the end. He'd said, *My dad...*

It seemed to prompt some fuzzy recollection—oh no.

I recognized his face now, with the unnaturalness of his high gone from it.

Oh, hold on. That can't be right. No fucking way. He can't really be who I think he is...

I hunkered down—and inside me, in some way, I hunkered down too, into some dark corner of myself—and I unzipped his fanny pack. Found his Velcro-closed bicyclist's wallet. Found his driver's license. Read the name on it.

Gary Ledbetter.

"Fuck," I said out loud, standing to stare down at him.

Banyan was a nickname. I put it all together now, because I had met this man a couple of times before. He was Mr. Ledbetter's second-youngest son. Son of Lawrence Ledbetter of Ledbetter Books. The son the old man had trouble with.

It wasn't a coincidence because Frankie sometimes came to work with me. Once, when I had to work through lunch, Frankie had gone to lunch with Mr. Ledbetter's son, Gary, who sometimes worked in the office on a kind of probational deal with his dad.

Gary "Banyan" Ledbetter had persuaded his dad to invest a lot of money—money blown, as it turned out—in trying to start a banyan fig plantation in the States, with trees transplanted from India, because he was fixated on banyans. He'd had a hashish vision under a banyan, and now people called him Banyan.

Mr. Ledbetter's son. I had unintentionally persuaded some people to help me kill, among other people, Lawrence Ledbetter's son. He had looked *way* different last time I saw him. He had his hair then, had a beard, had eyebrows, had no stoned-out gleam in his eyes. Totally different effect. And Banyan Ledbetter knew Abel. Of course, he did. He'd heard Frankie was into skateboards.

Really? You into skateboards? There's somebody you ought to meet, man. Friend of mine got his own shop. Ocean surfer gone sidewalk surfer. Got some interesting experience over there. You like rave mixes?

So it was Frankie, probably, who'd introduced Victor to the drugs through Abel. Not the other way. Banyan thought it was just X, but they were mixing fentanyl in everything now.

I remembered that day at the office. I, myself had introduced Frankie to Gary "Banyan" Ledbetter.

I shook my head in sick amazement, thinking life likes to fuck with you. Or maybe that thought was just a way to avoid blaming the real culprit.

"Come on, Tex...you crazy...motherfucker," Wendell was whispering. "Let's go." A bag under each arm and another hanging from her right hand, Dulcet was looking down at Wendell, as if trying to comprehend.

I thought I could just make out the sirens approaching, still a long piece off. It wouldn't be long.

"I don't think I should go, Wendell," I said. "Y'all go ahead. I think I should stay here and face all this. You take the cash, all of it."

Latesha looked at me, her eyes red. There was blood

dripping from her lips, and she was newly missing a couple of teeth on the right side of her mouth. "Tex—Slim Jim—we gone need you now."

Her voice was bubbly. She spat out pieces of teeth.

"Jesus, you're hit, Latesha," Dulcet said, with real concern. "We gotta get you to a doctor!"

Wendell looked at Dulcet. "You...hear that...little White ho? She don't say, 'Take Wendell to a doctor.' She already write me off." Wendell said it almost fondly.

Dulcet said half-heartedly, "No way, Daddy Wendell, I didn't write you off. No, sir. No sirree, sir." She looked at the satchels of cash and couldn't resist adding, "Three bags full!" Then she looked at me. "Tex, you got a hole shot in your ear! Ooh, it's like they used one of those hole-punching tools. You can put a gauge in there!"

Wendell said, "I got another little hole-punching tool right here for you, Tex." Then he tilted his pistol up at me.

"What's up with pointing that gun at me, Wendell?" I asked.

"You got to go with us...Can't...you talk to the police... They ID us..."

"You probably got prints all over here," I said, "and it's not as if your prints aren't in their computer. No time to get rid of them. I wouldn't tell the cops anything about you anyway, man."

He lowered the gun, realizing I was right about the prints. He grimaced in pain. "Editor Boy," Latesha said, blood foaming at the corners of her mouth, "Tex? You got to help us with him."

The siren got louder.

I sighed and decided I couldn't abandon Latesha, at least, and that meant going with them.

Now I remembered something Gary Ledbetter had said about the classic cars in the warehouse.

Where would the keys be? I went to the office desk, opened the drawer, and saw the brass ring of old-fashioned car keys. They had little paper tags on them identifying the model.

"Wendell," I said, "we're gonna travel in style, man. You want the Rolls or the Bentley? Your choice."

He smiled wanly at that. "Always wanted a Rolls..."

———

Dulcet got the loading dock open and the Rolls rolling while Latesha and I were carrying Wendell out. He groaned and ground his teeth in pain as we loaded him into the luxurious back seat of the saloon car.

Dulcet had the Rolls moving down the street, *oohing* over driving the Brit car from the "wrong" side of its cab, before we got the car door closed.

We pulled around the corner maybe eight minutes before the cops pulled up to the warehouse. That's what it looked like, anyhow, from the whirling lights I could see over the rooftop of the adjacent building.

Later, I found out the cop had gone to the wrong building at first. There'd only been a vague report of gunfire in the area. It took them a while to spot the broken glass from that shot-out window.

In some ways, we were lucky.

———

Wendell was propped up in the back seat, between Latesha and me. Latesha was leaning up against him to help keep him upright. She had one hand on his leg and the other on her swollen jaw.

"I wish I had a chauffeur's cap," Dulcet said, driving up a ramp to I-80 toward Oakland. There was a doctor in Oakland that Leon had told Latesha about on the last working burner phone before he'd summarily hung up with a "Just don't bring him here."

Dulcet went on, "A chauffeur's cap. That'd be cool. I could use it in my act too."

I glanced at her. She was still topless. "You're driving with your tits hanging out. Could be a smidge conspicuous. Pull over. Put on my jacket."

"Oh, well, fuck," she said. "Okay, but it's not my look." And right before the freeway ramp, she pulled over long enough to put on my jean jacket, buttoned most of the way up. She checked her hair in the rearview mirror.

"But now you're topless, Tex," she said.

"Girl," Latesha said, "get this motherfucking car back on the road! Wendell's...he fittin' to...he needs a doctor!"

Dulcet put the car in gear, struggling with the clutch. It lurched a couple of times before she got it rumbling on. "I haven't driven a stick shift since I was a kid."

I wondered how badly Latesha was hurt. But she was watching Wendell like a mother with a grievously sick child. You could see the veins pulsing too hard on his forehead. He had lost a lot of blood. There was probably some pretty bad internal bleeding.

He was still smiling. "Rolls-Royce Silver Shadow. Nobody going to call this bitch in stolen...not for a long time, if they ever do, right? This bitch here is mine. She mine..." He ran his hand over the white leather seat. It was only slightly smeared with blood.

"How much...how much money we get?" he asked, his voice weaker, his eyes dimmer.

Latesha said, "Near half a million dollars."

"Motherfucker...that a lot of money. You girls...you take your share too. You put your money...in...you...invest it... Latesha..."

"We all gonna invest our money together, baby," she said, sort of mush-mouthed through her wrecked mouth, so it was harder to make out what she was saying now. But I thought after that I heard her praying for him.

Wendell noticed it too. "Don't you...save my soul... bitch, who you..." But Wendell put his hand over hers. "You sure stuck by me. Look at this, a Rolls...we scored...like a motherfucker. Those Cuban pencil dicks can kiss my black...Latesha?" He coughed up a little blood. "How much money we got?" he asked again. "You count that money, Latesha?"

"I think it's near a million dollars, baby," she said this time.

I saw Dulcet looking in the rearview mirror at us. Maybe those were tears in her eyes. Maybe they were gleaming at the talk of all the money they had in the trunk of the car. Closer to three hundred grand.

"Maybe..." Latesha was saying. "A million and a half..."

Wendell's voice was a croak now. "Tex...what you gone do with your share..."

"I thought we should stick together," I said. "All of us go to Las Vegas, start one of those Mustang Ranch places. Best Little Whorehouse in Nevada. The girls can supervise. I can be head of personnel. In charge of hiring..."

Wendell made a raspy sound that might have been laughter. "Tha's right...we gon' to Vegas...Mustang Ranch... Wendell's...Love Ranch..."

"Barry White playing all day," I said. "It'll be great. We'll get you patched up and head out there tonight."

Latesha looked at me and then looked away.

Wendell's voice was getting softer and softer. "Wait till...my brother Ray Bob...wait'll he sees me drive up in this bitch...I'll toss him a roll...go out and have you'self a time motherfucker...damn he...Look at this Raybobby, you raggedy-ass motherfucker... look...this...." He closed his eyes. "Didn't get enough motherfucking... sleep. Fucking ho drain my..."

"You just rest now, baby," Latesha said.

Wendell didn't answer.

———

We carried Wendell between us, Latesha and I, his arms over our shoulders, his feet dragging, up a back staircase, into the office where the doctor was waiting. We'd arranged the whole thing through the doctor's beeper.

The doctor was a semi-retired elderly Chinese in Oakland's Chinatown who didn't ask questions if you waved enough cash. And Latesha had brought in a paper bag full of twenties and fifties.

I'd started out on this mission with a young Asian doctor. Now the mission was old, and so was the Asian doctor. He stared at me for a long, puzzled moment. I'd just about forgotten I was unclothed from the waist up.

Dr. Jiang said this was going to cost plenty because we'd dragged him from his bed, but actually, he was wearing a rumpled three-piece brown polyester suit and smelled of cigarette smoke. It seemed more likely he'd been playing Pai Gow poker with the boys in some casino. He scarcely glanced at the bullet holes in Wendell's clothes, the bloodstains on all three of us. This was not his first rodeo.

We stretched Wendell out on an antique, white-painted metal examination table, a deeply worn leather pad under his head. On one wall, there was a chart with the outline of a man on it, arrows from ideograms pointing to different blockage points for chi flows in the body. On the other was an old promotional poster for Eli Lilly showing various pills for various ailments.

Jiang had a neat little white mustache and watery eyes. His office was over a dim sum restaurant, and it was so redolent of Chinese cuisine, I felt sick to my stomach and hungry at once.

The doctor pressed two fingers to Wendell's jugular, kept them there for ten seconds or so. Then he shook his head.

But glancing at Latesha, he wisely put on a show of making sure with his stethoscope. "He is dead, miss. Maybe fifteen, twenty minutes," he said. "I cannot bring him back. If I could, his brain would be no more, you know?"

"You're saying...you're saying he's dead."

"We try for half an hour to revive him...everything, everything. There was a blood clot in the lung from a breaking vessel there, and the blood clot goes into artery, stops heart. We try to break clot up, restart heart, but he came to us already gone...Going to need good pay for all this. Lots of good pay."

Latesha pressed another stack of bills onto him.

"*Try*," she said.

Jiang shrugged and bustled around, opening drawers. He injected adrenaline—or the doctor claimed that's what it was. It might have been water, for all I knew, into Wendell's forever-limp arm. No response. Then he wheeled an oxygen tank over in its rack, put an oxygen mask over Wendell's slack face, and tried to force oxygen. No response.

Jiang looked at the money, deciding probably he needed to make sure it looked like he'd earned his pay, and climbed up on the table to straddle the body, his clasped hands pumping Wendell's chest. He went on for a full minute. He listened to Wendell's chest. Shook his head.

He shrugged sadly at Latesha. And shook his head again.

Latesha groaned and took a step back. She stood there, swaying—

And I caught her when she fell and dragged her to a chair.

I said, "Hold still a minute, girl. Lean back and open your mouth." And I looked in her mouth myself.

The bullet had shattered two upper right teeth, and it was lodged in the gold filling of a lower back tooth. I was kind of blown away by that. There was the bullet, half crumpled, wedged like a dud rocket in an old wisdom tooth filling. Ballistic oddities were dogging me.

"Not my specialty," Jiang said. "Tomorrow, a dentist... my brother-in-law, very good."

I almost hit him. But instead, I just looked hard at him. He got the message.

He muttered in Chinese and made her lean back in the chair while he probed in her mouth with forceps, wrenching out the remains of the two smashed upper molars, then working on the wisdom tooth, prying at the crashed spaceship of the bullet.

Latesha seemed to have mentally gone somewhere else. She twitched with the pain when he worked over her, but she never cried out, and her eyes never came into focus.

I wondered about Dulcet. She was supposed to be waiting outside in the Rolls. She had all the rest of that money with her. I hoped she'd still be out there when we got back to the alley.

The doctor finally dug the bullet out, looked at it in his forceps with arched eyebrows, then tossed it into a metal dish. He took out a big set of keys, said he was going next door to the office of a dentist—maybe the brother-in-law, since he had the key.

Then he stopped at the door, came back, took the money we'd brought for him, and took it out with him.

Maybe two, maybe five minutes passed. I was beginning to worry he'd gone for the police when he came back with some temporary filling paste and a little dental tool.

He worked on the tooth in an impromptu sort of way. He gave her some codeine pills. I made her swallow a couple.

She hadn't said a word the whole time.

Finally, the doctor put antiseptic on my ear. I looked at it in the reflection on a shiny chrome tissue dispenser. It was true. A neat round hole punched out most of the lobe, leaving a half-moon shape. The little wound burned. I gave the doctor three twenties. "That's to cut off the piece hanging down, sew it up real quick. Rather have a scar than a weird little fleshy earring thing."

He snipped it off, which made me swear, and he sewed it up in four stitches, which made me cuss four times.

He gave us some antibiotics and pain pills for Latesha and then turned to look at Wendell's body. "I have this..." He opened a cabinet, showing a couple of body bags—he made a point of claiming he'd never needed them before— and the two of us grunted through zipping Wendell in. I carried Wendell's body down the back stairs, over my shoulder. I make it sound easy. It wasn't. The stairs complained with creaks at every step, and so did my back.

Showing tenderness I didn't expect after his avaricious opening salvo, Dr. Jiang escorted Latesha, helping her down the stairs.

I realized then that the old doctor wasn't the venal, indifferent old prick I'd taken him to be. He simply assumed we were criminals, with whom he worked only for the sake of the inheritance of his children and grandchildren. And he didn't like or trust us. But seeing Latesha's grief had moved him.

In the alley, the doctor helped her into the Rolls. She climbed in beside Wendell's body and pulled his bagged-up head onto her lap. The doctor patted her arm before closing the door.

Dulcet stared at the body bag for one protracted moment, then turned firmly away and started the car.

———

We drove Wendell's body around for a while, more or less at random. We were quiet, even Dulcet. Watching for cops but not really caring where we went. Latesha just sat there, staring out the window. I came out with, "Um...Latesha. I didn't actually kill Victor. I let the kid go," hoping it would cheer her up.

She gave me a tired smile. "That's good, Slim. That's good. I kinda thought so."

We stopped at a house in Alameda with a "Free" sign on a box of clothes sitting on the curb. Dulcet got out, fished around, and found a pink button-up sweater, a little too small for her. She took off my jacket and stood there nude from the waist up, cooing over the pink sweater. "It has a unicorn on it!" she called out.

Latesha opened a window and hissed, "Girl, get your ass back here!"

Dulcet put the sweater on and buttoned it up. She picked up a tote bag with a big pink satin rose sewn to it, stuffed a few other truly random selections of clothing in it, and hurried back to the car.

"Here's your jacket, Slim."

I put on the sleeveless denim jacket. Now, no one was topless.

We only stopped once more, on the old steel bridge over the estuary into Alameda. I got out, glanced around. It was late, dark. A Ford Bronco drove onto the bridge, passed us, and then it was gone. I reached into the Rolls, got the guns out, and tossed them into the estuary. We didn't linger there.

Okay, to be perfectly honest, I tossed *most* of the guns away. I couldn't bear to toss Tuck's nice Colt .45. I tucked the silver revolver in the gun belt and hid it under a girder, in deep shadow on a rusty ledge of the bridge, where no one would be likely to find it anytime soon. I might need it.

We finally fetched up at a "lookout point" turnout, near the top of Grizzly Peak, overlooking Berkeley, Oakland, and the Port.

Berkeley was spread out below, mostly dark, with lights glittering in clusters. I could see the angular freight cranes jutting gigantically along the bay, so tall they were crowned with bright lights to warn passing choppers. Beyond the long sweep of the Bay Bridge, the San Francisco skyline was sharply outlined in lights.

It almost broke Dulcet's heart, but Latesha, coming out of her fugue, insisted that we burn the Rolls—with

Wendell's body in it. A Viking funeral kind of deal. She said *The Vikings,* with Kirk Douglas, had been one of Wendell's favorite movies. Saw it on TCM.

Dulcet liked the Viking funeral idea, but she hated losing the Rolls.

"Wendell was probably wrong that we got away clean with this car," I pointed out. "They probably have a list of the cars by now, and chances are they're looking for this one."

She pouted. "My beautiful Rolls!"

"It was Wendell's," Latesha said rather severely. Dulcet shrugged.

I didn't even consider saying, *Actually, it was Banyan's Rolls.* In my mind too, for no clear reason at all, it was Wendell's Silver Shadow.

Dulcet and Latesha almost fought over what to do with Wendell's cut. Dulcet, naturally enough, thought we ought to split it along with the rest of the money. I was pretty surprised myself when Latesha insisted on starting the fire with Wendell's share of the money.

She got her way. She took Wendell from the body bag and piled most of his share of the cash onto his chest. She lit it with his gold Zippo and then lit a big handful of hundred-dollar bills.

Dulcet backed away from the Rolls, saying, "Whoa Nelly, girl," as Latesha stuffed the wad of burning hundreds down into the gas tank.

I shouted, "Latesha, get the fuck away from that car... now!"

Murmuring a prayer to Jesus that would have pissed off the Vikings, Latesha was shoving the burning bills down into the tank with a stick.

I ran to her, grabbed her upper right arm in my two

hands, and yanked her back from the car, having to drag her, thrashing, to the cover of a couple of steel trash barrels.

One step ahead of the devil...

Dulcet was already crouching, calling a cab on her iPhone, telling them to send it to an address we'd picked out, up the hill. Still mad about burning the car and Wendell's share of the money, Dulcet snapped at the dispatcher when they didn't understand her the first time over the sound of the explosion.

As the Rolls gave out a deep-throated *whoosh*, and burst into flames.

But then Dulcet danced a little, waving her arms over her head in front of the pyre, wearing her pink unicorn sweater and her short shorts, a sylphic silhouette in front of a burning luxury car. Saying goodbye to Wendell her own way.

There was a dark, hard lump in the middle of me. It felt as if my stomach had petrified. It wasn't so much for Wendell, though I did feel something for him. It was just that, watching the car burning, maybe, after all, I felt some regret about not going to Frankie's funeral.

I shook my head, like I was trying to shake off mosquitoes. I forced the tears down, thinking that I had to get moving again...keep moving out ahead of it...

We were only half a block up the hill when the police cars and fire trucks came.

One step ahead of the Man.

The cops and firemen stared, bemused, at the pyre of the burning Silver Shadow, where Wendell's body burned joyfully.

You can only run as far as you can.

———

The cab found us in front of a dark mini-mansion in a stand of eucalyptus. The driver was an octogenarian hippie with braided white hair, the tips of his big white beard braided too.

"Look," Dulcet said, "it's fucking Willie Nelson come to get us."

The cabbie chose not to take offense, and said, "Hey, what's happenin'? Late to go out on the town, huh? But whatever's your...your..."

He broke off, looking us over. We were still blood-spattered and shabby after the fight. We probably smelled of gunpowder and blood and gasoline, Dulcet clutching the remaining two satchels.

He stared for a moment, then he glanced in the direction of the burning Rolls. Though from here, it was just a flicker of flame down the hill, a tremble of red light between the dark tree trunks below us, the counterpoint blue strobing of first-responder light bars. He must have rubbernecked the pyre scene on the way here.

I gave him the same look I gave the doctor, and he said nothing and took us where we were going.

An address on the East Oakland flats.

———

The Easter Hill Church of Our Loving Savior was a long, narrow wooden building that looked like it had probably once been a medium-sized discount shoe store. At the bottom of the hand-painted sign nailed onto the false front, next to a Christian cross formed out of glued-on sparkly stuff, silver lettering read "The Reverend Huey Kearnes." Below that, there was a butcher-paper banner in the window: *Save Easter Hill Church! Come to the Bake Sale and Witness for the Lord! (Yes, we will have Mrs. Hoaglin's Sweet Potato Pie!)*

We stood awkwardly on the sidewalk in front of the makeshift church—a makeshift clapboard chapel for a makeshift denomination. The cab was waiting across the street.

There was one light on in the back of the improvised church. But I couldn't see much in there.

"You sure they're in there, Latesha?" I asked.

She nodded. There was a certain peacefulness in her expression now. "Reverend Kearnes lives back there."

Dulcet shook her head in wonder. "You're not *really*, are you, Latesha?"

"I got no reason not to give myself to the Lord now," Latesha said. "Everything happen for a reason."

"No, I mean—the money. You aren't going to give them your share of the money, are you?"

"This place going to shut down, it don't get some money. The neighborhood 'round here can't afford to support it, but they do some good here. Organize food drives for peeps got no food, they got a program to get the kids off the street."

"Whatever. I just don't like—"

"And she's getting my share too, Dulcet," I said. "I already put it in her bag."

Dulcet pouted. It was not a cute pout. "That going to get you off the hook, Tex? Make you feel all right about what you've done...and what you didn't do?"

"Dulcet," I said tonelessly. "Shut the fuck up."

She looked at me, and her eyes softened. "'Kay!"

"Anyway, I'm not a complete dweeb. I kept five grand."

She clapped her hands. "That's my Tex!"

"Take your share, Dulcet, that *one* bag, and go wait in the cab. Maybe you can get Willie to sing for you."

"'Kay. Can we get something to eat later? I'm hungry as a wolfy."

"Sure. Go on now."

She looked at the satchels with a theatrical pout, then reluctantly gave one to Latesha.

Latesha held out Wendell's gold Zippo. "I think he'd want you to have that, Dulcet."

Dulcet brightened and snatched the Zippo. "Thanks!" She started across to the cab, turning around halfway across the street just long enough to say, "Bye, Latesha!"

"Bye, Baby." Latesha turned to me, kissed me on the cheek. "Thank you, Tex. I'm sorry about your little boy."

I swallowed. I wished she hadn't said that. "I'm sorry about Wendell. If it weren't for me..."

"I don't blame you, Slim."

I nodded stiffly and turned away, looking at the waiting car, but just standing there. Not wanting to get back in that car, either.

Up the street, I saw a teenager sitting on a small Y-handlebar bike, rolling it back and forth under him with little motions of his hips as he talked to his friends under a streetlight. They all had those black durags made out of stretchy material on their heads, with the flaps that hang down in back.

Latesha patted me on the shoulder, then she went up to the door and knocked. I waited to make sure she got in all right.

After a few minutes, I heard a gravelly voice, muffled through the door, "What devil's wickedness is that?"

"Reverend Kearnes? It's Latesha? You remember me?"

I heard the door unlock and open. "Girl, what you doing here this time of night?"

"You said I could come day or night, if I wanted to pray."

He smiled, yawned, and said, "You want to pray with me, come on in. What you got there?"

She went in without looking back. The door closed behind them. I waited a moment. Then I heard him shout something I couldn't quite make out. It was a joyous sound unto the Lord, though. And I definitely heard the word *miracle*.

I walked back to the cab and got in. I leaned forward and tapped the driver on the shoulder, reading his name off his identification card.

"Hey, Jason Winslow Becher," I said.

He looked at me. I noticed his bristly eyebrows and the marijuana stain on his mustache. "Yeah?"

"Did you call this stop in?"

"No, we aren't where we're going yet. But o' course, strictly speaking, I'm supposed to tell them wherever I stop in case..." He broke off and licked his lips.

I leaned toward him and fixed his eyes with mine. "In case? Not in this case. Jason Winslow Becher, you remember *no details* of this fare at all. You don't remember what the people looked like. And you didn't drop any of them here. You understand? You pretend I'm fucking Obi-Wan Kenobi here, and I'm erasing your mind. You *don't fucking know.* Are we clear?"

"Um...yeah."

"I mean this. Because if you do cross me on this, no matter what or why, I'm going to find you and kill your ass dead. And that's a flat promise. Okay?"

"Right on," he said, though *right on* made no real sense just then.

"Okay. Where you want to go?"

"Denny's."

"Denny's? For real?"

"I'm hungry."

"Seriously?"

"So very serious, ohmigod. And that place is open, and nothing much else is."

The driver set off immediately, in a hurry to get this fare over with.

I looked wistfully through the rear window, back at the storefront church.

I wished then that I could believe in the whole story about Christ. About repentance and forgiveness and heaven. I wished I could believe in God. But I can't.

I sure as hell can't.

11

ABOUT AN HOUR AFTER DAWN, we had breakfast. I had coffee, two eggs, and toast. Dulcet ate a whole Denny's Grand Slam. On the floor, protectively between her feet, was the tote bag. Inside it, under the tatty free clothes, was nearly $90,000 in cash.

We didn't talk much, then. There were only a few customers in the place, but they made me nervous. After she pushed her plate away, Dulcet told me that one time she'd had a customer who took her all the way to Paris and London in a private jet. She loved London. Wanted to go back there. "Where you want to go, Slim?"

"Back in time," I said.

"Back to when you were shooting that Ricky Kwai and that Abel? So you could watch that again?"

"No, no. Way before that."

"I'm going to London. But first, I'm gonna invest! Get my own place out like where the Mustang Ranch is. Run the girls myself, make a million dollars, and take trips to London and Pay-ree."

Afterward, we went outside and sat on a little bench by

a cigarette-butt urn, so Dulcet could have a smoke. With one arm around her tote bag, she lit a cigarette with Wendell's lighter. She crossed her legs, wagged the crossed-over foot, and smoked, watching the lights on the freeway.

Then, looking at the gold lighter, she said, "Wendell... ohmigod, he's just *gone*. Like if the Coit Tower just vanished away." She tapped ashes onto the cement walk. She said in a low voice, "You know, he never hit me."

"I take it he hit Latesha sometimes."

"Couple of times, because she was acting out. It's not really...it wasn't..." She cleared her throat. Was she holding back tears for Wendell? "Wasn't in his *nature*. I mean, Jeezy Louisey, he could be pretty tough. I saw him shoot a guy who stole some money from him. Guy wanted to get whole, pay him back with interest. Nope. But...he had a third gal, Sissy. I feel like she left because he *didn't* hit her."

"Some women get twisted around by stuff they've been through with men. And by the life."

"I was born twisted around, Slim." She tittered at that, with her eyes squinched shut, but I thought she felt it was true. She glanced at me and said, "But I don't allow anyone to hit me. Unless maybe a little sexy spanking. Now, Sissy, boy howdy, she had the scars too. Her stepdad broke one of her legs with a steel bar."

"Christ!"

We were quiet for a minute, and then I said, "I liked Wendell. Which...I didn't expect."

"He was a funny bunny. He had some bad luck. And you know what, he had a real big score once, and he put some money down for his luxury condo in the Sunset."

"Latesha told me. Wait. We could've stayed in a luxury condo instead of a Travelodge?"

"Nobody but me and Latesha and one dealer dude he liked ever got in there. Not even Leon."

She blew smoke into the air. "I got something for you." She opened her purse and took out a cheap cell phone. "It's an extra one I got so I could call Latesha and talk to her without Wendell knowing." She coughed a little, then took another drag on her cigarette, and the words came out along with the smoke. "I know she don't want to be in touch. But you might want to be in touch with me."

I took the phone. "Thanks." Doubted I would use it. She was a very attractive woman, but she seemed to me, to use an expression my father had, nuttier than squirrel poop. She made me think of Alice in Wonderland, if Alice had stayed and gone all Queen of Hearts.

"Were you in love with Wendell?" I asked.

"Me?" Her scanty eyebrows rose. "No, uh-uh, Texy Slim. I was just being part of something. In a place that was pretty okay with me. And I like Latesha. I'm going to miss that girl. Latesha, she was *maaaaaaddddly* in love with Wendell." Stretching out the word madly with an odd sort of delight. "I don't fall for a man. I do a dance with them and make sure they don't step on my feet. There's one who I think is into me. He comes around the club sometimes. Offers me a job every time. Unless you want to make me an offer, I'm going over there."

She looked at me like a waitress waiting for a customer's order. Waiting to see what I said to *unless you want to make me an offer...*

"Me? Um..." I shook my head. "I'm going to the police, see about what went down at Ledbetter."

"Ohmigod! You're turning yourself in?"

"That's about the size of it. I won't say anything about you."

"You promise?" She gave me the little girl pout, but the look in her eyes was icily serious.

"I promise ten ways from Sunday and all the way to Texas and back."

She tittered again and puffed on the cigarette, narrowing her eyes at me. "You really didn't kill those people at the office?"

"Nope. I did not."

Dulcet nodded, a little disappointed. She sighed. "I guessed you probably didn't do it." She flipped her cigarette butt, so it twirled neatly into the urn, trailing circles of smoke. She gave me a smoldering look she'd copied from some old-time movie star and said, "I betcha you change your mind about the police."

"Maybe," I said, not believing it.

"If you do go through with it, dump the phone I gave you before you turn yourself in."

"Okay." I stood up and stretched. The horizon was turning gray blue. "You ready to get another cab?"

I dropped her off south of Market with a tall, skinny, sartorially exquisite Black guy by the name of Jacques, with neatly jerry-curled hair. He came out of his spotlessly gentrified building to meet her at the cab. Jacques heard the news about Wendell impassively. He talked to me briefly, asking about Latesha, with no street English at all. It seemed he owned a small but thriving hip-hop recording company, with a sideline in girls. The girls did outcalls, along with servicing rap artists as required. Dulcet had told me Jacques had an MBA from San Francisco State. But he had the gold at his wrists, the gems on his rings. He'd once tried to *buy* Dulcet from Wendell.

I was sorry to leave Dulcet with him. A background hum of violence came off Jacques, despite his surface amiability, his limp handshake. But then again, I figured Dulcet was at least as dangerous as he was.

I just raised my shot-up cowboy hat to her and said, "Ma'am," to make her laugh. And she did.

Then I left her there with Jacques, deciding I shouldn't worry about Dulcet. I should feel sorry for Jacques.

Drag-ass tired, I took the cab three and a half blocks more to the cheapest hotel I could find, where the bathroom wouldn't be down the hall.

––––––––

The next day, I showered and shaved and strolled into the brand spanking new offices of the nearest SFPD District Station and asked for homicide. I said I had some information. No one was taking particular note of me.

The desk officer was a muscular White cop with a flat-top, gay if I'm any judge. He directed me to an office down the hall. "Sergeant Morito takes tips if he's got time. If he's busy, come on back, and I'll find someone."

Down the hall, I found the designated homicide cop, a uniformed sergeant, just hanging up the phone. He was a plump, mustached, middle-aged Latino. He looked up in a friendly way, but inquisitively. He seemed like a bright, amiable guy. A nameplate on his desk said, "Sgt. R. Morito."

There were framed pictures on his desk and a couple of framed certificates on the wall. I sat down across from him, took a deep breath, and said, "You're looking for me. James Purdoux. Those killings at Ledbetter..."

He stopped me with a raised hand. "I need to record this. I should have the lieutenant there. Might take a while, he's out somewhere."

"Sure, fine. But I want to get it all out now."

He seemed to hesitate. Then he got up and closed his office door. He went and sat back down and took a small digital voice recorder from a desk drawer, spoke his name and the date and time into it, and said, "Taking a statement from James Purdoux regarding the shootings at..." Another address, another date. And then he nodded at me.

I realized I had the phone Dulcet had given me, despite promising to ditch it. Well, they'd take it and make nothing of it.

I talked for a long time. I told Morito about Frankie, then about Eickhoff, and about accidentally shooting Eickhoff and how that'd happened. I told him about running off and hiding in the Tenderloin. "But I want it known that I did not kill those people at Ledbetter, except Eickhoff accidentally. I was drunk and crazy over my son's death, and then the cop was shooting at me. I just...ran. But, uh..." I took another deep breath and was about to tell him about killing Abel and the deaths of Ricky Kwai and his men. And yeah, Gary Ledbetter.

But then Morito hit the pause button on the tape recorder.

"Appears you don't know. Eickhoff isn't dead. He survived. He's in pretty bad condition, but he's alive in a hospital under twenty-four-hour police watch. He exonerated you completely. Plus, a secretary he shot survived. She named Eickhoff. You got the gun?"

"Threw it in the estuary, off the bridge into Alameda. Maybe you can fish it out."

He looked annoyed. "You threw it away? When you didn't do the crime?"

"I saw a newspaper headline. Said you were looking for me in connection with the Renquist thing." I was feeling dazed, dreamlike, hearing about this.

"We were never looking to *arrest* you for the Renquist shootings. What happened with you and Eickhoff was more or less understandable, under the circumstances. We just wanted your side of the story. Confirm things, close the case. It never was about you."

I stared at him. "Well, shit."

He nodded. "That's right."

I thought about it, then I shrugged. "That's a good 'un on me. But—"

He raised a hand to forestall me. "We'll do a more detailed breakdown of what happened for the report. You need some coffee, or something?"

"Listen, um..."

I should tell him about the men I'd killed on purpose. Shouldn't I?

"I was you..." Morito went on, "I'd keep a low profile. Hide out, but don't leave town. The damn reporters will be all over you if you don't get clear."

I nodded. "Yeah...a coffee. That'd be great."

"Wait till Detective Bruno hears this." He went to the door and called out, "Hey, Bruno, guess who just walked in! It's that guy Purdoux!"

I sat there thinking that getting to walk out of the police station meant justice would come to me when it was ready. And it would do with me as it pleased.

And now, finally, when I should feel relief, I felt a depression crash over me and drag me down. I kept seeing Ricky Kwai's brains splattering the floor. I didn't feel bad about ending his life. But the image was slapping me in the face. And I remembered him saying, *"Reno, in Reno..."*

Two more hours in the station and they cut me loose. Not even a mug shot. A vague request that I stay in touch. I gave them the phone number of the shitty hotel I was staying in. But Morito didn't think they'd need anything else from me.

I thought maybe I'd better go get the Colt .45 before the cops found it. Or some kid. That thought sent a chill through me. Anyway, I was probably going to need a gun.

I bought a cheap backpack in a thrift store, took a couple of buses to Alameda, and found my way back to the bridge. I found the gun and stuffed the silver revolver and the gun belt into the backpack.

I stopped in an overly air-conditioned tiki bar in Oakland, sat alone at a rattan table under the grimace of a tiki mask, stared into a "tropical tequila," and thought, *Now what?*

Morito had advised me to stay on the down-low. That felt right. I decided not to go back to my apartment. Besides reporters, maybe some of Ricky Kwai's people might have worked out who I was. I was worried that Dulcet might get talkative with Jacques. Guy like that would know some big-time local dope dealers. The Kwais could be waiting at my place for me.

Worse was just living with what had happened. Bad memories were noisy roommates, crowding my skull. Frankie's dying at the hands of poison vendors and Eickhoff leaving dead people like bloody debris on the carpet, and then me snuffing people out—people who'd lived their whole lives just to end at my feet.

And Gary Ledbetter. Sure, he'd provided the Molly, the lure that drew Frankie into the deathtrap that was fentanyl. So maybe "Banyan" deserved what he got. Gary Ledbetter? A schmuck playing with psychedelics, playing gangster, a stoned doofus without a clue. No, come on, Slim. He needed rehab and therapy, not bullets.

And what did *I* deserve? I just kept circling back to life

losing its meaning. I was no big-eyed young stud bubbling with hope. I was at the tattered end of my thirties, dead-ending at a concrete wall spray-painted *You got no more reason for living*. No Frankie and no career. Just a feeling that I didn't belong anywhere. San Francisco didn't feel like home.

My mission...truncated. Decapitated. Because who else could I go after? I had followed all the trails I had.

But there was...something. *Reno*, the guy had said. That's where they were based.

I had to go *somewhere*. I could head that way, think about what I wanted to do on the way. Maybe identify the top brass of the organization that killed my son in Reno.

It seemed insanely beyond my reach just then. If I tried to go after the national bosses, how many more Gary Ledbetters might there be—not exactly innocent but not deserving of being shot down—caught in the line of fire?

I sipped the fruity cocktail and shrugged. Head in the general direction of Reno and think about it.

And maybe get a clear perspective about what was squirming around in the back of my mind, hissing that it knew what I really wanted to do.

Telling me I should just take down the guy who'd failed Frankie: James Purdoux.

I didn't finish the cocktail. I left the absurd, almost empty tiki bar and took a BART to the city.

I bought some clothes and some toiletries at a sidewalk shop in the Mission, then went back to the fleabag hotel. I cleaned up and shaved, put on some new jeans, a new white cowboy shirt with pearl buttons, and a new Levi jacket, complete with sleeves. I ditched the old one. I bought some ammo for the revolver at a gun shop.

I decided to rent a car. I had five grand in credit on a card. And to hell with staying in touch with the SFPD.

The next morning, I rented a Mustang GT with only four hundred and sixty-five miles on it. I drove northeast, on and on, toward the Nevada border, in a hurry to put a lot of miles between me and San Francisco.

————

I drove halfway to the border of Nevada and felt an avalanche of emotional exhaustion tumble down over me. I had to get out of the car. I had to think it all through.

Was it fight or die?

Right now, I didn't feel like living.

I stopped in a little town named Jumping Trout on a river of the same name. This pothole of a town fed on the passing tourists, truck drivers, and fishing enthusiasts. There had once been good fishing on the river. Now it was over-fished, but people still came and tried, in a fitful way. Mostly, they sat around RV camps, smoked weed, drank, and argued politics.

Me, I got a motel room, paying cash, then went to the little post office, mailed my apartment key to Meredith with a note telling her she could have anything in the apartment she wanted. There were mementos of Frankie and a couple of antiques worth having. I told her to leave the rest for the landlord to clear out. I sent him a cashier's check to pay for that process and a brisk apology.

Maybe after I rested, I'd know what to do. Should I just end it here or hit Reno head-on with what I had left?

Thus commenced three sodden, vacuous weeks.

I settled into the one-size-fits-all motel room. Evenings, I went out and drank too much, listened to the internet-based jukebox at the roadhouse, puzzling the locals with song selections snatched off distant weaves of the web. "Who the hell is Mojo Nixon? Who the hell are Iggy and the Stooges?"

Got into one inconclusive fistfight because some guy thought I was staring at him. I had a sloppy affair with a freckled bottle-blonde waitress named Daphne. That lasted for two nights until her truck driver boyfriend got into town. Fine, she's all yours, pal.

Some nights when I couldn't sleep, I talked to the ceiling.

It was something I learned to do in prison. You find ways to cope with the stir, with the monotony, the routine humiliations, the thugs in and out of uniform. Most of that was coping you did inside yourself, out of sight.

On the ceiling over my top bunk, there were scratches and cement patterns and cracks, and in the shadows of the night, there was a place where all those marks formed into the rough outline of a face. I found that if I concentrated, I could make it any face I wanted it to be. Then I could talk to it, in my mind, unless my cellmate was snoring loud enough, in which case I'd whisper. I could make the face turn into my mom, and then later my dad, both looking gravely back at me, listening to my apologies, explanations, and sometimes my complaints. Then, nodding their understanding.

I spent a lot of time talking to Meredith that way. Come on, I told her, you know, I wasn't dealing drugs. I just got a chance for an ounce cheap, and I was being a hog. I shouldn't have done it at all. We all know that. Sure, I know that, but I was never dealing. The fucking Sheriff's department just decided they needed a bust—politics and shit—so they said I was a dealer. Because, you know, it's fucking Texas!

And she'd say, "That doesn't bring you back here when I'm all alone and pregnant and..."

And I'd say, "Look, I was just out of my mind. I had three weeks clean, and Deaver gave me a bump, and I just went off..."

Around and around. But in the end, on the ceiling, if not in real life, she'd agree with me and forgive me.

Now, in the motel, I was staring up at the ceiling at three in the morning and seeing Gary Ledbetter up there, looking down at me in open-mouthed confusion. Did they shoot me?

"Yeah, they shot you, man. I'm sorry. I didn't recognize you, just seemed so different, and...you didn't seem to know about the fentanyl. Least, I don't think so. I'm sorry, man. I'm sorry for you and for your dad. But you know, you were in deep waters already. At some point, those Kwai pricks would probably have dumped your body out at sea, man. But I'm still sorry."

And he seemed to forgive me. He nodded. And I teared up.

Then he faded away, and Frankie took his place. I talked to him a while, telling him I would always love him, and I was always proud of him, and I was sorry I hadn't protected him. And then I realized that he wasn't listening. The face I was looking at was the one in the hospital morgue. It was just Frankie's dead face.

———

I changed bars, thinking the one at the Red Lion might be a slight upgrade, and continued to wallow in disgust with myself for drinking so much. But drinking took me out of the head that told me Frankie was dead, and I'd failed him, and by the way, have I mentioned that Frankie is dead and you've failed him? It numbed me. It let me drift into a boozy little eddy in the stream of being alive.

At the Red Lion lounge, a witty, well-dressed gay dude offered me a line of coke. I had the plain common sense to say no. But we had a couple of drinks and talked about what we admired about James Dean, Kirk Douglas, and Daniel Craig.

I stayed in my room for days at a time, watched formulaic old movies and one or two good ones, and ate bad takeout and drank. One day blurred into the next. I read swaths of the Gideon Bible, finding it more discouraging than otherwise. In the motel office, there was a stack of yellowing paperback westerns and several British detective novels, and I read them to keep my mind busy. One book blurred into the next.

I was sleeping badly, as you do when you overdrink. I went three nights with no sleep to speak of, partly because I was afraid of the nightmares, which had been steadily about the shootings at Renquist. I started thinking seriously about killing myself.

I talked the town's only doctor into an Ambien prescription, bought a fishing pole and some camping gear, and managed four scroungy days by the river, where I started hearing voices in the sounds of the crickets and the rushing river. It sounded like Frankie talking to Wendell. Sometimes Abel chimed in. They were talking about me. None of it was heartwarming.

I went back to the motel, showered, ate a scanty meal, went for a drive, and realized I didn't want to go back to

Jumping Trout. But I did, just long enough to pack up and check out.

Fuck this place. Maybe the road will clear my head.

———

I got two-thirds of the way to Reno, feeling the black wave rising behind me, hearing it roar louder and louder. I caught myself driving faster and faster. But you can't out-speed self-hatred.

Finally veering off onto a ramp, I screeched onto a road that hooked up with Rt. 395 to Reno. Heading to Reno on the 395 just to have some place to go. Was it because of what Ricky Kwai had said about Reno? Not consciously, it wasn't.

The highway passed through land that got rockier and more arid almost by the mile.

It came to me then. That's what I wanted. The desert. That big aloneness. You need aloneness to make certain decisions.

I crossed the border into Nevada. I saw a sign. *Reno, eighty-five miles.* Could I really take on the Kwais there? Right then, I felt like I couldn't take on a drunk wino. Depression makes a repulsive caricature of your big plans.

I could blow what was left of the five grand at a casino. That'd keep my mind busy.

I tried to drive faster than the thing that was pursuing me inside, but it caught up and poised itself over me now. Caught up with me effortlessly, just because it was ready.

Dad? Where you going?

"It's okay, Frankie," I said, nodding. At least I think I said it out loud. "I'll balance the books."

I drove off the highway onto a side road, just dirt and

gravel stretching straight as a die, into flat, scrubby desert. Out into the desert, like a migrating bird that got blown off course. In the distance, empty-looking blue-gray hills seemed to rise sharply out of the horizon.

Close to sunset, the sun squatting down to watch me like a hunter watching a rabbit, I parked the car in a big, empty, flat, dry lake. There weren't even any rocks or bushes there. Just the smell of dust in the lowering sun. It was like a perspective plain in a Dali painting, without the surreal structures. I brought those. A gigantic image of myself melting as I raised a gun to my head.

I took the six-gun from the trunk of the GT, walked out into the desert, following my long, starved shadow. I got maybe fifteen strides. Then I fell to my knees.

It all poured out of me then, in dark waves, roaring through me. I started to sob.

Frankie...

I was out there for half an hour as the sky got dusky and the sun sank lower. I had the gun in my hand, waiting for the right moment.

Finally, I took a deep breath and thought, *Get it done.* I cocked the pistol—and headlights flashed at me. I ignored them, assuming there was someone passing on the dirt road. They'd go away.

The headlights didn't go away. They came right at me, getting bigger like a nightmare's opening eyes. Then, the shape of a car formed behind them, and I saw the outline and indigo color of an SUV with tinted windows that I'd seen three times on the way here. It seemed they'd been following me. It couldn't be anyone friendly. Ricky Kwai was part of a syndicate. Maybe someone had gotten to Latesha or Dulcet.

Someone sent here to kill me? I could roll with that. A

big swallow of pain, and then it's over. I probably should let them kill me. Suicide by gangster.

But something prodded me to get up. I decided I didn't care to be executed. Why not die fighting? There was dignity in that.

Gun in hand, I ran back to the car, posting myself so it was between me and the SUV.

The hulking SUV veered, its wheels spurting dust, and slung around toward the back of the Mustang GT. The driver's side window droned down, and Dulcet called out, "Hiya, Cowboy Curtis!"

12

DULCET HAD CHANGED HER LOOK. Now she had a bob
curving to points at her chin. The cut was a little ragged
around the edges, like she'd scissored it herself. She had lost
the blue highlights.

I lowered the gun and walked to the car. "How the fuck
did you find me?"

"That phone I gave you." She wore an old scarlet
Fabani swing coat with big buttons on it, like something my
mom had as a teenager in the 1960s, a red polka dot blouse,
and Wendell's sunglasses, which no one had presented to
her. Her upper lip seemed a little swollen. She touched it
with the tip of a finger. "This is Jacques's car, and he's got
an app that tracks his girls' phones, where they are, and I
put that phone number into it. It pointed me right here."

"I think I saw this car a couple of times following me.
Hanging out at a gas station and following me some more.
Why didn't you just say something there?"

"Waiting for a place with no security cameras."

"Security cameras. And you have Jacques's car. In
Nevada. And no Jacques. You on the run?"

She tucked in her chin and rolled her eyes like a cartoon girl. "*May*be."

"Dulcet, what'd you do? Did he try to take your money?"

"I covered that money in the bag up with dirty clothes. He never went in there. He's fastidious."

"Come on and tell me. I need to know."

She tapped her newly oxblood fingernails on the steering wheel. "Jacques was okay for a while. But he started to figure out I had money I wasn't telling him about. Said I was being a bad, bad girl, and he was going to break me in by making me do a threesome with a couple of guys. And they were going to film it. He's starting a porn website. I said no, and he gave me a crack on the mouth."

I nodded sympathetically. "You got kind of a fat lip there."

"It's getting better. Anyway, he wouldn't let me leave, so I had to fuck him up with my box cutter."

"You carry a *box cutter*?"

"Fits good in my little purse. You threw my gun in the estuary. So...box cutter."

"You kill him, Dulcet?" Now I was looking toward the highway, half expecting Nevada State Troopers.

"I don't think so. Gave him two or three good cuts. Might lose some motion in his right arm, I betcha. But yeah, when he was yelling and bleeding, I got his wallet and his car keys and ran out!" She gave me a grimace-y Valley Girl grin, all teeth. "He called the cops from the hospital and made up a big story about how he was auditioning me for a recording and how I went crazy on him, all for no reason and all that. He's got a boy in the SFPD, so...I had to leave town. Didn't know where to go. I thought you'd have some ideas."

"My ideas get people killed."

"Long as it's not *me*," she said, spreading her hands and tilting her head to mimic a bad teenager. Then she looked me up and down admiringly. "New shirt, new jacket, shaved. New man!" She took in the gun in my hand and said, "Ooh, I got good timing, seems like."

I gave my head a noncommittal shake. Then I said, "You better leave his car here. Being as it's stolen."

"Do I have to?"

"Be the smart thing."

"'Kay. Um...but wait. Aren't the cops looking for *you?*"

"Nope. Turns out they knew I was innocent in the Renquist shootings. They cut me some slack for running off because, you know, they found out what happened with Frankie. And they sent me on my way."

"You didn't tell them about Kwai or...I guess, you didn't."

"No. I was going to give them an edited version. Leave your name out and all. But when they said, 'Take a hike, son, we don't need you,' I guess I thought, *Don't be a jackass, Jim.*"

Dulcet got out of the SUV, bringing a big canvas tote bag with her. Spiked heels of a pair of blood-red shoes poked up from lacy underwear. "It feels weird to just dump this car here," she said. "It's worth a lot of money. I bet we could get two or three grand for this car in Henderson. Nothing like what it's worth, but there'd be no, no, *nooooo* questions asked. I know some shady fuckers there."

"To do that, we'd have to drive it to Henderson. And that car's listed as stolen by now."

"I guess. Fuckin' phooey." She hefted her tote bag full of dirty clothes and thousands of dollars. "Good to go, Texican Jimmy."

"Come on, then."

I slid behind the wheel of the Mustang GT, wondering what the hell I thought I was doing. Dulcet had brought me her mess, and I was diving right into it. But somehow, despite her not needing protection, and despite my perhaps needing protection from her, I felt protective of her.

I put the Colt under the driver's seat as she got in the shotgun seat, hugging her bag of money and dirty clothes. Then I drove back to the dirt road and off toward the highway.

"Your nice GT's getting all dusty, Cowboy Curtis."

"Where do you get the Curtis part of that? Just looking for alliteration?"

She made a *tsk* sound. "You don't know who Cowboy Curtis is? That cowboy from Peewee's Playhouse? You're not Black like him, though. Too bad. Black cowboys are extra sexy."

"I never saw that show. You date the actor?"

"I wish. Where we going?"

"I'm going to Reno."

"To gamble?"

"In a way. Last thing Ricky Kwai said was 'Reno, it's Reno.'"

"You still on a mission, Slimby?"

"I don't know. Wait...I'm Slimby now?"

"Like Gumby, but Slimby."

"Who's Gumby?"

"A Claymation thingy. My crazy mama was so into Gumby. She had videos. Who's *that?*"

We were coming up on a silver sedan, tinted windows, a fairly new Cadillac C5. It was pulled over beside the dirt road facing toward the dry lake.

Its windows were tinted so I couldn't see who was in it,

but as we passed, I could make out exhaust at the tailpipe. It was sitting there, idling. Just close enough to keep an eye on us.

"I don't know," I said. "But it's making me paranoid. First, you're following me. Now this."

"It was pulled up at the gas station when I got some gas, right after you left, about forty miles back."

"So...that car was following you?" I looked in the rearview. The car had pulled onto the road, and it was following us. Not real close, but not likely to lose us anytime soon. "You think that could be someone working for Jacques?"

"I don't know. Maybe. Why didn't they jump me?"

Because, I thought, *maybe they were following you to me.*

"How'd they find me if they're working for Jacques?" she asked.

"Most likely, he's got one of those apps that tells you where his car is, almost like the one that tells him where his girls are by tracking their phones. Car gets stolen, it shows you on a map where it is."

"Oh. I should've thought of that. But he's in the hospital. I cut him pretty bad."

"He just called in a favor. What'd you tell Jacques about me?"

"Nothing, nada. I mean...hardly."

"Hardly?"

"Well, that you were with me when Wendell got shot. I was an el stupido girl when I said that, huh?"

"Muy stupido. Were you high?"

She looked sheepish. "Kinda, yeah."

I blew out a long breath, enough I could see it blur a spot on the windshield. "I was afraid that'd happen. That car might be people looking for me. Was there anything in the news about..."

"Two things. That Rolls-Royce burning got national news! They're trying to identify the body. Oh, and the cops found the bodies and all the dope in the warehouse. Yep, they did. Last I saw, they thought it was gang-fight stuff. Some triad busting on another triad. But they got to be wondering why nobody took the dope."

"Like, *Chinese* triads? They still around?"

"Like, the children of the triads. Young gangs from that scene or something. I betcha they're adorable kids."

"They didn't connect the burning Rolls with that?"

"Naw, but they'll figure out who owned the Rolls, I betcha. So..."

It was getting dark. I switched on the headlights and asked, "My name didn't come up in these reports?"

"Only name I heard was Gary Ledbetter, Slimby."

I thought of Officer Morito. Would he connect Gary's death with me?

I drove onto the highway and swung toward Reno. The rearview showed the Cadillac still following us at just about the same distance. Like they were waiting for their moment.

It was too much of a coincidence, that car being out there same time we were. It's not like it was a national park or something.

I shook my head. It didn't seem like cops in a new model Caddy, which made me wonder if it could be the Kwai outfit.

The GT needed gas, and up ahead was a gas station. I figured, why not stop and see what these fuckers do? I had the gun handy. Best to know what's up.

"Keep an eye on that Caddy for me. Tell me what they do when I pull over."

"'Kay."

I pulled off the highway and turned in at a gas station.

"They're driving on," she said. "They kinda slowed, but now they're driving on. And now...I can't see 'em no mo'."

I should have been relieved. But I was disappointed. I wanted them to be the Kwais. The moment I thought, *It's them*, I started feeling better. I was no longer thinking about offing myself. I was thinking, *Here's another inroad to the mission*.

Now they'd moved on. That left me feeling down again.

Dulcet looked at me. "What you chuckling about?"

"Laughing at myself is all."

————

It was dark now. Just outside of the light from the gas station, as I screwed the gas line cap back in, I could see Dulcet smoking a joint at the corner of the building. She kind of waved it at me to offer me some, and I shook my head and closed the cover.

When we were back on the highway, she was as weed-sleepy and as discursive as I'd figured she'd be. She had reclined her seat and was looking up at the desert stars through the window. The sunglasses were put away.

I noticed something up ahead on the right. Within sight of the gas station, the silvery Cadillac C5 was pulled up off the road, its lights off. When my headlights lit up its rear bumper, I memorized the license plate. I passed it.

Looking in the rearview, I saw its lights switch on. It pulled onto the road and followed us. That same distance back. "You see that Caddy?"

"I saw it," she said. "Not surprised. We got to lose them, Slimby."

"We will somewhere in town."

We drove on, and after a couple of miles she said, "The stars are followin' right along with us too."

"Yes, ma'am. They can be counted on, despite being countless."

She let loose a grudging laugh. "You're funny. I thought I could count on you till I saw you looking like you were thinking of putting a bullet in your ol' ninny head."

I winced. That's why she'd sought me out. I was someone she could count on.

"You had to be there. I was...I've had suicidal ideation on and off since I was a kid. I took Prozac for a while, which made it go away, but I didn't like the bottled-up feeling the drug gave me, and sexually—"

"Leaves you dead from the waist down after a while," she said.

"Yeah. So I just dealt with it my own way. And with cognitive therapy, and all that, in recovery. Had it pretty much under control till Frankie died. And then *boom*, it's back, bigger and badder than ever."

"Don't do it while I'm with you. Or even while I might be somewhere close by. Deal, cowboy?"

"Deal," I said. "Aces."

"Did I save your life, coming there?

"Maybe."

"You just remember that, Slimby. My mama now, she was suicidal. I was always more like the opposite. I wanted to kick their asses, not my own, when I was sad. Like hitting outward, not inward."

"Probably makes more sense. If it's not going to get you arrested."

"Oh, it did. Juvenile detention. But Banyan, he's the

first person I ever killed all by myself. He was just so amazingly in the way..."

"In the way of the money?"

"Totally."

She wasn't as crazy as she seemed. "Banyan was so out of it. I don't think he knew his stuff was going to be mixed with fentanyl."

"A moment's thought would tell you that, bro." She imitated Wendell's voice. "That's how shit be now."

"Gary didn't seem capable of a moment's thought. Too much Molly, too long. I guess X is okay within reason, but he was delusional." I felt sick when I thought about Banyan, Ledbetter's son. Wrong place at the wrong time. He didn't deserve that. "You really had to empty your gun in him?"

"We weren't wearing masks. I would've been okay if the shooting hadn't started. Anyway, he made me want to do a trance dance and pretend I was on X."

Why, I asked myself, was I traveling with this woman?

"Did you know that guy?"

"No. Yes." I badly wanted to change the subject. "Forget it. You see that glow?"

She turned to look at the horizon ahead. "Oh! Reno!"

"Yeah. Not as big a horizon glow as Vegas, but it's got some roar in its aurora."

"You funny, Slimby." She yawned. "You know, I left my money in the car with you while I went to the bathroom at that gas station. I guess I do trust you. That's weird."

"Yeah. That Caddy's following us the same distance back as before. Don't seem to care if we know."

"Still not surprised."

"Did you say anything to Jacques about who got shot at that warehouse?"

"Um..."

"Dulcet!"

She put her hands over her eyes. "I wanted him to think I was badass so he wouldn't be an asshole with me. That didn't work."

"Did you tell him who shot Ricky Kwai?"

"Sort of. Maybe. I could've kinda."

I glanced at her. She dropped her hands from her face and gave me an I'm-a-naughty-little-girl look. Dulcet always communicated theatrically. Sometimes cartoonishly.

She went on, "I...I was stoned and just sort of talking about how fucked up the whole thing was, like it was a real firefight, and I think I might've said, 'The cowboy killed Kwai.' Maybe. Possibly."

"So does that give us a clue who might be following us?"

"The 14K guys?"

"Who?"

"Triad. Chinese American gangs. Kwai was one."

I sighed. The Kwai family. That gave me mixed feelings. I might want to finish what I started with the Kwais if they were involved in pushing fentanyl. But that could mean another firefight. Maybe there'd be more collateral damage—like Gary Ledbetter.

It appeared, anyway, I wouldn't need to shoot myself. I could commit suicide by gangster.

And really, I felt better, thinking about the Kwai giving me an opening. A chance to feel like being alive was meaningful.

"Hey, check out that sign," Dulcet said, nodding to the right.

It was a truly large billboard with an artist's prettied-up conception of a housing development. And above the painting of the houses, ponds, and paths, it said, "Watch this spot for another KWAI & Sons Development." Behind the sign, flagged stakes and bulldozed earth marked out a future construction site.

I grunted. "Reno. That's what Ricky said. 'It's Reno.' Could be they rake in cash with cheap, imported synthetic heroin sales, they launder it through the casinos and invest the laundered liquidity in developments."

"Sweet setup," she said, almost admiringly.

That made me grimace, but I let it go.

We were passing through Sparks, once a little town, now mostly a suburb of Reno. Small casinos, bars, developments, shopping malls. The lights of Reno were going from auroral blur into sharp focus.

"Dulcet, we're coming into Reno. I could get a room in a place with a parking garage. In a parking garage, you could get out before they saw you. These vultures in the Caddy are probably after me. You could take your money and launder it some way, maybe in the casinos. And put it in a bank. Get a plane to New York, and then London."

When she didn't answer, I glanced over. She had an exaggerated scowl, furrowed brow, full-on sulk going. "You trying to get rid of me, cowboy?"

"No reason you should have to deal with these assholes. That wouldn't be like the Dulcet I know. She takes care of herself."

Her pout deepened. "You don't know me, Slimby."

"You don't want them to get all that money, do you? You should take it where you and the money will be safe."

"You *are* trying to get rid of me!" she said in an angry whisper. "Asshole."

We drove in tense silence for a while. "Dulcet, there's the Biggest Little City in the World sign." We were about to pass under the Reno Arch, the big white and blue bow curving over Virginia Street, declaring the city's slogan, capped by the massive, almost art deco RENO and a 3D starburst topping all. The town had periodic earthquakes, and I wondered if the sign could someday fall and crush some tourists. Crushed under kitsch. Speared by a starburst.

Dulcet looked around. "You can just put me on the sidewalk right over there. I love the arch. I want to look at it for a minute. And then I'll go lose myself."

"What if they're after you and not me?" We pulled up at a traffic light. "Those people are two cars behind us. They could get out and chase you down. Or shoot you out a window, if they're working with Jacques."

"I should've finished his fancy ass off," she said softly. "But...just put me out there by the sign. I'm good. I'll take a walk, find a hotel. Maybe take a bus somewhere. I don't know."

Checking the rearview mirror, I didn't see the Caddy. Maybe they weren't what I hoped they were: Kwai operatives. I glanced at Dulcet. She was hiding her face from me.

I knew what she wanted me to say, and...I buckled. "You can trail along with me if you want."

She looked at me with her best thespian style, chin lifted, pretending a regal indifference, and said, "'Kay."

Then I looked in the rearview again and saw the gray and silver Cadillac C5 coming up behind us.

13

I DECIDED we needed the biggest, most central hotel I could afford to make it harder for whoever was in that Caddy to come after us without witnesses and hotel security around. A bigger hotel is easier to hide in.

I noticed a shiny new one. Tall, blocky, and glassy. Just as the traffic light changed to red, I cut into the right lane, got honked at for pulling in front of another driver, turned the corner, and whipped down the block. I looked in the rearview. The Caddy hadn't managed to follow me around the corner. Traffic in its way.

"Ohmigod, good move, Slimby," Dulcet said.

"That mean you're not mad at me anymore?"

"You're on probation."

"You'd be some parole officer."

I whipped around another corner, raced up a narrow street between the hotel and the river, and came into an access driveway. I parked in a temporary spot outside the lobby. A couple of maintenance workers on ladders were taking down the grand-opening banner over the big sign over the lobby: The Truckee Lucky Hotel and Casino.

It was two connected buildings, one tall and looking like a stack of standard modern hotel rooms with a high-roller's penthouse up top and the other about a third as tall with a blinking, sparkling display of four aces and a king of spades fanned out, traced in marching lights. A smaller sign said, "Riverside view!" Beneath that, a digital sign announced some country singer was playing nightly.

"It overlooks the Truckee," I said. "Nice river. Runs right through town."

Clutching her tote bag, Dulcet got out. I took my one small piece of luggage out of the trunk of the GT and brought it to the driver's side door. I looked around. No one was watching. I bent over, got the gun belt and pistol out from under the seat, put them in my bag, zipped it up, locked up the car, and looked around for the Cadillac C5. I couldn't see it.

We went inside, and I rented a room with two queen beds, second floor overlooking the Truckee River.

Naw, it wasn't that easy. If anyone was looking for James "Slim" Purdoux, they could just ask for him at the desk. I did not want that. We held back a little, watching the chunky White guy at the front desk, maybe thirty years old, and looking like he was sorry he'd taken the job at the new casino. He had the sides of his head shaved, a cap of brown hair on top, and a doughy, quietly discontented face. He kept checking his watch. Probably almost time for him to get off work.

I waited until no one else was checking in and then took three hundred-dollar bills out of my wallet. I still had most of that five grand. Dulcet and I walked up to the counter, and she beamed at him. "Everything here is so shiny and new!"

"Yes, ma'am, only open a few weeks now," he said.

I grinned at him and flicked the three hundreds absently, like a player riffling cards. "So"—I read his nametag—"Kieran..."

"Checking in, sir?" His eyes went to the hundred-dollar bills.

"Thinking about it. They pay you enough here?"

"Oh, well..." He glanced around. Shrugged. "Sure."

"You somebody's nephew? Like one of the managers?"

His eyebrows went up. "How'd you know that?"

"Just a crazy guess. They talked you into the job, and they're not giving you much more than minimum wage. I can increase your wages today by three hundred bucks. And fifty more tomorrow, and fifty the day after that if I'm still here. All just for you, in cash. Me and my sweet Susanne here need a room without my name associated with it. And...we need your discretion." I leaned forward and spoke confidentially. "Angry husband's lurking around. You know how it is."

Dulcet pointed at her still slightly swollen lip and said, in a stage whisper, "See that? The husband did it. Don't want him knowing I'm here, Kieran."

"Uh...okay." He looked nervously past us, as if expecting to see a big, angry husband with a gun. "I mean —" He looked at the money again.

"Honey, stop waving the money around," Dulcet said. She took a Reno brochure from its little plastic display rack and handed it to me.

I put the three hundred under the brochure. Kept my hand on it. "Can you make it work, Kieran?"

He cleared his throat and tapped on the computer keyboard. "I got a way to make a room available without, um, putting it in the system. It's for the owner's family and stuff. I guess I could do it. Probably no one notice. If..."

I pushed the brochure across to him. He took it, put it on the lower counter by his computer screen, and started tapping again. "Got one on the second floor, overlooking the river."

"Sounds good." I wanted a room on a lower floor, close to the exits, in case we had to get out fast.

He did some more tapping, then handed us two keycards.

Humming a song, Dulcet buzzed into the lobby gift shop and, in short order, bought a T-shirt, a western-style woman's blouse, socks with horseshoes on them, yoga pants, and some toiletries. I went to the front door, looked out, and didn't see the Caddy. I did see a young Latino guy with a half-grown mustache in a valet's livery. I tipped him to put the Mustang in a back corner of the hotel's basement parking garage.

I scoped out the people coming in and out of the lobby. Families, a few college boys, all of them pulling wheeled luggage behind them. None likely to have been the crew following us.

"Ooh," Dulcet said, bustling up to me. "Let's look at our shiny new room!"

It was not a suite, but it had a sofa, a safe for valuables, a mini-fridge with overpriced candy and little bottles of liquor, and a good-sized bathroom. Everything smelled of new carpeting and fresh grout. "I should've asked if you wanted your own room," I said, as we looked around. "I just thought this would be safer."

"Depends what kind of safe you mean, cowboy. Ooh, look!" Dulcet cooed over the view out the window. There was a balcony, but neither of us wanted to go out there and become a good target. "Lookit the river, Slimby! It's got goosies and duckies sleeping on the riverbanks!"

I joined her, and we stood there together looking at the Truckee glittering from hotel lights. Below the opposite bank, shadows under a row of quaking aspen and pine made the river's pools dark green. On the hotel side to the left was a fenced-off swimming pool where kids were splashing around and shooting at each other with water guns. Their father watched from the side, one hand in his pocket, the other one raised as he glanced at his watch. I figured he'd agreed to watch the kids for a while, but he was planning on hitting the casino as soon as his wife let him off the leash.

"You think they got a restaurant open?"

"If you want to go to the casino part. They always have some food going. Crap probably. You want the better food... room service."

"Ooh, let's see what they got!" She kicked off her shoes and found the room service menu.

Dulcet got a rare steak with mushrooms and onions and a baked potato with sour cream. And chocolate cheesecake. I ordered an omelet and made myself eat it. We ate at a little glass-topped table near the balcony door. We got a bottle of cabernet too, bottled at some vineyard on the outskirts of town. It wasn't bad.

I wasn't drinking much. But I wasn't fooling myself that I had any sobriety. I just didn't *care* anymore. I was still convinced I'd be dead fairly soon, one way or another. I just didn't want to get really drunk, because I might need a steady hand with the Colt.

I looked at the dresser, where I'd hidden the gun in the top drawer. I had my knife in my pocket too.

"You're thinking about your gun," she said. "You going to strap it on?"

"Don't be ridiculous."

She stuck out her tongue at me. "Too late. I'm always ridiculous."

I smiled at that. "Self-knowledge is important."

She nodded gravely, and then we laughed.

I went on, "Anyway, the door's double locked. So is the balcony. There's a little video box by the door, you see it? Latest hotel gimmick. Shows who's in the hall. If I see anybody at the door and I'm not real sure they're working here, I'll get the gun out."

"Where could we buy a gun for me without waiting out the rigmarole?" Her tone was as casual as asking to buy a pair of new shoes.

"Have to ask around. In the casino, probably. But you don't need a gun. Last time, you emptied the pistol into a guy high on ecstasy."

"I was just *playin'*."

I had to laugh. "You sounded like Latesha."

"I was doing her voice. That's what she says if she hits somebody. She knocked a streety down and said, 'I was just playin'. Don't make me get serious, bitch.'"

"I hope she's okay."

"Oh, she's happy as a bunny on Easter, praying for Wendell's soul every morning and night. I know her. I'm-a miss her too. Hey, Slimby?"

"Yeah?"

"What you going to do if that whoever in the Caddy doesn't find us? What if they give up? What then?"

"Somewhere, Reno's got a dope camp. Most every town does. There'll be fentanyl heads there. They'll know who sold it to them."

"You're really, truly, for God's sake, *still* on a mission?"

"Need to find out a few things before I can answer that."

"*Or* we could just enjoy ourselves for a while, Slimby." And with that, she stretched out a leg under the table and rubbed her bare foot against my crotch with surprising dexterity.

———

Sure, you betcha. We made love. After I had a couple more drinks.

Making love to Dulcet took me out of myself. It made me forget the dark wave, the wave sweeping Frankie's dead body toward me, as if he were a dead surfer. It made me forget Gary Ledbetter. It made me forget the bodies, the pools of blood at Ledbetter Publishing.

It could have been vanity, it could have been an honest effort to connect with someone, but making love to Dulcet, I felt good. She responded like a woman enjoying herself, but I just couldn't achieve that feeling of connection I had, at the best of times, with certain other women. The feeling that you're not just doing the low yo-yo, you're reaching into someone and plugging into who they are. And they're trying to make that same connection back.

I didn't feel that with Dulcet. I felt like I was knocking on a door, and someone opened it a crack but left the little chain in place and talked to me cheerfully through the door. Happy to see me. Happy to have a nice long conversation through the door. But not willing to let me in.

No, she didn't ask me for money afterward. She just gave me a particularly tender kiss and then spooned with me until she went to sleep.

I lay there in the warm bed, curtains closed, trying to sleep. But sleep was a train an hour late for the station.

While I waited, I started thinking about what I was planning to do tomorrow. Where it might take me.

I didn't have to do it, I told myself. I could just go to the casino and play poker. I could drive us both to Yosemite and rent a cabin. I could take Dulcet to London.

Dad? What are you going to do?

"I'll know tomorrow, Frankie." I am *pretty* sure I said it out loud.

———

Dulcet woke me from a nightmare—a truly fucked-up one I don't want to describe—by waving a steaming cup of coffee under my nose. "Wakey-wakey, cowboy."

I sat up and took the mug. "Than*kew*, ma'am."

"You were squirming around in your sleep, and your trigger finger was twitching," she said, going to answer the door. She was wearing a hotel bathrobe. She checked the hall cam and opened the door for a steward pushing a big metal cart in. "I'm paying for breakfast, Slimby. You've been getting everything."

She winked at the pimply young guy pushing the cart in and tapped her chest. "I'm the one with the most money, honey, not him!"

"Oh, ha, sounds great," the kid said, unloading the covered dishes from the cart.

She tipped him, watched him leave, and turned to grin at me. "I got us way too big a breakfast. We gonna put some padding on your skinny ass, Slimby. That way you won't get saddlesore. You ever even ride a horse?"

"I preferred a Kawasaki. I miss that rice burner. I did have some horse-riding lessons when I was a teenager."

"I always wanted a horsie. Come and eat some French toast and eggs Benedict."

Some of my appetite returned that morning. Afterward, I locked my gun in the room safe, and we went down to the hotel's business center. It was a cubicle of glass in a metal frame, containing several rentable workstations with full internet. None were in use.

I sat down and did some pointed research about Reno. The town had a homeless population, but not as sizable as it had been. Reno had invested in an enormous transitional center, with clean beds, twenty-four-hour security, counselors, and psychiatric technicians, and it had thrived. The city provided free "tiny homes" by the hundreds. Homelessness was much reduced. But there were still drug camps over on the east side, abutting Sparks. A tent camp threaded along the railroad tracks.

The stats suggested Reno still chalked up regular overdose deaths from fentanyl use. Fewer than Las Vegas but more than Salt Lake City.

Dulcet was on the PC next to me, skimming San Francisco news. "I don't see anything else about us, Slimby," she said.

I glanced at the door. It was shut. No one was close by. "They don't mention identifying Wendell's body? Nothing like that?"

"Not that I can see, Texy Slim. I don't even want to know either. I'm gonna look at…"

I turned to look. She was scrolling through glamour shots of women on horses. "You can afford a horse when you get some land to put it on," I said. "Why don't you stay here, check out all the pretty horses, and Google the regulations covering a Mustang Ranch around Las Vegas. I'm going to go have a pleasant chat with some unhoused drug addicts."

She turned me a pout, her head cocked. "You're going to buy drugs without me?"

"You know I'm not going to buy drugs. But I'll have to watch my back. Don't want to have to watch out for you too. Anyway, I'll be dressing down for the occasion. You'd have to hobo-it-up. Not really your look."

She snorted. "I had enough of places like that. Wendell had business in the Tenderloin, and we were there most every day." She gave me a plaintive look, not as theatrical as usual. "Why don't you let it go, Slimby. We could slip out of town tonight..."

"Maybe tomorrow night. Today, I need to know some things. I'm not getting into a fight. I'm not even taking the gun. I'm just going to ask some questions. You got a swimsuit?"

"A swimsuit? No."

"You could get one at the gift shop. Go out to the pool, have a swim. Maybe a couple of mimosas. Take a nap in the sun. Live the life!"

"What if those guys in that Caddy come around here?"

"I figure they're looking for me more than you. And you'll be safe out in the daylight, with people around. I'll come back in a few hours at the most. I promise."

"You're not going to drive, are you? If they're looking for you, they could spot that Mustang."

"I'm going to just walk in. Act like I'm trying to score."

"You don't have to get those questions answered. You can guess."

"I need to know for sure."

Her expression shifted from plaintive to a mask of indifference. "Whatever."

I turned back to the browser and searched for "get vehicle owner by plate," which took me to a semi-legit website. I inputted the Cadillac C5's license plate and state, and it came up with the right model and year, but wouldn't give me the names of the owners...yet. I had to swear I was not going to use the information illegally. I had to click through to several follow-up pages, and eventually, I used a credit card to pay a fee.

There it was. Owner of that silver Cadillac C5: Kwai Brothers Construction Inc.

14

I WALKED through the hot summer morning with my cowboy shirt's pearl buttons unsnapped. I was getting sweat stains on my T-shirt, under the arms, and over the sternum. And that was a look I wanted.

I hadn't shaved. I had put a dent in my cowboy hat and thumbed a little grime along the brim on one side. Along the way, I found a place to dirty my fingernails and the knees of my pants. With great regret, I scuffed up the toes of my boots too.

The expression on my face was more important. I was still trying to decide on it as I walked by street people panhandling in doorways. Some of them looked to me like gambling addicts, trying to build up a little stake. Their expressions were artificially friendly in a fatigued sort of way. Some looked stunned—perpetually stunned. The untreated mentally ill were there too, talking manically to themselves.

Before I got on the bus, I bought some cigarettes and a Bic lighter. They could be useful today. My gun could've been useful too. But I didn't bring it. The Peacemaker was too bulky to hide in this outfit.

After the bus, I had a long, sore-footed walk in my cowboy boots to the railroad tracks, sweating in the growing heat, but once there, I couldn't miss the encampment straggling along a cinderblock wall to one side of the tracks. The tents were mixed in with a half dozen makeshift shanties, scrap-wood lean-tos draped with paint-spattered tarps. Cook fires loosed sluggish brown smoke to coil close over the tents. It was close to a rusted, disused railroad track. A few campouts wandered tent to tent, maybe bartering.

Some thirty yards to the west, a much-graffitied freight train was waiting inertly on a working track. To the east, beyond the cinderblock wall, rose the high, ocher-painted rear walls of an industrial zone. Beyond the camp, toward the north, the cinderblock wall ended, and bulky concrete pillars lifted an overpass buzzing and growling with traffic.

I ambled toward the camp, like I knew where I was going but was in no hurry to get there.

We were well-schooled in tent towns back in San Francisco. Three kinds of encampments predominated. One form was mostly working people priced out of the rental market. They lived in parked cars, trailers, or tents. Just people who'd had a string of bad breaks, or whose working income didn't measure up to high rents

Other encampments were made up of untreated psych patients, self-medicating chiefly with alcohol. Those two forms of camps could overlap.

The third kind, less common, is all about drugs. The big four are fentanyl, meth, hydroxy and some combination of the first three. Heroin, and crack have started to fade, replaced by fentanyl and crystal meth. Fentanyl is cheap and powerful. It's a growth industry. Crack is around, but it's losing its fan base. Smoking meth has mostly taken its place. Sometimes people from the first tent town, just down on their luck folks, started sharing in drugs to escape depression, and became addicted. And they drifted into the third kind of encampment. I had been in Narcotics Anonymous and AA, in San Francisco for years, just to stay clean. I'd been an NA sponsor, trying to help street addicts to recovery. I went to visit recovering addicts; got to know some of those camps intimately.

The ground here was littered with used-up Bic lighters. That told me this camp was occupied by homeless addicts.

The smell—a mix of burning trash and unnamable squalor and mysterious chemical reeks—was about the same as the city dump. Not unbearable. But the heat made the stench thick and syrupy.

I could see the opioid-addicted sitting in the doorways of their scrappy habitations, hugging themselves, shivering, rocking in place. I saw a young guy engaging in "fentanyl yoga." You see them standing but bent over double, the same position for hours at a time, as they tweaked with fingernails at itch spots on their bloodied ankles. Between their ankles were crumpled pieces of blackened aluminum foil, lying next to a tarry ash pipe and a lighter.

From time to time, they pinched little bits of the tarry stuff from the crumpled foil, a compound that was partly fentanyl, stuck it in the pipe, applied the lighter flame, took a hit—all without straightening up. Then they'd go back to shredding their ankles.

This boy looked a couple of years older than Frankie had been.

It was painful to watch. Genuine, unadulterated sympathy rose up in me at the sight. If my Frankie hadn't overdosed on the pill form, he could have ended up like this.

In some piss-soaked doorway, bent over double, hour after hour, pinching fentanyl, pinching his own flesh, alternating laughing and weeping and muttering.

I felt punched in the gut. The dark wave was rearing over me again.

I looked away and strode on, telling myself to focus. Get this *done,* goddammit, Purdoux.

I passed a tent where a gaunt face incised with paranoia poked out under an entrance flap, eyes fixed on me as I passed. But some of the other campouts, these men and women were cheerful, in a subdued way, though they had a hunted look about the eyes. They waved to each other. They helped their friends carry overstuffed plastic trash bags of empty cans and bottles, and they petted the dogs that roamed the camp. I heard two of them gossiping about who'd lost their shopping cart loads in a police raid. All the time, their eyes were checking the terrain, but they were smiling, a little, with a kind of weary confidence. Enjoying the talk, like men in a POW camp when the guards weren't looking.

I tried to adopt that look for myself now, cheerful but warily nervous. I was aware of the campouts watching me as I took out the pack of cigarettes. I puttered along, checking the terrain but smiling slightly, tapping out a Marlboro Light. I lodged it in the corner of my mouth, raised the Bic to it…and didn't light it. I was staring down at a crumpled piece of tinfoil with a smear of blackened tar left on it. I bent, scooped it up, and shoved it in my pocket, like something a guy short on his drug of choice might do.

A campout laughed softly at me. "Not gonna get nuthin' off that, cowboy," he said.

I glanced at him and lit my cigarette. I hadn't smoked in twenty years, and I didn't want to have an unseemly coughing fit, so I just rolled the smoke around in my mouth and then blew it out.

The scraggly bearded campout—shirtless, wearing only cut-offs—sat cross-legged in front of his lean-to. His lean body was sunburned scarlet in some places, tanned dark brown in others. Long, sticky-looking blond hair hadn't experienced shampoo for a long, long time. His teeth matched the color of his hair, except for some green close to the gums. His eyes were reddened, eye sockets ringed in puffy purple skin. He was the poster boy for drug addicts.

Beside him were three plastic bleach jugs. He held one up to me and waved it. "Give you a huff for a ciggy," he said, grinning.

Ah. He was an inhaler of cleaning fluids and glue when he couldn't get his drug of choice. A huffer.

"Only thing I'm fixin' to inhale is fenny," I said. Hoping the slang was up-to-date enough.

"Yeah," he said, nodding, tossing aside the empty jug. "Wait, you got anything else? Like"—he licked his cracked lips—"even codeine?"

"Nah. But you can have a ciggy, I guess. Just one. I can't be handing these fucking things out. Only got the one pack."

I tossed a cigarette, and he caught it, but didn't ask for a light. He set it on the gravel to one side, maybe thinking to trade it for a puff on a glass pipe.

"Hey, Huffy," came a woman's voice. I turned and saw a woman walking up. "Shelter give me a couple of bottles of water. You look like you need one."

She looked to be a mix of Black and Native American, maybe thirty-five. A good-looking woman with high cheekbones and an aquiline nose. Her hair had gone wild, and her very-short shorts and blouse, once white, were blotched with dirt and spotted with what looked like red wine stains. The blouse had fluffy ruffles going down the middle, like it was a scrap of someone's discarded prom outfit. She wore rope flip-flops, the fibers coming unraveled. A fanny pack hung on her left hip. Maybe syringes in there, I guessed, maybe a knife or a small gun.

"Yuh, thanks, Nadine," Huffy said, taking the water bottle without looking at her. He put it to the side, with the Marlboro. Could be adding it to the barter pile. Still without looking at her, he said, "You got anything?"

"Not yet, I don't," she said. "I'm waiting for that guy Eric to come."

"Supposed to be here about noon. I got no money, though. You got any extra?"

"Sorry, Huffy." She looked toward the north end of the camp and then sidelong at me and said, "You new around here, ain't you, cowboy?"

I was surprised at how white and perfect her teeth looked. Her smile and her crinkling eyes captivated me for a moment, to a degree that surprised me. Then I said, "Came out from San Francisco. Trying to do a geographic, get away from the dope. Got into trouble at the casino."

"Trying to trade the dope for casino chips? You just get addicted to two things at once. I know. I've been there. Can't afford no casino now."

"Can't either. Pretty busted except I got forty bucks for my watch. Looking to get high and forget all that bullshit for a while. Somebody told me I could buy the shit out here."

"Maybe from him." She nodded toward the northeast side of the camp, where two men were sauntering through a shatter gap in the cinderblock wall. "I think that's Eric in that red hat. Not sure about the other guy."

Both men were burly. The tall, bearded one was

wearing a hoodie, a baseball cap, and some new-looking cargo pants. The shorter one was Asian. Broad-shouldered, he wore a crisp short-sleeved white shirt, a quilted maroon vest, and matching high-top sneakers. Expensive ones.

Huffy swayed to his feet and squinted toward the newcomers. "I don't know neither one. Never heard of no Eric."

"He was here the other day. You were off trading cans in. Saw him on Virginia, passing out candy."

I nodded. Passing out candy was an old, wry street expression. Handing out hits of dope to select people to propagate new clientele.

"Surprised they bother to come to this camp," I said, hoping to get her to say more about Eric. "Seems like there wouldn't be enough money here."

"See that hole in the wall over there? That goes to the nearer end of West Industrial. That's the main drug market over there. But you got to have money. You'd laugh, seeing who shows up over here. Saw a woman drive a new Prius in there, buy some fenty out the window. She had her a two-hundred-dollar hairdo an' sparkly nails. But I see she was dope sick. One time, a guy roll up over there on a Segway—"

"One of those two-wheeled things you stand up on?"

"Oh yeah! He looked like he had money. Wanted some heroin or fenty. College kids come there, office workers on break, all them. Eric, he goes there for that crowd, and then he checks over here to see if anyone's got their SSI money or pulled a trick or something, wants to buy. But they don't spend but a minute on this camp. Over *here*, it's just where you end up after you bought over *there*. Prius lady, she'll be here someday. If she don't OD."

A very observant woman, I thought.

"That Prius lady," I said. "She'll just go to one of those ten-thousand-dollar rehabs."

"And then she'll leave, and relapse, and her ass'll be right back here. And now look at me, I'm going to see if Eric's got a couple of dimes for me." She laughed dryly at herself and started over toward the two men.

Hands in my pockets, I walked along casually beside her, Huffy trailing behind us. One of my hands was on the closed-up Buck knife, just in case.

We got within four paces of the dealer and the wide-shouldered Asian guy I took to be a bodyguard, gun butt just slightly showing in a pocket of his vest.

It was too warm for that vest. But he seemed unaffected except for sweat. His every motion was supremely confident. There was boredom on his face, but no lack of alertness.

Nadine nodded at the bearded guy. "S'up, Eric."

He and his companion stopped, and the bearded guy with the droopy eyes and hawk nose rumbled, "What y'all looking for?"

"How about a forty?" I said, pulling two twenties from my pocket.

"Hey, hey," said Huffy, stepping in close to the big guy. "Listen, I can do some work for you if you front me a dime. I can—"

The slick guy in the vest straight-armed Huffy, his arm a blur of speed. Huffy staggered and fell on his ass.

"You got no money, keep yourself away," clipped the Asian guy.

Eric said, "I coulda done that, Renny."

"Then do it next time," said the guy in the vest. Renny, it seemed.

"I didn't mean to crowd nobody," Huffy said, raising his

hands in front of him. "But..." He stood up, grimacing, looking like he might burst into tears, and said, "If you just—"

Nadine turned to him, blocked him, and said in a low voice, "He's got a gun. You just keep your distance, and we'll talk."

"Okay, okay, it's on you, Nadine," Huffy said, turning away, shivering and hugging himself. He walked slowly back toward his shelter.

Interesting exchange, I thought.

She turned back to Eric. "Couple of dimes of fenty," Nadine said, rubbing her hands together.

He shrugged, reached into one of his cargo pants pockets, and pulled out three little balls of tinfoil. He rolled them in his hand. "Twenty each."

I handed over the money, and he gave me two. I saw from the corner of my eye Nadine had a hand inside her fanny pack. There was a hole on one side of the pack. I thought she'd take the money out with that hand, but she reached into a shorts pocket for cash. She counted out a five, then five ones and a ten, handed them to him, and collected her dope ball.

"All right, anyone else here worth talking to?" Renny asked, looking past us.

I glanced back. Some of the campouts were looking wistfully our way. Seemed nobody had any cash.

"Seems not," I said.

"S'long," rumbled Eric, turning away. Remarking to Renny, "Don't seem worth the trouble."

"You come the right day," Renny said. "You can clear a thousand, fifteen hundred from them. People get their checks."

I saw I'd been wrong. Renny wasn't a bodyguard. More

like a street captain, breaking Eric in. Like the trainer who stands behind the cashier trainee, showing the ropes, but for dope dealing.

I watched them walk back toward the gap in the wall and the street beyond. I figured I'd follow, see what else I could find out.

I started after them, deciding I'd just let Nadine do her thing.

But she put a restraining hand on my arm. "Hey. They won't like it if they see you trailing after."

I nodded. In a low voice, I asked, "Is Renny there with the Kwais?"

She looked coldly at me. "I don't know what outfit they belong to."

"No? Your task force hasn't found out that much?"

Her face went blank. "Task force?"

"Show me what's in your fanny pack."

"Fuck you. You don't get to mess into my stuff."

"You changed your diction when you were talking to Huffy. And acted like you had some kind of understanding with him." I looked around to make sure no one else was close enough to hear me. "You give him dope for information, officer?"

She snorted. "What the fuck."

"I saw that motion with your index finger. You videoed me buying the dope. That little camera in your fanny pack's probably got sound too. You're gathering evidence for a bust. Probably a city narcotics task force."

We looked at each other. She saw I wasn't going to be bluffed out. "And what are you supposed to be? The guy who busts the narcs?"

"Just an investigator. The private kind."

"If you're a PI, we can go somewhere else, you can show me your license."

"If you show me your badge."

She glanced toward the end of Industrial, a few people in the mix down there, a biker on a Harley talking to Eric. Past them, a camper truck with its back windows blacked out.

"That camper truck...your backup team in there?" I asked.

She glowered at me. "Think you're pretty smart? Maybe I'll take you in for questioning."

"Shall I show you my ID?"

"Not here."

I grinned. "Yeah, that'd look kind of funny, wouldn't it? Is the bust going down today?"

"We're gathering information. You don't keep your mouth shut, I'll find a reason to detain you."

I nodded. "You got a car nearby? Can you get one?"

"For what?"

"I want to follow Renny and Eric." I pointed toward the street. "Looks like they're getting into that Cadillac."

She looked and saw Renny and Eric getting into the C5. This one was jade green. I guessed it was part of the same fleet as the one that followed me and Dulcet.

"You follow them, they'll spot you," Nadine said. "And you're not following anyone, cowboy. We've got you buying dope. This isn't Oregon. This is Nevada. You can do ninety days for possession of even that much shit."

"You can't arrest me here, bust open your whole setup. I'm not keeping the shit anyway. I'll give one to Huffy and one to that fentanyl yoga human pretzel back over there."

"So now you're distributing?"

"Giving it away for free. This once. These people..." I

nodded toward the camp. "They're victims. They fell into a trap. I was a drug addict back in Texas, years ago. I know where that's at."

"What's your deal?" she asked. "What's your agenda?"

"I want to take down certain people responsible for..." I didn't want to tell her the story. "Doesn't matter."

"Take them down? Meaning what, exactly?"

She had dropped the street English entirely, I noticed. "Degree in criminology, Nadine? A police detective, for sure. Probably a lieutenant?"

"None of your business. What's your name?"

I found that I wanted to tell her. I was trying to extend my time talking to her. I felt like I'd known her a long, long time. Like she was important to me. And I did not know why I felt that way.

"I'll tell you, if you tell me. Is Nadine your name? I'm guessing not."

"You're guessing wrong. I use my real first name. That's all they know. What's your name?"

"Jim Purdoux. People call me Slim."

"Slim, get out of here. Keep your mouth shut, and I won't arrest you."

"Come on, talk to me a minute. You can keep an eye on me that way."

I started back toward the camp. Huffy was standing about fifty feet away, staring at us, one hand tugging at his own hair, pulling it to distract him from the dope sickness.

I walked toward him, and after a moment's hesitation, Nadine followed.

"When did you work it out?" she asked, not much above a whisper. "Back at the camp?"

"I started to wonder. You didn't seem like someone seriously strung out. Your teeth looked too good. Then there was that slip in diction. And I was pretty sure you had a camera in that fanny pack."

She grunted. "I got overconfident. Most people out here aren't too with it. They're either stoned or focused on getting there."

"I admire your outfit, especially those ropy flip-flops. And that blouse with the fluffy things on it. So random. That seemed right."

Then Huffy scuffled up to us. "I got an old watch, and... I can get some money if..."

I took a tinfoil-wrapped dope ball out of my pocket and handed it to him. "Knock yourself out."

He gaped at the dope in his hand and then jogged off toward his hovel.

"Can't believe I'm giving the shit out," I muttered.

"Someone close to you..." she said, glancing at me. She couldn't keep the compassion out of that look, which gave me my first glimpse into the real Nadine—into her real character.

"My son," I said. "It killed him."

She shook her head. "Happens way too much. We find a body or two every week."

"It's the Kwais, isn't it?"

She frowned, but then turned it into a rueful smile. "It's not hard to find out. Yeah, that was Renny Kwai. Nephew of the cartel boss, Murray Kwai. Renny's not much more than a kid, really, putting in his street time. He'll be a boss someday unless we can lock him up. Wouldn't like to lock you up, Slim Purdoux. You better stay out of it."

I had nothing to say to that. We walked on, back into the reek and simmer of the camp. We came to the fentanyl yoga guy, and I dropped the other dope ball at his feet. "You can have that shit," I said. "Don't do it too quick, it could kill you."

He looked up at me from the vicinity of his ankles with real astonishment. "Thanks! Wait, is this?"

"It's not a bust," I said. "But..." I wanted to lecture him about getting out of the scene. Tell him that most communities had some free rehab programs if you got on a waiting list. But this wasn't the place. And it wouldn't work anyway.

Stomach churning, I just shook my head and walked on. Weird to have a police detective walking at my side.

"You're not a licensed PI, are you, Slim?" she asked.

"Well, I'm an investigator, and I like to keep things private," I said. "And far as I'm concerned, I've got *license* to do what I damn please."

She gave a slight laugh. "You mean you're a fraud."

"Pretty much! But I'm doing what I can. You don't bust users for possession?"

"I don't, myself. It's the dealers I'm after."

We continued down the railroad track together. I looked at the old freight train padlocked up on the other track, way across the cinders. "That train ever move?"

"I've been working around here for a month, and it's been that same one just sitting there," she said. "Why?"

"That's how the police department is about stopping this drug from killing people. Like that train sitting there, getting tagged and gathering rust."

She winced. "We have some follow-through issues. I've got Renny and his muscle there for dealing now. But if we take it to the DA, he tends to drop that stuff. Low priority, he says. Jail is too full, he says."

"I saw a sign for a district attorney running for reelection."

She nodded. Her mouth looked like she'd bitten into something bitter. "Carl Wessen."

"You think he's taking bribes?"

"Might be just political bullshit. But sometimes I wonder. The bastard makes me feel like I'm spinning my wheels out here." She glanced at me. "And you're not helping much either."

"I'd like to, Nadine."

She gave me a long look, then snorted and shook her head. "I've got to go back now, Slim Purdoux," she said, stopping in her tracks. "I'm going to just let you go now. But I'll be putting you in my report."

"Hey, come on, Nadine. I'm letting *you* go." I looked into her eyes. "It's so strange."

"What's...what's strange?"

"I just feel like I know you. And I do not know why." I laughed at myself. "But I tell you what, you just rattle off your office number, and I'll remember it. I've always been like that. I might find out something about the Kwais you want to know. Maybe I'll take a chance that train'll move after all and I'll call you, tell you what I found out. How about that?"

She gazed at me for a long moment. "I'll tell you what's strange." She prodded me in the chest with a forefinger. "*You* are, Slim Purdoux." She made a dismissive gesture and said, "Okay then." She told me her office number and added, "Ask for Lieutenant Graves." She started back toward the camp, then stopped, and turned back just long enough to say, "If you tell anyone on the street my last name, or that I'm a cop, I'll show you my badge, all right. And then I'll show you my official police revolver, and that'll be the last goddamned thing you see."

Then she turned and walked off and, for some reason—some *strange* reason—despite the fact that she'd just threatened to kill me—I was smiling.

15

ALMOST BACK TO THE HOTEL, walking through a crowd of tourists in sun hats and loud summer shirts, everyone giving me a wide berth, I saw Frankie walking with some teenagers going to an ice cream shop. I froze, so somebody bumped into me, and said, "Fucking junkies!" when they had to skirt around. But I was busy staring at the kid.

Not my son, of course. Just a kid who didn't even look like him that much. I was always unconsciously scanning for him, though I knew for definite and absolute certain that he was dead, quite dead. Extinguished like a snuffed flame, not even a drift of candle smoke.

Someone honked a horn at me and yelled, "Hey, cowboy!"

It was Dulcet, pulling up at the curb in a big pickup, a particularly big, black Dodge Ram. She was wearing a new lady's cowboy hat of pink-dyed straw. "Come on, take a ride!"

"What the hell's up with this beast, Dulcet?" I said, getting into the truck. She bulled into the lane, tooled off down the street, someone's brakes screeching behind us.

"You like my new ride?" she said, with that toothy smile, eyes beaming wide. She was wearing pink overalls and a black lace bra, which was visible on the side because she wasn't wearing anything else I could see. Not even shoes.

"Um...yeah. Nice ride." I had one hand on the dashboard, the other holding the strap over the window. "You're driving barefoot."

"It makes a girl feel intimate with her big machine," she said, taking a hard right. "I always wanted something powerful like this. Look down on everyone from up here."

"I'd think you'd want a pink Barbie car or something. You with the little girl stripper act."

"My act—that's me too. But you wouldn't understand how those two are the same thing. That's powerful, what I do."

But I thought I did understand it. "You rent this thing?"

"No, I bought it with cash. Just nine thou. I called somebody who called somebody in Reno."

"Nine thou? For this? So it's a stolen vehicle?"

"He said it was all good now. They got a new license plate, a registration that some old DMV somebody got bribed for, and it's *alllllllll* good. Anyway, it's like eight years old, but not a lot of miles on it. I did have to do the guy a special favor to cut a few thou off."

"Oh, I see."

"Yeah, but you *don't* see." She was turning right, heading toward the river. "This guy's into withholding pee."

"Withholding what?"

"Peepee. Piss. Wee-wee, cowboy. It's a fetish. Those people, they get together, and they *don't pee* when they have to pee *real, real bad*. And they kind of squirm around like that together, and for some reason, a princess just don't know, it gets guys like this off. So I had to drink some beer with him and then *not* pee while we were naked in his hotel room, and it took like two hours, and it got weird—"

"It *got* weird?"

"And finally, we both have an explosive pee together in the bathtub, and he has an orgasm—"

"That's enough detail. You didn't let him touch you?"

"Not the fucky kind. I'd've charged more."

"If he gave you a two-grand break on the truck...kinda expensive just for not peeing."

She tittered. "Paying for not peeing!"

We both laughed. "You've got a new outfit and a new truck. Okay."

"But see, those shitheads in the Caddy know that Mustang GT you're renting. So I got this. Because they found us."

That tightened me up. I glanced in the side mirror. "I don't see 'em."

"They don't know where I am now. Leastways, I don't think so. But see, it was your big idea for me to go to the pool. So I did. And people going by outside on that river walk, they can so totally see you. Hey, you know they got a tiki bar at that pool? The bartender wears a lei and a Hawaiian shirt. I got a Mai Tai. It was *goooood* so I had two. Then I called around about the truck and got a number for a guy in Reno—"

"Dulcet? Back to the people following us?"

"Yeah, these two Asian guys were grillin' at me from the other side of the pool fence. They were these muscular dudes in suits without ties, and they had looks on their faces like they wanted to kill something, right? They just stopped on that sidewalk by the river and mugged at me through that wire fence, and I mugged back, and then they went on. But I saw 'em go into the hotel back entrance. They waited till someone was using a keycard to go in, and they followed 'em in. So I, like, ran in through the pool entrance and up the elevator and put on a skirt over my swimsuit, and I went down to the parking garage, and I saw them looking at the GT. Then they turned and saw me."

"Oh shit."

"So I jetted out of there and got a cab quick as I could and went to talk to the guy about the truck. Because now we really need one 'cause you got to get rid of that rental."

"I'd have to drive the Mustang back to San Francisco."

"You can turn it into the rental company here, and they charge you to send it back, even if they decide to keep it here."

"It's a big damn fee. But I guess I can use the cash I got from the scumbags."

"How much you got left?"

"Almost three thousand."

"You shoulda taken a bigger share."

"I just took it for emergencies, and I felt bad about taking even that much dope money."

"Oh. Your son."

"Yeah, my son."

"Here's the hotel. Should we go in and you can grab that car and drive it to turn it in, and I'll follow you there?"

"Maybe. I'm not armed. They probably are."

"I got your gun. It's under the seat there."

"Yeah? Go into the hotel outdoor parking, near as we can to the doors."

She steered the big pickup into the too-small spaces of the parking lot, having to take excruciating care not to hit parked vehicles.

"Basically, you bought this hulking gas-hog thing because you had two tiki bar cocktails?"

"You betcha, Slimby."

———

"Hi, boys. I'll meet you at the *poo*-ool!" Dulcet called out.

The parking garage elevator was within sight of where we'd parked the rental. The two Asian guys from the Kwai outfit were waiting, watching from the shadows across the garage lane, but visible, if you were looking for them.

I watched from behind a mommy van as they reacted to Dulcet and started toward her.

"See you at the pool!" she said, pressing Close Door as they started toward her.

I watched as they strode to the elevator. But she was already up to the first floor. They spoke in low voices and waited for the next elevator. When they took it, I went to the Mustang, had a good look around in case I'd missed additional minions, beeped open the car, punched the starter button, and was on my way to the rental place to turn it in.

I was worried about Dulcet. Just my instinct. But once more, I should be worried about the people who were a threat to her. Last one got himself seriously carved up with a box cutter.

The rental office was only two blocks away. No line, nobody behind me to take notice of a gun bulge in my shirt at the small of my back, and the whole process took me ten minutes.

Sweating in the late afternoon sun, I fast-walked back to the hotel. I buttoned up my shirt on the way and used the men's room off the hotel lobby to clean up a little. I didn't want the security guards to hassle me. The way the sun was angling outside, I thought I might need sunglasses. I'd need my eyesight unimpaired once the ball opened. I stopped at the lobby gift shop and bought clip-on sunglasses, then hurried to the hotel back door that led onto the courtyard between the hotel and the river. Still sweating, I stalked to the concrete walk along the river and up to the hurricane fence around the hotel pool.

There were a lot of people at the pool, including a grinning security guard chatting up a young blonde in a bikini. Kids splashed in the chlorine-blue water. Parents in sunglasses and swimsuits drank cocktails in the lounge chairs. The air was scented with sunblock.

On the other side of the pool from me, Dulcet was yacking merrily with the two Kwai gunnies under the bamboo overhang of the tiki bar.

One of the men seemed amused by her. The other, a little older and thicker around the waist, looked at her grimly. They had their hair cut short, both wore gold-tinted sunglasses, both had a visible gun bulge in the back, just like me. People only notice those things if they're actively looking for them.

I waved cheerfully at her. She waved back and then pointed me out to the Kwai enforcers. I could read her lips, more or less, from here. "There he is!"

The two men turned to look at me. Now both had the same cold expression.

We were going on a risky assumption that these guys, who might well be here to kill me, wouldn't do it in front of all these people. I reckoned they probably would be discreet about it, because they'd followed us from the desert at a careful distance. They hadn't pulled up beside us and started shooting.

Right now, they had the look of two men who would like to start shooting. But they glanced around and then looked at one another. One said something to the other in an aside, and then they got up and walked over to the fence.

"Mr. Purr-dox?" said the older one. He had a mild Chinese accent.

"It's pronounced Pur-doo, more or less," I said. "You men looking to have a word with me?"

"That's right. In private."

"Okay. What about?"

"That's going to be private too," said the younger man, putting a fist up on the fence. No accent at all.

I nodded vigorously. "I get you. Seeing as you boys followed us from the boonies all the way to Reno, I've been wanting to talk to you too. Meeting of the minds. You got a card or something?"

I expected a no, but the older guy took a business card from his pants pocket and passed it through a link in the fence. It read *Charles Deng, Field Supervisor, Kwai Brothers Development*. There was an 888 number that would send you to some automated answering service.

"Charles," I said, "how about I meet you gentlemen up the river there." I pointed along the walkway. "There's a little sculpture garden down there, under those pines. Monuments to some Reno founders. Flowering cactus, raked sand, Zen garden, right? Nice and quiet. I'll wait there for you, and we can talk."

Charles shook his head. "You wait right where you are." He hooked a thumb at the other man. "Han will wait here with you. I'll come around to that side of the fence. Then we talk."

Interesting tactic, I thought. Their way of making sure I couldn't ditch them or get behind cover.

"Y'know, I think the garden is best." I flipped the clip-on shades over my glasses. "I like those Japanese-style gardens, where emptiness kind of celebrates the life coming up in the midst of it. The empty calls the living things out, makes 'em stand up proud, and you see every detail. Know what I mean?"

They just stared at me. The older guy seemed angrier than ever and thought I was fucking with him.

I was, and I wasn't.

I touched my hat to him. "See you there."

I turned and walked off upriver. It wouldn't bother me much to die, right here and now, with a bullet in the back. I'd be disappointed as I went down that I hadn't had a chance to go with some dignity. My gun in my hand, at least.

But I didn't care that much. Let them kill me if they wanted to.

Right, Frankie? *Right.*

Too many witnesses, and no quick escape route. They didn't shoot me right then and there.

I kept walking, raising my hand once to lift my hat and wipe some sweat away. Thinking that at least Dulcet was out of this. Chances were, they wouldn't bother hunting her down afterward. And she wouldn't wait to find out. She'd get in that truck and slam the pedal to the metal. Maybe head out to Storey County, set up her own little Mustang Ranch out there like she'd planned. Maybe head down to Las Vegas or LA. Or to Austin. I'd talked Austin up to her. There are some who would like her, in Austin.

I picked up my pace. Too much open space to my left. Maybe they'd get in that Caddy and shoot me out the window and barrel away before anybody noticed the plate.

Up ahead, a copse of bristlecone pines shaded the rock and statuary garden.

I had an impulse to run to it, but decided that would be stupid. It would tip my hand.

I could feel sweat running down my back, making the slant-tucked gun slippery. It'd be embarrassing if that revolver worked out of my waistband and fell to the ground.

I glanced behind me, saw the Kwai hardmen about seventy-five yards back, not quite running, but leaning into their stride, coming at me side-by-side. I gave them a thumbs up and kept the same pace, which got me into the garden before them. A man and a woman were walking their French bulldog, and they left as I arrived. No one else was around. Gaming machines are a bigger draw than Zen gardens in Reno.

I walked in my best imitation of casual no-hurry-at-all toward the middle of the rectangular garden, passing a statue of a Northern Paiute Indian, to a big red sandstone outcropping that had been made the park's centerpiece. It was surrounded by waves of carefully raked sand. Like the most deplorable philistine, I walked across the neatly raked sand. Stepping behind the outcropping, I untucked my shirt, drew out the gun, and looked it over. I used a shirttail to carefully wipe sweat from the trigger and grip. The gun was loaded, and I had six cartridges in my left front jean pocket.

To my right was a bronze statue of a miner, kneeling at a curve of river rocks suggesting a stream, his pan dipping, his hat angled down, his face optimistic. To the left was a little group of rocks in an artful tumble. A bonsai grew from dirt packed into their midst. I contemplated the shaping of it, the marrying of the random and the intentional, as I thought about which one of the men I was going to kill first. The most experienced one. The older guy. The younger might be the better shot, though. Youthful acumen and reflexes. Could be he'd kill me when I killed his boss.

I didn't care much. But it would be nice to get both of them.

One problem was firepower. My Colt revolver against two guns, likely automatics, faster at spitting bullets than a revolver. More rounds to squeeze off before reloading too. It meant I'd have to fire coolly and with precision and at not too great a range.

The sun was bright, past the trees, and the two Asians in the blue suits were stalking toward me, entering the shade edging the garden, both of them raising nine-millimeter handguns as identical as their suits.

Here they came, maybe twenty-five yards away, two guys who wanted to kill me because I killed Ricky Kwai and screwed with their fentanyl operation.

I glanced around. No one nearby, but parked on the road paralleling the river walk was a Cadillac Escalade. Tinted windows. Engine running. No one was getting out to join the party. I guessed the two gunnies had called in a ride to get out fast once they took care of me.

Two rounds cracked by, close enough to my head that I could smell the air burning, and I ducked behind the boulder. Another two cracks, then a third, knocking chips of rock off the outcropping as I lifted up just enough to lay the barrel of the revolver across the stone cap and centered it on the nearest target. I'd expected Deng, the older guy, to use the cover while the younger one charged me, but it was the opposite. Han was ducking behind a pine, shouting a warning.

Deng was angry, and he was baring his teeth and firing as I lined up the sights on the gun and squeezed the trigger. The top of the rock kept the muzzle from wavering, and the top of his head flowered with dark-red blood and misty blue brain matter. His eyes rolled back, and he fell flat, firing spasmodically into the sand. I heard Han shout in anger, something about a motherfucker. Eyes stinging from gunpowder, I cocked the Colt and fired at the gunman behind the tree. Tree bark spat out, and Han ducked back. I lost sight of him, then saw him sprint to my left. I fired and missed. Sand spat up just past him. The gunman returned fire as he went, and boulder dust sprayed.

"Shoot straight," I heard myself yell, turning toward him, clasping the revolver with two hands, arms extended. "You keep missing me!"

He skidded to a stop, squatted behind the tumble of stones at the bonsai, and fired. A shot cut by my face, burning by at my cheek, and I fired twice, yelling, "You're fucking up!"

I saw him jerk backward, heard a hoarse yell. I kept my arms extended, cocking the pistol, and stalked toward him. "You need to calm down and kill me!" The words grinding out between my clenched teeth.

He was trying to sit up, but his neck was spurting blood, and it pumped from another wound in his chest. He raised his gun. His hand wobbled.

I spread my arms. "Get it done!"

But his eyes glazed, and his hand dropped, and his gun was silent as he died.

"What the hell," I muttered, lowering the gun.

Was it me yelling at him to shoot straight, to get it done?

It was. Where had it come from?

But I knew. Frankie knew.

I heard police sirens then. I stepped closer to Han and saw the blood sinking into the Zen-combed sand. Saw that Han was not quite dead. He was trying to speak.

"Yeah, sorry about that, man." I kicked his gun away from his hand. "But you and your friend Deng, you're just a finger on the hand that killed my son."

I knelt beside him, keeping out of the blood, and pulled his wallet. When I looked at his face again, I saw he was dead. His eyes looked with a frozen wonder at the empty sky, as if in shocked realization that its emptiness was his own.

For some reason, I patted his hand. It was still warm. Then I went to the other body—it was even messier—and I took his wallet too.

I was hoping it might look like a robbery attempt that got ugly. And there might be information in those wallets. Something I could use to get me closer to the Kwai.

I hid my gun under my shirt and jogged off toward the river.

The sirens sounded pretty close.

16

I DIDN'T CARE about getting killed, but going to jail was no longer something I was willing to contemplate. I had too much to do. I just walked at a good clip, afraid running would catch the attention of tourists on the river walk. As in, "Guy in a cowboy hat was running from there, officer."

The cops were showing up at the Zen park when I reached the pedestrian bridge. There were some tourists on the walk near the park, staring at the cops, three cars with light bars whirling and loud radio voices, but no one was pointing my way as I walked, quite slowly now, across the bridge. River smells came to me, and its soothing white noise.

The bridge led to a small parking lot for tourists on the other side, where the black Ram was waiting for me.

She might have her affectations, I thought, but this woman can be counted on.

Then I remembered how she'd gotten stoned and said too much to Jacques. Okay, she could be counted on most of the time.

I got into the pickup. As usual, before I could strap on

the seat belt like my old mama had taught me to do, Dulcet gunned the vehicle into action. Once more, I steadied myself between the dashboard and the seat.

"They dead?" she asked.

"They are. I got their wallets. Tried to make it look like a screwed-up robbery. That probably won't work." I put on my seat belt and dug the wallets out of my pocket. "Not much cash here. Eighty-five dollars total. You can buy yourself a few Starbucks drinks. We shouldn't use their credit cards."

"Oh, but Slimby, I could sell those cards for cash, like thirty bucks each."

"Not worth the trouble."

I opened the glove compartment, shoved the money in it, and noticed I was laying money atop a Heckler & Koch VP8SK pistol. "There's a gun in here."

"It sorta kinda came with the truck."

"Sorta kinda?"

"I gave him three hundred for it. It wasn't his. He took it off a guy, he said. That's all he said about it."

"Okay. A gun not registered to you that might relate to the commission of a crime is in your truck. What could go wrong?"

"I like it. It's not too big but bigger than my other one. I wanted a kick-ass gun for my kick-ass truck!"

"Well, if a cop stops us..."

"And if a meteor hits us. That's what Jebus used to say."

"Jesus said that?"

"Jebus. Old boyfriend of mine."

I closed the glove compartment on the gun and the money.

"Ooh, Slimby, was it gnarly when you shot those guys?"

She seemed happy and cheerful, asking the question, so

I couldn't help a snort of uneasy laughter. "Naturally, it was gnarly." I told her about it, but not in bloody detail.

"I wish I could've been there. Those guys were really creepy." She glanced at me. "You don't seem like someone who was just in a gunfight. Except you got some blood on your cheek. Looks like it's yours."

"Blood?" I looked at myself in the rearview. "Oh, a little graze."

"There's some wipes in the glove compartment."

I found the wipes and dabbed at the contusion. "You didn't ask what happened at the addict camp."

"I've seen enough of those."

"But...guess what."

"What?"

"I ran into a cop. Undercover!"

"A narc pretending to be a fenny head?"

"Yeah. And I confirmed that the Kwais are selling the shit on the street around here."

"What was the cop like?"

"A lady cop. She was convincing, but she made a couple of little mistakes, and I called her out on it—in private. She kind of threatened me. But we had a nice chat."

"A nice chat with a lady narc? She hot?"

"You asking for your information?"

"Ha, omigod. Who knows? But is she?"

"Not really."

Why was I lying about that? I told myself there was no point in lying. Dulcet's not my girlfriend. We have no attachment except by chance and a peculiar interlocking of contrasting personalities.

Come to think of it, though, people have gotten married behind less than that.

Still. No need to lie. I guessed it was just about not

wanting any needless tension between us. I wasn't entirely sure how Dulcet felt about me.

"Anyway, she figured out I wasn't who I was pretending to be either, and I told her about...Frankie. That got her a little bit more on my side. In a tough-lady kind of way. She gave me her card in case I found out some useful stuff."

"You're going to be a narc too? I mean, killing them, fine, but...narking?"

"No, I'm looking to see if I can get some information out of her."

"You think she's hot. I know that."

"She was in grubby clothes and all sweaty."

"Sounds hot."

"You get our stuff out of the room?"

"I got it. We not telling them we're checking out?"

"They'll figure it out. Meanwhile, it'll confuse the Kwais and the cops."

"Uh-huh."

She was silent. A rare thing. I could tell there was something she wanted to say. "Go ahead and say it, Dulcet, my dear."

"*Am* I your dear?"

"Sure. But that wasn't your question, was it?"

"Um..." Then more silence. She was headed toward the freeway south. She'd talked me into staying at a motel on the northern fringe of Carson City, like twenty-five minutes' drive from Reno. Far enough away from our trail, but not too far for what I wanted to do.

Accelerating onto the freeway, she said, "I try to just do stuff I want to do."

"Not unreasonable. And you don't want to get caught up in my mission again. I get that."

"You trying to get rid of me again?"

"No, I'm kinda getting used to you."

She smiled faintly. Then it vanished, and she said, "That bullet was like an inch over, you'd have a shattered jaw, Slimby. You know?"

"I know."

"And that would've knocked you down, and he'd have finished you."

"I know that too."

"So don't you think you got lucky?"

"I did some good planning, but yeah. I got lucky." I shrugged.

"You're really good at that 'I don't care' thing," she said. "That's what impressed Wendell."

"It's not a thing. I actually, really, don't care." Except my heart was still thudding from adrenaline.

"But you killed two of them. And Ricky Kwai. And that other guy...Arby or whatever his name was."

"His name was Abel. Are you going to do this every time I kill one of these guys?"

"Probably not, because what's the odds next time they don't get you?"

There was a nearly inaudible catch in her voice when she said that.

She cleared her throat and said, "I will hang with you for now because when I'm not terrified, I'm having fun. And being terrified is having fun too."

"It is?"

"If it's the kind where you're not totally trapped and there's still a way out—yeah."

"Lordy, Dulcet, I don't know who's more fucked up, you or me."

"Oh, Slimby, you're so ro-*man*-tic," she said, pretending to be a hillbilly girl from some old movie.

I laughed. "I meant it in a very tender way."

"Anyway, Mr. Slimby Texas Tequila boy, I'll stick with you till it gets looking like it's no fun no' mo, which might be any second now. Hey, *tequila!* You need tequila! You're all, like Tex Mex, Slimby! It's your lifeblood! Let's get some tequila and fajitas!"

———

We did get fajitas and tequila. But first, we checked into the Struck It Big Motel. We paid cash, extra cash, to keep from having to show ID or a credit card. Dulcet remembered the place from "some work I did a few years ago" in Carson City. Its sign was topped by a rusting cowboy on a rearing horse. The grinning, cigarette-smoking cowboy was waving his hat at the moon. Only two of the sign's lights weren't burned out.

Our room smelled of cigarettes and the mysterious musk that you get from a really old motel. Looking around, Dulcet said, "It's even worse than when I was here before!" She seemed pleased.

The bed was a brass four-poster set up on a worn braided rug spread on most of the wooden floor. A pre-flat-screen Motorola TV sat on a desk across from the bed. A beat-up padded rocking chair waited near the bed. A small dining room table was set up in a corner under a microwave oven.

I kneeled by the bed. "Are you going to pray?" Dulcet asked.

"Checking for bedbugs," I said, lifting up the mattress and looking at the springs.

"'Kay."

"I guess it's all right. And the sheets have been changed."

"Those your minimum requirements, Slimby? Clean sheets and no bedbugs?"

"Now you know all there is to know about me."

Dulcet set about unpacking, and I sat on the edge of the bed and went through the wallets I'd stolen from the Kwai gunmen. The older guy had a card for a tennis club and a small, aged snapshot I figured was of his family: a wife and two kids. I didn't look at it long. It made me feel sick with self-loathing. Then I reminded myself, *He was going to kill me. He knew what the Kwai brothers sold. He enabled them. He was part and parcel of Frankie's death.*

The self-loathing ebbed. But I didn't look at the photo again.

In the younger guy's wallet was a card for a strip club.

There were driver's licenses: Choa Deng and Lo Han. There were credit cards.

There was something I hadn't noticed right off in Deng's wallet. A little card printed for customers by Kwai Brothers' Storage in Reno. On the card was a handwritten door code and "Unit 31."

I pocketed the storage facility card.

Dulcet snatched up her purse and spun it around like a lasso. "Oh boy, cowboy, I'm gonna go get a bottle'a tequila an' two orders of fajitas. There's a liquor store next to the Mex place."

"I've been thinking, what's the chances Deng called in a description of you? Maybe sent a cell photo of you."

"Called it in to the cops?"

"More likely to the Kwais. What's the chances they got no dirty cops in Reno?"

She swung the purse on its strap, pendulously from one

finger, as if in a more thoughtful mode. "Um...less than zero?"

"Sounds right. There could be an APB with pictures of us both out there. They knew my name."

"You trying to scare me away again?"

"I'm saying it might be dangerous to go out unnecessarily tonight."

"It's *necessary* to get tequila and salt and ice."

"You risk getting busted for that?"

"For the fajitas too."

I grinned. "Okay. Here, take these wallets and get rid of them somewhere they won't be found. Do not keep or sell the credit cards!"

"'Kay." She took the wallets, bustled to the door, gave me a little girlish wave, and wafted out. I soon heard the roar of the Dodge Ram.

What about Nadine? Her phone number was there in my memory, crisp and new. Was I going to call the narc? I didn't have a phone currently. Didn't want to use the one in the room. There was a convenience store near the motel. Sometimes they carried burner phones.

I got up, went out, and bought a burner. Then I sent a text to Police Detective Lieutenant Nadine Graves.

———

I was sitting in the old, padded rocking chair, adjusting the TV with the remote, trying to get *Sesame Street* to come in. Lady Gaga was the guest. I thought Dulcet would like it. That's when Nadine called me.

"Lieutenant Graves?" I said.

"Purdoux, you didn't tell me you were a suspect in a mass murder."

"Women always greet me with that one on the phone. It's disconcerting."

"Yeah, hi, but...I guess it's not real surprising you didn't mention the mass murder."

"If you checked up—"

"I talked to the investigating detective."

"Then you know they didn't think I was a suspect for more than like ten minutes. The shooter confessed."

"I did get that, yeah. But...you kill those two in Reno?"

"Just to watch them die?"

"Not funny."

Okay, she knew when I was referencing a Johnny Cash song. She was even cooler than I'd thought.

"Which two in Reno?" I asked.

"There were more than two?"

"No, I mean—hold on now, what am I being accused of?"

"I'm not accusing. I'm asking a question, is all."

She didn't sound like a cop coming hard at a suspect, to my mind. It came across as much like banter as cop talk.

"If you're going to make accusations, make 'em in person, Nadine. When we meet at the storage lot."

"Or you could just give me the door code."

"Or...not."

"Now you're withholding information? You haven't told me how you got this door code."

"Got lucky."

"I notice the wallets are missing from the two Kwai enforcers we found shot dead. Could the code have been in one of those?"

"I could've got it, um, on the internet." I winced at that one. "Somehow. Or other."

"Another thing, a man fitting your description was

staying at a hotel a quarter mile walk from the park where we found the bodies."

"And was that man seen shooting these enforcers?"

"Not so far as we've been able to find out yet. We do have you on a security camera heading in that direction."

Ah. That was not good. "Lots of people heading in that direction is my guess. If you're checking for me on security cameras, does that mean there's an APB out on me?"

"It was suggested you be picked up for questioning. But Lieutenant Rynerson from homicide...he said no, not yet, because he was pursuing other leads, and he thought that would muddy the waters. Some bullshit of that kind. Seemed to me like he might have his own agenda with respect to Slim Purdoux."

"Why would a cop have his own agenda 'with respect to Slim Purdoux?'"

She sighed. "I can't get into that."

"So...he's on the Kwai payroll?"

There was silence on the line but for a faint cell crackle. Then she said, "I have no proof."

Sometimes ambiguity is clarity. "The Kwais don't want me picked up, taken where I can talk. They'd rather have me cut down on the street. They tell their man in Reno PD to find me, but keep it low."

"You don't know any of that. But suppose it's so. Why do the Kwais want you dead, Purdoux?"

Uh-oh. "I heard that the Kwais distributed the shit that killed my boy. I went around... asking questions about them. They must've heard about it."

"Doesn't seem like something they'd go to that much trouble over—a guy asking questions."

"You never know what paranoid people will do."

"I looked into reports of recent violence relating to the

Kwais in the San Francisco area. It seems Ricky Kwai and several associates were shot down by unknown persons in the East Bay."

I was glad to hear it was still unknown persons. "Yeah? Can't say I'm sorry to hear it."

"Nothing more you want to say about that?"

"Ask me again in person."

"We're back to this. I might be able to get a warrant to look into that storage unit."

"And the word might get to the Kwais, and then they'd clean it out before you could get in there."

More silence on the line.

I went on, "Or...we could just go look."

"You're insisting on being there?"

"All unofficial and stuff. I can make myself absent if you find anything interesting."

She made a growling sound. Then a small laugh. "I don't know why I'm so indulgent with you."

"I know why. Tell you when I see you. How about tomorrow sometime? Like when you're off duty, so you don't have to account for the time if you don't want to."

"Yeah, okay. You meet me there at seven thirty p.m.?"

The door lock rattled, and Dulcet came in. "Yep, it's a done deal," I told Nadine. "Gotta go. My dinner's here."

I hung up. Dulcet stood there, sacks in her arms, looking at me. Her mouth was sort of pooched to the side. "Um... you got a burner?"

"I did."

"Who you talking to on the burner, Slimby?"

I figured she didn't feel good about my talking to a cop. And, worse, making an *appointment* with a cop.

But I just did not want to lie to Dulcet. I owed it to her to be straight up. "I was talking to Reno Police Lieutenant

Nadine Graves. If I give her something she doesn't have on the Kwais, she might just tell me some things that can help me."

"Did you tell her where you were staying? What motel and all?"

"No, hell no. She doesn't know where I am. Not telling her."

"Ohhhh, Slim-*beeeeee*," she said, going to the little dented Formica-topped table. "You're making a date with that hot cop. Don't lie to your poor Dulcet."

"It's not a date. It's business. For Frankie."

She put the sacks down and took out the Styrofoam containers of fajitas. "I think I'd like it better if you got jiggy with her instead of did cop stuff with her. Just come and eat this food and drink this tequila. I got some margarita mix too. Is that Lady Gaga on *Sesame Street*? Cool!"

———

"Look what Mr. Big Weenie is doing! What an idiot!"

"Looks like he's having fun. But the girl looks kind of like she wants it to be over."

"Yuh. She got her some sad eyes."

"Yes, she does."

Flicking the remote around a bit drunkenly, Dulcet had hit the motel's adult channel. X-rated stuff.

"He looks like a dog when he does that," she said, laughing. "Hey, does porn get you off? Am I ruining your horny buzz?"

"Porn never did much for me. Though when I was in middle school, I traded my lunch money for *Penthouse* centerfolds." I looked at the laminated television listing.

"You like old movies, right? Says here they got TCM on cable."

We found it and watched Elvis singing "Love Me Tender" in his first movie. "Oooh, that gets *me* worked up," Dulcet said.

We made love, but she seemed distracted. I thought about telling her I had no expectations when she wasn't in the mood, but I decided she might find a way to feel insulted at that.

We each had a fourth margarita, which was for sure too many, and then she curled up next to me with her eyes shut and said, "Tell me a story about when you were a cowboy in Texas."

"I wasn't a cowboy. I was a music scene stoner and then a college student and then a drug addict and then a guy trying not to get raped in prison. But before prison, I was in some target shooting and Fast Draw competitions. Cowboy Fast Draw, they call it."

"That's being a cowboy."

"It's not. But...one time I was in a World Fast Draw Association competition, and they checked your draw time to the split second. And this guy got mad when I won, said I was using a fanning technique that was not allowed, but the camera proved it was a thumbing technique, and then he shouted at me that the judge was a friend of mine and—you won't believe this—he literally asked me to meet him in the parking lot and..."

But she was asleep. Anyway, the story was anti-climactic.

I turned off the TV and the light and lay down next to her. It took me more than an hour to go to sleep, and I dreamed about the kids I saw in the photo from Deng's wallet. They were coming after me and waving guns at me, and I had a gun in my hand, but I couldn't shoot some little kids.

I woke up at three in the morning, which is what happens if I drink hard liquor. I lay there with a headache and a raw dryness in my mouth, wondering what Frankie would think about me now.

I sat up, winced, slumped miserably on the edge of the bed, listening to Dulcet softly snoring and remembering suddenly her gleefully shooting Gary Ledbetter.

Was it necessary to kill Gary?

My companions in the raid hadn't worn masks. And Gary could identify them. But could he? He was so stoned.

Wendell, of course, wasn't going to take a chance. He'd have done it if she hadn't.

Had she really delighted in shooting Gary? Or was it an act?

She was always playacting after all.

I just shook my head and asked myself why I was with her. But I knew. She kept the wave of darkness at bay.

Weariness flooded back into me, and I crawled into bed and spooned her.

———

We got up late and had breakfast at a twenty-four-hour coffee shop attached to something called the Silver Horseshoe Card and Roulette Room. We lingered over coffee, with me looking through a Carson City newspaper—the local rag only published twice a week—and Dulcet reading a yellowed paperback copy of *Gigi* by Colette. *The Nevada Appeal* had a mention of the double shooting in Reno. It claimed there were no suspects. Was that claim Rynerson's doing?

"You're reading Colette," I said, tossing the newspaper aside.

"Yeah. *Gigi.* I read it before." She spoke in a kind of toneless whisper that wasn't usual for her. She didn't look up from the book. "I wanted to read it because I liked the movie. It's so much *not* like the movie."

"Who's the translator?"

She shrugged and put the book down. "Some professor lady."

"Colette was a great writer." I remembered that Colette had a flirtation with fascism late in the war. The whole Vichy thing. I thought about asking if she knew that. But why spoil Colette for Dulcet? "How come you pretend not to be as smart as you are?"

She shrugged. "'Cause it's safer."

In her world, it was. I picked up the paperback and leafed through it. "Colette was bisexual. Had some serious girlfriends. But she seemed to like men too. Or maybe they were just useful."

"Yeah, I'm bi if I'm in the mood." Still, the toneless whispering as she turned a page. "We going to do a three-some with that hot narc of yours?"

I laughed softly at the thought. "Yeah, right."

"We should go," I said, "if you're giving me a ride to Reno."

"You could take the truck. I'm thinking of going to Lake Tahoe." She put the book aside, and her voice returned to something like normal. "There's a bus that goes there from this casino in about an hour." She waved a flyer at me. "I never been to Lake Tahoe."

"Really? I went with Frankie and his mom when I was still married to her."

"Is Lake Tahoe the jewel of the world and shit, like people say?"

I grinned. "The jewel of the world and shit?"

She looked at me blankly. "You making fun of me now?"

"No. Just a funny juxtaposition. Sorry. Lake Tahoe is not as pristinely beautiful as it once was, not like the way Mark Twain described it. Because, you know, real estate and speedboat pollutants and all. But it's still amazing. You could wait, and we could both go."

"No. You're not going to be happy till you find out what you wanna know. You go whisper in that narc's ear."

"You don't really think I'm going to tell her anything about you...or Wendell or any of that?"

"Maybe if she's offering you a deal--or something. Like pussy maybe." She snagged up her purse. "I need a cigarette. Come on."

"Ohhhh-kay." I followed her outside.

We sat in the truck, out in the parking lot. She smoked and stared off through the windshield.

"I swear to you, on Frankie's soul. I would never turn you in. I'm not making any kind of deals with the...the narc...except to find out more about the assholes who killed my son."

"You know—and you can get mad at me and hit me, whatever—but your son killed himself. No one made him take that shit."

A ripple of iciness went through me. I wanted to shout at her. Then I just wanted to be away from her.

I took a deep breath and said, "He didn't know there was fentanyl in it. He was an innocent."

She shrugged and blew smoke out the window. "I wish I could have been an innocent. I try, best I can."

Then, I seemed to see her more clearly than I ever had.

She was remembering her childhood. I could see that. It was the pain in the set of her lips. Her eyes were wet.

"You know, Dulcet, I feel like...I don't know..."

She tossed the cigarette butt out the window and said, "Like you want to leave me."

"I feel like I'm *using* you because right now I'm afraid to be by myself for too long." She'd been in the life since she was pretty young. Who knows what she went through? She was used to hooking up with men to find her way safely through the world. On impulse, I said, "You and I do have a...you know. We talk and we laugh and we have a good time in bed. Anyway, I do."

"You think I don't?"

"I think you do, but...I still feel like I'm using you."

"Oh, so it's you're leaving me because it's the best thing for me? Women know that one. Don't give me that shit about using me. Ohmigod, we use each other. Everyone uses everyone else. It's a...what's that thing they call it?"

"Transactional?"

"Exactly. Transactional relationship. But if you're about to narc me out—"

"I'm not. Listen, Dulcet, I can tell you're mad at me. I'm totally for-real aware that you've *been there* for me. Probably those Kwai security pricks would've caught me at the hotel and killed me if you hadn't warned me. And you and me planned it out—"

Now, her mouth softened into a faint smile. She thumbed some tears from her eyes, as if she were wiping away grains of sleep. "We did totally set up those assholes, didn't we?"

"We did. You handled them. But that outfit's not done with me. There's a dirty cop who'd like to catch me alone.

Guy named Rynerson. He's a homicide detective who'd like to commit a homicide with me in mind."

"No shit?" She looked at me. "That what hot detective bitch said?"

"She's a decent cop. There are some, you know. They could have held me in San Francisco, but they were okay. Yeah, she kind of let me know about Rynerson. So...you want to be around when that goes down?"

She flicked her hair back from her forehead. "I'd be stupid to keep hanging with you, with some cop hunting you."

"Well, exactly."

She turned on the radio. It was a country music station. She tapped along with it on the steering wheel. "Yeah, it'd be stupid. But you'd fuck everything up all by yourself."

"I...well..."

"Omigod, I don't believe I'm gonna say this, but I'm gonna stick around and play it by ear. But you better not be getting me in lockup."

She handed me the keys to the truck. "Here. I'm going to go get that bus to Tahoe." She got out of the truck, and I got out and came around to the driver's side. I put my arms around her, and after a moment, she slipped her arms around my waist. We stood there for a moment, sort of swaying in place against each other. Then she stepped back and pointed at me. "You be back at the motel tonight. With my truck. Okay, Cowboy Curtis?"

I nodded. "You got it, Miss Yvonne."

She looked pleased. "You know who Miss Yvonne is?"

"I looked up *Peewee's Playhouse* when we were back in San Francisco."

I climbed up into the Dodge Ram. She said, "When I

get back, I'm gonna stop by the Walmart over by the casino. You need anything from there?"

"Yeah," I said. "If you go to their sporting goods, they'll have a gun-cleaning kit. Get me one of those."

"'Kay."

"And if you talk to any of your shady friends, see if they know where the Reno PD detectives do their drinking. Word about that kinda thing gets around."

"'Kay."

I started the truck, waved to Dulcet, and headed for the freeway to Reno.

———

Kwai Brothers Storage was one of those sprawling metal-walled complexes you find next to industrial parks at the edge of town. This one looked fresh, its units alternately painted utility-beige and dull white. It seemed like it couldn't have been around for more than a year.

About fifty feet away, Lieutenant Nadine Graves, arms crossed, was leaning on a Chevy Tahoe the same jet black as her hair. She was wearing a dark-blue pantsuit. The Reno Police Department badge on her belt glowed in the sunlight. On her right hip, just showing under her blazer, was a holstered gun. On her left was a compact two-way police radio.

I sat in the truck a moment, thought about bringing along my gun, and told myself I'd be a damned fool to do that. Suppose more cops showed up—and my gun was seized? A few ballistics tests on the gun and the bullets I left in Deng and Han, and I'd be on a fast track to the state pen. I shouldn't have brought it at all, considering that. Ought to have dumped it and gotten a different gun.

But it felt right in my hand. I was good with that model of gun, and I was feeling superstitious about it. The Colt had been working for me like a charm.

I left it under the truck's passenger seat.

I got out of the Ram, locked it, and walked down the strip of storage facility parking to Nadine.

"Lieutenant Graves, I believe!" I stuck out my hand to shake.

"Slim." Nadine shook my hand, her expression rueful. She nodded at the pickup. "You drive a Dodge Ram? I guess I shouldn't be surprised, but I am."

"Way too awkward a vehicle for me. Even just climbing in and out of that thing. I borrowed it from a friend."

"After taking your Mustang GT back to the rental?"

I gave her an "I'm so impressed" look. "You sure scooped the Purdoux data." I looked into the Tahoe and saw it had a police radio, but no prisoner grill between front and back. "Nice unmarked car. Shotgun in the cargo space?"

"None of your business, but hell yes. Slim, you said you'd answer questions about that shooting, face-to-face."

"Did I? A shooting?"

"Deng and Han? Kwai enforcers? Shot dead?"

"Will you answer a question first?"

"Which is?"

"Are you going to lie to me?"

"Lie to you?" Her brow furrowed. "About *what*?"

"About anything. Like if I asked, 'Are you wearing a wire?'"

She scowled. "I'm not wearing a wire. And no, I'm not going to lie to you. I'm not working undercover when I'm talking to you."

"Okay. You won't lie to me. And I don't want to lie to you, Nadine. Don't make me do it."

"Is that your weird way of saying you shot Deng and Han but don't want to say so on the record?"

"Look, if you're convinced I committed a crime, arrest me. No door code, though. You'd have to get a warrant to open it."

"I should get a warrant. But I don't want to wait for that. I'm afraid someone might warn them to truck the stuff out of here. And I have a workaround."

"Let's work around," I said, shrugging.

"You got a gun on you?"

"No."

"You got one somewhere?"

I hesitated. Then said, "Yes."

"Registered to you?"

"Uh...I don't want to lie to you."

"Don't start that again. Come on, let's check out the storage unit."

"It's number thirty-one."

We walked past the office of the storage lot, where a scruffy guy with blond hair and an Amish beard was watching us through the window. He raised a cell phone to his ear.

"You know anything about that guy?" I asked as we went down the concrete paths between steel buildings. Hot sunlight bounced off the white-painted metal. Sweat vapor started to blur my glasses.

"Not exactly. But the Kwais are working with some Russian outfit. Might be one of their people."

"Russian as in Russian Mafia?"

"That's the rumor. Russian and Chinese organized crime are buying businesses and property in Vegas and Reno. There's Pavel Abdulov. Russian 'investor' he calls himself. Word on the street is, he's Russian Mafia. His outfit runs scams on the casinos they don't own. Seems the Russian and Chinese cartels work together sometimes, mutual money laundering, drug wholesaling. It's some old arrangement going back to the KGB."

"There's no KGB anymore, is there?"

"It's called the GRU now. Basically the same thing, I hear, apart from the communist context. But I'm not a federal agent. Here's row three." We walked down the long row toward thirty-one.

I glanced at her. Something about her profile...

"You grow up on a rez, at all?" I asked.

She looked at me sidelong, not entirely pleased. "How'd you know that?"

"You have a slight rez accent. And your profile—so Paiute. Like maybe Pyramid Lake Paiute?"

She nodded slowly. "Not bad. You got some native blood?"

"Smidge of Comanche. Maybe an eighth. And some North Aztec-Mexican. Mostly French ancestry, apart from that. But my mom was mixed blood. In college, I minored in anthropology and Native American studies. Wrote a thesis on the Northern Paiute and the Washoe. Got a B plus, and the paper was published. Kept up my reading. Had a...a friend was Tonkawa." I didn't say that friend was my girl-friend in high school. *Reena.* My first and only really serious love, run down by some asshole college kid drunk-driving in his shiny new Camaro.

"You've got secret depths, Slim," Nadine said, only a little snarky. "Yeah, I'm a rez kid. Quarter Washoe, a lot more Paiute, some African American. Only person I looked up to on the rez was my uncle. A tribal cop. Sometimes I think I'll sign on with the tribal police. Big pay cut, though. I want to get narcotics out of the rez. Heroin killed my sister. I thought working with Reno police might get me to the sources."

"You want to hit the sources. You and I have something in common."

"You flatter yourself, Slim." But she smiled as she said it. "Here's thirty-one."

"The code is—"

"Don't tell me yet," she interrupted. Puzzling me. "Write it down on here."

She gave me a little pad, the kind cops use to prep for incident reports, and a pen.

I wrote it down and handed it back. She didn't look at it. "Now, hey—what's that over there?" She turned her back. "If someone were to open that when I wasn't looking..."

I got the message and used the code. A little green light came on next to the lock, and the door clicked. I opened it, reached in, hit the light switch. "Jesus!"

"What? You find something?" she asked, as if surprised. "Oh yeah."

We both stood there, looking in, with perfectly matched smiles of wry satisfaction.

The rectangular room, about five yards by three, was stacked half full with plastic-wrapped bricks of white powder.

17

"YOU GOT A TESTING KIT?" I asked. "Not like I think it might be plaster of paris, but..."

Nadine shook her head. Then contradicted herself by saying, "Yeah, I do." She took her radio off her hip. "But it's in the car. Anyway, if this is fentanyl, we'd need high-quality masks and gloves at the very least. Let a small cloud of fentanyl dust out, it can kill you. I figure it's fentanyl. No way they have this much white heroin in one place. Too expensive. And cocaine, meth—this stuff doesn't have that glisten." She held the radio up to talk into it.

"Um...wait. You going to call this in right *now?*"

She lowered the radio. "Obviously. I got to report that due to someone opening this storage unit in my presence, I have probable cause for calling in a SWAT team and a tox squad. Dangerous substances specialists."

"So I should make myself scarce."

"No, stay here."

"I'm supposed to hang around here and explain how I got the door code?"

"You're a CI, a confidential informant. I filled out that

form for you already. Not that I won't arrest you if you give me good reason, because I will. But see, the confidential part means I can get you out of here. Okay? Only you have to sign something that says you opened this unit. Which—" She reached into her jacket, took out a folded piece of paper. "I brought it along."

Nadine handed it to me with a pen, and I signed, holding the paper against the wall.

She took the form back. "I'm gonna have to take a picture of you here too. Then I call SWAT. When they take the scene over, I walk you out. I need them to see you here."

"What if SWAT wants to swat me?"

"They'll take their cue from me on this."

Then Nadine got on the two-way, and she called it all in.

I was visualizing my life in jail, where I'd be helpless to do anything but brood on Frankie and wait for the Kwais to kill me through their prison contacts. And if the Kwais kill me there, they win.

She must have seen the uncertainty on my face. "There are no warrants out for you. I've got your back, Slim."

I leaned against a wall, hands in my pockets. Nadine exchanged cop code on the two-way and explained the situation to Captain Somebody-or-other. I was thinking about Frankie and the dead Eickhoff had left with their insides oozing out on the floor of the office. And about Abel and Canadian Red and Tuck the Bounty Hunter and Ricky Kwai and the Dutch guy and the weightlifter and Gary Ledbetter and Deng and Han.

It was the first time I saw the kill corridor. It's traumatic ideation, more than thinking. Mental pictures, sharp and all lined up, coming at me like flashcards. I could see a long corridor of people dying and dead. It was hard to take in. I found myself breathing hard.

What we'd found in the storage unit was a big deal. About six minutes later, we could hear sirens. I heard confirmations of imminent arrival on her two-way...which is when Lieutenant Rynerson, homicide, showed up. Minutes before the secure-the-scene cops.

He was a tall, heavy-bellied, red-faced man in a black suit with a red tie and a white shirt. Maybe early fifties. He had a military haircut and a gingery mustache that merged with his frown lines. His badge gleamed on a western-style brown leather belt with a rodeo-style buckle showing a gold horse on a silver field. Next to the badge was a brown leather handcuff holster. In his meaty left hand was a hefty Glock automatic pistol, pointed at the ground. He had flinty blue eyes and far more lower lip than upper.

"Lieutenant Rynerson," Nadine said. She looked at the gun in his hand, seemed as if she might ask him why he'd drawn it, and decided not to.

"No one here but me and my CI," she said, with a sideways tilt of her head toward me.

Rynerson looked at me. "This your CI?"

I touched my hat and shrugged ruefully.

He just stared. "Isn't this that guy? Purdoux?"

"It is," Nadine said. "I've got him where I can arrest him when I'm ready."

"There are no warrants out on me," I said.

He glared at me. "You're a *suspect*. That's good enough to bring you in." He turned to Nadine. "I'm gonna to collar him, right now."

She frowned. "Just you?"

"Yeah. Why not? Everyone's busy with this mess."

"How'd you get here so early?" I asked as if just casually interested. "That guy in the office call you?"

Rynerson swiveled toward me, and his hand tightened on the gun. "Turn around and put your hands on the wall!"

"The plan is to take me out of here, act like I tried to escape somehow, or just turn me over to the Kwais?"

"Shut the fuck up! I said turn around, hands on the wall! You're obstructing. You're going downtown."

"Let me clear up something for you," I said, staying so calm it surprised even me. "When they made you a homicide detective, that didn't mean you could commit homicides."

He raised the gun. "Last warning!"

"Uh-uh!" Nadine barked. "This is my collar." She stepped between me and him. "I've been waiting for the right time. You going to push it, Marv, then it's right now."

My mouth went dry. Waiting for the right time? Is that what she'd been doing?

"Now look—" Rynerson began.

She turned to me and, in the same movement, got her handcuffs out. "James Purdoux, I'm placing you under arrest. Hands on the wall."

I stared. She stared. Then she rolled her eyes and mouthed, *Just do it.*

I turned slowly around and put my hands on the wall. She patted me down and said, "Hands behind your back."

I complied, and she cuffed me.

"You can cuff him," Rynerson said. "But I'm taking him. You've got to stay with your evidence."

"Lieutenant Graves?" A woman's voice.

Three uniformed were cops walking up. Two prototypical male cops and an Asian woman. The woman had sergeant's stripes.

"Sergeant Lee," Nadine said. "Can you secure the evidence till SWAT and the DS team get here?"

"That's why I'm here, ma'am," said Lee.

"Nadine, dammit," Rynerson began. "Listen—"

"I've been working on this one for a couple of days," Nadine said. "This one's mine. Check with the captain."

"Damned right I will!"

She grabbed me by my upper arm and tugged me none too gently along the walk toward the parking lot.

Rynerson followed, trying to argue. She ignored him, and she quickly performed a complicated maneuver: activating the fob to unlock the car, switching hands on my arm, opening the back door with the other hand, and snapping, "Duck your head!" as she shoved me in the back seat. I managed to writhe into the back as she closed the door and hurried around the car.

An armored Bearcat pulled up nearby. It had "Reno Tactical Squad" emblazoned on a door.

Rynerson was saying, "Goddamn it, I'm going to follow you to the station, Graves!"

"Lieutenant Rynerson!" called a uniformed SWAT lieutenant, getting out of the big Bearcat. The SWAT boss was wearing a Kevlar vest. "What's homicide doing out here? We got a four-twenty?"

"Nah, Jasper," Rynerson said. "I just—Whoa, hold on, Graves!"

His rage-red face gaped after us as Lieutenant Nadine Graves accelerated the Chevy Tahoe out of the parking lot, just as fast as she could get away with.

———

I was complimenting Nadine on her cleverness in extricating us from Rynerson when I noticed she was driving out into the desert.

What was that all about? It crossed my mind that the desert would be a good place to kill me. Maybe she was working for the Kwais after all.

"Well, hell. Why not?" I said.

She looked at me in the rearview. "Why not what?"

"Rather have you execute me out in the desert. Be a bummer to have Rynerson do it."

"Is that some kind of weird sarcasm I'm not getting?"

"What? No."

"When you were talking to Rynerson...Okay, he doesn't deserve respect if he's dirty, and I know he is. But taunting him about it, Purdoux—your cute *homicide* remark—I might have gotten us out of there without dragging out the confrontation if you hadn't run your mouth like that. As it is, right now, he's reporting me to the captain, which will get me a write-up, possibly a suspension, which is why I've got my radio turned off. I'm supposed to be off duty nowanyway so maybe I can get away with that."

"Giving you time to drive me out into the desert. With my hands cuffed behind me."

She looked at me in the mirror with an exaggerated sad look. "Oh, *poor* Slim."

"The cuffs are more uncomfortable than sexy."

Nadine laughed and shook her head, then suddenly swung the car onto a potholed asphalt road. We bumped through scrubland, past a couple of ranch-style houses, until the landscape got a little greener. Fenced-in horses and goats grazed to either side.

She took another turn, drove two more miles, and said, "You're on the rez, now."

"You going to stake me down on an anthill?"

"Sadly, those days are gone. No one appreciates the old traditions enough."

We passed a row of identical old FEMA houses, boarded over and deserted. She swung the Tahoe into a development that looked like it might have been set up in the 1970s. I saw tribal children running and clambering about on a small playground set between two of the houses. In the distance, I caught the blue shimmer of Pyramid Lake.

Nadine slowed at the last house of the last row and pulled into the driveway. "People see us, they're gonna think it's kinda weird when I let you out of those cuffs here," she said, getting out of the car.

"Look even funnier if you left me in 'em."

She opened the back door of the Tahoe and said, "Turn around in there." I turned around, and she reached in and unlocked the cuffs. "Come on out, prisoner Purdoux."

I got out, stretching my arms and rubbing my wrists. "Okay, I think I've got my joints reconnected now."

"I had to keep you cuffed for appearance's sake."

"All the way here?"

"Okay, the last ten miles were just for fun."

I managed a small laugh at that and looked at the house. Another 1970s one-story ranch-style, dusty-brown and yellow. The front yard was a mix of high yellow grass, sage, and cacti. There was red dust on the windows, but I could make out curtains. "You live here?"

"I've got a townhouse in Reno. But I come out here sometimes. It belonged to my aunt. She left it to me. Died of diabetes."

"I read somewhere, 30 percent of people on the reservations come down with diabetes."

"Yep. Lots of factors. Come on in. We can have a drink,

and we can talk about what an asshole you are for not coming clean with me and all."

———

It was over warm and stuffy in the living room. "That a Paiute rug?" I asked.

"Washoe." It was blue and white, with borders of chevrons, and a native sun symbol in the glowing yellow in the center. She switched on the air conditioner. "But the rug's machine-made. Okay, rez reds ran the machine, but even so, not authentic handmade. I got those early 1920s Paiute baskets on the shelf. And that painting of the cayuse in the sunset." She nodded toward a framed oil over the fireplace. "It's by a Paiute artist. And there's the sofa, authentically made in a Sears factory decades ago. Sit down, it's late enough in the day for me to pretend it's okay to drink tequila."

There was an Indian blanket with yellow and red geometric designs on the sofa. I sat at one end and looked at the CDs in a rack beside an old boombox. There was native music, but most of it was classic rock with a good deal of Joni Mitchell. "This music belonged to your aunt?"

"Oh yeah. But I got into it."

She went into the bedroom for a minute, then came out and mixed the drinks in the kitchenette. She brought me a tequila and tonic and sat down, drink in hand. I saw she'd taken off her gun, badge, and jacket, and let her hair down. It fell all jet black down over her shoulders. She kicked off her shoes.

"Damn, you're like almost human now without the cop gear, Lieutenant Graves."

"I'm all too human, cowboy." She raised her glass. We clicked them and drank.

"Holy *shit,* you made that strong."

"My nerves are wound kinda tight. Anyway, I gotta chill so I can think. Make up my mind if I should run you out of town—town in this case being the entire state of Nevada—or...work with you. Or what? I'm pretty sure you've flouted the law already."

"So the strong booze is all about getting me to admit something? I'm supposed to slurringly blurt that I...that I *what?*"

She grinned. "It'd be your word against mine." She moved closer to me on the sofa. "Don't worry about it."

She took a drink, looking at me over the top of the tumbler. Looking in her eyes, I let go of a weight I wasn't aware of until it was gone. The absent weight had to do with the effort to not constantly think about everything that'd happened in San Francisco.

And there was a softly delicious feeling in the air. I could almost hear it humming. "You put something in this drink besides tequila?"

"Like what? Thornapple? We don't use datura anymore. Or we're not supposed to. You never know what some *puhagim* is gonna try."

I nodded. *Puhagim* is Numu for a shaman.

"So..." She went on, "No drugs. Sorry. Used to take psilocybin when I was in college."

"Really! Sacred mushrooms are more Viking than Plains Indian."

"Was a time I'd rather been a Viking shield maiden than a nice Numu girl frying up a suckerfish."

"They still get fish out of that lake?"

"Sure. If you don't mind a mild case of mercury poisoning. Pick out a CD and put it on. But choose wisely, young one."

"I'm older than you, Nadine."

I got up, feeling the drink, and trying not to show it. I put on *Exile on Main Street*. The player had slots for follow-up CDs, so I put an album of dour love songs by Waylon Jennings and then the first album by All Them Witches.

Hearing the first Rolling Stones track, she said, "You pass the test. Have a seat."

She patted the sofa closer to her. I sat closer, and we both took a drink.

"You feel that?" I asked.

She looked at me curiously. "What'd you mean? The tequila?"

"No. Totally different direction than tequila. It's like... there's something humming in the air. Lot of energy to it. Maybe I'm hearing the air conditioner is all..."

"What kind of something?" she asked, looking at me like a doctor trying for a diagnosis.

"Like I said when we first met. There was a sort of thrumming in the air and it brought...don't roll your eyes at me...a feeling that I've always known you."

"This line usually work?"

"Not on cops. Anyway, it's not a line." I raised my right hand. "I swear on my honor I've never said any such thing to anyone before."

She looked in my eyes and said, "I believe you. A feeling in the air." She poked me in the chest. "Maybe we should *clear* the air. Just between you and me. You kill those assholes in the park by the Truckee?"

I shook my head. "You can't help being a cop. I still think you could be wearing a wire."

"I give you permission to check." She put her drink on the floor and spread her arms.

I laughed. "Yeah, right. You'd tase me."

"You see a taser? Come on, don't make me sit here with my hands up."

Well, what the hell. Don't be a dweeb, Jim.

I put my hands just under her arms and slid them down. "Don't feel anything but a brassiere strap. But technology can be miniaturized. It could be in that brassiere."

"You'd better check that then," she said, shrugging, her face impassive.

"I...okay. Fine." She wasn't wearing a wire. But role play is a delightful thing.

I unbuttoned her blouse, opened it, reached behind her, and very, very carefully, unhooked the bra.

She was a lot bustier than I'd thought. I stared at her areolas, the color of chocolate.

Nadine rolled her eyes. "Stop ogling and kiss me, dumbbell."

And that's what did it. The kiss. We both arched our backs at once, feeling it.

We were just taken by it, as if a cloud of desire descended from some Hindu deity of copulation. She gave me a hoarse command to "Get my pants the hell off, for God's sake."

A couple of hours later, we came out of it. We had made it to the bed after the first half-hour. And we were lying there on our backs, in the ruin of the bedclothes, my hand atop hers, staring at the cracked ceiling.

"That was..." she whispered. "Um...it was..."

"It was, yeah," I managed.

"Now you think I'm easy, huh?"

"That wasn't easy. It was exhausting."

She laughed. It was a good sound. "You seemed to go right along real easy to me. But you know that's the first sex I've had in a year and a half. How's your energy right now?"

I wiped sweat from my eyes. "You're kidding, right?"

"I thought...maybe once more..."

"That tractor won't run without fuel."

"I've got some tamales I could thaw in the microwave."

"Sounds like manna from heaven."

Groaning, she got up and went naked across the room to the hall. I heard the refrigerator door open, and then the whine of a microwave oven and the tinkling of ice in tumblers.

I glanced at the lamp table by the bed. Her gun and badge were there.

And I thought, what the hell have I got myself into?

18

WE ATE LIKE WOLVES, microwaved tamales tasting like the food of the gods. We had one more drink. Nadine proposed we take a shower. After the shower, she put on a bathrobe and said, "I think I need a nap. I got up at dawn."

"I'll lie down with you a while," I said, as I got my pants on. I didn't want to lose the feeling of being close to her. That feeling of *this is so good, it's all there is, all that matters.*

For a short time, I had escaped. For this little while, I didn't have to think about what had happened to my son.

We lay down on our backs, holding hands. She had her eyes closed, and I was looking toward the window, wondering if Dulcet was back yet. I had plans for her. They were not sexual.

I noticed Hulk Hogan staring at me from the opposite wall. "Nadine, why is there a big, framed poster of Hulk Hogan in here? Is he really your type?"

"My auntie's type, I guess. But in the hall, there's a signed picture of Tatanka."

"Sitting Bull?"

"Pretty good, Slim. They did call Sitting Bull 'Tatanka.'

This Tatanka is a native wrestler, real name Chris Chavis. But he's Lumbee, not Lakota. Kind of like to date Tatanka myself. Chavis, not Sitting Bull. 'Course, Tatanka is sixty-three, but so what..."

"Did you make up your mind, Nadine, or what?"

"About whether I date you or Tatanka?"

"About if you were going to run me out of state or work with me."

"Oh, that. Sort of slipped my mind when you seduced me."

"I seduced *you*? Ha! You *kidnapped* me in cuffs and then ravaged me! It's police abuse of a person in custody, is what it is."

She laughed. "You didn't try to escape, bro."

"You couldn't have chased me out of here with a gun."

She let out a long breath. "Something came over me, for sure. You know, I felt it too, back at that junkie camp, in that most romantic of settings. I felt like I'd always known you and...okay, there was an instant attraction. But I didn't *kidnap* you. I was trying to cover for you, with the cuffs and all."

"That's what it was? And then you totally lost control..."

"That was you, lost control."

"Me!"

We both laughed. I hadn't felt that good in a long time. I really did not want to leave her side. "You ever read that Ray Bradbury story, or maybe you saw *The Illustrated Man* movie..."

"I saw that on TV when I was a kid."

"Me too. These astronauts are on a planet where it rains perpetually, and they're having to trudge on foot for days to get to shelter. They're going crazy with the endless rain in this jungle, and then finally they get to the sun dome, and they go in this dome and tear off their clothes, and they can't hear the rain, and there's a little sun globe in there, and Rod Steiger is just so relieved and happy to be in there and..."

"Whoa, no more tequila for you."

I was abashed to say the rest of it, but I did anyway. "And right now it feels like you're my sun dome."

Nadine just looked at me for a moment. Her voice a little choked, she said, "Um...that's...nice." Then she pointed a finger at me. "Wait! Are you comparing me to something on another planet in a weird old science fiction movie?"

"Technically," I said, "yes, I am."

She shrugged. "I'll take it."

"Hey, you got a totem animal, Nadine?"

"A spirit animal? Like, I believe in that stuff. Except I think I know what yours would be."

"I'm scared to ask. Armadillo?"

Nadine shook her head firmly. "Nah, coyote. Seems like you're lean and mean and a trickster like coyotes in the stories. Coyote with a gun."

"But if you did have to have a spirit animal?"

"Wouldn't mind a cougar," she said, clawing at the air with one hand.

"Didn't know you could scratch like that." She laughed, and we kissed for a long time, and then she nestled her head against me and asked softly, "You got to be somewhere?"

Did I? I did. Did I want to be somewhere else? I didn't. But...

"There's something I have to follow up on."

"You going to tell me what?"

"Best if I don't."

Her eyes closed, she sighed, and said, "Oh god. Well, I can't see running you out of town...or Nevada. Not yet."

She yawned. "But um...you're not going to go all in on the Kwais, right? I mean, you can find where a bunch of them live, or their offices, but before you got shot down, you'd be killing anyone associated with them. Not all the Kwai family is involved in dealing fentanyl. So you get killed... and take down some innocents too."

"Not going to do something like that. I really want to know where their manufacturing gets done. Seems to me that big supply of fentanyl they had was probably not smuggled in. What I hear, more people are making it right here in the USA."

"There are reports that's happening. But we haven't heard a whisper about where that happens around here. Or no one is telling me, anyhow. Maybe Rynerson knows."

"I'm not going off half-cocked."

"I could make a joke, but I won't, 'cause I've got class. But damn, I'm so...sleepy."

We dozed. Maybe I even slept a little. When I opened my eyes, the sky through the window had a tinge of indigo, and there was some pink on a skirt of clouds.

I wanted to stay right where I was. But I made myself sit up. "You awake, Nadine?"

"I am now."

"I've got to get a ride. If you can't go, maybe you know somebody I could hire?"

She groaned. "You're going to go somewhere and get yourself shot and me in trouble with Internal Affairs, aren't you, Slim?"

"I definitely do not plan on either one."

"That's not a no."

"I left the pickup at that storage place. If it's not already towed. It was borrowed." I was thinking of that gun under the seat. If the cops had decided it was part of the crime scene, they'd have gone over it. I needed to know.

She sat up and swept her hair back with her hands and said, "Just get dressed, *wasi'chu*."

I winced at that. *Wasi'chu* is a Lakota word to call White people. It's not a term glowing with friendliness. "Hey, I'm an eighth Comanche."

"More like a one-thirty-second, I bet."

———

I turned down another drink, and we had a mostly silent drive to Reno. But she found a Waylon Jennings mix on Amazon Music on her phone, and we listened to it in the car. "I love listening to his gristly old voice," she said.

"Tom Waits for true gristle. You going to let me see you again?"

"Sometimes a girl knows she is as likely as not going to do something stupid. This is one of those times."

"I'll take that. Nadine...is there anyone, like maybe a snitch somewhere, who knows where the Kwai's dope factory is?"

"We're guessing it's somewhere out in the desert, but no clue where. We've tried following them out there, but they always seem to know someone's tailing them."

"Could be Rynerson telling whoever's got him in his pocket."

"No proof of that. But..." She shrugged. "Don't quote me, but Rynerson would be my guess. What would you do if you knew where it was?"

"Don't know."

She shook her head. "You just don't want to tell me."

I didn't have anything to say to that, because it was true.

We kept driving, another fifteen miles of tense silence as the dusk thickened around us. Then she swung off the freeway, and the two blocks took us to the storage facility. "Looks like the truck's there."

There were some leftover police incident cones, yellow tape, and a new chain with a big lock on the door to the office. But I didn't see any cops.

She pulled up beside the pickup. "Go on, Purdoux, and try not to kill anyone. It'd be good if you tried not to get killed too."

I sat beside her for a long moment. Then I said, "I don't think I should kiss you right here. Put you in a pickle if someone sees it."

"Who said I'd let you?"

"Okay, so I was thinking optimistically about that. You mad at me?"

"My feelings are way too complicated for that description."

I nodded. "That's almost encouraging. I did help you get a major dope bust. You think that'll give you cover from whatever Rynerson says?"

"Good chance of it."

I moved my hand closer to hers on the seat and waited. She growled to herself but took my hand in hers. She held it and then grabbed hold of the steering wheel with both hands. There was visible willpower in that motion.

"Nadine, I'll be in touch. If you have no objections."

"I'll take your calls. Got to. You're my confidential informant."

"Always with the mushy talk."

I got out of the Tahoe, unlocked the truck, and climbed in—and glanced over to see she was already driving away.

And then the plunge came. Hard drug users know what

I mean. A sickening falling feeling when your high wears off. You're coming down...after.

I was coming down after Nadine. When I was with her, Frankie's death, the dead at Renquist's, the kill corridor, the dark wave pursuing me—it was all kept at a distance.

Now I felt like a cigarette butt hissing out in a urinal.

I leaned against the steering wheel and clutched it, holding on hard. I shook. I ground my teeth.

Get on mission, Purdoux, I told myself. Move on. For Frankie.

I felt a wave of numbness then. I passed through it to a cold, hard purpose.

"What do you think, Frankie?" I murmured.

There was no answer, of course. Despite what you might think from *Macbeth*, the dead aren't a talkative lot.

I reached under the seat. The gun was still there.

———

"Ohmigod, I can't believe I got a sunburn on that lake," Dulcet said. She was lying on the bed, wearing only a bathrobe, a cold washcloth on her forehead. Her wet hair was wrapped in a small white towel.

I was at the little table, cleaning my gun with a brush tool and oil. I like the smell of gun oil.

"Summer day, Dulcet. Water reflects the sunlight. Yeah, you can get burned. You want some more lotion?"

"I'm already like cake frosting. I just hope I don't start peeling. That would be so gross. Like the Mummy."

"You still up for helping me out tonight?"

"You're not going without me." She shot a narrow-eyed look at me. "I notice you took a shower before you came back. Was she *good*?"

If I changed the subject, Dulcet would know, just from that. "It was...sudden. She kind of overwhelmed me. Christ, we barely know each other."

Dulcet snorted. "I knew she was looking to get in your pants. You going to move in with her?"

"Fat chance. She feels weird about the whole thing. I'd be bad for her career. How about you? You meet any millionaires on the lake?"

"Like they'd go on a tourist boat. But I was thinking about millionaires. No, *billionaires*. Maybe an Arab sheik with a gold-plated private jet."

"You might find yourself locked up somewhere, you marry a rich oil billionaire. That's happened to people. So your guy said the Busted Flush was the cop bar?""There's two of them. He said the one that the detectives go to is the Busted Flush. You could sit out there all night, he might not show up."

"After what happened, Rynerson's going to be pissed off. He'll want a drink."

"Or he's just out driving around looking for your ass so he can shoot you. 'Slimby, Slimby, he's insane. Lookin fo' a bang-bang in the brain-brain.'"

"That an original Dulcet lyric?"

"From a Swee-Toof rap. Except for the Slimby. You should get rid of that gun, Slimby. Use mine. Police could get you on forensics and ballistics and all like dat rat-ta-tat-tat."

"*Dat rat-ta-tat-tat*, that's Swee-Toof too?"

"That's Wendell. Liked to say, 'all like dat rat-ta-tat-tat.'" She sighed. "Poor Wendell."

I thought Wendell spent most of his time finding ways to rip people off. But I didn't say it. "Yeah, I should get rid of the gun. But not tonight. Not for what I have in mind."

"You know if it's a cop bar, duh, it's full of cops. They're gonna be friends of his. They'll all stand up with him."

"Not if I get him out away from them."

"You going to follow him home?"

"Could be. Or you could lure him somewhere for me."

"Might be a long fucking naughty-night. And we gotta drive *allllllla* way back to Reno." Dulcet sat up, wincing. "I got stuff to make us sandwiches and coffee."

———

Almost nine o'clock. A busy summer night in Reno.

Cool baths, ibuprofen, and aloe lotion muting her sunburn, Dulcet sashayed into the casino. She was dressed in a tight, canary-yellow silk dress offering an abundance of cleavage and shiny-red spike heels. I ambled alongside her, figuring anyone checking us out would focus on her, and with luck, I'd go mostly unnoticed.

The Winner's Rocket was one of the oldest casinos still standing in Reno. At the entrance drive, a towering sign, outlined in lights, showed a cartoonish rocket ship eternally blasting off. The Populuxe front of the casino was a space-age arc, like the shape of a roller coaster, over a gigantic spray of windows.

The gaming machine maze was in a stadium-big room, loud with bells ringing—"happy sirens"—and electronic voices. It was mostly video slots, like Knock 'Em Rock 'Em and Silver Dollar Stacker, with celebrities winking from shining play surfaces, flashing digital handfuls of hundred-dollar bills. The games shouted at us as we went by. The players hunched at the games made me think of bees with their heads in flowers or wasps clustered, wriggling with focus on forgotten scraps at a picnic table. I had left my cowboy hat in the truck, was wearing clip-ons over my glasses, and a long dark brown leather coat that Dulcet had bought for me before she went to the lake. It partly buttoned up to cover the gun belt. I thought it conspicuous in the warm weather, but no one stared at me. Security men yawned. Waitresses carried trays of drinks to slot players.

Me, I checked out everyone from behind my shades, trying to see Rynerson if he was here, before he saw me. We crossed the fading pop-art carpet, passed out of the ear-rattling maze, and threaded through tourists waiting to see a pop singer named Aleena Zazu in the Space Room. We passed the roulette and craps and blackjack tables, the poker rooms, and '007's Baccarat room'. Signs led us to the Busted Flush Bar and Grill. I held back at the door, watching as Dulcet walked with enticing authority to the bar.

It was dimly lit with dark wood and brass, neon beer signs glowing like nebulae through the cigarette smoke, and the sound system loudly playing "Killin' Time" by Clint Black. I saw Rynerson almost immediately. He was at the end of the bar, looking up at a broad flat-screen showing a baseball game, the Oakland A's versus the Orioles. Sports betting figures rippled by underneath.

Dulcet had found a picture of him on the Reno PD website. She approached him and looked up at the game, clutching her purse nervously. She passed a few words with him—probably about the game, mentioning she was from the Oakland area—and posed to show him her cleavage without seeming too in-your-face about it.

"You have talent, Dulcet," I murmured. "Could've been a movie star."

19

I TURNED AWAY and headed back to the parking lot, the same noisy, strobing route. All the way to the pickup, I was thinking about Nadine. Where was Reno Police Department Lieutenant Nadine Graves right now? Back on the job, probably. Explaining things to her captain.

I found my way to the Ram and drove it slowly around the building to a lot overlooking the back of the casino, and on the way, the radio news gifted me a little something about Nadine.

"This massive seizure of fentanyl was prompted by Reno PD detective Nadine Graves, following a tip by an unnamed confidential informant." Nadine's voice came on. "'The large amount stored here seems to corroborate rumors that drug syndicates are doing less importing and more manufacturing right here in the United States.' That was Lieutenant Nadine Graves at the press conference this morning. Kwai Brothers Storage has issued a statement denying any knowledge of the illicit drugs and emphasizing its willingness to cooperate fully with the investigation. In sports, the Oakland Athletics trounced—"

I shut off the radio.

Dulcet and I had reconnoitered the back lot. The front was brightly lit, and the back was mostly dark except for a few small lights for delivery and security. There was a small employees-only parking section on the street side of the back with no one watching it. Past that, at the casino's rear load-in doors, were delivery trucks for food and liquor, an armored car, and a couple of armed security guards gabbing and smoking cigarettes.

They were a good fifty yards away, taking no notice as I slid the pickup into employee parking, right next to a big Chevy Silverado, making sure I had maximum room between the two vehicles. I was going to need the space if the setup worked out. I substituted my wire-rimmed glasses for the shades, pocketed the Ram's keys, and climbed out, leaving the truck unlocked. That was part of the setup.

I knew we were taking what Frankie would call a big-ass chance. It could be that Rynerson would decide the smartest thing to do, whatever the Kwais wanted, was to call for police backup. Shout, *He's going for a gun!* Or he could bring half a dozen cop pals from the bar. They'd be half drunk and ready to pull the trigger.

"Got to risk it, Frankie," I muttered.

I stationed myself behind the Chevy Silverado, took out a cigarette, and made a show of smoking. I was imagining Dulcet telling Rynerson her story.

"Detective Rynerson? I finally got away from him, but he's here looking for you."

He demands to know what the hell she's talking about.

She wriggles and looks at him big-eyed and speaks with her best earnestness. *"I don't know his name. Said to call him Slim. He took my truck. We're staying right here in the casino hotel. He scares me. I saw you on TV talking about*

*that big drug bust, and when he went out, I came downstairs
to see if I could find someone to help me and—"*

"What's this man look like?" he'll ask.

*"Tall and kinda skinny. Cowboy boots and hat. He left
that gun in my pickup, but he might have another."*

Sitting up straight at that, Rynerson demands, *"What
kind of gun?"*

"Colt .45, one of those old six-shooters."

Which would match the ballistics, Rynerson knows, in
the shooting of Deng and Hu. Once I was dead, he could
show the Colt to ballistics, proving he'd nailed the bad guy.

"Show me this truck of yours, lady," he'll say.

*"Okay. He's kind of drunk. Left the Ram unlocked, if
you want to look through it..."*

That's how it was supposed to go. Something not far
from that went down, because in under ten minutes,
Rynerson was striding ahead of Dulcet into the employee
parking lot, Rynerson figuring to check out the truck and
then call for backup.

I tossed the unsmoked cigarette away and unbuttoned
my coat.

Dulcet pointed out the black Dodge Ram. As Rynerson
got close to the pickup, I crouched behind the Silverado,
then slipped around so I'd be behind him. Dulcet held back.
She was lighting a cigarette and chuckling to herself.

I straightened up, drew the Colt, and watched
Rynerson open the pickup's door and step up to reach
inside. He shook his head and bent to look. "Lady, you sure
he put that gun under the seat?" Rynerson called out.

"Gun's right here, detective," I said.

His back stiffened. He straightened up and turned
slowly to me, his right hand going to the gun under his
blazer.

Then he froze, mouth open and eyes wide, seeing the Colt pointed at his chest from four feet away.

He lowered his hand, leaving his gun in its holster.

I smiled. "You're a quick study, Detective Rynerson."

"Not much of a judge of character, though," Dulcet said, coming up beside me, cigarette waggling in the corner of her mouth. She beamed at Rynerson and did a happy little girl clap with her hands.

"You fucking whore," Rynerson snarled.

Dulcet pretended outrage. "*Most* ungentlemanly!"

Rynerson glared at me. "What do you think you're getting away with here? There's guards right over there."

"What you call 'right over there' is a long piece away," I said. "They won't take any notice of us. The trucks block their view."

He licked his lips. "You shoot me, they'll hear it."

"They won't leave their posts. You start yelling for them, I'll shoot you in the mouth."

"What the fuck do you want?"

"Could citizen's arrest you for breaking into that Dodge Ram there," I said.

Dulcet giggled and said, "Can I help shoot him?" She took her gun from her purse.

"Naw, the fewest guns on display the better, Dulcet. I've got this."

She pouted, but she put the gun back in her purse.

I could see Rynerson's shoulders tightening, his hands fisting at his sides. He was scared, thinking of rushing me. "Don't make me shoot you before we get a chance to talk, Rynerson," I said, shaking my head. "I've arranged this meeting for two purposes. One, to ask a couple of questions. I know the answer to the first question. If you lie when I ask it, then I'll know you're just going to keep lying, and I'll shoot you and go have a drink somewhere. Here's the first question. And remember, *I know the answer*, so don't come out with bullshit. Question is, where is the Kwai factory for manufacturing and packaging of fentanyl? And don't say 'what factory.' You pretend you're not part of this, that'll get you shot too. I *know* you're part of it, and I know they're making their own fenny out there, and I know where it is. Just want you to say it."

"I..." He looked at the gun.

"You seem undecided," I said and cocked the gun. An action known to spur decision-making.

Rynerson let out a long breath and said, "It's at the old Air Force base. Nobody else uses the place anymore. Curtis LeMay Air Force Base, about fifty-five miles northeast. I've only been there once. But I saw the shit in hangar three."

I considered his face as he gave the answer, and afterward. My pretending to know had already done the trick. He wasn't lying.

"I'm no drug dealer," he blurted. "I was just there because..." He tried to glance past me again.

"Dulcet," I said. "Move out of the space between the trucks. Go somewhere discreet and stand watch. *Please.*"

"Oh, phooey. You are such a *buzz*kill," she said. She went off behind the trucks, trailing cigarette smoke.

"You were saying, detective?" I prompted.

"I was just there because they gave me some money to help 'em get Murray Kwai out of jail and, uh, it was more money than I ever saw in one place before and...I don't know. They made me go out there to pick it up. I don't even know why."

"Because they wanted you totally *in*, man," I said. "They wanted you to know you were in it up to your ass. And if they went down, you'd go down."

He stared at me. Evidently, that hadn't occurred to him. "Uh...yeah. Maybe." He glanced around again. "You said you had a, uh...another question?"

"Yeah. You ever see someone die from an opioid overdose?"

"Long time ago. When I was a patrolman."

"That's how my son died. He thought he was taking another drug, but the Kwais mixed fentanyl in. Just a teenager. You know how many people die of fentanyl overdoses every year in this country? Last year, it was one hundred twelve thousand three hundred and thirty-two—that we know of. Lots of others unidentified out there too. And the Kwais, among others, sell the shit all over the country. And you protect them so they can do it."

"*That*'s what this is about? Your *kid?*" He raised his hands between us, palms outward, and shook his head hard and fast. "Listen, I had nothing to do with that. I don't sell the shit!"

"You're part of what keeps it on the street. And you profit from it. But since you're a step back from dealing, and since I really don't give a fuck what happens to me, I'm going to give you a way out. Here." I gestured with the gun to my left. "Keep your hands away from your coat, and move over there slowly, facing me."

He licked his lips again and walked crab-like a few steps to where I'd told him to go, with me turning to keep facing him.

"Now hold on, goddamn it," Rynerson said, his hands clenching and unclenching. "There's a security camera right up there on that light pole."

"We made a stop at Walmart, bought some wire cutters. Before we went into the casino, I cut the camera cable. It's gone blank. No one seems in a hurry to fix it, if they've noticed. We can do all this in private."

"Do all what?"

"We can fight it out like two men. Gun to gun."

His eyes widened. "We could...we could put the guns down and fight with our fists."

I shook my head. "I'm not in your weight class. I'll use the equalizer."

I could see in my peripheral vision Dulcet watching through the window of the Silverado. She'd climbed up on its mounting step to watch and had her back to the guards. She was not doing what I'd asked of her, which put us both at risk. But I couldn't let myself get distracted by that now.

"Now, detective," I said. "I'm going to holster my piece. Count one, two, and go for your gun. And we'll see who comes out of this."

"Now hold on with this cowboy bullshit!" he hissed, teeth clenched. "My gun's under a strap with the safety on! That's not fair, asshole!"

"You make a good point," I said, nodding calmly. "Tell you what, very slowly, like the slo-mo on ESPN, reach in there, take the gun out. I'll let you take the safety off and hold it by your side. That'll give you the advantage. You won't even have a holster to pull it out of."

"Slimby, you're being stupid!" Dulcet called, louder than she should have. "He'll shoot you when you holster it!"

"Another good point," I said. "And do please curtail the commentary, Dulcet. Someone'll hear you."

"They'll hear the damned *guns,* dumbass," Rynerson growled. "How about we both just back off, and you go about your shit, and I'll go about mine! I'll fucking resign from the department!"

I shook my head. "You've been looking to kill me, and

you won't give it up, that I'm sure of. But here's what we'll do. Even more advantage for you. I'll holster the gun right now. And I'll give you time to take the safety off."

"Slimby, don't!" Dulcet called.

I smiled reassuringly at Rynerson and took two steps back. We were about nine feet apart now. My blood was playing a drumroll in my head, but I was unnaturally relaxed as I eased the six-gun's hammer off cock and holstered it.

Then, I lifted my hand away from it.

My gun hand didn't want to do that. It wanted to stay close. It wanted to draw right now.

Staring fixedly at me, mouth open, breathing hard, Rynerson reached slowly into his coat. There was a second when I saw a little twitch under the cloth of his blazer when he opened the strap and flicked the safety off. Then, with all the speed in him, he drew the gun, pretty damned fast, snapped it up at me—

I drew the Colt and, in the same motion, cocked and fired, and a red hole appeared on Rynerson's forehead just above the bridge of his nose.

His gun hand clenched as he died, but he was falling backward, and the shot went into the air.

I holstered the Colt, and Dulcet rushed up to my side. "Slimby!" She walked over and stared down at him. "Oh, lovely days! Can we take his money and his wallet and his gun and stuff?"

"Fuck no."

"How we going to monetize all this?"

"For God's sake, Dulcet, get in the truck. We have to leave."

"You were so fast and sure, Slimby, when you drew that

thing," Dulcet said as we got into the car. I started the engine. "Wendell would be proud of you."

I snorted and drove away quick but not too quick. "Wendell would be proud of me. I'm so touched."

"You are such an old grouch, Cowboy Curtis."

———

We went straight back to the motel. Dulcet absolutely insisted she was going to give me "the hummer of hummers, Slimby, after that duel with the creepy cop." I was thinking about Nadine and wasn't in the mood to celebrate shooting someone's brains out, not even that asshole. But I didn't want to hurt Dulcet's feelings. And she quickly got me into the spirit of the thing.

After that, we ordered dinner from a Chinese place that delivered and had some tequila. Dulcet informed me she had an appointment in the morning to get her hair done.

Dulcet had no problem immediately going from seeing a man shot in the head to discussing her haircut. I pictured her sitting cheerfully in the stylist's chair, nattering with the hairdresser, saying nothing about the gunfight. She'd ask for a recommendation on where to get her nails done and never mention seeing a man's brains splashed on the tarmac the night before. She was not foolishly indiscreet—except that one, stoned time with Jacques. And there would be no cognitive dissonance, no post-traumatic anxiety, as her hair was blown dry.

———

The next morning, I dropped Dulcet off at the hairdresser, saying I was going to get a local map and see if I could buy a rifle. She didn't ask me what I wanted with the rifle. She just kissed me and said, "Take your time. I'll walk back to the motel from here, just a few blocks. Don't have sex with any police personnel, though, okay? I think that'd be a stupid move."

Then she went into the hair studio.

I sat in the truck, staring at my burner phone for a while, before finally calling Nadine.

"Lieutenant Graves, narcotics."

"Hi Nadine. You do know it's me, right?"

"All too well. You see the news this morning?"

"No, I did not." I guessed what it might be.

"Just a second." A pause, then she said, "Had to shut my office door. Rynerson turned up dead. Tell me about that, Purdoux."

"Rynerson's dead? You sorry to see him go?"

"You're going to pretend you didn't know he was dead?"

"You got a record button pressed down somewhere? Or maybe it's always pressed down at Reno PD?"

"It's not. I'm pretty sure if we look at the security cameras inside the Winner's Rocket, where Rynerson was last seen alive—"

"Lots of people go to casinos around there, I understand. Something about it being the main industry in Reno."

"And when we check the ballistics—"

"Does this mean I don't get a second date?"

There was a long, crackling hesitation on the line. Then she said, "I was crazy to go there with you. I just...it felt right. But...I can't let you go around...doing what you're doing."

"Any chance we could have a drink and talk about it?"

Another long hesitation. "I'm on duty."

"How about lunch with your confidential informant? The CI is paying. I'll...inform you confidentially."

She snorted. "I'll let you know."

And she hung up.

——————

I had another stop to make. About a mile outside of Carson City was a small stadium. The digital lights on the sign outside advertised a two-day gun show. You can get a gun fast in Nevada. That's not even a phenomenon I approve of. I think waiting periods and thorough checks are a good idea. I mean, think of Eickhoff, for example. He was on psych meds, but he had a legal gun. He might well have bought it in Nevada.

But that day I felt different about it. I wanted two rifles, and I wanted them quick as I could get them.

I drove into the parking lot, noticed a number of men sitting on open tailgates, talking earnestly with men looking at something in the truck beds I couldn't see. The unauthorized sales, I figured.

I paid my way in and strolled by the booths on the main floor. Automatic weapons were the dominant weapons on offer, and semiautomatic. I passed a booth offering AR-15s, carbines, AK-47s, M16s, and flat-out tripod machine guns advertised as "only for novelty and non-functional." But I'd been to gun shows before. The dealer would wink and quietly tell you how to make the machine guns functional. Or you could Google it.

The big room echoed with male discussion. The place was crawling with guys in paramilitary desert-camo outfits, complete with bloused pants in military boots. There were a good many bushy-faced men in overalls too. There were a few women with their hair cut like country music singers, some of them towing kids with them.

Tables between booths were decked with good associated with the gun trade. They were festooned with pamphlets extolling White Nationalist groups, "sovereign citizen" videos, and combat knives. They sold T-shirts, camping equipment, police scanners, American flags, political bumper stickers, and books.

I found a booth that had what I was looking for. I asked a few questions of the burly, bearded man in a faded NRA T-shirt and pointed to the rifles I wanted, a scoped Remington .308 rifle and a working Winchester 1892 replica. We made a deal, and he said I had to fill out a form so he could run the federal background check. Nevada doesn't require the checks, but the feds do. "It'll come back, clearing you or not, in just a few minutes," he said. I complied and waited. He came back to me frowning. "Says delayed. Might take a few days."

"Delayed why?"

He shrugged. "You'd know better than I would."

I figured Rynerson had put some kind of red flag out there. Or it could be left over from the Renquist case.

I nodded. We canceled the purchase, and I headed to the door, thinking about the guys at the tailgates.

I walked past the outer hall and into the parking lot, past a tent where they sold ammo. They wouldn't sell it inside where a terrorist or some lunatic might conceivably load a display weapon and use it.

I strode into the parking lot, lifting my hat long enough to wipe away sweat. The sun was beating down hot, lancing bright from countless windshields. I walked to the Ram and, discreetly as I could behind the truck's open door, took the Colt and the gun belt from under the seat, buckled it on, and tied the holster down. Then, I put on the long brown leather coat I'd left folded on the seat. Hot for a coat like that, but I wanted the gun with me. I didn't trust the tailgate sellers.

I looked over the scattering of tailgaters, picked a rail-thin guy sitting on a folding lawn chair between the open doors of a high-roof cargo van. He wore an oil-stained red ball cap and sunglasses with camo-style frames. Long, dirty black hair fell to his shoulders, and a graying mustache drooped on his V-shaped face. His beaky nose was whitened by zinc oxide against the sun. He wore a faded red and blue Hawaiian shirt, looking out of place with his camo fatigue pants. His forearms were blue with blurry old tattoos.

"Help you?" he asked in a gravelly voice. Behind him, the inner walls of the van were racked with rifles, several AR-15s, two 7.62mm light machine guns, a rack of extended-magazine pistols, two Uzis, a civilian sniper rifle that looked to be law enforcement surplus, a Winchester replica, and a combat shotgun. I spotted an MK13, a SOCOM sniper rifle. I wasn't checked out on that, and couldn't afford it anyway.

On the floor behind the dealer were two long, narrow crates. One was marked M20.

"That a bazooka?" I asked.

"It ain't a vacuum cleaner."

"Does it launch?"

"It will. Has to be jiggered for that."

I was tempted by the bazooka. But I didn't have time for jiggering.

"You do background checks?"

"Fuck no," he said, snorting. "Why'd I be sitting out here?"

"That Remington M700 police sniper rifle need jiggering to work?"

"Fully functional and fire-ready."

"And that Winchester, that a prop from an old movie or what?"

"It's a working replica. The best one: Browning .44 mag. Close copy of the Winchester 1892. Ready to rock and roll."

Same kind I'd had back in Texas. "They're both used, I assume."

"Yeah, but in great shape."

"What are you asking for those two weapons?"

"A thousand for the Remington, and two grand for the Winchester."

I shook my head. "That's double the going price."

He shrugged. "It's an illegal sale. You pay more for my risk. You could be ATF."

"I look like a fed to you?"

"Nope. But them's the prices."

"You know what, you'll sell these two to me at the legal rate. I'll give you an extra hundred per weapon for your risk. That'll be six hundred for the Remington, and eleven hundred for the Winchester."

"You know what?" He shook his head. "I don't like that 'you'll sell them to me' shit. Fuck off. Get away from my van."

He stood up, reaching behind him for a hideaway pistol I'd been expectingI swept the right wing of my coat back, drew, and had the muzzle of the Colt pressed against the zinc oxide on his nose before he could bring his pistol into play. He froze, and his eyes crossed as he looked down at the Colt's silver barrel.

I said, "Take your hand slowly from that gun or your last breath'll be through a new hole."

His face reddened. His nostrils flared. I thought I was going to have to shoot him. It would be a messy situation. It could ramify badly.

But then he slowly brought his empty hand back, palm up. "Whatever. I got hardly no cash for you to steal. I mostly use Venmo and PayPal."

"I'm not going to rob you. I'm going to pay you. The rate I quoted...in cash."

"Somebody's going to see you with that gun, buddy."

"I doubt they'll call the cops. Turn around and keep your hands where I can see them." He did, and I holstered the gun. "I'll let you keep that piece in its cute little back holster there. You go for it, I'll kill you."

"I'll be chill. You're fast as I've seen. So you wanted the Winchester and..."

He climbed in, got the guns down, put them in a long cardboard case, and, head ducked under the roof of the van, pushed the case toward me.

I said, "If these guns aren't in good working condition, I'm going to find out if the license plate on this van is legit. One way or another, I'll find you. I've killed a number of people in the last month or so, and I don't give a fuck anymore. You believe me?"

He looked into my eyes. Then he nodded.

I nodded back. "Turn around. I'll count out the money. I'll put it here under your copy of *Guns & Ammo Magazine*."

The gun dealer grunted with suspicion, but he turned around. I counted out the exact amount I'd promised him, put it down on the floor of the van, slapped the periodical on top of it, then picked up the case and carried it, kind of awkwardly, to the Ram. I got the case in the cab, behind the seats.

After I made a stop at the ammunition tent, I got back into the Ram, thinking as I went, *That gun-get could have gone south. Would I have shot him? Will I go after him if the guns are no good?*

I thought about it and then I answered myself as I drove out of the parking lot. "Yes, and yes."

———

The restaurant was called the Biggest Little Diner. Noisy with people having lunch. Country music played on the sound system. Lots of comfortable, high-backed booths. Rusty mining gear hung on the faux-rock walls.

Nadine was wearing a crisp, tailored suit. Her hands were cradling a cup of coffee. Her hair was tied tightly back. Her eyes were a little red, like she hadn't slept well. Her gun was visible on her right hip, as compatible with her suit as any fashion accessory.

"Hey, detective, what's up?" I said softly, sitting down across from her.

She pushed a menu toward me. "Brunch. I recommend the eggs Benedict over the smoked salmon."

"So be it." I was aware of Nadine looking me over as I waved to the waitress.

"You look like you just freshly shaved."

"Shower, clean clothes, shaved. A guy can hope."

She smiled wryly. "Not today, you can't. Not with me." She lowered her voice. "So Rynerson fired his police special before he was shot down."

"Did he?"

"And he was shot with the same weapon that killed Deng and Han. Likely a Colt revolver. Old school."

"Um...could we go somewhere, and I could check you for a wire, like you requested last time?"

To my surprise, she blushed at that. "Not appropriate, Purdoux."

My heart sank. "Is that where we're at now?"

She gave a shrug so small it was almost invisible. "I don't know what happened to me that day."

"What happened was us," I said, leaning toward her. I wanted to take her hands in mine, but she was all copped up, and I didn't want to embarrass her. Nor did I want to let myself in for the feeling that'd come when she snatched her hands back. "Chemistry is chemistry, Nadine. And recognition..." I wasn't quite sure how to say it. "It just is what it is. I recognized you."

"What, you're claiming, like...reincarnation?"

"No. Just...two people who are so alike in some ways they can see right into each other. It felt right, Nadine."

She closed her eyes, shook her head. "It doesn't now."

Then she leaned close and made a come-here gesture with her forefinger.

I lifted off my seat, over the table, and she whispered in my ear, "You are still *killing people*. That is not a turn-on."

Feeling gut-punched, I sat back in my seat, and the young lilac-haired waitress came and took our orders, chirping "Perfect!" to everything we chose. She bustled off. We sat in silence, hearing voices from other tables talking about irritating new gaming regulations and tourists who think they can park just anywhere.

Then she leaned close and said, "I'll prove there's no wire, right here."

I blinked. "Uh...really?"

She nodded. "I am not sorry that Lieutenant Rynerson is dead. It's probably for the best."

Nadine waited. Then, I got it. "Oh. You wouldn't have said that if—"

"Right. Now listen. You shouldn't have done it anyway, Slim."

"I'm sorry, Nadine." I shook my head. I could taste the bitterness. "Frankie wasn't your son. You judge me when you've lost a child that way."

"That wasn't Rynerson."

I just looked at her. She sighed and poured herself more coffee from the plastic carafe on the table. "Okay," she said. "I get it. It's an organization, and he was part of it. But you can't stop that organization by throwing your own life away."

She cared if I lived or died. That was something anyway.

"I can make a dent, detective. That would save some lives. At least, I hope so. It's a reason for living."

She whispered, "Killing is a reason for living? You know how that sounds, Purdoux?"

"You know what I mean. I'm talking about killing murderous bottom-feeding drug dealers."

"They might deserve it but that doesn't keep you outta jail."

"Look, —maybe you could talk me into leaving it right here. If...you're willing to leave with me. Right now. Today."

She leaned back. "Leave...with you?"

"We could go somewhere else. I'll go with you to a Paiute rez in another state, if they'll let me live there. You could do law enforcement there. A rez always needs a good tribal cop. We could, you know..." My mouth was dry. I wet my lips and took the plunge. "Get married."

"I..." Nadine closed her eyes. Her lips buckled.

"Right." I went on, "We barely know each other. In some ways. But in another, we do know each other."

There was a glistening at the corners of her eyes that became very small wet pathways. "*I can't.* I should...I should marry one of my own people. And...and anyway, we'd still be on the run anywhere we went. I mean, if they figure out these killings are down to you. The Kwais can get the word out. I told you about Wessen."

I nodded. "The DA. He might be their man."

Nadine thumbed the tears away, scowling because she didn't want me to see that. , Then she made a show of having a cup of coffee, like there was nothing else on her mind.

"Nadine, forget I said anything. About you and me.—"

"No. I'm not going to forget it. I'm...It's something good to remember. That you asked, despite the craziness of it. If we'd met in some different way. If you didn't have the history you do. I even feel like we could maybe be happy. But—"

"You can't consider being happy?"

"Or it could be hell! And I'm not going to step out of a career for any man, I don't care who."

I nodded. Checkmate. "How about Tatanka the Wrestler? Would you do it for him?"

She pretended to ponder that seriously. "Okay, maybe for him."

We both laughed a little at that. Rueful and sad laughter. Then the waitress brought our food, and we ate it mechanically, saying almost nothing.

"So if you're still not wearing a wire," I said, pushing my plate aside. "Then..." I leaned toward her a little and lowered my voice. "Rynerson told me the dope factory is at the Curtis LeMay Air Force Base. The place is officially abandoned. Only it isn't unoccupied. Hangar three, he said."

She put her fork down and stared at me. "You believe him?"

"I think he was telling the truth. He was pretty scared."

"And then—what'd you do?"

"I let him draw on me. Let him get his gun out before I drew mine."

"You're kidding."

"Nope."

"That's...this is the real damn world here, Slim. You don't take chances like that."

"I was pretty confident."

She wiped her mouth with a napkin, put some cream in her coffee, and watched it billow. "You're not going out there, right? To the old base? You know how outgunned you'd be. I know you're a bright guy, and that would not be smart. So you're *not going out there*. Right? Say, 'right.'"

"Haven't made up my mind yet." I had 95 percent made up my mind. But technically, I wasn't lying.

"What am I supposed to do with the information you gave me, by the way?"

"You could push for a raid. Get out ahead of me."

"A raid on what basis? 'My CI heard this from a guy he killed'? Or—I heard chatter on the street? The first one would get you arrested. The second one would not be taken seriously."

"They could watch the place. Figure it out. But..." My voice rumbled in my throat. "The word would get to the Kwais that their factory was going to be watched. Before the whole thing could get organized."

She nodded. "They'd pull out—lock, stock, and barrel."

"You could go to the DEA. They might start an observation without alerting the local cops. I mean, it's thirty miles out of town."

"They take a long time to make a move."

"Okay." I shrugged. "I felt like I had to tell you, Lieutenant Graves. Somebody should know."

"I am not dismissing the information. I'm just saying nothing's going to happen till I can get more evidence their little factory is where you say it is."

The waitress came and asked if we wanted more coffee, and we said no. Nadine frowned silently at her cup, and I tried to think of another way to get her to see me alone. Then the bill came, which I insisted on paying with cash.

She said, "Should I ask where you got that hundred-dollar bill?"

"Rather you didn't."

"Because you don't want to lie to me."

"Nadine. What do you say we go sit in the pickup and talk? I can put on the air conditioner."

She gazed at me for a long moment. Then looked away. "No, no, I don't think so, Mr. James Purdoux."

"You don't want to be alone with me?"

"Something like that." Her phone chimed, and she looked at it. "Got to go to a meeting with the captain. Still explaining a lot of stuff regarding my CI, and my not answering my phone on the way to the rez. And..."

"I'm a pain in the ass, huh?"

"Yeah. But thanks for lunch."

She stood up, straightened her jacket, and said, "Come on outside a minute."

We stood outside in the shade under a concrete overhang. It was hot in the shade. Was going to be hotter out in the sun.

Nadine glanced around before saying, "I'm going to make some discreet inquiries at the DEA and some other places where I trust the people. It'll take me a few days to figure out, and get the right people on the line. Don't do anything stupid while I'm working on this."

"I...won't do anything stupid."

She looked at me skeptically and took my hand, held it for a tantalizing moment, and said, very low, "Slim, thanks for asking. About...you know. In another life..." She squeezed my hand and turned away. Then she stopped, turned, and pointed at me. "Nothing *stupid*, Purdoux. Remember."

"Smart as I'm capable of."

"That's what I'm afraid of."

I watched her walk over to her Chevy Tahoe. And right then, I made up my mind about what I was going to do next.

I was at 100 percent.

20

I DROPPED the Ram off at the motel and started walking east along the highway. I could feel the lowering sun searing the back of my neck.

There was a used car lot within a half mile of the motel. With scarcely a word, hardly looking at my driver's license, a heavy-set older Native American guy with a quid of smokeless in his cheek sold me a slightly dented dark-blue 1996 Toyota Tacoma, with a mountain of miles on it, for most of the rest of my cash. I didn't figure I'd need the money.

I drove the Tacoma to the motel. The engine sounded good. Those old Toyota trucks run forever. As I parked next to the Ram, I saw Dulcet scowling at me through the front window of our room. She had her arms crossed on her chest.

Can't seem to get right with women, I thought.

"Why the Toyota truck?" she asked, before I'd quite made it through the door.

I closed it behind me, took off my hat, and sank into the musty rocking chair. *Let's Make a Deal* was on the television, muted, a contestant pretending to dance in silent delight.

Dulcet was wearing only a knee-length teddy, like something from the 1940s. The antiquated air conditioner under the window was loudly grinding away, and it blew on the skirt of the slip, lifting it a little. Her new hairdo was blonder and cut in a short, wavy bob, like Marilyn Monroe in some movie I couldn't remember the name of.

"Your hair looks nice," I said. "You're looking even more like Monroe. Or maybe Jayne Mansfield."

She closed the curtains on the window. "The truck, Slimby."

"I've got to go recon that place in the desert tonight. I don't want to use your truck. Could be the Ram was reported related to that Rynerson thing. And it's big and noticeable and noisy."

She looked at me closely. "You are so full of shit. You don't think you're coming back, and you want to leave me my truck."

I winced. She had me.

"Well..." She went on, "I'm going with you. So I hope that stupid little Toyota truck can make it back."

"Dulcet..."

No way was I taking her with me. I shook my head firmly. "You know what? I had a rough day. Almost got into a gunfight at the gun show."

"A gunfight at a gunshow? Too on the nose, Cowboy."

"It was kind of stressful. Make me feel better if you could sit on my lap, and I could hold you and tell you the story."

Her scowl became a pout. She ran over to me on her tiptoes and slid onto my lap. I put my arms around her. We canoodled, and she murmured, "You shouldn't bullshit me, Slimby. I want to help."

"I know." She felt good in my arms after that chilly lunch with Nadine.

"I found those rifles, Slimby. Hiding something under our bed is pretty weak."

"I wasn't hiding them from you, just wanted them out of sight."

"You didn't buy those for reconnoitering. And you bought *two*. I betcha one was for me!"

I smiled. "No, my darling Dulcet, no. I will need them both, alternately."

"You said darling. *Am* I your darling?"

"Sure." I've never been clear on what a darling is.

"So I'm coming with you."

"It's going to involve crawling through the desert at night on my belly, maybe for like a quarter mile."

"You liar."

"Nope."

"You're kidding."

"I'm not."

"You'll crawl through cactus and get a scorpion up your ass."

"See? You wouldn't be into crawling through dirt and cactus and maybe getting a scorpion in your panties."

She pouted. "I guess not."

"I'd rather have someone to come back to."

"*Would* you come back?"

"Sure. You want to order pizza, later?"

"Yes, please, and ooh, tell me the story of how you almost shot someone today."

————

But when it got dark, and it was time for me to go, Dulcet was pacing back and forth, arms crossed like an angry wife waiting for a tardy husband.

"Only thing you're missing is the rolling pin," I said as I started loading the Remington. I had already checked that the rifles were cleaned and oiled, and all the moving parts were working.

She flickered a smile at that and then put a thumb knuckle in her mouth and bit down on it.

"We both know you're smart, Dulcet," I said.

She looked at me with her head cocked. A little startled.

"You're intelligent." I went on, "And you *know* this excursion is something you can't help with. I'd be constantly distracted, worrying about you. You're a second target for them."

"That's one less bullet for you then," she said.

"I don't want either one of us to get shot." I was pretty sure I'd get shot tonight. But no reason to share that hunch with Dulcet.

She sighed and slumped into the rocking chair. "You even know where it is?"

"Found the base on the internet. Not much detail about it. But I know where it is."

"Whatever, stupidhead Gumby Slimby, whatever. You cleaned those guns, but did you clean your glasses?"

My turn to smile. "Yes, I did."

"Letting some four-eyed lunatic out there in the middle of the night with..." She shook her head. "Where's the tequila?"

"Over there with what's left of the pizza."

I had a small plastic sack I was dumping the rest of the ammunition into.

"You think that's the way to carry your stupid bullets?" she asked. "Rattling around in a white plastic sack?"

"Um...no. I should have bought something for that at the gun show. But I was kind of in a hurry to get out of there."

"There's a Salvation Army store by the laundry place. I saw some army-surplus stuff in the window. I bought a green army backpack, not very big. Was a present for you. I was going to wrap it. It's in the closet there."

"You...are so thoughtful."

"You...are not."

I went to the closet and found the pack. Green cammie. Looked Vietnam War-era. Jungle gear. I organized the ammo in the back of it and in the side pockets. Then I put the rifles back in their cardboard cases, for now, and carried them out to the truck. I came back in and strapped on my gun belt.

I took a deep breath, decided I needed to pee...and I needed a moment to chill. I had a feeling climbing up my back like an icy rat.

I went into the bathroom, peed, and then went to the sink and had a look at myself. Who was that crazy fucker?

That feeling bit into me, and I felt my heart sinking. Suddenly, the bathroom smelled funkier, the walls looked more cracked, the mirror grimier, my eyes more sunken. I turned around and saw every speck of old-time grime in the bathroom. Saw the rust on the bathtub-shower combo. Saw mold on the old plastic shower curtain. Saw stains on the ceiling. Saw the tiles curling up in the corners.

This is what you're seeing soon before dying, Purdoux, I told myself. *This is where you are. With a half-psychotic woman, a damaged child in a woman's body. You're surrounded by guns and liquor, and still angry at everything, and this is where you find yourself. This moldering motel bathroom.*

"What do you think, Frankie?" I asked softly.

He answered with his silence. His eternal silence would always tell me what I needed to know.

The black wave came—and washed over me. I shivered and clutched the edge of the sink. I just let it come.

Get it together. You've got something to finish.

I turned around, ran some water in the rust-stained sink, and splashed some water on my face.

Didn't make me feel better.

Turned off the spigot, dried my face, and said inside myself, *The mission matters, Purdoux.*

I put on the brown leather coat to protect me from the underbrush and maybe provide a little camouflage. Underneath it, I had my black cowboy shirt. I wore jeans and my boots. Not ideal boots for this expedition. I would be wearing no hat. "Hey, Dulcet. Can I borrow Wendell's lighter? Might need it."

"Ohhhhh...kay." She took it from her purse and handed it over.

I tied down my holster. Dulcet started singing her twist on a Johnny Cash song as I picked up the keys to the Toyota truck. "Oh, don't take your guns to town, son! Leave your guns at home, Slim..."

"I promise not to take them to town," I said.

I blew Dulcet a kiss and went out the door. I hoped she'd be okay.

But my mind was on Nadine.

———

Yeah, sure, I exaggerated about crawling a quarter mile through the desert.

With the Remington and backpack strapped on behind, the Winchester in my hands, I trotted along, bent over low, wending through the scrub and around boulders, watching for cacti clumps, and trying not to think about scorpions. I could smell sage and pinyon pine. I heard the choppy call of a nightjar. Saw the golden eyes of a shoco owl looking out at me from its burrow in an outcropping of gray rock. As I looked, the little owl's eyes closed.

There was a half-moon. Just enough light to help me set my boot steps on the uneven, sandy ground.

The Toyota pickup was parked a half mile west at the end of a dirt road, partially hidden in an abandoned construction site where someone had started to build a house and given up before it was finished.

About two hundred yards east of me was the nearest corner of the chain-link fence around the defunct Curtis LeMay Air Force Base. There was a light mounted on it, illuminating a small area of fencing, making it look like reptile scales. Another light was in the distance on the farther corner of the fence. I could pick out the dark shapes of old utility buildings and barracks beyond the fence. The only other light showed as a yellow glow over the top of what was probably an administrative building. I figured that light from farther east was coming from the hangars. Maybe hangar three.

The desert is hot during the day, and temperatures drop sharply at night. It was nice and cool out there. Fragrant, like a moonlit garden, right up to the edge of the fence.

Boots crunching in rubbly dirt and sand, I headed toward the lake of darkness between the two light poles. The closer I came to the outer perimeter of the base, the louder my heart pounded. It was more like anticipation than fear.

Going to get it done. Lay the burden down for good. One way or another.

I made it all the way to the fence, barely lit at this angle, by the thin moonlight.

There was razor wire along the top of the fence. Highly inconvenient, new-looking razor wire. The shiny braces for it had been bolted on top of the old chain-link frame. The cartel was quite sensibly trying to keep people off the property.

Looking through the fence, I could see the dark angular shapes of the abandoned buildings, weeds and cacti growing up between them. Just enough light to show at least half of the windows had been broken out. I reckoned that in years past, before the fentanyl factory was set up, the abandoned base had been raided by looters looking for copper and other metals. The razor wire and the lights were supposed to discourage thieves and homeless campers, so the cartel didn't have to bother burying bodies out in the desert. I'd seen a light over the front gate too. And a security camera on a pole out there. It was a big, ramshackle, overgrown property. With any luck, they hadn't set up a lot of security cams.

Or maybe I'd already used up all my luck.

Right now, my concern was that razor wire. There was concrete along the bottom of the fence. I found a place where it had been bent back. Not enough to crawl through, but enough room for the Winchester. I pushed it through, gently as I could.

Then I took off the Remington, laid it down carefully on the ground, keeping its muzzle and scope out of the dirt. I took off the backpack, took out the wire cutters we'd used to sever the cable at the casino parking lot, and a pair of heavy leather work gloves. I looked around and saw no gang sentries. But I knew there'd be some tramping by. Got to move fast.

I put on the gloves, clamped the cutters between my teeth, grabbed hold of chain links, stuck the pointy toes of my cowboy boots in the links, and started to climb. It was awkward and noisy. Softly cussing, I got my shoulders parallel with the bottom of the razor wire, held on with my left hand, and used the other to cut through the narrower parts of the wire. The outline of the anti-personnel wire was silhouetted against the peeling white paint of the building beyond the fence. It was hard work, but the strips of thin metal parted, twanging apart one by one. Using the sharp-edged jaws of the cutters, I pushed the loose wire down so it hung toward the other side of the fence, away from me. I moved laterally on the fence, thinking how vulnerable I was to being shot up there. I moved a yard down the fence line and pushed down the other ends of the clipped wire.

I dropped down outside the fence, put the gloves and the cutters in the pack, strapped it on, and then strapped on the Remington. Then I climbed the fence below the gap I'd made, grunting as I slung a leg over the top. My pants crotch caught on some of the chain link at the top, but I writhed free, got the other leg over, and dropped to the ground inside, landing with a wince on the balls of my feet.

I crouched, picked up the Winchester—

And froze, listening. Worried about all the noise I'd made.

I heard voices. Two men talking, not so far away.

I couldn't make out what they were saying, except a guy with a high kind of voice said something about a schedule.

I walked as quietly as I could to the nearest building,

probably a barracks, because it was long and only one story high. I sidled slowly along, close to the wall, stepping irregularly—like I'd learned when I was hunting with my dad—to keep from making the obvious sound of approaching footsteps. Pausing at the corner of the building, I heard the staticky background buzz, the raw stuff of men's voices from a walkie-talkie.

"Copy," said one of the men, clearly.

I was still in deep shadow and risked a slight peek around the corner. I saw two men in silhouette against the white-painted building. I could just make out that they were in uniform. Standard security guard outfits.

It could be some shell company owned by the Kwais had bought the abandoned property from the military. For appearance's sake, their guards were in security uniforms. Guys who knew exactly what this property was being used for.

But what if they *didn't* know?

Were they just security guard hirelings, who knew nothing past their paycheck and days off?

If that was the case, then by my internal book of rules, killing them would be cold-blooded murder. There'd be no justice in it. None at all.

One of them lit a cigarette, and I saw their faces in the red lighter glow. I could see they had walkie-talkies clipped to their belts, and each man had an AK-47 strapped over a shoulder. An old model of assault rifle, but sturdy and deadly...and Russian. I remembered the cartel involved cooperation between Russian and Chinese gangsters.

Still...they might just be ordinary security guards.

I had to know.

Then the guy with the cigarette said, "Nah, I don't bowl. I play some Pai Gow. That's my idea of a sport."

The other guy laughed scoffingly, and then cigarette guy walked away, giving a small parting wave. He had his rounds to finish. The other one turned my way, and I eased my head back under cover.

I listened, holding my breath, and heard the approaching footsteps of the guard.

He was whistling softly to himself.

Just a security guard? Or a hired killer protecting the people who'd killed my son?

He was walking right up to the corner of the building. If he wasn't one of them, I'd have to try to knock him cold. Something I'd never been trained to do. It's not like you can just slam a guy on the head and he drops silently, out cold. Not in real life.

If I shot him, the gunshot would bring the others running. How many others? I had no idea. But I figured a sizable force of armed thugs protected the operation. Better not fire a gun until I got close to my real targets.

I took my Buck knife from my pocket, thumbed it open, and waited, picturing stabbing right through the voice box, and from there, slashing his jugular. That'd smother his outcry. I am no commando and wasn't sure I could pull that move off. Never stabbed a guy in the neck before.

The sentry was close now. Too close for me to elude. Even if he knew what he was guarding, did that justify killing him? I had no problem with killing the men at the top and anyone who tried to go after me down below. But this guy?

What do you think, Frankie? Should I kill him?

21

HE MADE up my mind for me. He was looking to the right when he stepped out, and he was yawning, not at his most alert. I was to his left. The sentry didn't see me, which was a relief. I didn't want to kill this guy unless I had to.

He walked off to the east, his back to me, down along the fence line. Going away from the place where I'd broken in. He wouldn't see those slashed anti-personnel wires.

I let out a long, slow breath, folded the knife and put it away, and looked around the corner of the building again. All clear.

I turned the corner and prowled down the graveled, weed-grown lane between the two buildings. I watched for security cameras, but didn't see any. The building ran to a main road that cut down the middle of the base, one end dimly lit by a light mounted on the main gate. The road was two-lane concrete, cacti and weeds growing up from the numerous cracks. In places, you had to look closely to see the road.

Turning, I saw the other sentry walking away from me toward the runways on the other side of the base.

I laid the Winchester down, stretched out flat beside it, and peered around the corner of the building, looking west toward the hangars. One of the hangars was lit up. It was a little to the north of the road, maybe four city blocks down. Two men with rifles—probably more AKs—stood together talking. Their body language was all boredom. That was good. Boredom meant weak alertness.

Me, I was feeling pretty goddamned alert. My mouth was dry, my heart was thudding, and my hands were sweaty. I was nervous as all hell.

But afraid? Not so much.

Because I still didn't care what happened to me. I did hope that when they got me, it was a clean kill. I knew there was a chance they'd grab me wounded but alive. Torture would follow like night follows day. It'd be one long, long night. They'd want to know who had sent me, and wouldn't be inclined to believe I was alone in this.

I made up my mind not to surrender, no matter what.

Getting to my feet, I moved up east, pressed against the building in deep shadow. I came to the next weedy lane between buildings. Looking to the left, I saw a sentry walking by to the west near the fence. He was going to see that slashed wire soon.

I waited until he passed, then I started running, feeling the heavy jiggle of the Remington police rifle on my back, the stock bumping against me. Not the slickest setup.

I passed a building with a rusty sign labeling it the officers' mess, then came to the administration building. Two floors high. Next to it was a military air traffic control tower. The tower was dark, but there were lights on the first floor of the admin. And there were three vehicles out front: a Jeep, a silver and black limousine, and a white GMC Sierra late-model pickup.

The limousine caught my eye. Who was here who warranted a limousine? This might be my lucky night.

"Could be destiny, Frankie," I muttered, jogging toward the truck.

Then I saw the sentry, and he heard the sound of my quick footsteps crunching in gravel. I heard him react. "Who's there?"

I crouched behind the white truck. The tailgate was down, and I could see a four-gallon container of spare gasoline strapped into one corner behind the cab. It gave me an idea.

The sentry was moving, muttering into his walkie-talkie as he stepped out onto the lane between the buildings. He had his AK-47 in his left hand. He said, "Copy that," replaced the walkie-talkie on his belt, and took the AK in both hands.

Hunched over, I crept around the truck, came up behind him, and slammed him in the back of the head with the Winchester. Hard.

Hoping it would take him down. Hoping it wouldn't kill him.

He went to his knees, groaning. I gave him another hard tap, and he fell forward.

I gave a moment's thought to appropriating the AK for myself instead of the Winchester. A matter of firepower. But I didn't know what the fuck I was doing with an AK-47. No experience with them at all.

I moved quickly to the side entrance of the admin building, found the door unlocked, and stepped in. There was light coming from a room down the hallway, and the sound of a machine running with a flapping, fluttering sound.

I walked as softly as I could along the creaking floor—tile over wood—and peeked around the edge of the open door. Two guys inside, burly men each with a Glock 45 on their hips. They stood with their backs to me at a money-counting machine. One was feeding loose cash into the machine. The other was watching. The taller one was blond, and the other had receding black hair. Both were wearing expensive golfing clothes. Why, I do not know.

They were talking in Russian. Occasionally, they used English words or phrases, like "big interest" and "real estate," which clued me that they were talking about investments.

The cartel paid them well because the temptation had to be big. In the middle of the room, about five feet by six feet each, were two stacks of cash bundles. All pressed and neat from the machine. I could see twenties, fifties, and hundreds.

Must be a couple of mill there.

I brought the Winchester to my shoulder. There was a round in the chamber, and the safety was off.

"You guys come out here from the golf course?" I asked because I didn't want to shoot them in the back.

They turned, both of them blue-eyed and with high cheekbones, the blond one with a neatly trimmed beard. He had drawn his gun as he turned, so I shot him first, through the heart. I worked the Winchester's lever and shot the second guy as he drew his Glock and rushed me, snarling. He got so close that the rifle's muzzle left a powder burn on his forehead around the bullet hole.

He dropped limply at my feet, blood pooling around his head. I stepped back to avoid the red puddle and hurried back to the side door. I heard shouting in the distance, risked a look into the hall—no one coming yet.

I took a deep breath and ran down to the side door. All clear outside. But it wouldn't be clear for long.

I took four long strides to the GMC Sierra, leaned my Winchester up against a wheel, climbed in back, unstrapped that gas can, lifted it, grunting—it was heavy with six gallons in it—and carried it to the tailgate. I saw flashlights probing toward me from the main road.

I set the gas can down, jumped to the gravel lane, turned, and grabbed the big gas can with my right hand, nearly pulling my arm out of its socket as I slung it down. Snatching up the Winchester with my left hand, I went back into the building as fast as my burden would let me.

I carried the can into the room with the money. I set it down near the stack of cash. I leaned the Winchester against the stack of money—there was something pleasing about that—and took off the backpack and the Remington. Then—because I'm not a dweeb—I took $20,000 in cash, two bundles with currency straps from one pile, as a gift for Dulcet, should I ever have the chance to give it to her. She could add it to her money for starting a business. The bundle went into one side pocket of my backpack. Another two bundles went into the other side to send to Latisha at the churchin the unlikely event I'd get the chance to send them.

Fast as I could, I put the backpack on and slung the Remington over a shoulder. Then I poured the gasoline on the two piles, tossed the can at the money, got out Wendell's lighter—

Shouts from outside. Sentries coming.

I crouched, touched the edge of the spreading pool, lit the gasoline, grabbed the Winchester, and had to backpedal fast as the flames flashed up the money with a big *whoosh*. I sprinted to the door but I jumped back into the room with the burning money as someone at the side door fired an AK burst at me.

Bullets smacked up the hallway, and flames roared at my back. I felt hairs singeing off the back of my neck, and I thought, *Brilliant, Purdoux, you're going to burn to death.*

I levered a round in the Winchester, took half a step into the hall, swinging left. I caught a glimpse of the AK shooter, and as I centered the sights on him.

I fired, and he fell backward. I levered another round in. The heat behind me was intense. The flames were reaching the dead men by the money counter. I could smell human meat cooking. Shreds of burning money drifted past me like fiery butterflies.

Gunfire cracked from the open door to the outside. I saw the muzzle flash from behind a car on the gravel lane. I fired, levered another shot in, fired, levered, fired, again and again, two shots a second, until I'd used seven rounds. Maybe three left in the rifle. I'd be sorry to lose the rifle but...I fired three times more, clicked on empty. There was no return fire—not yet. Someone was keeping their head down. Or maybe I'd hit them.

Feeling flames licking at my heels, I turned, tossed my rifle into the fire to take care of fingerprints. I drew the silver revolver, and ran down the hall to the right, the Remington clanking against me. Smoke billowed, giving me some cover. That's when the bullets in the Glocks worn by the dead men started to go off, some of them banging through the doorway behind me.

More rifle bullets cracked up close to my left, and then I was on the stairs, panting, pounding up to the second floor. I ran to a window looking out onto the big sheet-metal hangars. They were set off to the right a little, and there was a runway stretching down to the landing field road. Fighter jets and small planes and choppers would come in on the landing field, trundle down and turn into the hangars.

There were huge hangar numbers painted in red on the corrugated metal buildings. A clot of sentries stood in front of the nearest Hangar, number three. Some of the sentries were pointing at the admin building, others waved their hands. They eemed to be arguing about what to do. They'd heard the explosion and the gunfire, and were getting updates on walkie-talkies. I don't think they knew I was so close.

The big corrugated metal doors of the hangar were partly open on number three. Inside, in a pool of light, were a slim Asian man in a suit and a stockier man in golf togs, who I thought might be the Russian boss, Pavel Abdulov. What's with the golf clothes, Russians?

The two men were looking around in alarm, one of them cupping a hand to shoutat the sentries.

Smoke roiled around me, pluming up the stairwell. But the smoke and fire and the Glock bullets going off randomly —as if the dead men were adding their own chaos in protest —all of that was keeping the sentries from coming at me from behind.

The two bosses, if that's who they were—the only guys not obviously armed—started away from what looked like a gray brick wall behind them, about to exit.

Don't do that, boys. Stay inside.

I drew the Colt and fired at the big window in front of me, three shots, so part of it shattered and fell away, clashing around my boots. I fired the rest of the rounds at the cluster of sentries, and one of them fell. The others ran back into the building for cover, waving their arms at the bosses. *Get back, get back!*

I holstered the Colt and knelt. I took off the backpack and the Remington, flicked the safety off on the sniper rifle, and used the bolt to slam a round into the chamber. I stood up, stepping back from the window. Smoke was thickening around me. The light came from outside, but I was partly hidden. A sentry was firing toward the window, and glass shattered above me and fell away.

I laid the barrel on a half-broken pane of glass sticking up from the frame, made a quick adjustment to the scope, and the picture sharpened. The two bosses were silhouetted against that gray wall, which I could now see was made up of blocks of material in transparent plastic, exactly like the ones in that storage room I'd found with Nadine. Each stack was about six feet high.

"You idiots should wear a gas mask in there," I said, coughing as smoke wreathed around me, wishing I'd thought of a gas mask myself.

I held my breath, aimed carefully, and fired at the blocks between the bosses. A gray-white plume gouted out from the blocks. The two men saw it and turned to run. I had already worked the Remington's bolt-action to lever another round in and fired again at the bricks of fentanyl. More pure drug dust came spewing out, and a cloud of it covered the two men.

They both fell, twitching. Lungs full of pure fentanyl— those sons of bitches were dying.

I knew they would die as surely as I knew that bullets were shattering the glass close by me, as surely as I felt something slash at my face and right ear. If the sentries got me, they got me. I was in a fixed state of mind, a kind of pristine fury.

A mental picture of Frankie on that slab...

I dropped the scope's round and located other targets in front of the hangar. I fired fast as I could, reloading again and again, and gunmen fell, and then the Remington's clip was empty. I wasn't going to have time to use it anymore because flames were rushing up the stairs and bullets were cracking by. I tossed the Remington into the flames and knelt, squinting and coughing, reloading the Colt from my gun belt.

Flames were looming over me now and sucking away the breathable air.

Gasping, I slipped on the backpack and then turned right, looking for a way out, thinking maybe if burning to death seemed inevitable, the only way out would be to put a bullet from the Colt in my own head, and why not, the mission was done so far as I could carry it out.

Then I saw a door, lit from the firelight behind me, that said "Emergency Only" across it.

The Colt in one hand, I ran to the door, slammed against the release bar, and stepped out onto the top landing of a rusted iron fire escape. I gulped clean air and then caught my breath, seeing at the bottom of the fire escape stairs, just starting up, was a gunman with an AK, a Russian guy, raising his assault rifle toward me.

I fired. The angle was awkward, so it took two rounds to cut him down.

I pounded down the metal stairs, jumped over his body, and landed on the gravel verge beside the concrete road. Flames were roaring through the admin building's windows. Bullets cut by me from behind. Smoke rolled thickly out the nearest window, and I used it to cover me as I ran across the road into the deep shadows next to a mess building, coughing as I went.

The front door of the mess building had been knocked down by copper looters. I ran inside and down a hallway strewn with broken glass and random junk. The walls had been sledgehammered open in places, and stubs of wires showed where the copper had been.

I got to a back entrance, the door missing, looked out into semidarkness, and a man almost blew my head off.

The AK burst shattered the doorframe to my right. Splinters sprayed, and a piercing pain jolted deep into my right shoulder. I was reflexively firing the six-gun back at the midsection of the gunman's shape.

He spun and went down, groaning. Striding past him, I saw that the dying man was Eric, the dealer from the homeless camp. I pushed myself into a sprint, heart drumming as I pelted along the southerly fence.

A Jeep pulled onto the lane fifty feet in front of me, its headlights near-blinding me. I fired where I thought the driver was sitting and then dodged to the right between two buildings, and up a wooden set of three stairs, through another door smashed by looters, down past the empty bunk beds of the barracks, through dust and cobwebs and spiderwebs, and reached the door that opened onto the main road. I heard the Jeep roar by as it searched for me.

I hunkered down and heard more of them coming from the direction of the hangars and the Jeep screeching in a U-turn. Someone had spotted me.

This is what you wanted, I told myself. *Go out and meet it.*

My hands shaking, I reloaded my Colt, got up and—smiling to myself because now it was all going to be over and done with.

I ran outside, firing toward the men piling out of the Jeep. One of them went down, but I saw the muzzle flash from another, and felt like I was hit in the right side of my chest with a sledgehammer.

Then I was flat on my back. I lay there, fighting for breath, cocking the Colt.

I sat up—a bigger physical effort than I'd ever made,

sitting up right then. My vision was blurred, and I looked for someone to shoot at, maybe get one more for Frankie.

I saw a sentry with an AK-47 standing by the Jeep, silhouetted against the firelight from the admin building. He was swinging the weapon toward me just as I was raising my shaking hand to try to squeeze off one more shot from the silver revolver.

22

THEN CAME the angry rumbling of a big engine and a steely *bang* followed by screeching of tearing metal--and gunshots to the west. The guy with the AK and I both looked...and saw a big black Dodge Ram pickup roaring down the middle of the road, part of the front gate stuck to its grill. The Ram smashed a patch of cacti, sending it flying, and struck the gunman, sending him spinning through the air. Then the hulking, steaming, black pick up, half dragging the front gate, came roaring right at me.

The pickup swerved, skidded to a stop next to me, just missing my legs. I reached up and grabbed the door handle and, gritting my teeth against waves of pain from the wound in my chest, I pulled myself up, opened the door, and writhed cursing into the passenger seat. I almost lost consciousness right there. My mind went—and came back.

I saw the windshield was mostly shot away. More bullets ricocheted off the fence gate stuck to the warped front fender, spitting red sparks.

A round smashed the small back window behind Dulcet. She ducked, shouting, *"Shit fuckity fuck!"*

My voice sounding weak and strange, I said, "You almost ran over my legs."

She tossed me her HK pistol and snarled, "Shut up and shoot people, Slimby!"

She gunned the truck, spun it in a donut turn, accelerating hard toward the west. Bullets clanged into fenders on the right side. My voice was thick, my mouth not working so well, as I said, "How'd you come to be here?"

"Knew where you were going, came out, and heard everybody trying to kill you! Who else they be shooting out here? *Just use the guuuuunn!*"

We were in sight of the busted gate. I opened the passenger window. Bullets clattered off the rear of the truck as I fired at the muzzle flash from an AK-47. I squeezed off rounds at two men running up with rifles. My eyesight was blurring, but I saw someone crumple.

Dulcet yelled incoherently as two more AK bursts hit the truck, a couple of the bullets ricocheting inside, buzzing by, one shattering the dashboard radio.

I hurt. It was getting hard to breathe. I leaned out the window a little, and looked to the east. I saw another muzzle flash, fired three or four times at it—I'm not even sure—and the clip was empty just as we drove through the gate.

I leaned back, dropping the gun on the floor. Strength was draining out of me. There was smoke coming out of the front of the car and the engine was sputtering.

Dulcet glanced at me, reached up and turned on the truck's overhead lights, illuminating the very, very red blood flowing copiously from a deep groove through the meat on my right shoulder and the bullet hole in my upper right chest. Gray smoke rose from the Ram's engine, whipping away as the truck bumped along.

I figured dazedly that the engine was likely to die under

us, pretty much any second now. The gate stuck to the truck's grill creaked--and fell away. We thumped over it. That was painful.

I caught my breath and said, "Turn right at this dirt road. Yeah. Keep going. My truck's up there. Like a quarter mile. We'll switch over."

"'Kay," she said, her voice hardly audible. I looked at her, saw she was wobbling in her seat, leaning forward to squint into the wind coming through the big gaps in the windshield, the wind fluttering her hair back.

"There's bandages in the glove compartment," she said, her voice kind of warped as if she were straining to talk.

But Christ. What she'd been through. I pictured her smashing the truck through the gate under heavy sentry fire. The girl was insane. God bless her insanity.

I opened the glove compartment, the motion spearing pain into me. I found the little box of bandages, tore one out, and pressed it against the wound on my chest.

"Am I still wearing my backpack?" I asked. Things were getting misty around me. I couldn't feel my back.

"Yeah." She was panting, making little whimpering sounds now, one with each outbreath. "Uh-uh."

"There's money in it for you. They had a big stack. I took forty thou. I was going to send Latisha half, and the rest was for you. But you just saved my fucking life, Dulcet, so you should have it all. You shouldn't have done that, but—"

"Shush, Slimby," she said, her voice hoarse. "There's your stupid Toyota. Fucking brakes on my truck aren't working no more, no more, Slimby Jimby." That's when the pickup's engine died and we coasted into a Joshua tree and stopped with a crunching jolt. We both yelled in pain at that.

The overhead light was flickering, but still on. I looked at her and saw blood at the corner of her mouth. And dripping down the side of her seat.

"You're hit."

"No *duh*." She closed her eyes. "I feel like I'm going to spin away...*way* awayyy..."

"Where you hit? The bandages..."

"I saved you twice, Slimby." Eyes still shut, she clutched at the steering wheel. "You owe me something."

"Yeah, I do. Tell me where you hit, Dulcet. Come on."

"Never mind, never mind, Cowboy. I want...I just want..."

She made that little squeaky whimper.

"What do you want, Dulcet?"

"You just...just going on, is what. You going on. You have to just...You owe me... You find a reason. You go on."

"I will. I promise you." I put my hand on her arm. "But listen, I've got plans for us."

She sagged back in her seat. Eyes still shut. Murmuring, "You do?"

"If you're chill with it, we're going to use this money, start that business. Your own Mustang Ranch. We got to be really good to the girls though. Rules about that."

"That's right. That's good. That's what we'll do. No drugs, no bad johns. Good security. Protect the girls."

"Healthcare. Vacations."

"That's right. That's right, Slimby. I knew you were the..."

She coughed and couldn't say the rest because of the blood.

I saw lights in the rearview mirror. Someone was coming. Probably the Kwais' people. They were coming, and Dulcet was going, and I still had my Colt. I would take a few of them with us. "Dulcet?"

Eyes still closed, she flailed her hand out, trying to reach me. I caught it and held on. She coughed up blood. Spat it to one side. Wiping her mouth, she managed to rasp out, "Slim...my Jimmy Purdoux..."

"I'm right here. There's a doctor, Dulcet, a good one I know. The best. I'll get you to him."

"Yeah? He better be...a fucking miracle worker."

"You stay with me, okay?"

I looked in the rearview mirror. Was there pursuit? Couldn't tell. The mist was thickening. I felt weak enough that I wasn't sure I could draw my gun.

I brought her hand to my mouth and kissed it.

"I love you, Slimby."

"I...love you too, Dulcet."

She turned her head, sleepily opened her eyes. Gave me a ghost of a smile. "'Kay."

Then her eyes closed, and her head sagged down.

Her hand went limp in mine. I could feel life passing out of her.

But I kept hold of her limp hand. And gasping for air, I leaned back in my seat. Someone walked up to the window. I glanced over, wondering what kind of gun they'd use to kill me. AK or maybe a pistol?

It was Nadine. She shone a flashlight into the car.

Its light filled my eyes and seemed to burn me down to nothing.

————

I heard voices in the darkness.

I felt cold, and I was in the dark, so I thought I was in a

cavern of some kind. And the voices sounded like they were in an adjoining cavern. A man and woman talking of "his BP" and "a third transfusion" and "increase the drip to..."

And then they faded into dim echoes, and the darkness thickened.

I was gone, and then I came back, and this time there was a faint light in the cavern.

"He's opened his eyes...a little."

I felt a warm touch on my right arm.

"Dulcet?" I said.

"James..." It was not Dulcet's voice. A warm female voice I didn't know. "James? Can you hear me?"

But I was too tired to answer, and the darkness flowed back in. Numbness filled me.

Gone again.

I came back, I don't know how much later, to more voices and a sharp pain in my chest.

"He's in and out of it," said that warm female voice.

I felt so numb. It was hard to get anything to operate. But after a couple of tries, I got my eyes open.

I saw a short Asian lady, late twenties, in green scrubs and a doctor's white coat, a stethoscope around her neck. She was smiling at me. Her eyes seemed all lit up with goodwill. "James? I'm Doctor Chen. How are you feeling?"

"Where'm I?"

"Saint Mary's Regional, critical care. Moved you in here from ICU this morning."

Made sense. I was in a hospital bed, an IV line in my hand, a nasal cannula feeding me oxygen, and a catheter where catheters go. The ceiling light seemed harshly bright. I was alternately aching and numb. I wasn't handcuffed to anything. That was good.

Someone stepped into view on my left. *Nadine.*

Wearing a blue skirt, a white blouse, and a blazer. Her gun was in a shoulder holster this time. I caught just a glimpse of its strap. Badge on her hip. Her hair up, her face solemn.

I cleared my throat. Managed to get my numbed lips working. "Lieutenant...Graves." The words came out a little lispy.

"Mr. Purdoux," Nadine said. She did a little sideways motion of her head at the doctor and then gave me a significant look. *Stay formal, Purdoux. Careful what you say.*

Doctor Chen took hold of my right hand. "Tell me how you're feeling, James."

I looked at her. "How I feel...is numb. 'Cept where...it hurts."

"We've got you on some serious painkillers, James."

"How's about..." I licked my lips. "*You* tell me how I am."

"You were shot twice. You had a very extensive operation on your chest. You had some work done on your shoulder. Two wounds, lots of sutures. We had to intubate you for breathing. You had blood in your right lung. You were in the ICU for a few days. You've been mostly unconscious for a week."

"How long before..." I licked my lips to help get the words out. "Finish the opioids?"

She patted my hand. "Oh, don't worry, we're not going to snatch them away anytime soon."

Nadine shook her head. "I don't think that's what he means."

"To get off 'em," I said. "Want off them when it's... bearable."

Dr. Chen smiled. "You might want back on if you try that too soon. We'll see how you feel in four or five days."

"I'm...in recovery. From all that stuff."

Nadine raised her eyebrows. "Serious recovery?"

"Back to it," I said.

"That movement hurt?" the doctor asked.

I cleared my throat and shifted a little in the bed. A long icicle of pain went through me. "Numb, kinda, but some stuff hurts."

Nadine nodded. "Get some rest. We'll see if you feel like a talk tomorrow."

"Dulcet?" I asked.

She shook her head. "Your friend passed on. I'm sorry. She was gone by the time the ambulance got there. You almost went with her." She looked away, biting her lip. "Get some rest, Mr. Purdoux."

She turned away. I had questions. But I was too tired to ask them, even without the doctor in the room.

I closed my eyes.

———

It was four days before Nadine came back.

I was sitting up, trying to watch a movie on television. It was possible if I kept maximumly motionless. I wasn't quite as numbed out and couldn't move without pain. I was still hooked up to beeping machines, thankfully not the catheter. I tried to focus on Al Pacino in *Serpico*. A commercial came on. I muted it, did not want to hear about erectile dysfunction or the psychic call center or why I should send money to iffy ministries in India.

I closed my eyes and quietly marveled at how the black wave was gone, how a weight seemed to have slid from my shoulders. The grief for Frankie was there, like a raven that would always be perched on the bust, but I felt freer now. Was it just the morphine? I didn't think so. I could feel that the grief had moved into a different part of me. Like a shrine.

Seeing the Kwai boss and the Russian boss die together in a cloud of fentanyl, it did wonders for me.

Nadine came in just as the commercials ended, and Serpico walked into the NYPD locker room. I left the TV muted.

"See that," I said, pointing at the screen. My voice was hoarse, but I could articulate better now. "What they did to Serpico? See how corrupt cops are?" I grinned at her. "It's the shame of America."

She glanced at the TV and snorted, then gave me a snarky look. "You're more yourself now."

"Is that a good thing?"

"That's the question." She drew a chair up to my bedside.

"I was kind of surprised not to be manacled to the bed."

"Hasn't been easy, keeping you unmanacled. You want some water or juice or something?"

"What I want is to get off the OxyContin."

"Dr. Chen is right. The pain would kick your ass. They dug a 7.62-millimeter AK round out of you. Did a lot of microsurgeries on the veins in your lung."

"Who's paying for all that?"

"Not the county, if they can help it. That insurance card in your wallet still in effect?"

"I think so. Shouldn't we close the door?"

She nodded, got up and closed the door, sat down again, and I said, "I'm not going to ask if you're wearing a wire."

She sighed, grating her teeth a little. "*Still* no wire. And I've almost gotten busted myself, trying to keep you out of prison. You can't plead, 'All those guys I killed deserved it, Your Honor.' The vigilante card doesn't get you out of jail."

"They were all trying to kill me."

"Were they? The ones you shot with a sniper rifle?"

"Okay, so that part's more complicated. Maybe I will have some water. Constant cottonmouth."

She poured me a glass from a pitcher by the bed and brought it to me. I drank a little, and she sat back down.

"Slim, the only way to keep you out of prison was to *lie* you out, which will stop if I'm put on the stand. If they ask me about you, I'm *not* going to jail for perjury. I'll pretend I had the facts wrong before, but now, your honor, here's the goods

"How'd you even find me, that night?"

"I followed you there, Purdoux. Right from the motel. That's the first thing you've got to know. I wanted to be there when you were."

That was a thump to the gut. "You had me under surveillance."

"Just that day. It was obvious you were going out to that base. I didn't want to arrest you. I didn't have anything but hearsay about the base. No one in the department seemed interested in surveilling it."

"Which is pretty fucking suspicious. How many more Rynersons are there?"

"I don't think it's dirty cops. I think it's the DA."

"Wessen."

She nodded. "Glenn Wessen. He's big on busting undocumented immigrants and shoplifting gangs. But he ducked out on the drug cartels. Takes some odd trips overseas in private jets from time to time. I reckon he's a bought man. They'll prosecute if we catch low-level dealers on the street, but going any higher than that? For Wessen, there's never enough proof."

"That was why you...the whole thing out on the rez... That was just to find out what I knew..."

"No. That was—I was lonely, okay? And suddenly, when I was with you, all that loneliness just went away. And yeah, we had something, we did. But...I couldn't let you just pick targets and shoot them down. Couldn't let the cartel get away with everything either. I figured if I followed you, called in a couple of cars when things started to light up, I'd have probable cause to bust the operation."

"And...me with it."

"You always risked that."

I nodded. "You're right. But nobody likes being a sacrificial lamb, Nadine."

"Jim, you put yourself in that position. I figured you were planning to get yourself killed out there. Take some of them down with you. This way, it'd be worth something. And there was a chance of saving you. Once we got the tox squad in there, we found another mountain of that poison in hangar two. Their lab's set up in there too. It's all off the street now. We arrested six Kwai hardcases and a Russian. A couple of the Kwais are in another hospital, thanks to you. The rest are dead. I should say good shooting, I guess. Three cartel flunkies and a Kwai captain got away. But you got their boss man, Murray Kwai."

"What'd you tell the Reno PD about me?"

"Told them *my CI* was meeting me there to point out where the drugs were. And, near as I could figure, Captain, we stumbled on a gang war. Turf war between the Russians and the Tong. Because some in the Russian cartel have, for real, been grumbling about the Chinese connection. We floated a theory that this sniper, this gunman, was hired by some Russian captain who wanted to get rid of his boss and take over. And this hypothetical gunman got away..."

"Did he? I'm just asking as a hypothetical gunman."

"Far as they know."

"Should I send the Russians an invoice?"

"You're funny." She wasn't laughing.

"I'm stoned. They've got me on drugs."

"Just be careful what you say. Some reporter is likely to find out that my CI got wounded by stray bullets out there. Might want to interview you."

"So that's our story? A disgruntled Russian gangster did all that?"

"I hope to God it's one I can keep telling, Slim, because if I can't—"

"If you can't, you won't perjure yourself." I nodded. "I get that. I don't blame you, Nadine. And I get that you're already taking a huge chance with your career."

"My career? Hell, my freedom! I could go to prison, Purdoux. Wessen knows I suspect him. He'd love to get something on me. The DEA is on this now, and it's become a federal case." She scowled at me. "You're not thinking of going after Wessen?"

I shook my head. "Not going after any DAs. I've done what I could."

"Murray Kwai is dead. Pavel Abdulov is dead. You got lucky in your timing out there. Crippled them. The fentanyl cloud you set up killed three others too. But that doesn't mean *Renny* Kwai is going to buy the story about the Russian assassin. You can't stay in Nevada, Slim."

"Can you get me out of this antiseptic lockup here?"

"Not for weeks. You'd keel over."

"Nadine, where's Dulcet's body?"

"County morgue."

"How'd you fit her into your spin on what happened out there?"

"Gangster girlfriend. Came to help our missing assassin. He got away. She didn't. A tragic figure. Some people talk like she's a hero."

"She was, far as I'm concerned. You know, she wasn't supposed to be out there. I tried to keep her away from that base. She came out to save my ass. She's...she was..."

"I know about her, Slim."

I shook my head. "Hard to know her. She was way more complicated than she seemed."

"Okay. What was she to you?"

"You want to know? I think she was the best goddamned friend I ever had." I had to clear my throat. My eyes stung. "I want to get her a nice burial. A really good stone. Like with a kind of cameo of her profile on it. Something she'd like. Which reminds me, do I have any money left?"

"Yeah, about that. Did it ever occur to you that the two and a half million dollars you burned to ashes could have been seized and used by the county for good purposes?"

"It occurred to me that money *from the poison that killed my son* could go to the local government, yeah. Washoe County—which had let the Kwai operate on and on—they would take the profit from all that fentanyl. *So I fucking burned it.*"

She seemed a little taken aback by the anger in my voice.

I licked my lips and went on, "Anyway...anyway, I took some cash to give Dulcet—she was going to start a business —and some to send to...a friend. Someone who's part of a community church down there in Oakland."

"You expected to mail that money out from the grave?"

"I took it in case I got away. Forty grand."

She shrugged. "I know how much money there was.

Still is. I have the backpack stashed. I'm going to let you have it so you can get out of Nevada and keep your head above water. That's totally and completely illegal, giving you that money. Don't think I'm taking any more chances for you. This is about the fiftieth one, and it's the absolute last one. But..."

Tears welled in her eyes.

I pointed at her. "You're trying to take care of me. You *do* feel something for me."

She looked at the window. Shook her head. "We had one...just one adventure. Stupid, but...I can't be sorry about it."

"'Cause not everyone gets a chance to feel that way. I sure never did before. It doesn't have to be over—"

A perfunctory knock before the door swung open. Dr. Chen came in.

Nadine stood up like a triggered jack-in-the-box. "Okay, James. I'll check back in with you, um, in a few days."

"Could you actually wait and..."

But she shook her head briskly and turned away. "Dr. Chen, he's complaining about the police, so I guess he's back in form."

Dr. Chen chuckled and came over to check my vitals. I tried to watch *Serpico*.

———

Two days. No Nadine sightings. I couldn't call her. I shouldn't anyway. What could we safely talk about?

My only company was old movies, badly clipped back to make room for way too many commercials. Sometimes I tried to talk to the busy nurses, but they kept it brisk. They didn't trust me. You come in with bullet holes and a cop comes in to interview you, the nurses don't spend any more time around you than they hve to. . The nurses would detach the needle from the little fixture on my arm long enough for me to get up and go to the tiny bathroom. The toilet was like something on a passenger jet, except there was a small shower. I would use the toilet, take a perfunctory shower, and then walk around the room for a minute or two. Then the pain would get to me, and I'd ring for them, and they'd come back and re-attach me to "the dope pole."

Most of the time, I was left alone with my thoughts, which was like being in a prison cell with a real creep.

My thoughts see-sawed darkly between Frankie and Dulcet. Sometimes they yawed to Gary Ledbetter and the sprawled, still bleeding dead-- the victims of Eickhoff, like an omen laid out for me on the floors of the very building I worked in.

The opioid drip would build up in me, and I'd start to drift in and out of waking dreams. The kill corridor. People I'd killed on my mission for Frankie, all lined up.

Then I saw Frankie, hollow-eyed and pallid, at the other end of the corridor, walking toward me, stepping over the dead. "Dad? Why aren't you with the others?"

"I don't believe that's you saying that, Frankie," I said. "Something's put on your face like a mask."

"Then why call me Frankie?"

I didn't have an answer for that. And the dead began to bleed again and to shake with pain on the floor. "Frankie..."

I wrenched myself up and out of the nightmare.

That's a skill. If you've got PTSD, you can learn it.

Right then, I rang for the nurse and pushed her into getting Dr. Chen for me. I asked for one of those buttons where you can decide how much painkiller is flowing into you. Press the button and you get a little more. The machine limits you to only so much.

Dr. Chen was reluctant to set that up, but I talked her into it.

Five more days of weaning myself off. As I lowered the dosage, pain encroached. Mostly from my upper right chest, with a lower level of pain in my right shoulder. Some from my face, where I'd been cut up during the fight. They'd had to do some stitching on the right side.

On the sixth day of weaning from the clinical dope, I was feeling a little stronger, but less comfortable.

On the seventh day, right after I ate something that was reputed to be supper, Nadine came to see me.

23

NADINE WAS DRESSED JUST like before, but she'd put on a little makeup and let her hair down. She had her purse on a strap over one shoulder. Under the other arm, she was carrying a bulging manila envelope.

I pushed the tray on wheels aside, and she tugged a chair close to me. Her voice almost a whisper, she said, "I think...the spin is working." She bent over in the chair, put the manila envelope under my bed, and straightened up. "Seems like they're not going to come after you, not right away. But I can't be *sure*." She took a three-page document out of her purse. "I brought you something. You sign it, you'll be confirming our version of events that night. I'll witness it. Says you were there to give me critical information, to answer questions as I looked over the base from a distance, and then the gunfire broke out, and you caught some stray bullets. Otherwise, you'll be called into court to testify. This way gives us time, at least."

I looked over the transcription of what I didn't actually say, and I signed it. What's one more crime?

She folded it up, put it back in her purse, and said, "I'm

not at all certain about the Kwais. The youngest has taken over. We saw him out selling drugs, in person. Renny Kwai. He claims they had nothing to do with the drugs, that it was some outsiders and a couple of rogue family members, and... Wessen is letting him slide."

"Nothing suspicious in that." I rubbed my throbbing forehead. "That all you here to tell me?"

"How you feeling? I mean, not just the getting shot part."

"Like...there's a weight off my shoulders. The grief 's not going to leave me. But...it's better."

"I want to tell you...you will definitely look better shaved."

"I'll ask the nurse for a shaving kit. Anything *else* you want to tell me?"

"Then, when you're strong enough, you have to leave the state No arguments. Got to leave Nevada. I brought your money."

"You've been"—I glanced at the door— "hiding forty thou all this time?"

"The desert hid it for me. It was evidence that could be used against you. And...you'll need it. If you want to donate it to that church, whatever. But you take it. And there's something else in that envelope. Keys to the Toyota pickup."

"Still where I left it?"

"I moved it. It's in a parking garage about a block and a half from here. I paid for a month."

"You pack my bags too?" I asked. "You going to escort me to the town line to see I leave?"

She ignored the sarcasm. "There are a few things in the bag from that motel. And that goddamned redneck pistol of yours is there. I shouldn't have put it there, I guess, but...I didn't want you to be defenseless after...all this. Maybe the Russians know about you. I'm not sure."

"I'm not leaving till I get Dulcet taken care of."

"I was thinking about that. I'll arrange it for you. You can get people's photos etched on a tombstone now."

"Yeah, I've seen those."

"I found a photo of her online, at an arraignment a few years ago. She looks good in it." She took a phone out of her pocket, scrolled, and found me the photo. It made my throat constrict to look at it. She was an adult with glamorous hair and pretty, but the expression on her face was like a wistful little girl. A child who'd become lost—and gotten used to it.

"Yeah. That photo. With *Dulcet McNair*, birth and death date."

Nadine nodded. "I've got her birthday off her driver's license."

"That stone will cost."

"Whole thing, with a headstone, casket, cemetery plot... over nine thousand. Maybe over ten." She glanced nervously at the door.

"Take $11,000 out of the envelope," I said. "If there's any left over, you probably won't want to keep it?"

"Nope."

"Give it to a food bank."

"That works. Um...gonna pretend to use your bathroom."

Nadine got the envelope and hurried to the bathroom. I had a pad of paper and a pen by the lamp at the side of my bed. I wrote some lines on the pad. Nadine came back, the envelope a little lighter, her purse fuller.

"Actually, could you put that envelope in the closet there, with my clothes? The orderlies would find it under the bed."

Nadine nodded and hid the envelope as best she could in the closet. We both knew possession of a firearm in a hospital was illegal. Then she came back, and I held out the piece of paper. "I wanted to put this on the gravestone under her name. It's a paraphrase of Edna St. Vincent Millay."

She took the paper and, standing by the side of the bed, not quite in reach, read it aloud, *"Her candle burned at both ends; it did not last the night; but ah, my foes, and oh, my friends—it gave a lovely light!"* Nadine chuckled dryly. "Yeah, you changed the tense. Editorial neuroticism. But I don't think Ms. St. Millay will care. I'll get it up there. Mountain View Cemetery is the best choice." She folded it and put it in her purse. "Slim, I've still got a lot of stuff to... to make sure we're all squared away. Legally."

"I get it. Thanks for bringing me that stuff...and...the truck and...keeping me out of the calaboose. Listen, you want me to just...stay away? I mean—forever?"

"That's what it needs to be." Her lower lip buckled. "I don't know how it could have happened that quickly and that deeply, Slim Purdoux. It did—and it's hard to let go of. I don't *want* to let go of it."

"Then...come with me. You can resign Reno PD. Start over in some other state. Like—Texas. We could go to Austin. You'd get work with Austin PD, *boom*, like that in Austin. Texas is dying for good cops."

"Slim, I can't. My *people* are here. And I owe them. But...I did give notice at Reno PD. I'm joining the police force on the reservation."

I nodded, pretending that her not even considering coming with me didn't hurt. "Okay, well. Maybe after a year or two, I could—"

"No! Everybody knows you as my CI, and you're all

mixed up in what happened at that base, and...we just can't. In the end, I'd be constantly worried about living with a guy who should be in jail for murder."

I was hours from my last opioid dose, but there was a pain in me that overshadowed the wound in my chest. It cost me to say, "You're right." I cleared my throat. "Could I maybe call you...every so often?"

"Yeah, I guess. If you're careful what you say."

"Okay, so..." But I didn't say what I wanted to say. "Be... be careful out there, Nadine."

"I will."

I heard her walking to the door and opening it. I dropped my gaze to my hands when the door closed behind her.

———

Five more days of reducing the meds. The pain from the wounds was bearable now. On the sixth day, I got a nurse to bring me a pack of disposable razors and shaving cream. I took a shower and shaved.

That evening, I talked to Dr. Chen, asking if I could check out. She did not want to release me yet. I didn't want the commotion of insisting.

"Ask me in a week," she said. "Maybe then."

In the early hours of the sixth day, at four in the morning, I sat up in the bed and gave myself one squirt of opioid. Then I turned on the over-bed light, and very, very carefully, removed the IV needle and fixture from my arm. I used my left thumb to compress the small hole until it stopped bleeding, then I closed it with the tape they'd used to hold the needle in place.

I got up and found my boots in the closet. They'd given

me a clean white T-shirt that morning, because I'd bugged them to, and I had some sweatpants they give you when you walk around in your room.

I put the pants and boots on, threw off the hospital gown, put on the T-shirt, and took the big manila envelope out. I got my wallet from the little drawer in the bedside table. Carrying the envelope, I went to the door and looked down the hallway.

No one around. I saw a sign for the emergency stairs. I went down the stairs and came to the emergency exit door. My second time going out an emergency exit from a hospital. The first time was that day when I saw Frankie in the hospital morgue.

The door set off a warning clangor. Once more, I didn't care.

I slipped into the manicured bushes outside the hospital and found my way to the sidewalk.

All this hurt, you bet it did. My chest, my upper right arm. And I was still a little weak. But I rejoiced at being mobile and free.

There was an address for the parking garage written on the envelope, with a number for a parking space. I found it, slipped past the gate, and searched through the garage until I found the Toyota Tacoma. Not hard, the place was mostly empty at this hour. I unlocked the pickup and opened the small suitcase on the front seat. Clothes, my gun and gun belt, some toiletries. A United States roadmap. *Yeah, Nadine, I get it. You didn't need to put the map in.*

I was hoping to find a note from Nadine in the suitcase. Nope, nothing like that.

I put on a clean shirt and jeans. Then I drove out of the garage...and went looking for a casino.

It wasn't to gamble. It was because the casinos were

open all night, and no one would take any notice of me in the place.

I went to the nearest casino, called Cloud Nine. I hid most of the money under the seat of the Toyota, got out and locked it, and hoped to God no one broke in.

I changed a fifty-dollar bill at the coffee shop, got some coffee, and plain donuts. Read someone else's discarded newspaper.

Investigations Deepen Around AF Base Bust.

I saw quotes from Nadine. Nothing about me.

I shook my head in admiration. She'd have made a great fixer for some criminal mastermind.

They had an electronic jukebox, the kind where you can get most anything from online. I put on some jazz. Miles Davis, "Kind of Blue" for starters. I listened to that. I tried to make plans. Nadine kept coming into them. I kept seeing her shaking her head at me. *No, do not include me in your plans, Purdoux.*

I talked to a chunky white busboy who asked me to put some country rapper on the juke. I did and wished I hadn't. Fine, whatever, but just not my cup of joe. He told me he was going to become a country rapper himself, wait and see.

Around seven in the morning, I got some real breakfast —eggs and potatoes—and waited to see if I could keep it down. I did, though it was iffy for a while.

Then I asked where the nearest post office was.

I drove there and waited as the sun rose higher until the post office opened.

In the back of my mind, I did have a plan that included Nadine. Maybe three years off, I'd circle back to her. Find her in person. Be discreet.

Maybe she'd be married by then, with a little boy of her

own. If it was like that, I'd leave her completely alone. But I had to know.

There she was again, in my mind, shaking her head at me. *Forget it, Purdoux.*

I laughed softly at myself. *You're a hopeless chump, Purdoux.*

The post office opened. I stuffed ten grand—one bundle —in my suitcase, because I'm not a dweeb. Have I mentioned that? I'd need it to get the hell out of Dodge. Something to start over on, somewhere. The aching wound in my chest made me feel like it was okay to take the money.

Dirty money? Yes. Was it necessary to do what both women had asked me to do? Hell yes.

I was feeling ragged, tired, and in some pain. But I felt like I was going to be able to keep on.

I took the envelope into the post office, stuffed the manila envelope, containing 15K in cash, into a hefty Priority Mail envelope. I found some scrap paper in the trash can and used a post office pen to scribble a note.

Latesha,

This is a gift from Dulcet. She's passed away, and she went like a hero. She saved my life.

Dulcet wanted you to have this. I think she thought it should be half for you and half for whatever charity you want, but it's up to you. She's buried in Mountain View Cemetery in Reno, Nevada. I arranged a nice gravestone. You can find it there if you visit Reno.

Your problematic friend,

Slim Purdoux.

I put the note in with the money and dropped Wendell's gold lighter in too. I sealed the envelope and wrote Latesha's full name on it, care of Easter Hill Church of Our Loving Savior, and the address. Then I took it to the elderly lady at the post office desk.

"You're up bright and early," she said.

"Yes, ma'am. I want to have this kind of special delivered, if I can."

"That would be certified mail, sir."

"Sounds good."

"The fee for that is..."

I paid it. Gave them my apartment address in San Francisco, just to provide some kind of return address. Then I went out to the Tacoma, drove down the road a block, and stopped at a gas station with a convenience store. I filled up the tank and got a giant cup of coffee to go.

I got myself onto the freeway, heading south. When the right route showed itself, I'd take myself southeast, to Texas. To Austin. Because I didn't know where else the hell to go.

I wasn't sure what I would do in Austin. But I kept on driving. I had made a promise to Nadine to leave the state. And I'd made a bigger promise to Dulcet.

I have a new mission. I've been tasked to find a reason to go on living.

What do you think, Frankie?

A LOOK AT: EVERYTHING IS BROKEN

Forced into action; forced into adulthood.

When twenty-year-old Russ arrives in the oddly named town of Freedom, California, he expects little more than an uneasy visit with his estranged father. Instead, he finds a community cut off from the outside world by a mayor's radical experiment in "decentralization"—a place with few rules, minimal services, and more questions than answers.

Russ barely has time to take it all in before a monstrous tsunami devastates the West Coast. In the aftermath, Freedom's isolation becomes a curse. Supplies dwindle, tensions erupt, and the wave of human cruelty that follows the natural disaster proves far deadlier than the ocean itself.

As chaos closes in, Russ, his father, and a young woman named Pendra must summon courage they never knew they had. To survive, they'll have to forge unlikely alliances and learn that true strength comes not from standing alone, but from standing together.

A tense, pulse-pounding thriller, *Everything is Broken* is a gripping coming-of-age story about resilience, community, and the brutal choices we must make when survival is on the line.

AVAILABLE NOVEMBER 2025

John Shirley is the winner of the Spur Award for his western *Gunmetal Mountain* and the Bram Stoker Award for his story collection, *Black Butterflies: A Flock on the Dark Side*. His novels include *BioShock: Rapture, Blood in Sweet River, Suborbital 7, Stormland, the Eclipse cyberpunk trilogy, Cellars, Batman: Dead White, The Brigade,* and *Borderlands: The Fallen*. His new story collection is *The Feverish Stars*. He was co-scripter of the movie THE CROW, and wrote extensively for television.